The Wars For MAGISIS

NAMYA GUPTA
YAHVI AGARWAL

Anecdote
Publishing House
For the love of quality reading!

Anecdote
Publishing House
For the love of quality reading!

anecdotepublishinghouse.com
champreaders.com

Anecdote Publishing House
2nd Floor 2/15 Lane no. 2 Ansari Road, Daryaganj-110002
Email: info@anecdotepublishinghouse.com
Website: anecdotepublishinghouse.com

Published by Anecdote Publishing House

First Edition 2025
ISBN 978-81-98258-97-7
MRP ₹ 450/-

Book Promoted and Marketed by Champ Readers Pvt. Ltd.
Book edited by:- The Book Bakers
Cover design by:- The Book Bakers
Layout by:- Arivazhagi Balasundaram
Printed in India

The Wars For MAGISIS

NAMYA GUPTA
YAHVI AGARWAL

Dedicated to each other, because it was the coming together of our ideas that created this story!

ACKNOWLEDGEMENTS

I thank my parents for encouraging me to follow my dreams and continue writing this story. Without their unwavering support, I wouldn't have been able to complete this book—and even if I had, the story would have likely turned out very differently. They played a huge role in helping me get it published, and I couldn't be more grateful.

A heartfelt thank you to our agency, The Book Bakers, and our publisher, Sagar, for turning our dream into reality. I am also deeply grateful to my friends and family for their insightful feedback, which helped shape the flow of this story.

Lastly, I want to thank my co-author and best friend, Yahvi, for being by my side throughout this journey. We shared our ideas, built upon each other's creativity, and together, we brought this book to life in its best possible form.

Namya

First and foremost, I thank my parents. While they may not have contributed to the story itself, their unwavering love and support kept me motivated to keep writing. They never once discouraged me from pursuing my vision for this book, and for that, I am truly grateful.

I would also like to thank my close friends for their invaluable advice and help in editing the story. A special shoutout to our agent, Suhail Mathur from The Book Bakers, for making this journey possible and for working closely with our publisher, Anecdote, to bring our book to life.

And finally, my deepest gratitude to my co-author and best friend, Namya. She helped seamlessly blend our writing styles and ideas, making this book what it is today. More than that, she kept me going throughout the entire process. Because in the end, we weren't just writing a book—we were creating something special while having fun along the way.

Yahvi

Contents

1. The Freeup

On a bright sunny morning, Hilary, the leader of the Freeup, woke the learners of the Freeup early at 6 am. Her long wavy magenta hair and black almond eyes provided no comfort to freshly awoken eyes.

"Girls! Wake up! Come on!" Hilary yelled, entering the room. She went around to everyone and shook them awake.

"It's so early though! Can we sleep more just for today? Why do we have to start our classes so early?" Mia groaned, shifting in her bed. Her blonde hair streaked with pink was all over the place, reaching just below her ears. As she squinted, her eyes shone brightly in their bottle-green glory.

"Please?" Sia pleaded. Her neck-length sea-green hair was covering half her face, letting only one of her dark purple eyes to be seen. Hilary listened to them, frowning.

"No!" Hilary said angrily. "You need practice! All of you!"

"But why," Mary said, "do we have to do so much practice?" Her long silky jet-black hair was half on the bed and half hanging over the edge. She too opened her golden eyes and squinted at Hilary.

"Because the Ruleup is still out there! So we need to practice to gain the upper hand in the war!" Hilary said.

Nothing. No one moved. Only more groans.

"ENOUGH!" Hilary roared. "Get out of bed, all of you!" Then she stormed off angrily.

Freaking out, they scrambled out of their beds and got ready.

"Hilary's in a bad mood so much these days," Sia said, tying her hair in a ponytail.

"Yeah, I think it's because of all the war talk," Mia said.

"Maybe, but I feel like there is a lot of other stuff on her mind too," Mary said. "She's always under too much stress. Hilary needs to learn to relax."

"Yeah well, now we better go to practice," Nora said.

Soon, they were on their grounds, which had a long, wide grassy patch to practice in, and was full of different kinds of beautiful trees and bushes. The plants and trees had been grown by a few of the girls themselves.

They weren't able to concentrate on the class at first and got scolded a couple of times by Hilary, but after a while, managed to throw off their exhaustion and were able to concentrate well enough.

In the middle of the training, when Hilary was testing a few learners on what they knew and giving the others a break, Mia cracked a joke, sending Sia into helpless giggles until she tumbled off her chair. In the process, she accidentally kicked it, causing it to break—much to Hilary's frustration.

"Why're you interrupting all the students by making so much noise?" Hilary yelled furiously and glared at them. Hilary rubbed her forehead with her fingers and tried to steady her breathing. She always put so much hard work into teaching them, but they didn't seem to care.

"I-we're sorry, Hilary. We'll concentrate now," Sia said in a small voice.

"We promise not to disturb the others again," Mia said.

Hilary glared at them for a few seconds then said, "Fine. But if this happens one more time, then it'll be detention."

They nodded silently.

Detention by Hilary meant they would sit in a room, not allowed to talk, but rather think about what they had done. They would only be able to talk after the time is up. Then they would apologise to Hilary and tell her what they have learnt and what they won't do again.

They didn't disturb anyone for the rest of the training, so the class went smoothly.

"*Levitando!*" Sia cried, as the stick she was supposed to be lifting gave a small jerk and rolled on the floor. But she didn't give up hope. She kept on trying.

By the end of the lesson, they had all mastered their spells. Hilary was very proud of them.

"Now, there is *Nesciusement*. This spell makes a living thing unconscious. Practice it on cats." This was a medium difficulty level spell but soon everyone mastered it. They were all very happy with their results and discussed it excitedly.

"That time I was so close! My cat's eyes kind of lolled into its head but then it shook its head, and it was awake again!" Mary said.

"That's called resisting a spell," Nora told Mary.

"Nice job!" Emma said enthusiastically.

"Great lesson, right? So, tell us the great joke," Mary said with a giggle.

Mia laughed and said, "Well, all I said was, imagine if Hilary herself got up at 10 o'clock in the morning on a lesson day! Sia found that so funny that she just had to laugh! Isn't that weird?"

"Yeah, it is," Emma said in a hushed voice. "I just hope Hilary never hears this. If she does, then she'll put you both in never-ending detention!"

All of them laughed.

At snack time, Sia and Mia were joking again about 'Hilary getting up late' (they told Hazel too) but thankfully stopped just before Hilary entered the room. They had cookies and milk for snacks.

After snack time and training, they had a 45-minute break before training resumed for another two hours followed by dinner. They were all gathered in the living room, each engaged in their own activity. Mia and Sia were reading a joke book, while Emma and Mary discussed the trees in the training area. Rita swayed to the soft music that always played in the background. Nora, one of the elder learners, was immersed in her favorite book. Meanwhile, Hazel, Sally, and Amber chatted together.

After some time, Hilary entered the room and said, "Girls, time for your lesson. You will be transforming a strand of your hair into a sword by saying the spell '*Transformacioles*'," Hilary said, walking out of the room and into the grounds. "Your hair can be turned into any weapon with this spell, but we will be focusing on transforming it into a sword. First, you will need to learn the spell, then I might teach you all sword-fighting too."

"Ooh!" Sia said, like she'd always wanted to use a sword.

Finally, they began.

Mary was doing the best. "*Transformacioles!*" Her hair turned into what looked like something between a dagger and a sword.

Mia was having no luck at all. The strand of her hair turned into a very pointy spike and since she couldn't hold it, she threw it down. Unfortunately, she stepped on it and shrieked so loudly, it echoed. The pike was sharp enough to pierce through her shoes into her foot.

Scarlett gasped in horror and said, "I knew we shouldn't have been doing this!" She started crying and Olivia comforted her.

"Mia!" Hilary yelled.

Mia trembled. "I-I st-stepped on m-my h-hair…"

"Which had turned into a very pointy spike," Sia added, to rescue her friend since Hilary looked as if she was going to explode.

Hilary's anger drained from her face; she said, "Oh gosh, I'll have to see how to help you. I mean, what to put as a bandage. This is bad. Oh, I just hope they aren't all over…" Hilary mumbled as she hurried out of the grounds and into the Healing Room. She found a few bandages in the first-aid box that hadn't been touched for weeks. Sia helped Mia into the Healing Room. Once they were inside, Hilary wet Mia's leg, dabbed the place where she had gotten hurt with some cotton that had medicine on it. Then, she carefully wrapped the bandage around the wound.

Hilary said, "Now, that should help it. It will probably take a few days to heal. Until then, try to stay indoors, Mia. But I'll still give you crutches."

"Now what are you gonna do?" Sia asked.

"You'll play something with me?" Mia asked.

"Which game?"

"How about… Guess the words?"

"Sure!"

2. The Ruleup

Nearly one hundred miles away, there was another group: the Ruleup. They were evil and used dark magic.

The same day, Ruby got up early in the morning and changed. She was around Hilary's age, but her thin face, cold blue eyes, and tiny nose—perfectly proportioned with her thin-lipped mouth—gave her a maturity beyond her years. Her silky red hair with orangish yellow streaks hung loosely over her shoulders. She marched to her group's bedroom and yelled, "Get up! Come for breakfast!"

"Yeah! Coming!" Clara cried out in reply. Clara was a learner of the Ruleup along with thirteen others who were all around the age of thirteen and older. She got up and slipped right out of bed. "Hey guys, wake up!"

Soon everyone was awake, and they all headed to the dining area.

"So, Ruby," Daisy said, her light brown eyes shining with excitement, "today is the first big day of training to prepare for Freeup, right?" Her short straight light pink hair was tied up in a small ponytail. "I mean, we were always just learning defence and dark magic and all. This is exciting!"

Ruby grinned and said, "Yes, it is. I hope you'll train extremely well so that we can remove all the obstacles in our path to do our desired job: rule Magisis!" They lived on Magisis, a planet that was full of magic.

As Ruby was finishing her words, a cheer rose. "We'll win, Ruby!" Sarah shouted. Sarah's ombre green hair was wavy and reached till the bottom of her chest. Her black eyes shone with excitement and determination. She was sixteen years old.

"They've got no chance!" Alice yelled at the top of her voice, her sea-green eyes darting here and there, daring anyone to oppose her.

"Yes, yes everyone. Now please stop," Ruby said firmly. The cheers stopped as soon as she finished speaking. "Good. Now we should start our training."

They all got up and moved to their classroom, a beautiful room painted in a lush green colour. But what they learnt in that room was not nearly as beautiful.

"Today we will be learning the mass destruction spell," Ruby began. "The spell is *Destrucmasa!* Practice on these metal rocks. If they burst, then your spell is right. If they don't burst, then your spell is wrong. Go! Now start practising!"

"*Destrucmasa!*" Sarah cried, focusing on it, determined to get the spell right. She almost got it right except the spell didn't hit the rock properly and nearly made the entire room explode.

"SARAH!" Ruby yelled. "HOW DARE YOU MAKE MY ROOM EXPLODE!"

"I'm sorry!" Sarah said in a low shaking voice. "I didn't do it intentionally. I really didn't. I was just so determined to get it right that I lost focus." Now murmuring, she said, "And I didn't make it explode, it *nearly* exploded."

Ruby calmed down a bit. "Okay," she said. "If that's the case then don't focus so much. Too much effort can make your spell go haywire. Now, if you will excuse me, I will clean this room." She walked around the room, murmuring, "*Instaurixa*."

Suddenly, there was another explosion. "Now who's doing—" Ruby began angrily.

"I did it this time!" Sarah cried. She smiled her biggest and broadest smile.

"Oh!" Ruby cried, her expression changing suddenly. "Well done, Sarah! She deserves a round of applause!"

Everyone started clapping instantly. Sarah looked around, showing off.

"Show-off," Alice muttered under her breath, pretending to clap in sync with the others.

After the lesson, Andrea, Sarah's best friend came running towards her yelling, "Well done! It's so cool how you manage to be so awesome at dark magic!"

"Thanks, you'll never know what those words mean to me," Sarah said.

Andrea grinned. "Yes, I will. I am your best friend."

"Okay, c'mon now," Ruby barked. "We've got a lot of things to do today."

Everyone got up automatically and silently moved to the lush green practice room.

"Now, we'll practice the torture spell on these frogs," Ruby said, pointing to a pile of jars, which had frogs in them, kept on a table. "Remember, to help increase your concentration, you should think about how much you want to stop the Freeup! The spell is Doutelen. Three, two, one, go!"

As everyone began practising, the air was full of shouts, all of them saying the same thing, "*Doutelen!*" Alice was doing extremely well. Her frog kept on jumping here and there, trying to get away. "*Doutelen*!" she shrieked. Her frog went up and down, sideways, and finally belly up.

Everyone cheered her on half-heartedly, jealous that they couldn't get it right. Only one girl, Jane Rosier, had not gotten anything right. She was determined to become good at it and decided she would show them what she could do.

"*Destrucmasa!*" she yelled instead of Doutelen. The air exploded with dust from the floor and the blood of the frog. Her light purple eyes widened, turning red in panic. She was sixteen but her shoulder-length wavy frosty blue hair made her appear younger.

"JANE!" Ruby shouted. "Remember what you have to do! Now I don't have any more frogs and you don't need them because you are going for detention!"

"But Ruby, I really didn't me—" Jane began in a shaking voice.

"Quiet! I have had enough of your absent-minded brain! Go to detention! Now!"

Detention from Ruby was more like a punishment than a learning experience. The learners had to tie their own ankles to a hook on the ceiling of the room. The hooks were enchanted so as to keep the person from fainting, but the spell wouldn't stop the feeling of helplessness and despair.

Ruby still looked furious and said, "Now, we will do mind-control. Later, one of you will have to teach it to Jane."

Nobody really wanted to, but they didn't say anything. Only Luna did since she felt bad for Jane.

"Okay, so the spell is *Ecoutroler*. You have to think about what could be going on in someone else's mind."

"But how will we do this one?" Andrea questioned.

"Make these spiders get caught in their own webs. Off you go! Start!"

The best they could manage was the spider making the web (which it probably did by itself).

"*Ecoutroler*!" Daisy cried. Nothing happened and the spider just kept gazing at her in astonishment.

None of the others succeeded either.

"Argh!" Ruby shouted in anger. "Why is nobody getting this right? It's so easy!"

"It isn't, Ruby," Sarah said. "You just have more practice than all of us."

Ruby made a face at her but couldn't put a finger on it. Scowling, she said, "Lesson over, go to lunch."

Everyone went to the dining room, where Ruby served some rice to everyone and then left, not eating any herself.

"I don't like this," Mila complained in a whisper. "It tastes like it was made 4 days ago."

"Yeah, this is horrible," Rose agreed. "I would prefer to not have any lunch at all!"

Everyone who heard nodded.

After a while, Luna got up. "Someone has to remove Jane from detention! She can't just hang like that!" Luna's black eyes shone with determination. She flipped her wavy long lavender hair and walked out. Luna was a bit older than sixteen years.

The others burst out laughing as Luna scowled at them, storming out of the room.

"Luna!" Jane begged as Luna entered the room. "Please remove me from detention!"

"That's why I'm here," Luna replied, hovering herself up into the air and helping Jane do the same.

"Thanks for coming; I had no idea when Ruby would let me go, and I knew nobody would come to free me because you guys don't like me," Jane explained, her eyes full of tears.

"I'm so sorry," Luna said. "I didn't know. I would've befriended you before."

The words sounded like such a lame excuse to Jane that she thought Luna was just being nice. But she meant it. The two girls walked back, talking the whole time.

"Oh look, baby Luna has made a friend!" Lily mocked, who had been Luna's best friend until now. Lily was also sixteen like many others and Luna but wore her pastel pink hair with purple highlights to have an air of superiority about herself.

"I don't care if you mock me," Luna spat. "I've made a new and better friend. Because real friends never really turn against each other."

Jane looked at her, surprised. Maybe Luna meant it, after all.

Before anyone could reply, Ruby entered the room and said, "Okay, girls, I have some important things to take care of, so you have the whole day free."

"Hooray!" Everybody cheered.

"Remember to teach Jane the mind-control spell," Ruby said. She murmured something that sounded like, "Not that I expect she'll learn," as she handed over a spider in a jar.

"The mind-control spell is *Ecoutroler*," Luna explained. "You have to focus on what that spider can be thinking of and have to make it get stuck in its own web."

"Okay. *Ecoutroler*!" Jane cried. Much to both of their surprise, the spider made the web and instantly got entangled in it.

"You did it!" Luna gasped. "Wait till I tell the others; everybody would want to be your friend!"

Luna ran to the dormitory to tell the others along with Jane, who was dragging herself behind her reluctantly. "She did it!" Luna shouted, as she entered, panting. "Jane mind-controlled the spider!"

"I don't believe you," Lily said, not even bothering to look up from the book she was reading.

"Show her, Jane!" Luna said excitedly.

Jane nervously took out the same spider and cried, "*Ecoutroler!*" Once again, much to Jane and Luna's delight, the spider got tangled in its own web. Everyone cheered.

"You actually aren't the absent-minded person Ruby talked of!" Rose cried excitedly, jumping up and down.

"She's the best of us all—she just needs the right motivation!" Alice said with admiration.

Jane turned pink with pleasure and said, "I don't really care about being so good and popular, but I can't tell you how happy I am to finally have friends."

Sarah was jealous because she was always the best, but decided to congratulate Jane so that the others wouldn't think she was conceited. So, she said, "Well done, Jane!"

"Thanks!" Jane cried, unaware of the edge to Sarah's voice.

Sarah turned her back to Jane, deciding she wanted nothing to do with her, ever.

3. The Joke Comes True

The great joke started with Sia and Hazel, who incidentally got up at the same time.

"Good morning," Sia said, stretching her arms.

"Good morning," Hazel replied with a yawn.

"Gosh, it must be early, Hilary hasn't come to wake—*ACHOO*!" Sia ended with a loud sneeze.

"Stop making noises early in the morning!" Mary said in a sleepy voice, rolling around in her bed.

"I'm sorry, I woke up and felt like sneezing. And once a sneeze is on its way, nothing can stop it!" Sia said, laughing.

"Okay, let's just go t-t-to-sleep," Mary said, yawning loudly.

"Mary," Emma said slowly, "the time is…" She pointed at the time spell board for them to see in big, bold letters. It read **8:30 am.**

Hazel gasped suddenly. "Could the…could the joke have come…" She broke off.

Three of them suddenly yelled with laughter.

"Of course, it came true; of course, it came true!" Sia shouted, dancing around the floor. Hazel joined the laughter. They were making so much noise that everyone in the room got up!

"What is going on?" Rita grumbled.

"It's probably 5:30 in the morning," Chloe said sleepily, shifting in her bed.

"It isn't! It's 8:30!" Mary said, her voice quivering with excitement.

"And Hilary isn't awake! She overslept!" Sophia shouted.

"But I thought," Scarlett said, wide-eyed, "that Hilary slept with an alarm! A loud one too! I can't imagine how she couldn't hear the ring of an alarm clock like that one."

No one responded. They hadn't thought that anything could have happened to Hilary. But why else would she have not gotten up?

"We should check if she's okay," Nora said urgently once she realised, fidgeting with her turquoise shoulder-length wavy hair all the way to

Hilary's room. They found her lying on her bed peacefully. Nora's dark blue eyes stopped bulging with panic.

Just as Nora was about to shake Hilary, Mary stopped her, "Wait. We shall first check if Hillary actually is poisoned or if she's just asleep."

"But if she's asleep then she can tea—" Nora began.

"No, if she's asleep then there must be a reason for it! She must have slept late! If that's the case, then we should let her sleep."

"You have a point," Nora agreed. "There's this spell that tells you if a person is sleeping or something has happened to them. We could use it."

"I think the spell is Dormy-quess or something," Pat said, brushing her short, dark blue hair from her eyes. Her stormy grey eyes narrowed in concentration.

"Yeah, it's *Dormir eque!*" Nora said, pointing her finger at Hilary. "*Dormir eque!*"

Another Hilary sleeping on the bed appeared on the real one for a split second then it disappeared.

"That means she's okay!" Pat exclaimed.

"Now, let's let her sleep," Mary said, half-whispering. They nodded and crept out of the room.

"I have to tell Mia," Sia said with a smile.

Mia was half-amused, half-scared by the story. "But she's okay, right?" She asked.

"I suppose," Sia replied.

"Anyway, look at the bright side! The greatest of my jokes came true!" Mia cried. They started laughing loudly as Sia followed Mia hopping with her crutches into the dining room.

"You won't need this anymore, will you?" Sia asked.

"Oh yeah! We'll give the others a surprise later," Mia said.

***

Hilary shifted in her bed and then got up, rubbing her eyes.

"How come my alarm isn't ringing?" Hilary wondered out loud. She checked the time and gasped. "10 am! Why was I up all night researching?" Hilary quickly took a bath, wore her dress and ran into the kitchen where Pat was unsuccessfully trying to make pancakes.

Hilary asked worriedly, "What happened? Nobody's hurt, right?"

"No, we're okay, but how come you got up so late? Don't worry, we just started breakfast a while ago since we slept for a little while extra," Pat said.

Hilary sighed and said, "Come in the dining room. I'll tell everyone what made me get up so late."

Pat nodded and followed Hilary outside the room. Almost at once, everybody spotted Hilary and waved.

"It's nothing to worry about, really," Hilary said. "I was just up all night trying to figure out how to defeat the Ruleup."

The Freeup and the Ruleup were sworn enemies. The Ruleup had one goal ruling over Magisis, and the Freeup's goal was to stop them from doing so, as they believed in their freedom. They were constantly on the brink of a war.

"If that's the case then we all shall train harder! Only we can stop them!" Emma shouted. There were murmurs of agreement.

All of a sudden, Sia said quietly, "We're sorry for not learning properly. We just didn't realise how serious this situation was."

Everyone gave shouts of agreement.

"I'm glad you realised," Hilary said. "I hope you'll train harder from now on."

Everyone nodded, relieved that Hilary understood. "I'll make breakfast. You must be starving," Hilary said, walking back into the kitchen.

Soon, everyone was happily eating breakfast and praising Hilary's cooking skills.

"Good. Now let's get moving to the grounds for training," Hilary said. "Wait, where's Mia?"

"She went to the bathroom," Sia said, smirking.

"I'm fine! My leg's healed!" Mia shouted as she ran into the room.

"That's good! Now you can train properly," Hilary said. "I knew you would recover soon."

"Are we going to learn something defensive today, Hilary?" Chloe questioned.

"As a matter of fact, yes," Hilary replied. "We will be learning how to make a shield. The spell is *Protegerus*." She looked confused as to why they didn't start.

"Umm...Hilary?" Mary asked, afraid that Hilary was knocked off her senses.

"Yes?" Hilary asked. "Why haven't you started?"

"How are we supposed to know if we've made the shield or not? I mean, there's no one to put spells on us," Mary explained.

"Basically, when you think of making the shield properly then you will feel a strong repelling force between your hands. You have to move your hands around the area you want to protect. Get it?" Hilary explained.

"Okay. One more thing: how do we work against the repelling force if we want to make the shield smaller?" Sia asked.

"Well, if you think you need to make the shield smaller, then the repelling force will let you make the shield smaller," Hilary explained.

They nodded their heads and got to work.

"*Protegerus!*" Nora cried. She was good at magic and did it well. Her shield expanded easily but she was having trouble making the shield smaller.

Mary, who was almost as good as Nora, cried, "*Protegerus!*" She made a good shield, except for the fact that she could not change the size at all.

"Well done, y'all," Hilary praised. "Now that you've got the right motivation, you're doing much better!"

Soon, everyone got it right.

"Now that we're done with this, we'll start with another spell," Hilary said. "The spell is *Cresceret*. This is a growing spell and then later, I'll teach you the shrinking spell. Here, take these frisbees and make them bigger," Hilary said, giving them one frisbee each.

"Umm...*Cresceret!*" Scarlett, who was not very good at spells, cried. Her frisbee became half an inch larger. "Oh no," she whined, "why don't my spells work?"

"Actually, they do. I never said that you need to make the frisbee huge. I just said you have to make it bigger. Half an inch may be less, but it still is bigger," Hilary reassured her.

Scarlett smiled, basking in the praise.

"Yes, but still work on it so that you will be able to make the frisbee much bigger. It will be more useful that way, for instance, as a weapon."

Once they were all done, Hilary clapped her hands to get their attention. "Now for the shrinking spell. It is much harder than the growing spell. Make these bigger than usual frisbees small again using the spell, *Encogerse!*"

Most of them got it right. Some people like Scarlett and Olivia were having problems, and others like Nora and Mary were doing very well. Mia and Sia were halfway there. For example, when Mia tried to make the frisbee smaller, only the top and bottom part got smaller. So, it became like an oval.

Soon, it was time for lunch.

Hilary said, "The pre-lunch lesson is over. You all did well." Her eyes travelled to Scarlett and Olivia. "Except a few." She quickly looked away. "Have lunch, then you will have your break."

They had vegetable sandwiches and five different types of cheese for lunch. After everyone had eaten their food, they went for a break.

4. A Really Fun Break

Mia stretched her arms above her head. "Eating a lot of food makes me sleepy," she said to no one in particular, yawning. "I'm taking a power nap for, like, uh, 30 minutes."

"Sleepyhead!" Amber mocked. "Especially after you got up at 8:30."

"What's the problem?" Mia asked. "I'm sleepy because I ate so much."

"Okay, but why get up in 30 minutes?" Sia asked, trying to change the topic to avoid an argument. "We have a two-hour break!"

"No, I don't want to sleep the entire break. I will do something after I wake up. So, please wake me up in 30 minutes. It's 1:30 right now," Mia said, checking her watch.

The others went out of the bedroom, leaving Mia there to sleep. They went into the living room and played hide 'n seek for 45 minutes until Sia remembered she had to wake Mia up.

"Oh, I forgot to wake Mia!" Sia exclaimed, running to Mia's bed. "Hi, Mia." She shook her from side to side.

"Hi," Mia groaned, "what's the time?"

"Um, um, um, it is—" Sia stammered.

"Did you not wake me up on time!" Mia cried.

"Just 15 minutes," Sia said.

"That's okay! Now, let me play too," Mia said reassuringly. "What are you playing?"

"Hide 'n seek," Sia said.

Sia and Mia joined in. They played till they didn't feel like playing anymore. They still had around 30 minutes left for the break to end. Sia and Mia sat in a corner with Emma and Mary. Nora and Pat were talking among themselves, and Olivia and Chloe were doing a funny dance. Scarlett and Sophia were watching them, their sides aching with laughter. They were having so much fun that they forgot about practising spells. Olivia and Chloe's dance was just so funny, that everyone started watching them and laughing.

"Gosh, hasn't time passed fast? Look, it's already 2:45. Only 15 minutes to class!" Emma exclaimed.

"And we have to practice spells," Mary said.

"Oh no!" Scarlett cried, standing up. "Why didn't we start before?"

"We need to start," Sally said. "And we forgot to do it before."

"I wasn't asking—" Scarlett began.

"Let's start now, at least we will have some practice then," Mia interrupted.

They practiced some spells which they had learnt the day before.

"I don't know what to teach you for now," Hilary said, entering the room. "So, you all can take a break. Remember to practice."

"Oh, thanks, Hilary!" Mary cried, relieved.

"Thank goodness," Scarlett said, relieved. "I was super worried 'cause I'm not that good. I hope this will give me some practice."

"Remember this break is only for a little bit more than an hour, so let's start quickly," Emma reminded.

"Yeah," Mary agreed.

They all started to practice, asking each other for help when needed.

"Come for snacks now," Hilary said, entering the room.

"Good timing!" Nora said. "We were just wrapping up."

"That's great! We can talk about what happened while we have milk and biscuits," Hilary said.

They nodded and followed Hilary into the dining room. Pat told Hilary all that had happened.

"Did you find a spell to teach us?" Sally asked.

"Yup. I'll be teaching you the vanishing spell. But before I tell you too much about it here, you'd better come to the grounds," Hilary said.

"Snacks?" Sia asked.

"Huh? Oh, yeah! I'm giving y'all snacks, don't worry. Come to the dining room, let's eat first," Hilary said, laughing at herself.

"Good!" Sia exclaimed.

"The vanishing spell sounds hard," Rita said, frowning.

"It is," Hilary said, nodding. "But I'm sure you can master it; I have faith in y'all!"

"Is it really useful?" Rita asked.

"Yep," Hilary said. "You can hit the Ruleup without them even noticing!"

"Cool!" Mia cried. "Now, I can even hit Sia when she gets annoying!"

"Hey!" Sia protested.

5. An Argument

A terrible thing happened to the Ruleup after practice the next day. It was a Friday, so they had only one hour of practice. Two hours after the break, Sarah, the Ruleup's smartest learner, tripped over a large stone, fell flat on her face, and rolled down a hill.

Luckily, Jane saw her and told Ruby at once. Ruby was extremely scared because Sarah was terribly hurt, and she was her star learner. The news spread like wildfire; every Ruleup member was afraid they wouldn't be able to win without their star.

They all liked Sarah and were relieved that Jane had saved her; otherwise, Sarah might have been in worse condition. But Sarah was still hurt. Luna did her best to comfort Jane, who was shaken by the incident, especially since it had all happened right in front of her. Jane cried in Luna's lap.

"It's okay, Jane. Sarah will recover soon," Luna said reassuringly.

"But it would be better if I didn't see it at all then I wouldn't be crying like this," sobbed Jane.

"No!" Luna cried, shocked. "If you hadn't seen Sarah, then she could have been hurt very badly. We are so grateful you found her."

"You're just like everyone else, just caring for popularity. I just want a real friend. I thought you were my friend but you're not," Jane said angrily and she started to walk away.

"Jane!" Luna called after her. Why was she randomly mad?

"I told you before, I don't care about being popular!" Jane exclaimed, angry tears sparkling in her eyes.

"Jane—" began Luna but Jane had gone. Luna found her a while later, sobbing and when she tried to comfort Jane, she just pushed her away.

"Jane, please lis—" started Luna.

"You're not my friend," Jane interrupted, walking into the bathroom and slamming the door shut.

Luna burst into tears. Her first proper friend and she, Luna, had already lost her. Was that how bad a friend she was?

"Oh look, it's little Luna who thought about being friends with silly little Jane," said Alice mockingly, entering the room with Daisy.

Daisy put a hand up to stop Luna from objecting. "We heard what Jane said. We were just behind a bush relaxing when you two came on the other side of it and we heard."

"Argh! Don't talk to me!" Luna shouted in anger, throwing a big ball on them with as much force as she could muster. They dodged and went away. Angry tears sparkled in Luna's eyes as she went to see Sarah. "Sarah!" Luna said, panting, as soon as she entered the room.

"Jane?" Sarah asked weakly.

"No, it's me, Luna," Luna shouted, throwing herself in front of Sarah's face.

"Can you call Jane?" Sarah asked in the same weak voice. "I want to thank her."

"Um, um," Luna stammered, "um, I'll just tell her you gave her your thanks." She ran out of the room at top speed.

"Wait! Why did you come here in the first—?" Sarah began asking. But Luna was gone.

"I hope Sarah will be alright soon," Luna said to herself. "Then Jane will be happy again."

"Aw, look, baby Luna's talking to herself," Daisy said in a babyish voice.

"So what? You don't? Well, you're the first person I've ever met who doesn't talk to themselves!" Luna growled.

"Leave her be, I don't want to waste my time on her. Do you, girls?" Ava said, "And who cares? We'll call you whatever we want!"

"Yeah! We all know what happened between her and Jane and she still supports her," Clara said approvingly.

"I would be so happy if baby Luna and stupid Jane ran away," Rose said.

The idea lit her brain up. Why not? She could run away with Jane. Jane had once told everyone about being a better person when she was younger. Luna hadn't believed her before, but now she wondered.

Luna ran to the bathroom. "Jane!" she yelled. "Jane, come here!"

"What hap—oh, it's just you," Jane grumbled, opening the door because she thought it was Ruby.

"I need to discuss something with you late at night," Luna murmured. Jane scowled but agreed. "I'll give you some food. It's two hours past lunchtime, we had lunch at 1, you must be starving," Luna said. Jane nodded. "Here you go," Luna said, handing over a plateful of food.

"Thank you," Jane said gratefully and started gobbling up the food.

It was dinner time now and Luna had no choice but to go to the dining room to eat food. She entered the room silently with Jane. They both got a lot of glares.

"There's no water to drink," Mila complained.

Soon, Ruby entered the room. Daisy glared at Jane and Luna and told Ruby about the entire argument.

"Jane! How dare you even think like that! Detention for you!" Ruby yelled angrily.

"It wasn't Jane's fault! It was—" Luna began.

"Silence! Both of you get detention!" Ruby yelled. The whole Ruleup smirked at this. Jane and Luna looked so afraid but Ruby said, "You deserve it!" Jane and Luna were very angry, but they were afraid of Ruby. She was very scary and powerful. They didn't want to mess with her.

Luna and Jane were not allowed to finish their dinner. Ruby sent them straight to detention. They looked so gloomy that Mila felt sorry for them and after a while, helped them down.

"Thank you!" Luna cried.

"You're welcome, Luna. But remember not to go out of here. That will get me into big trouble," Mila said.

"Thank goodness she came!" Luna exclaimed.

"Yeah," Jane muttered. She leaned closer. "What did you want to tell me late at night? Can't you, like, just tell me right now?" She didn't want to admit it, but she was burning with curiosity.

"Can't risk it," Luna murmured. "Someone might hear us."

Right on cue, Mila appeared at the door and said, "Why don't you two sit on those chairs, I know Ruby won't come because she and the others are joking about you two. I wish I could end that stupid joke!"

"Thanks for that," Luna said. "Now, should I lock the door?"

"Sure," Mila replied, turning and closing the door behind her.

When detention got over, the two girls had only five minutes to get changed and go to bed. They ran to their bedroom and grabbed their pajamas.

6. Running Away

At 10:05, Jane woke up by the sound of her alarm, which was under her pillow. She rolled over in her bed and poked Luna hard with her finger.

"What?" Luna grumbled sleepily.

"It's time to wake up!" Jane said. "It's late."

"Wha—oh yeah that," Luna said. "Come into the bathroom. Wait, let's give Mila this." She filled Mila's bottle with water and shook her hard.

Mila jumped and got up. "Oh, thank goodness, there is water to drink, finally," Mila said, feeling thirsty when she saw the bottle of water. She drank the whole bottle and snuggled back in bed.

"So, the plan is, I will first set a spell on this dormitory, so that if anyone tries to get out, they will be thrown back. Next, I will dress as a Freeup person. Mila will see both of us together and will think that someone from the Freeup has captured you. I've made sure she'd go to the bathroom. We hide near the Ruleup for like two days and once the panic has died down, we will set off to the Freeup," Luna said quickly. The last dialogue surprised Jane a lot.

"The Freeup! Where I was supposed to be," Jane said, surprised. She instantly put a hand to her mouth.

"What?" Luna asked, dazed. "You were supposed to be what? Part of the Freeup?"

"Nothing uh, nothing," Jane said quickly. "I, uh, let's get on with the plan."

Luna tilted her head. She didn't want to give in, but it would just waste time. "Yeah," Luna said, peering out of the bathroom door. "I'll wear my disguise."

"You didn't put the spell!" Jane cried.

"Oh yeah!" Luna said, putting the spell. "Umm. *Fermer acle!* There you go. Now, let's put on the disguise." She removed a mask that looked somewhat like Hilary's face and put it on. "Do I look well disguised?"

"Yeah, you look kinda like Hilary," Jane replied. "I mean, I think Hilary looks like that."

"Then let's start," Luna said, getting up.

"And Mila?" Jane asked.

"Look! There she is getting up. Come on, quickly," Luna said, panicking.

Luna came out of the bathroom and dragged Jane out of it. Jane didn't expect her to be so harsh and was too scared to cry out. When Mila saw them, she rushed to the bathroom but when she reached the door, she was thrown backwards.

"Ugh! That Hilary has put a spell on this room, and she is taking Jane with her! And—no! Now, I won't be able to go to the bathroom! What rotten luck!" Mila groaned. She rushed to her bag, took out her strongest lock, and opened it. She broke the shield since it was a level-one shield, which could be broken by a strong lock opened by a key a millimetre away from the shield.

But Jane and Luna had gone. She rushed to the bathroom first because she couldn't hold it any longer. After visiting the restroom, she rushed to Ruby's room and luckily, she hadn't slept yet. Jane and Luna rushed away from the Ruleup's hideout as quietly as they could.

"You actually hurt me," Jane said angrily.

"I'm sorry," Luna cried. "I just had to make it look realistic."

"You didn't have to. You could have done it a bit softly because it was dark and Mila would barely have noticed," Jane said crossly.

"True," Luna said, "but I was just panicking."

Jane didn't respond. Once Mila had told Ruby everything, she ordered Mila to wake everybody up. They all started to look for traces. Ava found a small torn part of Jane's night-dress and Andrea found a note. It said:

Dear Ruleup,

Help! The Freeup has captured me and Jane.

If you want us, they want you to come on Hawk Mountain, when you are ready to surrender.

P.S: They forced us to write this!

Love,
Luna and Jane.

"How dare they," Ruby said angrily. Everyone else looked around at each other, smiling. "What is it?" Ruby snapped.

"Because those kids are gone and even if the Freeup tries to get a few secrets out of them, they won't be successful because Jane is such a scaredy cat and Luna will not speak at all because she will be comforting silly little Jane," Clara said. "Plus, we hardly let them into our secrets. We always told them the small ones."

"Ha! That's right," Ruby said, throwing her head back and laughing.

"What if they read both of their minds using a spell?" Mila asked anxiously.

"Those babies probably won't even know how to do that," Rose said.

"Yeah!" Lily said, snorting with approval. But she didn't look sure. She didn't look happy. Luna *had* been her friend, even if not a good one. Luna was great at spells, she just always hid it.

"Lily and Rose are right. Those babies don't even know the spell. They are too rule-following to even think of doing that! Come on, no more panicking and thinking of those kids. We need to train and be ready to fight," Ruby said scornfully.

"OMG! They don't think it's a big deal!" Jane said in shock. Luna and Jane had been listening to everything using the eavesdropping spell.

"I'm not really that surprised," Luna admitted. "They have no sense of bonding. Now that we know they don't care, we can set off to the Freeup."

"That means we won't have to stay here for two days?" Jane asked, grinning.

"Yes, but the journey is also super long. It will take us two days if we take breaks to eat, sleep and rest. We'll take those breaks, of course, so let's set off now," Luna replied.

"Yay!" Jane said happily. So, they bought everything they needed using their spare money. They set up a tent in the distance, concealed from view.

"They wouldn't be able to see us, would they?" Jane asked.

"No chance," Luna said happily. "And why would they bother to come searching for us here? They don't care." Luna's voice turned bitter. She couldn't believe that she'd tolerated such evil and heartless people for so long. She couldn't believe she hadn't talked to Jane before.

"Good. Now, let's sleep," Jane said, giving a huge yawn.

"I agree. It's late, eleven o' clock," Luna said.

***

"Good morning," Jane said, shaking Luna.

"Good morning," Luna said, sitting up. "What's the time? Nine already! We really should start."

Jane nodded. "I'll make some breakfast. It might not be awesome, but—" Jane quickly picked up some food from a nearby shop.

"Not bad," Luna said, eating the waffles Jane had made.

"Let's go to the nearest fly bike shop and buy ourselves a fly cycle," Luna suggested after she was finished eating. A fly cycle was a magic bike on which you could fly.

"Why?" Jane asked.

"Because it'll be much easier to fly cycle to the Freeup's place than to walk there," Luna explained impatiently.

"True," Jane said, shrugging.

They started walking.

"I seriously have no idea how to make my way around here," Jane said. "I've never been around much. It'll be more likely we've been taking circles than actually getting anywhere."

"Let's use a wayfinder spell," Luna suggested.

"Good idea," Jane said. "You just have to think about the place you want to find, right?"

"Yeah," Luna replied. She paused like she was waiting for Jane to do it.

"Um. Why don't you do it?" Jane said nervously.

"Sure. *El camino,*" Luna cried, thinking all about a bike shop. A map appeared above her hands. "It worked! Good. Now, we have to walk straight for 100 yards," Jane said, looking over at the map. "Right turn and another 400 yards," she panted after walking for some time.

"Finally!" Luna said, walking over to the shopkeeper.

"Hello ma'am," said the shopkeeper, not recognising them. "What kind of fly bike?"

"Two fly cycles, please," Luna replied.

"Here you go. 50 Magisos[*] for each fly cycle," the shopkeeper said.

"Thank you," Luna said, handing him a 100 Magisos bill.

"I have never done this before. How do you drive this thing?" Jane asked.

---

* The currency of Magisis

"You just have to tap these pedals. Right, left, right, left and so on and so forth. You just have to click on the green button, and it levitates 1 foot. The red one makes it touch the ground," Luna explained.

"I get it. Let's go. I'll put the strap on and cast a map. You can follow me. *El camino*!" Jane cried. She thought of Hilary and harmless magic. Suddenly, a map appeared. "Gosh, this route really is very long. It'll take us ages."

"I told you," Luna said.

"Yeah, you did," Jane said thoughtfully. "So, let's see. It's straight 1 mile then left turn 400 yards, right turn 200 yards, lef—this is enough for now."

"Let's stop for food," Luna said after a while. Jane and Luna pressed the red button and their fly cycles touched the ground. "Here you go. Take your salad."

Once they had finished lunch, they reached the border of the Ruleup's village, Yerminal. Now, they were going into the Freeup's village, Wenteron.

"It's getting dark. We should stop going and set the tent. We've been travelling for 7-8 hours, I think," Jane said.

"I agree," Luna said, her fly cycle touching the ground. "Let's put the tent up here." She pointed to a comfy spot in the middle of many shrubs, their leaves laurel. They travelled for another day and reached close. "The Freeup's not too far away. We can reach there in like 10 minutes," Luna said, after finishing her dinner.

"I vote we don't go now. It's too much stress at night and they may take it as an attack," Jane said.

"True." Luna sighed.

"We'll eat breakfast and then go to the Freeup."

They both crawled into the tent and put out their pillows and mattresses. Then they curled up and slept peacefully for the night.

7. Meeting the Freeup

"Good morning!" Luna cried, early in the morning at 6:30.

"Good morning!" Jane said, getting up. "Are you excited? I am."

"Me too, kinda, but I'm still nervous," Luna replied.

They walked to the Freeup headquarters in silence.

"Okay, we're approaching the protection. They'll know we're there, at the very least. Worst case scenario, it'll kill us, but I don't think the good people will do that," Luna said. She took a deep breath and closed her eyes. "Are you ready?"

"Yes," Jane said, trembling slightly.

"Then here goes nothing," Luna said. She put one foot inside the protection like she expected it to explode. For one delightful moment, nothing happened. Then suddenly, Luna let out an ear-piercing scream.

"Luna!" Jane cried, running forward to help.

BANG!

"Jane," Luna said.

"Are you okay?" Jane asked anxiously.

"I'm fine. The only thing is, I feel exposed." Luna shuddered. "Like everyone knows all my secrets."

"Maybe that's what the protection was there for," Jane said.

"Maybe." Luna shrugged casually, hiding her shock.

"But what was the bang for?" Jane asked.

"I don't know. Perhaps it's the only way to find out the whatever," Luna said.

"Well, we have to get in," Jane cried. "But let's do it quickly, so that we can get in without the screaming and miles and stuff."

They stepped inside. Neither of them screamed because they knew what to expect.

"We did it," Jane cried in joy.

"Yeah," Luna agreed.

"What are two members of the Ruleup doing inside our protection?" A hissing voice asked in front of them.

"AAHH!" Both of them yelled because they couldn't see who was speaking. Suddenly, a person appeared.

"What are you doing, come to spy on us?" she asked scornfully.

"I'm sorry, but who are you?" Jane asked.

"Nora."

"We have come here to betray the Ruleup," Luna said.

"LIAR!"

"We wanna hel—" Jane began.

"LIA—"

"What's going on, what's going on?" Another voice cried.

"Wh—oh, Hilary, these people from the Ruleup came here!" Nora said.

"What are your names and what do you want?" Hilary asked.

"I'm Luna."

"I'm Jane."

"Jane?" Hilary asked, dazed. "Jane Rosier?"

"Yeah," Jane mumbled nervously. But she was barely able to hide her excitement. Did she remember her? Then they would be admitted into the Freeup easily!

"Oh, I'm so glad you came back!" Hilary cried. "After Ruby stole you from me. C'mon, let's catch you up."

"Ruby stole me from you?" Jane gasped.

"Yes, of course. How else do you think you got there? C'mon now," Hilary said.

"What about me?" Luna asked.

Hilary and Nora looked at Luna uncertainly.

"Um," Hilary said doubtfully.

"She's okay," Jane cried. "In fact, it was her idea to come here in the first place."

"I think we can trust her," Nora said, "if it was her idea."

Hilary hesitated; she didn't want to take any chances. "All right," she said. "All right, she can join too. But before anything, here's your test. Without touching the quill, you will write your full name. This quill is special, the more beautiful your handwriting is, the better your writing will be."

"*Manu Moveri*!" Jane cried and moved her hand in the way to write her name. It looked like this:

Jane Rosier

Luna cried, "*Siguemi Mano!*" And moved her hand to write. Her handwriting was worse because the quill wrote things after she wrote it, not while she wrote. It looked like this:

Luna Jones

"You both can join," Hilary said happily.

"Yes!" Luna and Jane cried joyfully. Then they followed Hilary inside.

Everyone was having breakfast. They all looked up at the sight of two new children.

"Let me introduce y'all to two new learners of Freeup. This is Jane and this is Luna," Hilary said, pointing at them.

Everyone introduced themselves to Jane and Luna. Both of them were friendly and kind, so everyone wanted to be their friend.

"Well, these girls certainly fit in with us," Scarlett said.

"Yeah," Emma said enthusiastically.

"I am going to make the protection stronger," Hilary announced, "so from now onwards, no one but the Freeup can enter. The others can only enter if we allow them to. There will be a scanning spell without them knowing. That way, we'll know who it is without showing ourselves. Then we can let the person in by making the disabling shield if we want to."

"Good idea," Jane said. "I'm not complaining, but Luna and I got in very easily. It would be scary if the Ruleup decided to invade." She shuddered.

"Yeah," Hilary agreed.

"Now that it's class—" Mia began.

"No class now, we do that after lunchbreak. Now, you can learn more about Jane and Luna," Hilary said.

"Yay!" everyone exclaimed.

All of them spent a happy two hours together and then, it was finally time for class.

"Today, we will be learning the vaporising spell. Do it on these rocks and they must turn into vapour. The spell is *Vaporizar!*" Hilary said.

"*Vaporizar!*" Everyone except Jane and Luna, who were too nervous to try at the start, cried. It was a hard spell, so nobody got it right. The best was by Nora, who managed to make the tiniest of a fraction of the rock, liquid.

Jane took a deep breath. She concentrated hard and thought of what she wanted to achieve and said, "*Vaporizar!*" Much to everyone's surprise, it burst into vapour almost instantly.

Everyone gasped. It was such a hard spell and Jane made it look just so easy.

"Wow!" Hilary cried. "You are great at this."

By the end of the lesson, Nora and Mary managed to vaporise half their rocks. Nobody else managed to vaporise their rocks or even melt them, for that matter.

"Wait, Jane," Hilary called after Jane. "I want to talk to you."

"Okay," Jane said nervously, following Hilary into her bedroom.

"Ruby stole you from me because you were so good at magic," Hilary explained.

"That is why I was so bad at magic there. I'm not supposed to be doing that magic!" Jane exclaimed. "However, I realised that I could even do that type of magic."

"Yes. Now I see why Ruby stole you. You really are very good," Hilary said. "Now, you can go to lunch."

"This food is much better than the Ru—never mind," Luna said.

Chloe raised an eyebrow. "What?"

"Nothing," Luna murmured.

"All right," Chloe said suspiciously.

Nora and Hilary had decided not to tell anyone that Jane and Luna had once belonged to the Ruleup. The only reason Nora knew was because she had been in the protection area when Jane and Luna arrived. If everyone knew, many might not want to be friends with them. Nora had no problem with it, but she wasn't sure others would feel the same.

"Guys, I know I said I'd take class now, but I have to catch Jane and Luna up," Hilary said. "But y'all can practice the vaporising spell. Luna can do it during tomorrow's break."

"Works for me, except I don't know how to do it either," Nora cried, laughing.

"Everything doesn't need a teacher," Hilary said. "You can practice too while helping others."

Nora sighed. "As you wish." She walked away. As she entered the dormitory, she said, "Hilary has told us to practice the vaporising spell. I will practice it myself along with helping y'all a bit."

"You really are like our second leader, Nora," Mia said.

"Thanks," Nora said.

They practiced. Everyone was determined to get it right. Still, by the end of the lesson, only Nora and Mary got it right. Sia, Mia and some others managed to vaporise half the rock (the remaining half liquid). The rest of the learners at least managed to make the rock liquid.

Meanwhile, Hilary taught Jane and Luna everything. Jane was very good, so she didn't take much time. Luna was fine, not too good, not too bad but they managed everything in about an hour (for Luna).

"I'm done with them," Hilary said, entering the dormitory.

"Whoa, that was quick," Nora said.

"Yeah, well, they both were pretty good," Hilary said.

"I'd like to ask everyone something. Suppose someone from Freeup was abducted by Ruby when they were small and never liked the Ruleup's bad ways. Would you all accept them?" Hilary asked.

Nora understood what Hilary was trying to do.

"If that was true, we would accept that child at once," Pat cried.

There were general murmurs of agreement.

"And what if there was another person from the Ruleup who was a best friend of the person stolen by Ruby and didn't like being evil. Would you like both of them to join us?" Hilary said.

No one knew where this was going, but Rita said, "We would accept them at once if they were good."

The room was once again filled with murmurs of agreement, with some of them wondering what was going on.

"Well then, I have a very special announcement to make," Hilary said.

Jane shuddered. She didn't want everyone to know. But it *would* make her life here easier. Luna was even more afraid. She was the 'didn't want to be evil' person, not the innocent little girl who had got stolen. But they were good people. Maybe they'd accept her. They *were* saying that they would. But that was probably just because they were being nice and didn't want to contradict Hilary.

"Tell us now, Hilary," said Chloe, seeing that Hilary was hesitating.

"Yeah," Nora agreed. It would be just rude not to tell them.

"Okay. Jane and Luna were Ruleup students, and Jane was abducted. Luna was the other one who decided to come here. You can quiz them later about their great escape. They will stay here, be a part of Freeup and learn with us," Hilary said.

Nearly everyone looked horrified.

"But that's just terrible," Emma cried. "It's bad they were stole—"

"Only Jane was stolen," Hilary interrupted. "And the Ruleup is bad, they use dark magic, so don't expect anything good from them."

Emma just stared.

"Though I'm not sure if Luna's mother handed her over," Hilary added, with a half-glance at Luna.

"I don't know," Luna said, uncomfortable.

Jane related the whole story of their escape, leaving everyone amazed.

"I knew the Ruleup was very cruel, but I certainly didn't know they would be so callous, not caring at all if their own two students were captured by us," Scarlett said in amazement.

"Now, we should start with lessons," Hilary said. "Remember me telling y'all about invisibility spells? Then a dreadful storm appeared, and we couldn't do any practice? I forgot all about that later. So, I will be teaching y'all the vanishing spell now. C'mon." She walked out into the grounds.

Everyone followed.

"The spell is *indespectus*," Hilary said. "Think about transparent things. Then move your hands around anything you want to make invisible, and it wouldn't be seen."

Everyone tried their best to get it right but only Jane succeeded.

"Wow," Jane said softly. "How am *I* so awesome at it?"

Hilary, who had been watching her, said, "See Jane, you are made for this kind of magic, practice more and you might as well be a star."

Jane was not used to being praised, so she glowed (but of course, no one saw her because she was invisible). None of the girls felt jealous of Jane. In fact, they felt proud that at least one person could do it.

"Well done! You did it," Luna yelled, running towards her and Hilary. Everyone heard Luna's yells and looked over to find Hilary and Luna apparently talking to thin air. Then they all realised that Jane had succeeded in the spell. Subtly, everyone started looking up to Jane as their second leader instead of Nora.

Nora wasn't jealous as it would remove pressure from her to get everything right. Though there was a bigger problem in Jane teaching anything anyone. She was too shy to even think of teaching. But nobody minded because Pat was only too happy to take over. She was willing to give up her free time to teach them.

"So, Miss New Second Teacher," Mia said to Pat, "what are we going to learn today?"

"Hey! Don't call me that," Pat said, giving Mia a friendly punch. "We are gonna practice how to explode, Mia."

8. New Learners

"Now that those idiots are gone, we have to look for new learners," Ruby said. Even though Ruby pretended to be happy that Jane was gone, she was worried. *What if Hilary recognised Jane and let her study over there? What if she told Jane the truth about her being stolen? What if Hilary had caught Jane so that she could take her back?* Ruby would never admit it, but she was afraid of the truth. She lived in lies. It was the only way.

"How?" Clara questioned.

"We'll go around our village and find two people who want to join," Ruby replied with a wicked grin.

"Good idea. We'll find someone and scare the others," somebody said.

"Yeah, we'll need to see how we'll ask them," Mila said, with a touch of worry in her voice.

"We'll just ask them 'do you want to join the Ruleup'? Yes or no question," Ava said, laughing. She clapped Mila's hand and then doubled over with laughter.

Everyone started laughing. No one noticed how mad Ruby looked.

"Be quiet! This is no time for jokes. We need to think of a proper plan that will work. We need to think hard," Ruby said angrily.

"Okay, okay," Ava said, rolling her eyes.

This angered Ruby more. "Did you just mock me?" Ruby asked in a dangerous voice.

Ava was taken aback. "Of course not, Ruby. I'm sorry," she said, trembling. *Pretend to be scared, Ava. Otherwise, Ruby will be all like 'You dare stand up to me? Detention!' Ugh, I hate it! She's such a dictator! Do this! Do that!* she thought.

"Fine! Now, back to bus—" Ruby growled.

"Can't we just use some kind of spell?" Daisy asked, trying to stop Ruby from getting angry.

"I don't exactly know a spell to figure out if you're a destructive magic person. But I like the idea. I'll try and find or invent a spell that can do the needful," Ruby said.

There were shouts of agreement at this. Ruby started reading through some books to find out how to invent a spell. Unfortunately, she found nothing and went to bed angrily and woke up in a bad mood. The next day was not the happiest day in the world for the Ruleup because the minute Ruby got out of bed, she started yelling randomly.

"Come to breakfast! Now!" she yelled. "It's already 10 am, you're taking ages." They were doing everything at the speed of light and it was just 7. "Why are these books lying on the floor? Go and clean it up, Sophie!" Ruby yelled, when she had thrown them herself last night.

"*Desaparecer*!" Sophie cried. The books disappeared instantly with the vanishing spell.

They went to the village and saw a kid looking around nervously. She was around thirteen.

Her mother yelled out to her, "Come on, Tina! You know that you hate the Freeup and that they don't care for you, so don't wait for them to battle you. It'd be so good if the Ruleup came and took you," Tina's mother said.

"I know, Mom! You don't have to announce that to the world for the tenth time," Tina said. She had long wavy hair. The colour was dark orange at the top, lighter orange in the middle, and then finally yellow at the bottom. She had round sea-green eyes that shone with determination.

"If I heard right, you're Tina?" Ruby asked, walking over to Tina's mother.

"Yes, she is. What do you want?" Tina's mother snapped.

"I'm Ruby, leader of the Ruleup and would like to ask Tina if she wants to join us," Ruby explained.

She gasped softly. "Of course!"

"Yay! Now, I can fight that stupid Freeup," Tina said.

"Ruby will want someone with that spirit. I hope you are good at spells, otherwise she is gonna send you back home," Clara whispered to Tina.

"Well, I'm the best at it in my school," Tina said. "But here, magic might be different."

"Do you know anyone else who wants to be a part of the Ruleup?" Ruby asked.

"Uh. Um, yes! My friend Katie is also like me. I'm sure she'd want to join the Ruleup too," Tina said.

"That's great," Ruby said. "Tell me where she lives."

"Just next door. I'll just call her." And before anyone could stop her, Tina yelled, "KATIE, COME DOWN!"

"Coming!" An extremely high-pitched voice cried back. Katie appeared from the next house.

"OMG! You are one of the Ruleup now. Can I be one too?" Katie said in her high-pitched voice.

"Um, of course," Ruby said.

Katie took permission from her mom immediately.

"Yes, just one thing," Ruby said, slightly annoyed. "And please, if you continue speaking in such a high-pitched voice, I'm going to get a headache. Talk normally."

"Yes, I'll try," Katie said, her voice becoming very shrill now.

Ruby rolled her eyes. "Yes, c'mon," she barked.

Katie and Tina followed Ruby.

"We'll have a test to enter. There will be a big, heavy weight swinging at you, and you have to try to stop it from killing you," Ruby said.

She said it so casually that Tina and Katie took a minute to understand.

Katie put her hands to her mouth. "OMG! It will kill us. But this has to be safe. My mommy wouldn't—" Her voice was just so high that Ruby was shocked she could still hear her.

"Shut up," Ruby snapped.

"I don't like Katie, she is so babyish and just *so ugly.* Tina's alright, though," Alice whispered scornfully.

"Yeah, I know," Daisy whispered back.

"Quiet!" Ruby snapped. "We need to go now." They reached the Ruleup's headquarters and Ruby took them on a tour.

"But what about beds for us?" Tina asked as they reached the bedroom.

"You will take those two beds," Ruby said, pointing to where Jane and Luna's beds were.

"Cool. I love this bedroom. It is so cool, and this place is so cool and being with the Ruleup is so cool," Katie said excitedly.

"Wait till you see our practice room, it's even better," Andrea said.

"I am so excited to learn with you guys," Tina said, trembling with excitement.

"Whoa, calm down, if you behave like this all the time, Ruby will go mad!" Alice exclaimed.

"Come on, we need to go for your test," Ava said.

The heavy weight swung at Tina's face with enormous force. It would've killed her, but at the last moment, she cried, "*Romper!*" The weight broke into pieces.

"Well done!" Ruby cried. "Welcome to the Ruleup, Tina."

Next, as the weight swung at Katie, she pointed at the tip of the chain and cried, "*Procident!*" The weight broke off the chain and the chain swung at Katie harmlessly.

Ruby was disgusted at the way Katie did it. It was too in-destructive. But it had worked, so Katie had technically passed the test. Regretfully, she said, "You're in too, Katie."

"Yay!" they cried happily.

"Let's go for lunch," Alice said.

"Talk to them a lot," Ruby whispered to Ava. "Find out if they're hiding something."

Ava nodded and passed the message.

"So, where's your family living, Tina?" Daisy asked.

"My grandparents, my parents and I live in this village. The Freeup wanted me, but you took me first," Tina said. "Not that I wanted to go," she added hurriedly.

"Good. What about you, Katie?" Alice asked.

"Well, my family lives in Mentipel city. I live in our village Penus with my parents," Katie explained.

"Yeah and—" Alice began.

"Oh, I love it here," Katie interrupted in the highest-pitched voice.

"Learn some manners, like not speaking in such an irritating voice if you want to love it here any longer. And don't interrupt," Daisy yelled.

Katie was deeply hurt and started to sob.

"Cry baby!" Andrea said rudely.

"It's not my problem I've got such a voice," Katie said, sobbing.

"Well, then at least try to not use the stupid voice," Ava said, irritated by this new girl.

"And for goodness sake, stop crying," Daisy said scornfully. "How old are you, ten?"

"I'm—" Katie broke down in sobs and covered her head in her hands.

9. More Learners

"Get out! I don't want a cry baby in my Ruleup," Ruby shouted. Before anyone could throw an insult at Katie, she turned away and ran out. She grabbed her things and left the headquarters.

Tina cried, "Thank goodness Katie is gone! I hated her so much, but I just couldn't tell her that because then she would go and complain to adults and then I would be in big trouble."

Everyone was very surprised. The entire Ruleup had thought that if Katie had been turned out, even Tina would get up and go too.

"It's really bad luck for us," Ruby sighed. "To get a new learner and lose her within the hour."

"No, it's not, because I know where you can get new learners," Tina said in a determined voice. "Proper ones."

"Where?" Ruby asked.

"Near the river. There are five children. They always wanted to join the Ruleup but never could," Tina said.

"And how do you know this?" Daisy asked suspiciously.

"Oh, I have known them for several years," Tina replied.

"And are they like Katie?" Ruby asked.

"No, they are much better," Tina replied. "If they were like Katie, I would *never* suggest them."

"So, what are we waiting for? Let's go," Ruby said. "Tina, lead the way." She walked out of the headquarters.

Daisy was about to go through the trees near the river, but Tina stopped her.

"We need to go this way," Tina said, pointing left. They went left and they soon reached the riverbank. On one side, three houses were joined together, just ahead of the woods. Tina headed toward them. "This way."

"Are they all like you?" Clara asked.

"Uh, yeah, kinda, I guess," Tina answered.

"Well, then I don't think we will have a problem liking them," Clara said. Everyone nodded in agreement.

Tina blushed. Finally, they reached the door and Tina knocked.

"Hello," said a girl with straight jet-black hair, twinkling almond blue eyes and dark brown skin.

Tina greeted the girl and explained to her how she got into the Ruleup.

"Wow!" the girl said. "Come in," she told the Ruleup.

"Hi, I'm Ruby and I'm the leader of the Ruleup," Ruby said. "We're looking for new learners. Would you like to join?"

"We join the Ruleup?" the girl asked, trembling with excitement. Ruby nodded her head. "Of course!" she cried. "I'd love to join. I'm sure all my sisters will too."

They followed her into a small room with a table in between.

"Who are these people?" A woman asked, who must have been their mother.

"These are the Ruleup! Let me introduce you to us. I am Hannah, this is my twin sister, Lucy. Violet and Anne are identical twins and Bell is the eldest," Hannah said.

Lucy also had jet-black hair, but they were short, and her blue eyes were dark blue and cold. Her skin was a bit lighter than Hannah's.

"Cool. Now, are you going to join?" Ruby asked.

"Oh yeah! We are offered to join the Ruleup," Hannah cried excitedly.

"Please, can we join?" All the sisters chorused.

"Of course, it's way better than your current school. But what's with the strange name? What's 'up' with Ruleup?" their mother asked in an enquiring voice, facing Ruby.

"Oh, that's just because we are going to be the Ruling Group. We just decided that was quite a mouthful and named ourselves Ruleup for short. And that stupid Freeup just copied us! Got it? Now girls, quickly pack and let's go," Ruby explained and wanted to get done with this quickly, not wasting any more time.

The sisters packed their things at the speed of light and then everyone went to the headquarters. All of the five sisters just stood and gaped at the great building in front of them. Soon, they even had a tour of the headquarters.

"Wow! This place is great. It's hard to believe that I am actually gonna stay here," Violet said in amazement.

"I know, this is great," Anne said, agreeing with her sister.

"I have a test for you. It isn't the same as Tina's, though it's similar. A huge rock will be rolling at you, and you have to stop it," Ruby said.

Hannah went first and cried, "*Congelar!*" The rock froze instantly.

"Well done," Ruby said. "How about you now, Lucy?"

"*Liquefio!*" Lucy cried. The rock turned into lava. And so, it went on.

"You all are very good. Admitted into the Ruleup," Ruby said.

"Now, we should—oh my—it's nearly dinner time. I will have to see about your ability in learning magic tomorrow," Ruby said.

"All right. Let's have dinner now," Violet said.

When Lucy put her sandwich into her mouth, she spit it out almost immediately. "Yuck! This is burnt crisp!" she whispered, irritated.

"I know," Alice replied, "Ruby's food's always like this. She's the worst cook EVER. Everyone wishes she would make better food."

Luckily, Ruby didn't hear her.

"We can start with your lessons tomorrow," Ruby said, clearly not aware of the gossip regarding her.

"Okay," Bell said, choking with the effort of eating the sandwich.

Next morning, Hannah got up at 6, 30 minutes before Ruby came to wake them up. She was so excited to see how she was at lessons.

"There's no way I can sleep now," she said to herself. "If I get up early, perhaps I can make good food for myself. I'll give it to Lucy too."

So, she got dressed and went into the kitchen to make food. "Hmm. I think I'll make a waffle for myself." She made a waffle and tasted a bite. "This is much better than Ruby's COMPLETELY rotten food."

"Come for breakfast!" Ruby shouted. After she had woken up everyone, they all got up and went to the dining room. Hannah was sitting on a chair, reading a book.

"Oh hi! Good morning," Hannah said. Before anyone could reply, Ruby reappeared, holding what they supposed was their breakfast.

"Here is your breakfast," she said, handing them over a 1-week-old bread toast.

Just as Lucy was about to put it into her mouth, Hannah stopped her. "I made these for you and me," she whispered.

"Thanks!" she said, taking the waffle and throwing the toast in a bin near her.

It was great that Ruby didn't come poking around to see them eating, because if she found out what Hannah and Lucy were up to, she would be furious. Hannah and Lucy decided not to tell anyone else either. After breakfast, they had a break before their lessons. Everyone went into the living room and at once, started complaining about breakfast.

"It was a week-old toast!" Ava said, disgusted.

"Yeah! I saw her making that last week and she kept it in the store cupboard," agreed Clara.

"I even saw Ruby make some fresh food today! Tomorrow, I will wake up early and keep it outside, so that Ruby gives that to us. It's better than week-old toast," Andrea said.

Hannah and Lucy were pretty disappointed since they were planning to get up early tomorrow and make some breakfast for themselves. They decided to discuss this before bed because Ruby had arranged a meeting for the older Ruleup members, and they wouldn't care what the sisters were up to. Everyone was still grumbling about the toast, so they had a few minutes to quickly discuss when and where to meet.

"Let's go into the storage room near our bedroom, so that if someone does come, we can quickly slip into our beds," whispered Hannah.

"Yeah and in case someone wakes up to use the bathroom or something, we should make lumps in our bed so that we are not caught," whispered back Lucy.

"Yes! Our plan is totally fool proof," whispered Hannah.

They both stopped talking because Violet was coming towards them.

"We had way better meals at our home, didn't we? Over here, the food is so bad but I just can't bear to leave the Ruleup," Violet said.

"Well, you know that we will ma—" started Lucy but she broke off because Hannah stepped on her foot.

"Don't!" Hannah hissed.

Thankfully, just then, Bell called over to Violet so she had to go.

"You nearly gave away our secret," Hannah said angrily.

"Sorry, I didn't mean to," Lucy replied.

"It's okay. Anyways, our plans are made," Hannah said, calming down a bit.

"Yeah," Lucy said. "Well now, we need to go for lessons."

At the lesson, the sisters proved themselves to be very good, though Bell was by far the best.

"It's obvious she'll be better than us," Violet said. "She's way older. She's like sixteen, and Anne and I are thirteen. Lucy and Hannah are around fifteen."

"Maybe. But I think skills matter more," Hannah said.

Next morning, Andrea got up early and replaced the old food with the fresh one. It didn't take her much time. She was quick and did it without any problem. Just 10 minutes later, Lucy and Hannah went to make their food. Just as they were about to go into the kitchen, the delicious smell of biscuit and gravy took over.

"If we are getting such a delicious meal today, I can't bear to eat anything else," Lucy said to Hannah.

"I agree. We'll leave it for today," Hannah said. So, they went back to bed and tried to sleep.

10. The Story of Magisis

"Hilary, I really want to get some fresh air today. Please can we go for a walk?" Mia pleaded.

"Do you guys want to?" Hilary asked the others.

Everybody agreed, so the Freeup went for a walk on the west side of their town.

"Hilary, how was Magisis formed? How did everyone get magic? I don't know anything," Jane chirped suddenly.

"I'll tell you. C'mon, let's sit," she said, motioning everyone to sit with her. "10 billion years ago, our sun was formed in a large nebula called Prolopt in our galaxy, Whirlpool. But about 5 billion years after our sun was born, something terrible happened! Another star collided with ours, causing massive chunks of rock to break off from our sun.

"These are now the 8 planets we know; Magisis, Lepromin, Tachél, Remlofe, Holfens, Fakermuss, Selply and Negofer. But the only planet that got advanced magic was Magisis. How? Well, ours was the first chunk that broke off and it got hit by a massive solar flare. This left a lot of stardust on our planet; too much for life to use.

"But the stardust couldn't be left lying on the planet's surface. Something had to be done about it. It is thought that life decided to experiment what would happen if it added more stardust to it! As a result, magic was born. The other planets also got stardust but not that much, so only some people have magic there."

"That's so cool! But now that you've told me all that, what about us? I mean, how are there different types of magical people? And how come everyone got magic? Like *everyone*?" Jane asked curiously.

"Yes. If something good happens in evolution, then as a result, everyone will be like that." Hilary paused to take a breath. "People were merry and happy. They started making magical schools and doing advanced training. They would be taught by someone not much older than themselves. Take us, the Freeup, as an example."

Silence followed. Nobody spoke. Almost nobody knew all this in detail. It was so natural to them that they never even thought about asking.

"But if people were so happy and merry, then why would anyone want to change that?" Emma asked.

"Well, some people wanted more power. They wanted to be the rulers because they were more powerful than others. Because they thought they had more wisdom. All these things are obviously wrong. "People need and deserve their own freedom because all magical power is equally strong," Hilary said.

"It's not the Ruleup's fault they are Ruleup then," Luna said suddenly. "It's their ancestor's fault. They were persuaded by them because they weren't allowed to find out what good was."

Hilary stared at Luna. From all she knew, Luna hated the Ruleup. But somewhere inside, she hoped Luna was right. Perhaps, they just needed the right words to persuade them?

"Well, that may be true but it's too late," Hilary said.

"I wish I could do something about it." Luna sighed sadly.

The others stared blankly into space, wondering how to reply.

"But why do you favour them? Now, they're bad people. And they continue to be bad, wanting it that way," Olivia said.

"I hate them. Ha! I might even hate them more than you do. But if they had been allowed outside into the world before they learnt wrong things, I'll bet ANYTHING they wouldn't be what they are now," Luna cried. "And I don't *favour* them."

"But that's the point, Luna," Sia said impatiently. "They are what they are. We are what we are and have to stop them."

Luna sighed.

"Can you guys just leave it? We came out for a walk, not to argue," Mia said, getting up.

"Yeah," Mary said, getting up too.

They continued walking until they reached a mountain. It was the Hawk Mountain. No one wanted to climb, so they decided to levitate and reached the top.

"Now, we can slide down!" Scarlett yelled.

"Oooh yes, let's do that!" Pat cried.

"Woohoo!" Olivia shouted in joy.

They slid down the mountain.

"That was so fun, I wanna do it again," Sophia said excitedly.

"Maybe the next time we go for a walk. I have work," Hilary said.

Once they reached their town, Hilary found a nice snack shop and bought some biscuits, cookies, sandwiches and drinks for everyone. They neared a colony of houses.

"Where's Tina?" Hilary asked no one in particular when they reached Tina's home.

"I don't know. She was here last time," Mia said.

"Hi, where's Tina?" Hilary asked Tina's mother who just came out of her small house.

"None of your business, she has gone to a better place," said Mrs Smith scornfully.

"But she was about to join," Hilary cried.

"NO! She didn't even want to. You didn't respect her feelings. She has gone to the Ruleup and they took her in immediately. Not like you who just came and said that Tina was to soon join the Freeup! She was only kind to you because she didn't want you to make a bad name for her," Mrs Smith said.

"That's not my fault," Hilary yelled. "And I asked if she would like to join, and she had said yes."

"NO! She wanted to join so that she could betray you. She wanted to join on a condition, but you just went away," Mrs Smith shouted.

"Let's go, girls, apparently Mrs Diana Smith is mad," Hilary said, shooting a look at Mrs Smith. They glared at her before turning around and leaving.

"That was the craziest thing I've ever seen," Emma said after they were out of earshot of Mrs Smith.

"Yeah," Hilary cried. "And I thought Tina was good."

"Now what? Should we go back?" Sia asked.

"Let's just eat," Mia said, eyeing the bag of food which Hilary held.

"Yeah," Jane said, her mouth watering.

"Like a picnic!" Mary shouted happily. "I've always wanted to have one."

"Awesome idea," Hilary cried, cheering up.

Everyone gobbled up the food.

"Good food always makes me sleepy," Mia said, yawning.

"Let's go back now," Sia said with a grin. "Mia will finally be able to sleep."

"Hey," Mia cried angrily. Sia and the others burst out laughing. "I'm just sleeping here," Mia said, throwing herself on the grass.

Everyone chit-chatted while Mia slept. Hilary got some drinks because it was so hot. Finally, they started to walk back to the headquarters.

11. Sarah Recovers

Sarah had almost recovered from her wounds. The members of the Ruleup visited her every day.

One day, Sarah asked, "Where is Jane?" They all looked at her silently. They couldn't tell her the truth that they were happy she was gone. "Well, where is she?" Sarah asked again.

"The Freeup took her away," Daisy stammered.

"Oh no! That's so bad. We have to save—" she began.

"Okay, we'll tell you the truth," Ava said, panicking. They told her the entire conversation, which caused the whole Ruleup, except Luna, to be against Jane.

"Oh, she's a monster. How could I have liked her?" Sarah cried after they'd finished.

"I know. I do hope you will be alright soon. Here, have your food," Alice said, handing it over.

"And we have to go for our lunch. Bye," Ava said.

They left the room. Everyone took a seat at the dining table.

"I wish Ruby would make something better." Hannah sighed.

"Me too," Andrea said.

"We'll have to eat this for now," Violet said, putting the horrible food into her mouth.

"Yuck! What is this?" Andrea cried, spitting her food all over the table.

"This is cake," Ruby said from behind Andrea.

"This?" Andrea cried before she could stop herself.

"Yes," Ruby said coldly. "This is the best cake I've ever made."

"Which tastes like it's the worst," Clara murmured.

"What did you say?" Ruby hissed dangerously. The cake was completely soggy because it had been soaked for 5 hours. Then, they imagined, Ruby had left it to rot for two weeks.

"I SAID THAT YOUR FOOD IS THE WORST!" Clara shouted.

"Yeah," everyone agreed.

Ruby was taken aback. Since when did these guys get so much courage? she thought, feeling very mad.

"How dare you! My food is the best in the world," Ruby shouted.

"No, it isn—" Clara began.

"Be quiet! You've made her mad enough as it is," Alice hissed, secretly pleased. But she didn't want Clara to get hurt.

"Be happy with what you have. My mother didn't even give her Ruleup any food at all, which included me. And we learners were happy. Unlike you all, who always want more and more and more and more!" Ruby roared.

Everyone was shocked. Ruby had to starve! But that didn't mean that they also had to. They couldn't say anything and ate the so-called 'cake' in silence. Once they got out of the room, they all talked in low voices with each other.

"I really hope something makes Ruby make better food," Andrea said.

"And by the way, Andrea, Sarah is calling you," Ruby said, appearing from behind the door.

"Yes, I'll go and see her," Andrea said quickly, hoping that Ruby didn't hear what she had said about the food quality.

"Andrea, can you sleep with me today?" Sarah asked.

"Of course," Andrea cried. "I'll ask Ruby." She went out of the room and found Ruby sitting at the table.

"Ruby, Sarah wants me to sleep in the sick room with her and even I want to. Can I?" Andrea asked, using her most persuasive voice.

Ruby was still not happy with them, but she was perfectly happy with Sarah. If what Andrea said was true, then she couldn't forbid Andrea from sleeping with Sarah. "If she wants you to," Ruby murmured.

"Yay!" Andrea shouted and ran to the sick room. She set up a camp bed near Sarah's bed. "I am so excited to finally sleep near you."

"I know. It's been so long since we did that."

Andrea and Sarah hugged. A few hours later, it was dinnertime. Ruby had given some gravy and noodles; it was two days old. It still tasted a bit good. Suddenly, she got up.

"I want you all to know that I am going to try my best to make better food for you all because I just found out that Sarah developed an allergy to rotten food while she was sick. I don't want to take any more chances," announced Ruby. Everyone was happy that they would get better food.

"It is bad that Sarah fell sick but we are still happy that you will give good food to us," Ava said.

"If we have good food, we will be stronger and we can do our spells better," added Sophie, grinning widely.

Everyone had fun at dinner because Ruby finally made better food. "Well that was a good meal," Andrea said to Sarah as she entered the room.

"Yeah, I had freshly made noodles," Sarah said cheerfully.

"What! We had two days old gravy and noodles," Andrea exclaimed.

"Oh, well, I guess Ruby just got mixed up in trying to make good food for me and by mistake, gave you some old food," Sarah said, shrugging.

Something else was brewing in Andrea's mind. What if Ruby had given the rest of the Ruleup bad food while she made special food for Sarah? What if Ruby was planning to do this every day and continue giving the whole Ruleup bad food except for Sarah? Andrea kept tossing and turning on her bed that night. What was Ruby's plan?

The next morning for breakfast, they got two days old waffle with fresh chocolate sauce. The chocolate sauce made the waffle taste a bit better.

"It was such a good meal, right?" Sarah asked Andrea with a grin.

"Yeah, except it was two days old," Andrea said, not very cheerfully. The thought of Ruby giving only Sarah fresh food was still bugging her.

"Really?" Sarah asked disbelievingly.

"Yes. Really! Everybody is talking about it," Andrea cried. "I think she is making good meals just for you. I noticed she doesn't like to cook much. But you're her star, and you got the illness. She doesn't want you to stop fighting the Freeup."

"But she cares about you too," Sarah shouted.

"More for you," Andrea yelled. Jealousy was building inside her. And it was her weakness.

"I—" Sarah began.

"Girls, girls, cool it already," Bell said from outside.

Both of them ran over to her and started yelling.

"If you talk like this, I wouldn't understand anything," Bell shouted. "One by one! Andrea, you go first."

"Ruby favours her but she wouldn't admit it," Andrea yelled, pointing her finger at Sarah's face angrily.

Bell sighed. "Now you, Sarah," she said.

"I didn't start it. She started blabbering about giving them old food and me fresh. And she's jealous of me," Sarah yelled.

"I am sure we will sort this matter out later but for now, you need rest, Sarah," Bell said. "And you come with me, Andrea."

With a last scowl at each other, they walked away.

Once they were out of earshot of Sarah, Bell asked, "What happened, Andrea? How did it all start? What rotten and fresh food?"

Andrea sighed. She wished it hadn't happened and explained everything. Bell took her chance to speak as Andrea paused for a breath.

"Andrea, Sarah is ill. Don't upset her. Just drop the subject for now," Bell said.

Andrea scowled at Bell. She knew Bell was saying that because she liked Sarah.

"I don't care," Andrea snapped. She stormed away.

Bell thought about telling Ruby but decided against it. She didn't want to cause any trouble and decided to keep the matter between herself and Andrea. But if Sarah decided to tell Ruby, she knew Andrea would—or even she herself would be in big trouble. But Andrea didn't keep her cover, she told everybody—but in a twisted manner. When Bell entered their bedroom, complete chaos was going on.

"Ruby gave Sarah fresh food but not us," Clara was shouting.

"Sarah doesn't even admit Ruby cares more about her," Ava yelled.

"Yeah! Sarah's so rude, how could we have liked her so much," Daisy was yelling over and over again.

And there in the midst of it all, sat the culprit, Andrea, grinning at the tantrum she'd caused.

"Girls! Sarah's ill," Bell shouted all of a sudden.

"No, she isn't," Alice snarled. "She's neither hurt nor ill at this point of time."

"So, what will you do about it? Tell Ruby? Steal Sarah's food? Control Ruby's mind? Make your own breakfast," Bell yelled. She was so fed up, why was everyone making such a fuss?

"Since when have you become so ferocious?" Violet said in mock admiration.

"Shut up!" Bell shouted.

They all became quiet. "Good," Bell said, satisfied. "Now, tell me what you are going to do about this matter."

"Nothing," Andrea said in a small voice.

"There you go," Bell cried. "Drop the matter, there's nothing you can do about it. And why did you cause so much trouble? Seriously Andrea, why didn't you keep the matter to yourself?"

Everyone was shocked. Andrea could have solved the problem by keeping the matter quiet, but she was so jealous that she made complete chaos.

"If Ruby finds out, she will kill us all, just because of you, Andrea," Bell said in a dangerously calm voice.

"I already know," said a voice from behind. Bell jumped to see Ruby standing behind her. "Because I happened to be behind you when it happened, and it was a good thing too."

"All of you will go in detention, except Sarah. Your detention will be tomorrow and since we have no lessons, you will have it from after breakfast to lunch," Ruby yelled.

"Ruby, let me expla—" Bell began.

"I want no excuses or explanations, my decision is final," interrupted Ruby, clearly annoyed. Everyone was angry with Andrea that day. Andrea had thought that if she caused this ruckus, everyone would be against Sarah, and Sarah would be punished, not them. But her plan had backfired and now, she was hated by everyone in the Ruleup.

"How could we like Andrea," Alice groaned.

"Yeah! Now we have detention for like 3 hours or something," agreed Daisy.

This was the tenth time in that day everyone was groaning about detention.

"I'm sorry, guys! I didn't know there would be so much trouble and I didn't know that Ruby was standing right behin—" Andrea cried.

"Oh, just shut up! None of us believe you now," Ava said scornfully.

Andrea scowled. But she felt really sad. It hurt when all your friends spoke badly of you. And because of this tantrum, their food became as rotten as ever. Only Sarah had got all the good food and was very happy. That day for breakfast, they got three-week-old jam (three weeks over its expiry date) with two-week-old bread.

"I HATE this food," Andrea muttered. She could barely bear the smell of it and wanted to throw it in the dustbin. But she didn't.

"I hope Sarah will ask Ruby to give us good food too," Lily said wistfully. But she knew it would never happen. Sarah was too proud for that.

12. Rotten Revenge

A naughty scheme was forming in Lucy's mind. She decided to tell Hannah her plan and if she approved, they would tell it to the entire Ruleup, except of course, Sarah and Ruby. She found Hannah on a bench in the front yard.

"Hannah, I have a plan for revenge on Sarah and Ruby," Lucy said in a low voice.

"Tell me," Hannah said, her eyes glittering with excitement.

"Okay, so the plan is, we secretly make Sarah's food stale and tell Ruby not to make any food for any of us. This way, we can make our own food and tell Ruby she doesn't need to."

"That's a great idea. But what about Sarah's allergy to rotten food? If we do that, Ruby will know instantly that we gave her bad food, not the fresh one," Hannah asked.

"No, I think she would monitor us, not Sarah." Lucy replied. "She won't take any chances against her *star learner*." Hate flowed through her voice in the last two words.

"Let's do it," Hannah said cunningly. Both of them ran to the bedroom and found everybody still angrily talking about what Andrea had done. Andrea was silently sitting in the corner of the room, drowning in guilt and sadness.

"Guys," Lucy shouted as she entered the room, panting, "I have a plan to take revenge on Sarah and Ruby." She explained everything to them. "And I have decided to give Andrea a second chance," she added with a half-glance at Andrea.

"But we don't want Andrea," Daisy cried.

"She's such a traitor. Nobody wants to work with a trai—" Alice began.

"Just forgive me, will you, you horrid creature," Andrea cried. "Give me another chance."

"Everyone deserves a second chance," Lucy agreed.

"Okay, okay," Daisy said, still not satisfied.

Lucy explained the plan to everyone.

"So, all of us are in this, right?" Clara asked.

"Yes," Hannah replied.

"When do we put the plan into action?" Ava asked excitedly.

"Whenever you like," Lucy said. "Maybe tomorrow. That will be the best."

"Yes, yes, let's," they chorused.

"Okay. Then tomorrow," Hannah said, grinning.

"Wait. We can't just d—" Bell began.

"Oh, be quiet, Bell," Lucy snapped, "you know you want to do it as badly as we do. You're just afraid of being caught."

Bell smiled, because every word of the sentence was true. *It is safe*, she thought to herself. *It has to be. And what kind of big sister would I be if I didn't trust my own little sister?*

Everyone was very excited at dinner that day. They were all very fidgety.

"How is Sarah and her allergy?" Violet asked nervously.

"She is okay, thank you," Ruby snapped coldly. "Not that it's any of your business."

"We're her friends," Alice said.

"I like this gravy," Andrea lied.

"LIAR!" Ruby yelled. "I purposely made it rotten."

They stared. They had all guessed that Ruby would have made it rotten on purpose and now, they had proof. They said nothing for the rest of the meal. That day, before going to bed, they decided to tell Ruby not to make any food for them.

"Why? I thought you wanted more things, not less," Ruby said suspiciously.

"Those were only your thoughts, but we have decided to make our own food. We don't like your food," Ava said boldly.

"Because you always make it so rotten," Rose murmured.

Ruby glared at them.

"Fine. Do whatever you want. Don't come groaning to me that you are not able to cook," Ruby said, not believing they would be able to make food any better than hers. "I myself will give Sarah food, so that you don't give her bad food."

"We weren't going to give her *our* food," Alice said. "She's not worth it."

Ruby just scowled. "Good," she said and walked away.

"Now what? We wouldn't be able to give Sarah our old food," Lucy cried, concerned.

"It's okay. We'll switch Ruby's food with our own when she's left it for cooling. Then, Sarah will get the bad food," Hannah said.

"Good," Lucy said, relaxing.

"But won't she have an allergic reaction?" Lily asked, who was worried for Sarah.

"She deserves it. And Ruby can just give her medicine for the allergic reaction, it would be stupid not to have some if she knows Sarah has the allergy," Ava said.

"Okay, well now, who should make food? We should have at least 3 people on the job," Bell said. Violet and Lucy grinned.

"Bell, Anne and Ava can make the food for us," Lucy said, grinning widely.

"What? Not me," Bell said, starting to panic.

"Of course, you. You will be the head chef," Lucy said.

"Well, I am good at cooking," Bell said thoughtfully.

"Okay, so then that's settled. Bell, Anne and Ava will make food for us but if any of them is busy, we will need to keep a substitute chef," Violet said.

They decided that Tina was going to be the substitute chef.

"Great. So, our food problems are settled," Clara said. Soon, everyone went to bed. Ruby was very angry with the Ruleup except Sarah. She kept tossing and turning in her bed. *How dare those silly kids say that they would make food for themselves?* she thought. *They don't know how to do a thing. Hmph.*

"I bet those kids won't even be able to get up early in the morning to cook food," she said to herself. But the next day, Bell, Anne and Ava woke up early and made waffles. Ruby had just finished cooking when the three entered. Ruby just glared at them and walked out of the kitchen.

"Look! There is Sarah's breakfast, left for cooling. It's omelette," Bell said, pointing to a dish of omelettes. "We need to make these rotten with that spell we read in a book the other day."

"What was the spell again?" Anne asked.

"It's *Pourrir*," Ava replied. "Bell, you do it."

"Sure," Bell said. "*Pourrir*!" She thought about Ruby's noodles that had been two days old. She also thought about what had happened two days ago. The fresh food immediately looked like it was two days old.

"Now, it looks old, what next?" Anne asked.

"We just need to use a spell to make it look fresh when it isn't," Bell said. "*Rentus Veltus!*" The food returned to looking normal.

"Now, Sarah won't get fresh food," Anne said, laughing. By the time they were done, Ruby entered. She took Sarah's plate and put it on a tray, heading for the sickroom.

Ava grinned to herself at the thought of Sarah's expression when she would eat those omelettes. By the time the three girls came with the food, the rest of the Ruleup had come for breakfast. Even Ruby was sitting on the table, reading a book. The waffle looked very appetising. Ruby was about to take one bite from an extra waffle when Bell took the plate away from her.

She said, "This is our breakfast, cook something for yourself."

Ruby glared at her. "I am your leader, and you can't stop me. From now on, you will make food for me too."

"Ugh! Now, we have to make food for her," Bell said, taking a seat beside Lucy.

"As if we could ever make food," Lucy groaned.

"Can't be helped," Ava murmured.

"Yes, it can. We aren't going to give her our food. She can cook something for herself. She can have her disgusting food. We aren't gonna give it to her," Tina said, extra loudly so that Ruby could hear.

"You will make food for me," Ruby yelled.

"No, we won't! We won't give you our delicious food. You always gave us rotten and disgusting food. Now, have that yourself," Daisy yelled back.

Soon, everyone was yelling at Ruby that they would not make food for her.

"And you are our leader, but we are not your slaves," Andrea yelled. Everyone agreed and started yelling at Ruby. She got very angry and hit Andrea with a spell.

"*Doutelen!*" Ruby yelled, pointing at Andrea. Everyone gasped in horror as Andrea screamed with pain, rolling all around the floor.

"Yes, Ruby, we'll make food for you," Rose said, scared. Everyone else nodded.

"Yes, we agree," stammered Sophie. Ruby seemed satisfied and walked away to sit on a chair, her nose in the air.

"Serves you right for disobeying me, your leader," Ruby said, sitting down.

"Cheer up, guys! I don't have any problem making some extra food," Ava said cheerfully.

"Best waffle I ever tasted," Andrea said, licking her lips.

"Yeah, much better than Ruby's soggy ones," Daisy agreed, glaring at Ruby. Even though they were frightened at what Ruby had done, they were still mad at her for trying to torture her *own learners* and then make them work like slaves.

Sarah, meanwhile, got the two-day-old food and didn't like it one bit. After taking her first bite, she spit it out of her mouth and called for Ruby. Her stomach hurt really bad.

"Yes, Sarah? What is it?" Ruby asked, panting.

"You gave me stale omelettes!" Sarah yelled. "Now, my stomach is hurting, and I feel sick."

"No, I didn't," Ruby snapped. "I made them fresh."

"Yes, you did," Sarah hissed, holding the half-rotten egg in front of Ruby's face.

Ruby gasped, "Wha—?" She suddenly walked out of the room. "GIRLS!" Ruby shouted to the Ruleup, her face red with anger. "GIRLS! What did you do to Sarah's omelette?"

Andrea said, "Nothing. Like we would give her our delicious food." There were murmurs of agreement.

"No, you made it two days old," Ruby yelled.

"How? I don't remember any spell to make food old," Clara answered back.

"You stored it in the kitchen two days ago," Ruby yelled.

"None of us even went into the kitchen two days ago, let alone made food there," Clara yelled.

"Oh, I don't know what you did. Maybe you took my food," Ruby shouted, not convinced that she had made rotten food.

"And hid it where? In the kitchen drawer?" Clara asked, smirking. "Oh wait, that's what you used to do."

"SO, YOU, RUBY, DID MAKE ROTTEN FOOD FOR ME," Sarah yelled.

"I didn't! These girls did something," Ruby yelled. How could they prove her wrong so easily?

"I don't believe you," Sarah hissed and walked back into the sick room, slamming the door behind her. Ruby knew she wasn't supposed to have rotten food, and now, she was going to have an allergic reaction. She opened the medicine cabinet and tried to find something that would help her. She had read a book or two about magical herbs and medicines.

Though she couldn't understand how, she knew, she was sure, it had something to do with the other members of the Ruleup. She didn't want them to prove themselves smarter than her. How she wished she could pay them back. Once the girls had finished with breakfast and went into their bedroom, they all burst into laughter.

"Very smart trick, Lucy," Clara praised.

"Couldn't have worked better," Anne cried.

"Yes, yes, thank you. But we really should keep quiet just in case Ruby is listening at the door," Lucy said with a half-glance at the door. Fortunately, she wasn't. Meanwhile, Sarah, who had hated the omelettes, had to throw them away and stay hungry.

"Seriously, Ruby is so rude to us," Sarah said in disgust. "I got an allergy, and she still gave me rotten food."

"I know," said a voice as the door creaked open. Sarah gasped.

"What are you doing here?" Sarah asked.

"I came to tell you that I'm sorry. I want to forget this conflict and be friends," Andrea said.

"I'm sorry too. I should have asked Ruby to make better food for you all too," Sarah said apologetically. "And guess what? I've asked my mom to buy you all a treat. The chocolates must be arriving tomorrow. And I'm all right. Now, I can finally leave the sick room." Sarah's mood suddenly improved drastically.

"That's great," Andrea said cheerfully, "I'll tell the others you're sorry. And I found the medicine for your allergy." The new best friends walked to their bedroom. On the way, Sarah drank the medicine and felt a bit better.

"Hi Andrea," Violet greeted.

"Hi! Sarah's okay now," Andrea said cheerfully.

"That's, um, great," Ava said, trying to hide the dislike in her eyes.

"Well, that's fine but I still don't like you for what you did," Lucy said stiffly.

"She's okay," Andrea cried. "She's sorry for what she did. Please don't treat her like this. And her mom is giving us chocolates on her word."

"Oh okay, I'm sorry, Sarah," Lucy apologised, her mouth watering at the thought of chocolates.

"Oh!" Bell said, cheering up. "So that means we all can like you again."

"Um, yeah," Sarah said, not sure what to make of that.

"Thank you so much for forgiving Sarah," Andrea said.

"Sarah, we have started making our own meals since Ruby's is so rotten," Alice said.

"That's great. Especially now when Ruby has stopped giving me fresh food again," Sarah said.

They all went quiet at this. They felt guilty about their trick now. Anything could have happened to Sarah if Andrea hadn't found the medicine. But Sarah was in such a good mood that she didn't notice anything.

"Yeah," Ava said uncomfortably.

"So, let's play," Sarah said cheerfully. "Yay!" Everyone felt pleased to see Sarah so happy.

"You know, I sometimes wonder if Ruby gives us rotten food on purpose," Anne said suddenly. "'Cause I have seen her cooking fresh food and then keeping it in the store cupboard."

"What do you mean 'wonder'? Of course she does that. I've seen her many times," Andrea cried.

"I never knew," Anne said. "If you all knew, why didn't we catch her?"

"That wouldn't have worked. She would have told us about her mother if we did, then," Clara said.

"But it would have worked. If we—" Anne yelled.

"Guys! Keep it low, otherwise Ruby will come here and see what is happening," Clara exclaimed.

Anne stopped shouting at once.

"Sorry, Anne, we pounced on you like that, we all were just shocked and angry," Ava said calmly.

"Thanks for understanding," Anne said.

Alice smiled.

"Well, what do we do now?" Tina asked.

"You all have detention now, except Sarah," Ruby said, suddenly appearing at the door.

"Oh yeah, we had detention because Ruby favours little Sarah," Ava mocked.

"Be quiet! Otherwise, I might as well give you a double detention," Ruby yelled in anger.

"Well then, give me another detention," Ava yelled back.

Ruby was taken aback.

"Go and take your detention everybody," Ruby said, trying not to sound surprised. The whole Ruleup grinned at Ruby's surprised face.

They whispered another plan and did what they were told to do.

13. More Revenge!

"Ha! She is in for a huge surprise." Tina beamed, once they were out of Ruby's hearing.

"Yeah," Hannah agreed.

"Okay, I'll remove you guys from detention once Ruby puts you in it," Sarah said, grinning.

"Yup. That's the plan," Daisy said. Just a minute or so after they were put in detention, Sarah freed them.

"Let's show Ruby that we're smart enough to skip her stupid *detention*," Hannah said.

"Yeah, I bet it wouldn't occur to Ruby that Sarah could have possibly removed us from detention," Lucy said. Under her breath, she muttered, "*Detention*. More like torture."

No one heard her. But Lucy couldn't believe she had ever *wanted* to join this group. But the people here *were* nice. It almost made it worth it. Almost.

Once they came out of the room, Andrea cried, "Hi Ruby! How are you? Today's such a good day, isn't it?"

Ruby just stood there; her mouth wide open.

"Why don't you close your mouth, Ruby? A bee might fly into it," Alice suggested.

"How did," Ruby stammered, "how did you get out of your detention?"

"We have our ways," Daisy said, smirking at the surprise on Ruby's face.

"The whole Ruleup has had enough of you yelling and giving orders. Plus, we are smart enough to get out of detention," Ava said in a determined voice.

Ruby was lost for words. She stared at their backs as they walked back to their bedrooms.

"Did you see that look on Ruby's face? It was seriously *so* funny," Tina said, laughing so hard that tears were pouring down her cheeks.

"Yeah! I loved Alice's joke." Daisy laughed. "She is seriously funny."

"I have another surprise for Ruby," Andrea said. "If she hasn't had enough already. Not that she ever will." She grinned.

"What is it?" They all asked curiously.

"We will give Ruby completely rotten food," Andrea said wickedly.

"How?" Sarah asked.

"She makes her own food and she leaves it to coo—" Ava said.

"Then we will replace the food, yeah," Alice said.

"So, like I was saying, we will find out what Ruby might eat two weeks later," Ava said. "I have always noticed some kind of pattern in what she eats each day. We'll have to study it."

"What are we waiting for? Let's make the food and hide it somewhere," Anne cried, getting up excitedly.

"Hide it where?" Sarah asked. "And why can't we just use a spell?"

"We can't use a spell because we don't know one," Anne lied.

"Um, we'll hide it in our rubbish drawer," Violet said. All of them had a shared drawer where they kept the things they didn't really need but couldn't throw either. They got to work and soon.

"I found out what Ruby will be eating in the next two weeks. According to the pattern we've been following without realising, she'll be making *toast*," Ava said.

"Great. Now, we just have to wait for two weeks," Bell said, putting the toast in the drawer.

***

"Good morning, guys," Hannah said at 6:15 in the morning before Ruby woke them up.

"Morning," Sophie said, getting out of bed.

"It's been so boring lately," Andrea, who liked a joke, complained. "I hope it is our trick day today."

They all burst out laughing at this.

"Very soon, Andrea," Lucy said. "Just a day away."

The girls were very excited and restless. They just kept on whispering about it.

"Can't wait to see Ruby's face when she makes an old toast for herself," someone was whispering.

"The toast should have rotted completely by now. I will go and check on it," Andrea said, walking to the bedroom. She walked to the drawer.

"Yes! It is completely rotten and there will be no signs of it because Ruby is always putting so much butter on it," Andrea said happily, walking towards them.

"Okay, now, let's be very cool so that Ruby isn't suspicious of us, okay?" Bell said, trying to hide the excitement in her voice. Everyone agreed.

The next morning, Ruby decided to see what they were doing just in case. When she was watching Bell make the toasts, Anne quietly placed the old toast, which she had smuggled in the kitchen, on Ruby's plate. Just when she finished, Ruby turned her gaze to Anne instead of Bell.

"So that's my breakfast, I suppose?" Ruby asked.

"Yes," Anne replied.

"Good! Now I know that you haven't done anything suspicious," Ruby said.

They left the kitchen.

"It's done, I've replaced the toast," Anne said excitedly.

"How?" Clara asked curiously.

Anne explained everything to them quickly.

"Whoa, you really must be smart to trick Ruby right under her stern gaze," Alice said admiringly.

"I know! And the best part of it all is that now Ruby can't be suspicious of us." Ava beamed.

"Now, we just wait and watch," Andrea said. Ruby was very sleepy that day, so she didn't notice anything wrong with her bread. She took one bite and coughed because of the terrible taste.

"Ew! What's wrong with this? What have you guys cooked for me," she shrieked.

"Uh, what?" Tina asked. "I thought you saw our cooks make your food."

"I had! But it tastes completely rotten, almost as if it were weeks old," Ruby shouted.

"Well, I don't have any idea of what happened to your toast then," Sophie said.

"I didn't even ask you, so be quiet," Ruby snapped.

"Looks as if our plan is successful," Clara whispered.

"Yeah," Sophie whispered back.

Ruby was still looking at her toast, wondering how it was tasting so rotten. In the end, she decided not to eat breakfast at all. Alice was about to say something when Daisy stopped her.

"Look! Ruby is standing just behind the door, I can see her shoe sticking out, she suspects us. She means to stay here and listen to what we are saying," whispered Daisy.

The message was passed on. Nobody spoke about the toast and instead, they did all kinds of random talk. Ruby soon got bored, so she slipped out of her hiding place and went to her bedroom. Once breakfast was over, they all went to their bedroom and locked the door. Ava also put a spell on the room so that no one could eavesdrop.

"It was so funny when Ruby got that rotten toast." Sarah laughed.

"I know! It was hilarious," Tina said, also laughing.

Everyone was laughing loudly. Eventually, they all got bored and just started to do their own things. They also removed the spell and unlocked the door.

"I have nothing to teach you, so you all have free time," Ruby said, entering the bedroom.

Everyone just nodded their heads and continued to do what they were doing. Ruby went out of the room because they weren't doing anything suspicious as far as she knew.

୨ ୨ ୨

14. An Experiment

The Freeup was doing very well in their training. In fact, they were doing so well that everyone wanted something different; even Hilary wanted a change.

"Let's try and do some kind of experiment today," Mia said after an hour of thinking.

"Sure, but what?" Hilary asked.

"Maybe making your own spell," Sophia cried excitedly. "Even we want to know how to do that. Just like you, Hilary."

"That's a great idea," Hilary agreed.

"Oh wow! I never knew you could make your own spells, Hilary," Jane said admiringly. "I don't think even Ruby did."

"Yes, it's not easy," Hilary said with a shrug. "The ones I have made aren't that useful or well-known."

Soon, everyone started to read books to find a way of inventing a spell.

"Which book is right?" Mia groaned after going through a whole lot of books.

"Maybe you should read through all the books which you have seen, again," suggested Sia. "And this time, read it. Don't just flip the pages without reading properly."

"Ok then. But I'll do it later 'cause I can hear Hilary calling us for lunch."

Everyone ran to the dining room where Hilary was serving soup. After they were done eating, they went back to their work.

"Argh! I have read at least 50 books that are full of useless information about how to make already existing spells. They expect us to cheat? It's so boring," Amber shouted angrily.

"Maybe try coming out of the ancient books section and into the learning tips section," Mary said, laughing loudly.

"Yeah, I'll do that," Amber said.

She wasn't serious, but everyone who heard Mary's suggestion instantly walked over to the tips section. But none of them realised in which section they were. Anyone who didn't hear Mary went there too, just following everyone. The entire section became very crowded and there was a lot of pushing and pulling.

"Ugh. Just when I was about to open *The Birth of Spells*," Nora said angrily. *She snatched it out of my hands! Rude!* She thought angrily. Scarlett had taken the book from her. She had seen the book at the same moment but was further away.

"I'm sure this is the right book," Scarlett murmured. She went out of the room and into the dormitory. After reading the first chapter, she looked pleased with herself.

"Yes, I knew it! It was this book," she cried. No one was around, so they didn't come rushing over to read it.

"Now, it is your class time. Stop searching. Who has found the right way to invent a spell?" Hilary asked. "Or has no one found it at all?" There was silence. Slowly, quivering with excitement, Scarlett raised her hand.

"Tell me," Hilary said, hopeful that Scarlett had found the right piece of information.

"Well, you have to think of what you want the spell to do, then you have to find a suitable word in another language for it," Scarlett said nervously. "You have to think about how the user will think, so that the spell is possible."

"Correct! That is the right way you invent a spell," Hilary said encouragingly. "Which book did you choose?"

"The Birth of Spells," Scarlett said with some nervousness.

"I was pulling it out and she snatched it," Nora murmured under her breath.

"I saw the book at the same time," Scarlett cried. "I didn't know you had it."

"What?" Hilary asked.

"Nothing," both Scarlett and Nora murmured, blushing.

"Uh. Okay. So, now that you know how to make your own spell, how about you all do that in this lesson?" Hilary asked. "And don't discuss what you are going to do."

They quickly nodded their heads. Luna had been planning to make a spell that would send a person flying backwards. The only problem was that she didn't know if a spell like that already existed.

"Hilary, can I invent a spell that sends a person flying backwards? I mean, does a spell like that already exist?" Luna asked.

"Yeah, that spell already exists," Hilary replied.

"Oh," Luna said, disappointed.

"I never knew it was so hard to do even the first thing—thinking of a spell to invent that doesn't already exist," Pat sighed.

"I know," Nora cried.

"Hilary, can I make a spell that helps you fly not just levitate?" Nora asked Hilary softly.

"Yes. Surprisingly, that spell doesn't exist yet," Hilary said. She tilted her head to one direction.

"But how is that? It's so basic," Nora said.

"Somehow, people never really felt the need. We already had fly cycles by the time someone thought of it," Hilary explained.

"What is your idea? What is your idea?" Pat asked excitedly.

"No, we're not supposed to tell each other that," Nora said. "By the way, can I search my spell in different languages in our library?"

"Sure," Hilary replied.

"What about a dictionary for English to Latin? I think the word for the spell should be fly. Um," Nora said, flipping through the pages of the book. After a while, she found it. "*Volant*," she murmured. "Now, I need to think of what I need to think. Maybe all about fly bikes and birds and all the other things that fly. Maybe even the person flying." She went back to the others. No one else had got an idea.

"I'm done. I know the spell's wordings and what I need to think," Nora said, panting.

"Good, very good! Did you test it?" Hilary asked.

"Um, that's the only thing left," Nora stammered.

"Why don't you try it now," Hilary suggested.

"*Volant!*" Nora cried, pointing at Pat. Much to everyone's disappointment, nothing happened. Nora tried again, "*Volant*!" Nothing happened, Pat just stood there, rooted to the spot.

"Try once more," Hilary said, feeling much more disappointed than she looked. Nora tried at least twenty times, but she just *couldn't* get it right.

"I'm not sure what I'm thinking is right," Nora said nervously.

"It's okay, just keep trying," Hilary said. Nora shook her head. "Maybe what you are thinking isn't right," Hilary suggested.

"From all the experience I've had with spells, we always have to think about the things that can make your spell work, or the spell in action."

"Maybe you should start with say a smaller object, Nora," Hilary said. She was pretty disappointed herself but didn't expect anyone to get it right on their first try.

"Okay," Nora said, looking around. "How about that picture?"

"Yes, try that," Hilary said, looking to where Nora had pointed.

Everyone was looking at Nora, waiting for her to start the spell.

"*Volant*!" Nora yelled. Nothing happened.

"Oh, wait!" Mia yelled as Nora started to groan. "It's not working because you're supposed to do it to a person. Try it on me."

"You're right," Hilary cried. "Try it, Nora."

She did.

"Did you see that!" Nora yelled in excitement. "Mia rose a bit into the air."

Everyone had seen it.

"Yes. Keep on trying," Hilary yelled.

"Now, everyone, I want you all to try thinking of some more flying objects. I didn't think about giving you this book before, but now I will. It is a book full of words and things," Hilary said, taking a book. "I found this when I went to another empty planet. It had all the things a non-magic person would want. It looks as if someone from the non-magic world dropped this. It has all of the things that match a certain topic and will help you all to get an idea of what you need to make."

"But how do we know if a spell has been already invented or not?" Mary asked.

"I have crossed out those spell suggestions," answered Hilary. She duplicated the book using a spell.

They searched in silence for things that flew.

"Whoa," Jane said after 45 minutes. "There are billions of things that fly. Along with birds and fly bikes, there are clouds, dust, insects, dragons and so many more things. Do we have to think of all of them?"

"That may help," Hilary said.

"Okay, then let me try," Nora said. She pointed her finger at Mia and cried, "*Volant!*" Mia rose to the ceiling and banged her head. All of them except Mia cheered. While Mia grumbled, rubbing her head, Nora ignored her. "I did it!"

"Yeah, it's such an achievement!" Mia cried, just a slight hint of sarcasm in her voice.

"Well done! I love it. Now, everyone will start practising this spell," Hilary said. She was very happy and proud.

But it was messy work, because they had to point at each other. They managed it the best they could.

15. Need of Ideas

"Now, I want you all to create your own spells. Even to Nora, remember, practice makes perfect. You can also take ideas from the books which I gave you," Hilary said.

Everyone cheered. Hilary was very glad to see her learners so enthusiastic in inventing their own spells and she was also happy that they never found any of her magic boring. *They always learn with passion*, Hilary thought. Everyone went into the bedroom and started making space for the books. Then they all headed out to the living room to relax.

"You know, when me and Luna were in the Ruleup, the food there was absolutely rotten but here, the food is fabulous. Hilary is a wonderful cook. She makes awesome food!" Jane exclaimed at dinnertime.

"Well, Hilary's food is the best," Mary said cheerfully.

"Ahhh, now I can look forward to relaxing after that yummy meal," Sally said.

"Nuh-uh, you need to read through the spell book," Olivia said, dragging her friend into the living room.

"Oh, yeah, I totally forgot," Sally groaned. Soon, everyone was looking through their books.

After a while, Hillary suggested all of them to play a game. Everyone threw their books on their beds and started to play Get-it. In Get-it, you needed to choose a spell and then hide. The seeker would be blindfolded. If they bumped into you or touched you, you had to mutter the spell you chose. Then, the seeker will guess the spell.

If he/she was right, you would also get blindfolded and then help the seeker find the others. This would continue until only one person was left. That person was the winner. Also, you couldn't change your hiding place if you saw that the seeker(s) was/were nearing you. And if the seeker guessed your spell incorrectly, you got to hide again. To help the seeker guess, they could ask some 5 questions.

After an exhausting game, all soon fell asleep, dreaming of making new spells and defeating the Ruleup and bringing peace to Magisis. The next day, everyone was sleeping so peacefully that Hilary had to shake everyone until they got up.

"What were you all doing? Snuck out of bed and played till midnight or something, did you?" Hilary asked, laughing.

"No, no, we were just very tired that's all," Mary said, yawning and getting off her bed. She nearly tripped and was about to land face-first on the floor but Emma caught her.

"Oh yeah, some of us were *very* sleepy," Emma said, laughing.

"Okay now, sleepy heads, time to take a bath and come for breakfast.

"Tell me, what did you all do last night?" Hilary asked.

"We were playing Get-it," Emma replied. "It was fun."

"So, Hilary, when do we read those books?" Pat asked.

"Well, if you want, you all can read it in your free time, but we would still read it in lessons," Hilary said.

"We'll read it in some of our free time," Sia said determinedly.

There were shouts of "Yeah!" And, "Of course!"

As they were going for their lesson, Pat asked Hilary, "Can I invent a spell that helps someone recover from an injury, illness, wound, etcetera?"

"Yes! No one has made such a spell yet. And it will also be very helpful," Hilary said excitedly. Her mind was racing. A healing spell would definitely help them in a war, and in general too.

Pat was very happy. She went to the library to find the right words for her spell.

"Right. What language should I use?" Pat murmured, running her hand over a lot of dictionaries that translated English to other languages. "What about—?" Pat said. She paused. "Yes! I'll do it in Spanish," she said, her eyes catching an English to Spanish dictionary. She took the book and sat on a comfortable sofa in the library.

"Recover in Spanish is *recuperar*," she murmured, running her finger around the word.

"No, that's too hard to remember," she groaned, shaking her head. After a while, when she couldn't find anything, she took a Latin dictionary and started searching.

"Yes! The word in Latin is *Salve*," she said. "That should be my spell." She looked very cheerful. She ran inside to the living room where everyone was still struggling with their spells.

"Hilary, I found a wording for my spell," Pat said, running into the room.

"Awesome!" Hilary said. "What is the word?"

"It's Salve," Pat said.

"Nice! It's also easy to remember," exclaimed Hilary.

"Can I try it out?" Pat asked.

"Yes, let's go out in the grounds."

"Uh, how do I practice my spell?" Pat asked. "I mean, there is no one hurt or sick over here."

"Guys! Don't be idiots. Mia is right here, and the poor girl is hurt," Sia said, a crazy smile on her face.

"Wha—?" Mia began saying.

Sia pushed Mia playfully, Mia being Mia, fell down on the floor almost immediately. Mia started crying, "OWWWW THAT HURT! I SCRAPED MY KNEE. SIA, I WILL NEVER FORGIVE YOU, COME HERE." She tried to run after her but fell back down on the floor.

"It's okay, I'll just try my spell. *Salve*!" Pat cried.

Nothing happened. She tried several more times. Mia's knee didn't show any signs of healing. "SIA, I WILL MURDER YOU!'

"Hey! It ain't my fault, all right? Pat said she could do it," Sia said playfully.

"WHAT? It isn't my fault. Look, I can do it. I'll show you," Pat cried. "*Salve!*"

Mia's skin almost healed instantly. Everyone started clapping. Even Sia.

"See, Mia! I told you Pat could do it. You get angry for no reason," Sia said.

"What—you were literally just—" Pat stopped herself from speaking. "Forget it. Let's just celebrate my awesomeness."

16. A Day Off, Ruined

The Freeup were walking towards Hawk Mountain again. They soon reached and crossed it the same way as before.

"Now, you can slide as many times as you want because I have no work to do," Hilary said, once they had reached the peak of the mountain.

"Yay! Now, I'm gonna do it at least ten times," Mia shouted.

"Yeah, we are too," the others cried.

"We should use the flying spell to go up," Nora suggested.

"Good idea," Rita cried.

Soon, they were sliding down the mountain, screaming with joy.

"You all need a break from studies so that's why, we will camp over here for a few days. We'll buy tents and everything we'll need," Hilary announced.

Everyone jumped in happiness.

"But Hilary, no one is there to protect our headquarters so—" Nora asked.

"Don't worry, I have put a protection spell," Hilary reassured.

Hilary paired up four to a tent. Pat and Nora were in one tent with Hilary because she couldn't get any more tents and everyone else's tent was full.

"Exactly what I love. Camping out in the open with friends. Just wonderful," Nora said, sighing.

They all relaxed and enjoyed themselves.

***

The Ruleup had gotten up late today and were having breakfast now.

"I'm bored with your tricks," Ruby said. "These wouldn't help you. Like this, we'd never be able to defeat the Freeup." She glared at them. The Freeup! The entire Ruleup had forgotten all about them in taking revenge on Ruby. How could they have?

"Well?" she asked impatiently. "Do you want to defeat the Freeup or not?"

"Of course, we do," the Ruleup cried.

"Then stop your tricks. If we fight among ourselves, you can forget about fighting ANYONE else," Ruby shouted. "The Freeup will divide and conquer."

Ruby was thinking about the rotten food which the Ruleup had tricked her into eating. She'd found out when the girls were talking about it and had forgotten to put the anti-eavesdropping spell. She didn't bring it up to avoid an even bigger argument. Despite being angry at her learners, she didn't want them running away. Maybe she could improve her ways. Maybe just a little.

"I'm—we're sorry," Sophie said in a very small voice. "We should think of a plan to defeat the Freeup."

Ruby glared. "Fine, but you will think of it," she shouted.

Everyone thought that they had been spared. They had earlier thought that this meant twenty hours of detention.

"We will," Ava said, almost cheerfully. Even though they felt happy about getting no detention, it was almost as impossible to think of a plan as it was to come out alive from a twenty-hours-long detention.

"I think we should use a map spell," Andrea suggested. "Then we can go to the village near their headquarters."

"But how will we get there? It takes at least two days on a fly cycle," Ruby asked.

"Um, you can teleport," suggested Alice.

"Good idea!" Rose cried.

"But how would we see them if they're at the headquarters? I don't know what happens in their protection spell and I don't really want to find out," Anne said, shuddering.

"They will go shopping or go out at some point, silly," Hannah said. "When they do, we can catch them."

"I can defeat the Freeup alone, yeah," Ruby said sarcastically. "Good plan."

"Once you see if they're there, then you can teleport back here and take all of us there," said Alice.

"Yeah! But we'll have to stop in the middle because you can't teleport so many people such long distances," Bell said.

"It's decided then. Let's put my plan in action," Ruby said, determined.

Everyone was mad at her for saying it was *her* plan and taking all the credit. But they didn't show it.

"*Teleportar!*" Ruby cried. She thought about Hilary and her voice. She thought of what comes a bit further than their headquarters. She thought of all the magic people. And suddenly, she disappeared.

"Well, I hope it worked," Andrea said after a while. There was an awkward silence. They had always been under Ruby's stern gaze and suddenly, she was gone. Were they supposed to party and talk terrible things about her? Instead, they ended up talking about how bad it was that they'd forgotten about the Freeup.

***

Ruby reached her intended location. It was the town outside the Freeup's headquarters. Quickly, she muttered the invisibility spell.

"*Invisibilia*!" Ruby was invisible. Slowly, without making any noise, she started to walk. She wandered around a bit until she saw the tents the Freeup were using.

Hilary put her head out of her tent and said, "Well, I think this is just the perfect location to camp. We're staying for four days, girls."

Four days! Ruby thought. What good luck! Now she could go back and get her learners. The Freeup weren't going anywhere.

"*Teleportar!*" Ruby hissed. She thought of her home and reached there. "*Uninvisibilia!*" Ruby became visible again and walked inside her headquarters.

"They're there? Let's go quickly," Rose cried excitedly.

"Now, now, no hurry, girls," Ruby said. "They are camping for four days."

"Still, I wanna go now," Sophie said.

"Yeah, I'm so excited to defeat the Freeup!" Ava shouted.

"Alright, let's go then," Ruby cried. She was pleased that she was re-uniting with her learners.

"Everyone, just touch each other. *Teleportar!*" Ruby cried. They appeared a thousand miles north in one go.

"I'm hungry," Mila groaned.

"Here is some food," Ruby said, handing out boxes of food.

"Mmm, this is the first time I've had good food in a very long time," Andrea said before she could stop herself. Much to everyone's surprise, Ruby just laughed.

"I did it on purpose, as you might know," Ruby said, grinning. The others couldn't believe that Ruby was finally admitting the truth, but she seemed in an oddly good mood.

"But why, Ruby? Why did you do it?" Ava asked.

"Oh well, I guess you all should know now," Ruby said, sighing. "I was annoyed at you all. I thought that you were all spoilt brats, and this would teach you a lesson. I guess that I never thought it would cause a rebellion." She took a deep breath and closed her eyes. "I didn't want that. I wanted to complete what my parents had started, and I needed help for that. Anyways, now let's quickly finish this food and we need to get going. You don't wanna be fighting till midnight, do you?" Ruby said, laughing. But it seemed like a forced laugh. Like she was remembering something bad.

No one seemed to notice. They were too busy eating.

Is the food more important to them than me? Ruby thought. *Did I really treat them* so *badly?*

Once they were done, they teleported another thousand miles west and so on, until they reached the village. All of them put on the invisibility spell. They used the third level of it, so no one could hear or see them. They moved very close to the Freeup's tent and saw them eating lunch. Slowly, they opened their mouths and muttered a spell to make themselves visible again. The Freeup jumped to their feet at once and gasped.

17. A Fight and a Loss

"Ruby! What are you doing here?" Hilary asked.

"I have—" Ruby began.

"Jane! Luna! I thought you got captured. And when someone gets captured, they aren't let free to roam around," Sarah yelled, getting suspicious. "'Cause you guys might escape. Wait a second, why're you both not escaping?"

"It's time you knew the truth," Hilary said, somehow calming down at the question.

"Say it," Andrea yelled, jealous that Sarah was showing so much liking to Jane and Luna.

Hilary told the entire Ruleup, the story of Ruby stealing Jane and how Jane and Luna planned on running away. Ruby was acting to be fine with everything but deep down, she was scared. She had no idea how they could win with Jane on the other side. Even though Sarah was completely well now, she didn't know how good Sarah would be against Jane.

"I don't believe that it," Mila shouted in disbelief.

"'Course I did! Did you think that I would let someone so good at magic be in the hands of the Freeup?" Ruby shouted.

"But she isn't even that good," Sophie snorted.

"She is," Ruby said, "and she isn't a destructive magic person."

"Ruby, but how can you say this? Jane's horrible. She's stupid. She's shy—and ARGH! I don't even know what to say," Sarah yelled.

"And there's more!" Ruby said, ignoring Sarah, which surprised and annoyed her. "It's time you knew Luna's truth too. I took Luna from her Aunt and Uncle. Her parents died of a disease when she was very small. Her Aunt and Uncle took her in. They were bad and tricked her into thinking that the Ruleup was good. Luna wanted to be on the good side and that's why she agreed. Not until she was bigger did she realise that the Ruleup was bad. And her parents were good people."

"Ruby! How could you?" Clara asked, shocked.

"Be quiet, Clara! You don't want me to torture you just like I tortured Andrea, do you?" Ruby yelled. Now, the Freeup was horrified.

"RUBY! How could you? How can you torture your own learners? I can't believe how bad you are," Hilary exclaimed.

"Shut up, you—" Ruby began shouting.

"Enough!" Hilary yelled. "I've had enough. I feel very bad for these kids who have to work like your slaves and keep quiet if you ill-treat them."

"They don't care, do they?" Ruby said, looking around at her learners.

"No, we don't," Sarah said.

The Ruleup did not want to admit to the Freeup that they did not like Ruby very much and they didn't want the Freeup's pity, so they merely nodded. They might not agree with Ruby, but they *did* want to rule Magisis, and Ruby was the only person who could make it happen.

"LIAR!" Jane shouted. "I have overheard you once, complaining about how rude Ruby is. Complaining about how much you *hate* her."

Ruby's face paled, but not with anger.

"That's not true," Andrea lied.

"Yes, it is," Luna yelled. "Jane told me."

"Well, then she made it up," Anne yelled. "You all are just a pile of rotten LOSERS."

"Yeah! Your silly learners don't know a thing. They are babi—" began Ruby.

"Keep quiet, Ruby! You came here for a reason. What is it?" Hilary yelled.

All of this while, villagers had gathered and were staring at them because of so much yelling. However, when they realised that the argument was heating up between the grand Freeup and the silly Ruleup, they fled into their homes. For a few others, however, it was different. They realised that there was an argument between the wonderful Ruleup and the spoilsport Freeup. They too, however, fled into their homes.

"I have come here to declare war, and now I will," Ruby yelled.

"FOR MAGISIS!" Hilary cried.

"FOR A BETTER RULER!" Ruby cried at the same time.

Both groups charged.

"*Encogerse!*" Sia yelled, pointing at Clara. Clara shrunk to the size of a mouse.

"Hey!" Clara squeaked. "Make me big again." But Sia just laughed and walked away.

"*Transformacioles!*" Mary shouted, pulling one of her hair, and hurtling it towards the Ruleup. She had turned it into a dagger.

Ruby was shouting, "*Doutelen*!" Over and over again, which was torturing the people of the Freeup.

Most of the Freeup were making shields, yelling, "*Protegerus*!" To stop the Ruleup's dangerous spells.

"*Congelar*!" Rose yelled, pointing at the big rock which someone had sent rolling at her.

"*Fermer acle!*" Hilary yelled. Some of the Ruleup were rushing at her, so she cast the spell and they were all thrown back. The entire field was filled with cries of all kinds of spells.

"Mia! Behind you! QUICKLY!" Pat yelled.

Mia moved out of the way. Ruby had just thrown a big rock at her but luckily, Pat had spotted it.

"Hilary! Nora, help her! I'm too far," Mary yelled, dread filling her. Hilary had just gotten a big wound and fainted.

"*Salve!*" Nora yelled, sitting down on the grass beside Hilary. Hilary regained consciousness but was completely lost. Nora told her quickly that she had a wound and had fainted.

"What?" Ruby said in disbelief. "But this spell doesn't exist." A thought struck her, *they know how to make spells.*

"*Destrucmasa!*" Alice yelled, when Mia sent a piece of her hair, which had turned into a big sword, hurling towards her. The sword burst into pieces.

Alice used the torturing spell on Mia, but Mia quickly created a shield.

"*Indespectus,*" Hilary murmured, she turned invisible, and then quietly snuck up to Ruby. She used the shrinking spell on her. Then, she hurried behind a bush and quickly made herself visible again.

"Ahh! What happened?" Ruby yelled angrily. Unfortunately for the Freeup, Ava saw her and made her big again.

"*Nesciusement*!" Rita cried, pointing at Sarah. Sarah wasn't quick enough to block the spell and collapsed backwards.

"SARAH!" Ruby shouted in horror. She tried to shake Sarah back to her senses, but she was unconscious.

A level 3 unconsciousness spell was nearly always fatal.

"Good! Now that their most powerful and smartest learner is down, we can take down the other members easily, but of course not Ruby. Thank you, Rita, for hitting Sarah with that spell," whispered Hilary to her group.

"No, no, no, no, no, Sarah, are you okay? Please be okay," Ruby murmured worriedly.

Sarah didn't respond. Anger hit Ruby like a bullet. She knew it was a level 3 unconsciousness spell. And she *cared* for Sarah. "*Doutelen*!" Ruby yelled, pointing at any Freeup person she could find. She was so angry, and the spells were coming at the Freeup very quickly, so they were getting harder to block with every passing minute.

"Hmph! This proves that Ruby's favourite is Sarah," Hannah whispered.

"Yeah! She wouldn't do something like this for the rest of us," Lucy whispered back.

"Nora, out of the way! There's a—AAARGH!" Rita shouted. She was warning Nora about an approaching torture spell and got hit by one herself.

"Tell me, how to recover her and surrender to me. Then I'll stop," Ruby was shouting.

"If we surrender, then the whole of Magisis is in danger. Surrendering is the last thing we want to do now. How dare you even think about it," Hilary yelled back.

"But Hilary, what about Rita? I can't bear to see her in such pain," Nora said, very worriedly.

"We'll find a way but for now—" Hilary began.

"That's what you get for making my Sarah unconscious," Ruby yelled, laughing. She was continuously hitting Rita with torture spells.

"Stop it! If you, Hilary, are ready to give up one of your learners because of what you can do all by yourself, then you might as well lose two. I will make sure that even I am tortured," Nora yelled, heading towards Rita, who was yelling in agony.

"Nora, come back!" Hilary shouted, but it was too late. Nora was right next to Rita. Ruby started hitting both of them.

"Nooo!" Hilary yelled, as she saw both of her learners yelling in pain.

"Yesss!" Ruby yelled cheerfully.

"No, no, no, no!" Hilary said.

"Hilary, one's abilities alone should never factor in a war when everybody's life is at stake. We have to fight in unity," Rita said, breathing her last. She died because of all the torture Ruby had done on her. Hilary was pretty shaken up when she realised she had given up one of her learner's lives.

"Is she dead?" Sarah asked. She had woken up and seen Ruby torturing Rita to death because any spell that has been put by a person who is approaching death is weakened. Thus, Sarah was able to see what was happening even if she couldn't say anything before Rita died.

"Sarah, you are awake," Ruby said. And while Ruby was distracted Nora recovered and froze her.

"*Geler!* That was for killing a friend who saved my life," Nora yelled in anger. "*Transformacioles!* That's for being Ruby's pet without bothering to tell her off." Her hair had turned into a huge weapon, and it hit Sarah. Sarah got a fracture on her leg. Others from Freeup were also very angry but a few were more shocked than angry that Hilary thought she could do without one of her learners.

Hilary was so stunned that she couldn't even fight anymore. But her learners directed their anger towards their spells and that spurred them to fight harder and get better aim. As for Ruby, she was getting up because one of her learners had saved her. But she did not strike yet as her joints were stiff. Suddenly, a very peaceful song was heard. A long line of people appeared; the Calmup.

The Calmup was a third group on Magisis that wanted to spread peace using their powers. They had powers of singing that made people go to sleep. While Freeup wanted to bring peace too, they were ready to fight for it. The Calmup's songs made both the Freeup and the Ruleup sleepy. Soon, everyone fighting was lying on the floor.

The Calmup went away. But before leaving, they used their powers in a way that the Freeup would wake up sooner than the Ruleup, so they could escape the war for now. Soon, it got very dark and everyone woke up. No one had any more strength to fight and a temporary truce was called. The Ruleup just slept in some bushes and the Freeup was about to do the same, but Nora stopped them.

"Guys. We need to give Rita a burial."

Hilary agreed. Everyone felt a wave of sadness wash over them and nodded in unison. Hilary held Rita's body in her hands.

"*Lux!*" Olivia cried. A light appeared in her hands. She held it up so everyone could see.

"Move the light closer to Rita's face," Hilary said, as she gulped down a sob. She couldn't cry in front of her learners. She needed to be strong.

Rita's face was pale, eyes closed, but she looked peaceful. This had been a willing sacrifice, to save anyone else from Ruby's wrath. Mary sobbed, and Emma put a hand on her shoulder and pulled Mary close to herself, tears streaming down her face like silvery lights that glistened in the light Olivia had created with her spell. Nora, Pat and the others started crying too.

Hilary took a shaky breath. "Help me with carrying R—" She closed her eyes and took a moment to regain control. "Rita."

Pat and Nora rushed forward to help her. Together, the three of them carried Rita to the burying grounds, the rest of the Freeup following them, crying. It was beautiful, but in a sad way. There were coffins made of safen. Safen was a material which was a Magisis specialty. It was made by people who collected stardust and froze it to extreme temperatures.

Then, it was heated a bit to mould into various shapes. People used safen because of its natural beauty and glow. All around the pale coffins, there were enchanted plants so they would never die. Never lose their beauty and always radiate a beautiful sadness. They seemed to say—treasure the ones you lost. Bury them here, and they would be remembered forever.

Each coffin had a name written on it in white, barely noticeable from the coffin itself. The area had grass on the floor, but it felt like barren land. There were black fences with black flowers shaped into them, and a large gate. At one side, there were spare coffins and there was lots of open space.

There was only a man over there and he turned away when the Freeup entered. He had had enough experience to know that people who had lost someone were not comfortable with other people looking at them and displaying pity.

Hilary couldn't hold it back any longer. Tears poured down her face as she, Pat and Nora went to take a shovel. They could have used magic, but it felt rude to use magic since that was the cause of Rita's death. Once they were done, they carefully placed her inside. Then they filled it back in. The Freeup passed a coffin from the many lined on one side. Nora placed Rita in it.

"Rest peacefully, sister," Nora whispered, putting her hand on the coffin and leaving a mark saying Rita.

Hilary had finally regained control but watching Nora cry made her burst into tears again. Pat held back her own and went to Hilary.

"It was all my fault, all my fault. I should have surrendered. I could have stopped her somehow. That was all she needed. I could have—" Hilary was saying. She stopped talking and continued sobbing.

"Shh. It's okay, we can't change the past. But we can make a better future," Pat said, hugging Hilary tightly.

But Hilary pushed her away and said, "It's all my fault. I should have—" She couldn't continue, she choked on her sobs and nearly collapsed to her knees like Nora.

Pat caught her. "Hey," she said to Hilary softly. "You need to stay strong. To make Rita's sacrifice worth it."

"I know. But I was the cause, I was the cause of—" Hilary said, she couldn't say any more. She started sobbing so much that all her strength was gone, and she fell asleep, her face as pale as Rita's.

Pat sighed. "Let's all sleep. It'll do us good."

18. A Bad Time, for Everyone

When Hilary woke up, she was confused. Slowly, it all came flooding back to her. Rita's death, her burial and how it was all her fault. She woke everyone up.

"Girls, we haven't completed the tradition of a burial. We need to place flowers over Rita's grave," Hilary said, trying to speak without pain in her voice, but unable to do a good job of hiding it. Everyone recognised what she was trying to hide.

"Okay Hilary, let's go now," Pat said, sniffing.

Exiting the burial grounds, they all reached the florist.

The man at the counter looked very happy today. "Hello! Good morning. What kind of flowers would you like?" Jenks asked.

"Hi, Jenks. We need burial flowers," Nora said.

"Burial flowers? Oh no. I'll get some now," Jenks said, his happiness draining away.

Burial flowers were different and special from normal flowers. They were enchanted to never die. All the graves used only burial flowers in Magisis.

"We need pink flowers," Nora said.

"Pink your, uh—favourite colour?" Jenks asked.

"Yeah," Nora replied.

This was another tradition for the burial—flowers to be the dead person's favourite colour.

"Hilary, are you okay? Should I—?" Nora began, seeing Hilary crying again.

"I'm fine. Let's go," Hilary interrupted, quickly wiping her tears. "I'm fine."

Scarlett, Chloe, Sally, Amber, Hazel and Olivia had started to sob loudly. Nora, Pat, Emma and Mary went to them and wrapped them all in a hug. A few other villagers came along. They retreated as they saw the Freeup crying and holding burial flowers. After a few minutes, they reached the burial grounds. Hilary placed the flowers neatly around Rita's coffin.

"It's time we head home," Hilary said.

The Freeup reached their headquarters. They all ate lunch in silence.

"It's so good to find a safe place to sleep in when you're at war," Nora said dreamily after lunch was over. "Even if you have just—"

"Huh? What do you mean?" Pat asked.

"Uh-oh, um, nothing. Nothing at all. Let's sleep. It will give us more strength," Nora said, snapping out of her dream.

"Nora, what exactly do you mean?" Hilary asked.

"Let's just sleep. We all need rest," Nora said, getting up and heading for the dorm. She raced away.

Hilary raised her eyebrows at Pat and Pat just shrugged.

***

Ruby finally stirred after Freeup had gone, still sleepy. She blocked the tears in her eyes. Her learners hated her. In hindsight though, that was the most sensible thing they'd ever done in their lives. Her chest hurt. She felt so lonely. She took a deep breath. Maybe she had to be strict, but she would *no longer* be cruel to her learners.

The others started stirring. Clara got up first.

"Who were those random people interfering in our war?" she asked angrily.

"How am I supposed to know?" Ruby hissed.

"I just remembered who they are. Don't you all remember the Calmup? The people with magic powers that can make people go to sleep," Ava said.

"Oh yeah! I bet the Freeup called them. The cheaters," Hannah said angrily.

"No, I don't think Freeup called them, because the Calmup can control who goes to sleep with their songs, and the Calmup definitely won't put the people on their own side to sleep," Ruby said. "And they looked just as surprised as we were."

"True, but I still think that—" Hannah said.

"Let's just leave it. We need to find the Freeup. So that we can continue our war," Lucy cut her off angrily.

"Yes!" Ruby agreed. They all teleported nearly everywhere in the village but couldn't find them. However, Ruby knew *exactly* where they were but would never disrupt the tradition of burials. She didn't care that the Freeup were her enemy. She *wouldn't* stop them from giving someone a burial. That was beyond evil. Her parents would never do that. If it was what her learners wanted, she was not going to let them have it.

"They probably went to their headquarters," Ruby lied. "Well, let's go home." They teleported back home. "Let's practice our torturing spells," Ruby said after they had rested.

"Can we just do different spells? 'Cause then if everyone practices the same spell then we'd have mastered just one spell," asked Violet. "And we'll end up doing only one thing to the Freeup; torturing them."

"Alright, good thinking. You can practice spells which you think will be effective," Ruby said.

"Who will we practice the spells on?" Sarah asked.

"How about we get some bugs or animals and practice it on them?" Rose suggested.

"Yes, I will get some animals and insects right now!" Ruby exclaimed, surprising them by teleporting and coming back with a lot of bugs in jars and animals in cages. She had got a few parents (of the Ruleup members) to help her with the jars and cages.

"Mom! Dad!" some people from the Ruleup yelled.

"We have only come here to help," Tina's mom said. "We are going to teleport back as soon as we have finished helping Ruby."

Before leaving, they gave hugs and kisses to their children.

"Now, start practising," Ruby barked once the parents had left.

"But Ruby, some of these animals are wild. And they will run away if we open the cages. Even the insects could run away," Mila complained, who was secretly scared of wild animals and bugs.

"Mila, the cage bars have spaces in the middle, which is where you will direct the spell. And if you hit the bars, it won't matter because every spell can go through the bars. For the insects, you can put the spell through the glass," Ruby explained.

"Oh," Mila said, relieved.

Soon, the hall was filled with yells of different kinds of spells. Even Ruby started practising.

"Everybody, listen up. Nobody can use the killing spell. Understood? Because I haven't got any extra animals or bugs. One animal and bug for each of you," Ruby announced.

"Ahh!" Andrea yelled after a moment. "Help me, Ruby." Andrea had been working on a lion and decided to practice the enlarging spell. The huge lion broke out of the cage. A few people looked over, yelled, "Ahh!" and then ran away.

"*Parvus!*" Ruby yelled. The lion shrank to its original size. "What were you thinking, Andrea? Practicing an enlarging spell—AAHH!" The lion charged at Ruby, still out of its cage. "*Congelar!*" Ruby cried. The lion froze. "*Instaurixa!*" The cage repaired itself. Ruby opened the cage door and shoved the lion back inside. "What were you thinking, Andrea? Seriously, you have no control over what you're doing. Now, you will practice only on your bug. I am taking away your animal."

"I'm sorry, I just thought of the enlarging spell and then I used it," Andrea said in a small voice.

"And how would an enlarging spell help us? A shrinking spell will have some use. If you make the opponent stronger, then you can't win against them," Ruby yelled.

"I'm sorry," stammered Andrea, not daring to look at Ruby; instead, she looked at her feet.

"Ruby, I have an idea. Some of us should practice the enlarging spell on small animals because we could take a lion with us in the war and make it large. Then, one of us could mind-control it to attack the Freeup!" Sarah exclaimed, saving Andrea from trouble and coming up with a brilliant plan for the Ruleup.

"Hmm. Nice idea. Let's do it," Ruby said cheerfully. Clara, Bell, Hannah, Lucy, Anne and Violet practiced the enlarging spell with their small animals like rabbits, parrots, etc.

"The ones with large animals should do it on their bugs, right?" Ava asked.

"Why're you even asking?" Ruby snapped. "Isn't it obvious?"

Ava shrugged, and they all started practising.

19. Nora's Story

Everyone woke up around 4:45 in the evening. A few minutes earlier, Hilary was shifting in her bed and then got up. She yawned loudly and stretched her arms.

"Oh my! It's 4:25 already. I bet the girls are already up. They might be starving after their breakfast disaster last time. I don't think they will be able to make milk and snacks either," Hilary exclaimed, checking her clock.

She quickly took a bath and wore a shirt and some shorts. The Freeup hadn't taken a bath after Rita's burial. They had straight gone to bed. By 4:35, she was dressed. Hilary ran to the dining room but couldn't find anyone else. She ran to their bedrooms and found them all sleeping peacefully.

"Girls, time to wake up," Hilary said, shaking every girl slightly. By 4:45, everyone was ready.

Hilary made hot chocolate and gave them all some marshmallows.

After the food was over, Hilary asked, "Guys? Do you all want to train? If you don't want to, it is okay too. I won't force—"

"Hilary, we'll train. We need to defeat the Ruleup," Nora interrupted.

"Look," Luna paused, "I haven't known Rita for as long as you all have, but we could try talking to the Ruleup. Maybe convince them that everyone deserves their own freedom?"

Hilary sighed. She said, "In the beginning, I had tried to persuade her but it didn't work. Instead, it made Ruby more intent on ruling over Magisis. What she said was, 'if everyone has their own freedom, there will be chaos. Everyone will do whatever they want and start doing random stuff, and they might hurt themselves! So, Magisis needs a ruler! And I will be it.' I knew she was trying to convince me that her intentions were good but I wasn't fooled."

"But still, can't we try it again?" Luna asked.

"It's no use, let's train now," Hilary said.

"But—fine," Luna said, sighing.

"C'mon," Hilary said. "Let's do training."

They trained all afternoon and evening. That night, Nora couldn't sleep well and woke up at five in the morning.

"O—" Nora began shouting. Then she softened her tone. "OMG, it's just 5 am." She couldn't go back to sleep and hence decided to go for a walk in the grounds. She put her coat on and left the room. Suddenly, somebody tapped her shoulder.

"Ah! Oh! It's only you," Nora said, on the verge of panic. It was Pat. She hadn't been able to get any sleep either. She was worrying about Nora, about how she suddenly waved away the question and how she seemed uncomfortable when Hilary asked what she meant.

"What are you doing here?" Nora asked. "You scared me."

"I wasn't able to sleep and when I looked beside myself where your bed is, I found it empty. So, I decided to come looking for you. I guessed that you would have gone for a walk, because your coat was missing," Pat explained.

"Smart girl," Nora said in mock admiration.

Pat rolled her eyes but went on, "I, um, just wanted to ask, um, what happened yesterday, um, when you were not able to sleep thin—"

"I don't want to talk about it," Nora said sharply, her grey eyes seeming pure black in the darkness.

"I'm sorry Nora, I didn't mean to—" Pat apologised.

"I'll tell you what happened only if you promise not to tell anyone else until I am ready to tell them," Nora cut her off.

"Okay, I promise I won't," Pat said.

"So well, I was not brought up on Magisis," began Nora. "I was born here, but then someone lied to my parents that my uncle was sick. He was on another planet. My parents panicked and went there. Then, my parents found out that this person had lied to us. But we had to stay there because we didn't have access to a spaceship. When I was around six, a war started on that planet."

"What was the planet name?" Pat asked.

"The planet's name was Tachél," Nora replied.

"No way! Tachél is full of betrayal," Pat exclaimed.

"I know." Nora looked down; her eyes torn with pain. Pat had never seen Nora look so tired. It made her wonder what had happened. Nora began recounting her past from ten years ago when she was on Tachél.

***

"Larry, look here," Nina (Nora's mom) said. She had long turquoise hair tied back in a ponytail. She had Nora's eyes and a beautiful face, but at the moment, looked extremely pale and worried.

"What happened?" Larry asked (Nora's father). He had dirty blond hair and a very handsome face. He saw that the whole planet was at war. Nora was only six years old at the time.

"Oh no! What do we do? How do we save my Little Nora?" Nina wailed.

"Mommy? What is happening?" Little Nora asked, appearing from behind. Nina quickly closed the curtains.

"Uh, nothing darling, nothing. How about you go to the kitchen and have some of your favourite choco-chip cookies?" Nina said.

"I'll take you. Come on," Larry said, taking Nora's hand and leading her into the kitchen. Nina rushed upstairs to get a suitcase. She started packing their most important things, things they would need to survive. Just then, Nora came up.

"Mom? Why are you packing?" Little Nora asked.

"Oh! Um, I was just packing up for a holiday," Nina said. "Go get your most important things and we will pack it in here."

"Okay," Little Nora said. She went straight to her window but was horrified at what she saw. The whole village was at war. Some people were fighting while others running. Houses were being crushed apart. Children were crying and running everywhere to find their lost parents. Adults were panicking and grasping their loved ones and trying to flee.

Zombies were flying everywhere and attacking anything in their path. A man dressed in all black stood with a large remote in his hands. Little Nora gasped in horror. It was such a loud gasp that her parents in the next room heard her and came over.

"No!" Larry exclaimed, as he saw that Little Nora had taken a peek outside.

"Why didn't you tell me?" Little Nora asked, shaking with fear and her teeth chattering.

"Honey, we didn't want to scare y—" Larry began, and Nina joined him. But they were interrupted by Nora crying.

"Our home planet is gone. We will die. No!" Little Nora sobbed. "Why is this happening to us?"

"Don't worry, dear. We will be out of here in no time." Nina sounded like she was convincing herself more than Little Nora.

"Will we die, Mom?" Little Nora asked.

"No, darling, absolutely not," Nina said. Then, she and Larry hugged Little Nora.

"Whatever will happen to us, we will always be together," Larry said.

Little Nora wiped her nose on her sleeve. "I know, Dad. Then we will go on a proper holiday."

"Yes. We will get off this planet," Nina agreed.

"Yes. We will have lots of fun afterwards," Larry cried.

"Yay! Let's take a rocket now," Little Nora shouted. Her parents looked at her uncertainly and Little Nora felt shame burning down her throat. How could she have forgotten? They were at war.

"Yes, darling. We will," Nina cried, trying to lighten their spirits.

"We will," Larry joined in. Little Nora quickly put one of her favourite books and some clothes and her favourite toy in a bag. Then, Nina carried Little Nora in her hands. Larry took the suitcase, and they rushed out of the house. When they were just about to reach the place where the rockets were, a big building came crashing down on them.

KA-BOOM!

Little Nora was saved because she wasn't in her mother's hands anymore. She had managed to get out of the building's way at the last minute. But she couldn't find her parents and started to cry.

"Mom! Dad! Where are you?" Little Nora yelled. "No!" She fell to her knees. Why did this happen to her? She turned and saw the man in black approaching her. She didn't care. Nothing mattered right now.

Suddenly, some other man crept behind the one in black and yelled, "*Nesciusement*!" The man in black fell down.

"Nora, come here. I am your uncle. Your mother's brother," the man yelled.

"What is your name?" Little Nora asked.

"My name is James, but for you, Uncle James. Come here, I won't hurt you," James said kindly. Little Nora slowly approached, eyeing him suspiciously. It took almost an hour for James to convince her that he was a good person.

"Where are your parents?" James asked.

"They died," sobbed Little Nora. James put an arm around her.

"I'm sorry, I'm so sorry," James said softly. He himself felt very sad. He'd lost his own sister. But he had to stay strong, for Nora.

"I don't want to talk about it," Little Nora said, turning away.

"Okay, let's get you home," James said.

"My house might be in ruins," Little Nora said.

"No, not this home, your real home," James said.

"My real home?" Little Nora asked.

"Magisis. It's another planet, where you were born," explained James.

Nora stared at him, wide-eyed. "Really?"

James nodded. "It is. Do you need to take anything?"

"Hmm, maybe. I have my important things with me, but I want to take a photo frame from my home here." Little Nora cheered up. They went to her home and thankfully, found it in good shape. Little Nora rushed inside with James. She took the photo but just as they were leaving, the house exploded!

"*Protegerus!*" James yelled. He and Little Nora didn't even have a scratch on them.

"Wow! Is this magic?" Little Nora asked, her voice quivering with excitement.

"Yes, and even you should know it," replied James. "It's in your blood. I will teach you once we reach Magisis."

"Yay! Let—" began Nora. She stopped because as they reached the rocket place, all of the rockets were gone.

"No! No! I need to get you back to Magisis. This planet isn't safe for you," James yelled. The whole night, they searched for a place to sleep but found none. The next day was the same. Then the next and the next. James had got some food but after five days, they ran out; they were so tired that they could barely stand up.

"Uncle James?" Little Nora asked weakly. Her legs were jelly and she looked like she would pass out due to exhaustion any moment.

"I'm tired," she panted.

"I think I see a store. I'll go and get some sleeping bags; it's a camping store."

"Okay."

Uncle James returned shortly. "Nora, come here. Look what I found," James yelled after a while.

"What is it?" Little Nora said. "Wow, a rocket!"

"Yeah."

"Let's fly home."

"We'll fly high, then I will put it on autopilot so that we can sleep." Soon, they were sitting in the rocket. As soon as Little Nora sat down on a seat, she collapsed. James tried not to follow her example. Quickly, he started the ship and made it ascend until it was twenty miles above the surface. He put it on autopilot and went to sleep.

When Little Nora got up, she asked, "Where are we?"

"In space. Look at the stars, like tiny twinkling lights in a dark room," James said. "Aren't they beautiful?"

"Yes, they are," Little Nora agreed, looking at the stars with fascination. Suddenly, she noticed a sparkling planet; it was literally sparkling, like someone had sprinkled a billion tons of glitter on it. It was blue, green, red, orange and yellow. "That planet," Little Nora said. "It's beautiful."

"Yes. This is Magisis, my home, and yours too."

"Wow! I can't believe I'm actually gonna live in this wonderful world."

"But yes, you are." James smiled. Soon, they were walking on the planet's lush green grass and wonderful smelling flowers. James took Little Nora to her new home.

20. A New Friendship

"Well, that's my story," Nora said, trying to sound upbeat.

"Wait! So, then who is the man who you call your father?" Pat asked.

Nora sighed. "Don't tell anyone. It's my Uncle James. I pretended that it was him."

"What? No way."

"Yes, it's true, I never told anyone before. I couldn't tell anyone that my parents were dead. So, I pretended that he was my father."

"Oh my! So—" began Pat.

"Don't." Nora choked back a sob. "Don't tal—"

"Pat! Nora! Where have you been? We were so worried. It's already seven o'clock. We searched everywhere," Hilary yelled, running towards them.

"Hilary—" Pat began but she stopped. Nora ran away. She just couldn't stop herself from breaking down but didn't want to do it in front of Hilary.

"Nora!"

"No, Hilary, don't! She's really sad. Leave it, just tell everyone we are safe and sound," Pat warned. Her tone made Hilary want to do it unless she wanted to be screamed at and be sent flying backwards.

"Oh," Hilary said.

Soon, they were all sitting at the dining table.

"Where were you?" the others demanded when Pat came into the dining room.

"Me and Nora went for a walk and didn't realise the time since we were talking," Pat said, slipping into a seat.

Nora came after a while. It was clear that she had been crying. Her eyes were red.

"Nora—" began Pat.

"Stop it! I don't want to talk to anyone. Leave me alone," Nora snapped.

"Okay," Pat said, taken aback. Nora sat away from everyone and ate her food.

"What happened to her?" Hilary asked in an undertone.

"I don't know," Pat lied, "but I think we should give her some space," truthfully this time.

"Why?" Sally asked, getting very inquisitive all of a sudden. "Is something wrong? What happened?"

"Nothing. Just leave it," Pat said, getting up and leaving the room.

Everyone finished their food and left the dining room and went into the living room.

"Hello," Nora said, sitting next to Pat, who was sitting there.

"Um, hey, you okay now?" Pat asked.

"Yeah yeah, I feel better," Nora said.

"Hey Nora!" Mia yelled. "You okay now?"

"Uh-huh, though there's no need to yell as if some really loud music is going on," Nora said, grinning widely.

"Ha-ha! That's the old Nora I know." Mia laughed.

"Though seriously, what were you guys talking about, when you were walking?" Emma asked.

"Oh, um, I'm not sure if—" Pat began.

"Um, I'll think if I want to tell you later. Please excuse me," Nora said, getting up and leaving the room. Everyone had seen the expression of deep sadness on Nora's face and instantly wished that the question had not been brought up. A while later, Nora re-entered the room and her eyes were red again.

"I'm so sorry for my outburst," Nora said, entering the room.

"It's okay Nora, would you like to—?" Mary began.

"I'll tell you what exactly happened," Nora said. "Just, someone, go and get Hilary. She has every right to know as well."

Mia flew out of the room and came back as quickly, dragging Hilary with her. Nora told everyone, the story of her childhood. She choked back a sob as she told them how her parents had died. When she finished her story, everyone had a thousand questions. Nora answered all of them patiently.

"Nora, I'm so sorry," Hilary said, hugging Nora. Nora returned the hug.

"Um, Nora?" Jane asked.

"Yeah?" Nora said.

"Can you describe the man in black? I mean, like every single detail which you remember?" Jane asked.

"Well, except for what I told you. There was this weird red sign on his cloak, that's all," Nora said.

"How did the sign look?"

"It was like a circle with lines and some lines coming up at the top. That's all, why?"

"Can you show a drawing? Oh, and colour it?"

"Okay, I'll try to draw it quickly." Soon, Nora was done.

This was how it looked:

"No way! I know who he is, then," Jane exclaimed, after looking at the drawing.

"What!" Nora exclaimed, getting up so fast that her chair went flying backwards. "That's impossible."

"Yes and no," Jane said.

Nora looked confused. "What?"

Jane sighed. "I have heard of this guy, and I know him, well, kind of know him, because he is related to the Ruleup."

"What! Tell me who exactly he is," Nora demanded. It was all she could do from stopping herself from banging her fist on the table and yelling: NOW!

"He is Ruby's dad, and he used to destroy planets for fun," Jane said angrily.

"ARGH! I am going to kill Ruby. And I don't care that it is dark magic." Her expression was beyond hate. "Her father killed my parents. And now *I* will kill her." She stormed out of the room, her fists clenched, shaking.

"Nora, wait—" Pat began.

"Leave her be, Pat, she needs some time to herself," Hilary said calmly, but secretly worried. Soon, it was lunch time but Nora still didn't come.

"I am going to find Nora," Pat said, getting up.

"Pat, wait," Hilary said.

"Why?" Pat asked, clearly annoyed.

"She'll come. I still think that she needs some time to her—" protested Hilary.

"I don't care. I am her friend. I'm going to find her and comfort her. And she might need company. Someone to cheer her up," Pat cut her off, going off to find Nora. After a while, Pat found Nora lying down under her covers. At first, she hadn't been able to see her but then she thought she saw some movement on Nora's bed. So, Pat threw the covers and found Nora under them.

"AHHHH!" Nora screamed.

"It's okay, it's just me," Pat said, shaking with the effort.

Nora glared at her. "What?"

"Um, what happened to you when, um, we found out who the man was?"

"Later. Now, why did you come here anyway?"

"Um, I just came to call you for lunch, and when will you tell—?"

"Okay, I'll come for food. I was getting hungry anyways."

"Oh, um, what about my question?"

"I'll go and wash my hands. You go on ahead."

"Okay."

"I don't know when she will tell me what happened to her, but she is coming for food," Pat said.

"Hi, everyone," Nora cried, walking into the room.

"Hey, I was thinking about something. Why do you cook food for us, when you can just do it by magic?" Nora asked.

"Even magic has its limits," Hilary replied. "It's not possible to create food."

"Hmm, okay," Nora said, shrugging and taking a seat beside Pat.

When lunch was over, Hilary went to check her storage room. She gasped in horror. "Oh no! What happened? My storage room is completely empty. And what on Magisis has happened to my cleaning supplies? They're all gone. Oh my! Looks like I forgot to go shopping—probably because of the war. I even used up my backup supplies!" she exclaimed.

"Well, looks as if we have to go shopping," Mia said.

"Not we. I will have to go alone, you guys are staying right here," Hilary said.

"Hilary, we all need some things for ourselves!" Pat exclaimed. "Please let us come."

"Yeah! Please, pretty please. Let us come, Hilary," the others pleaded.

"Okay, okay! Take your money and let's go," Hilary said, rolling her eyes.

After a few minutes, everyone was ready to leave.

"Which shop are we going to, Hilary?" Nora asked. They'd gotten ready, but had forgotten one important detail. Where were they going?

"Mid-Mart," Hilary replied. Mid-Mart was the largest store in Anlemiss; it had everything you could possibly want. It was located in the main village because that village was the largest in Anlemiss. Anlemiss was the continent where both the Freeup and Ruleup lived. Every continent had one branch of Mid-Mart in their main village—it was almost as big as a mini-town on its own.

"But that's so far away. It's in Jafrer, the main village," Pat said. "It will take, like, more than a day even if we use a fly cycle."

"Who said we are fly cycling? We are going to use the speed-o-matic," Hilary replied. The speed-o-matic was a kind of train which was superfast. It was used mainly for getting to Jafrer; every continent in Magisis had its own speed-o-matic.

"Oh, yes, of course! We'll get there in 10 hours?" Emma asked.

"10 and a half."

"Cool," Hilary said. "I'm gonna get tickets for recliner seats 'cause you don't need beds in the morning."

"Yeah, beds are boring. Recliner seats are awesome," Olivia said.

All of them set off for the speed-o-matic.

21. The Speed-O-Matic Station

The Ruleup were also going to Mid-Mart, because even their supplies had mysteriously disappeared.

"Argh! I can't believe those kids are still playing tricks on me. I bet this is one of their tricks," Ruby yelled, storming out of the storage room. "KIDS! EMERGENCY MEETING! NOW!" As soon as the Ruleup heard this, all of them ran downstairs to the living room.

"What happened Ruby, why—?" Sarah asked.

"Sit down!" Ruby ordered. Everyone sat down quickly on chairs or sofas. "You have started your tricks again, haven't you?" Ruby barked.

"What tricks?" Hannah asked.

"Oh please. Stop acting innocent. You all have emptied out my storage. Don't pretend that you don't know that," Ruby yelled.

"What? Your storage got empty. I bet the Freeup—" Hannah began. Hannah hated the Freeup and even though she never admitted it, she always found a way to blame them.

"Hannah. There is a simple explanation for this. No need to blame the Freeup all the time for everything," Bell interrupted. "One explanation is that maybe because of the war and all, we got so busy that Ruby forgot to go shopping and we finished all of our supplies."

"Hmm. Yeah! That's probably what happened, but remember, I said probably," Hannah cried.

"Ha-ha! Hannah, you'll never change." Bell laughed.

"Okay. Guys, we need to go shopping. We are out of supplies," Tina said.

"Yeah, but," Ruby said.

"But what?" Alice asked.

"We will need to go to Mid-Mart in Jafrer," Ruby said in a hollow voice.

"What? Why? That's so far and—" Ava began.

"Argh! Silly, all of our supplies are over, so we will need to go to Mid-Mart because that is the largest shop and—" Hannah interrupted.

"Enough, you two. Stop arguing. We can't waste time like this," Ruby cried. "And do you all wanna come? 'Cause if you have things which you wanna buy, you can come and get them."

"Um, yeah. We'll come, all of us have something we need to buy," Bell said, saving Hannah and Ava from another scolding.

"Fine! Go get your money everybody," Ruby said, glaring at Bell. Once they were back, Ruby said, "Guys, I talked to the person who was managing the speed-o-matic and gave him money for our seats."

"You mean recliner, right?" Sarah asked. "I love them."

"No," Ruby said. "Just normal seats."

Her face fell. "Okay."

"Let's go," Ava cried.

"Yeah," Daisy agreed, "I'm excited to go on the speed-o-matic."

"Um, okay," Ruby said. "We're walking there. I'm not putting in the effort to teleport when it's not required."

"'Kay," Andrea said. "Can we go already?"

Everyone followed Ruby. Suddenly, Ruby stopped and everyone banged into her.

"Ah! Ruby? What happened? Why did you stop?" Sarah asked, who was front in the line and who had bumped right into Ruby, with more than ten girls banging into each other behind her one after another. "Ow! Ow! Ow ow ow ow!" Sarah yelled.

"I'm sorry, it's just that—" Ruby's voice trailed off.

"What happened, Ruby? Tell us," Sarah asked, who was very annoyed with Ruby for stopping all of a sudden.

"It's just that I saw something weird," Ruby said, still in a daze.

"Oh, what was it?" Sarah asked, her heart softened.

"Nothing really, um, let's go ahead, shall we?" Ruby said.

"You're lying." Sarah looked up, determined.

"No, I'm not." Ruby looked away and started walking.

Sarah raised an eyebrow. Everyone started walking towards the speed-o-matic station. Ruby was very quiet and so deep in her thoughts that she nearly banged into a lamppost but thankfully, Sarah caught her arm just in time and pulled her back.

"You okay, Ruby?" Sarah asked.

"Huh? Oh, um, yeah, I'm okay, how about you guys go and get some snacks from this cafe? There's still loads of time for our speed-o-matic to arrive. I'll get a table," Ruby said, clearly distracted.

"Hmm, okay. What should I get for you?" Sarah asked, still not satisfied.

"How about two to three mini cheese sandwiches? Oh, and here's a bunch of money, take it and buy food," Ruby said, handing Sarah a bunch of Magisos.

"Wow! Look at all these pastries and sandwiches and drinks," Violet exclaimed, as they went to see what was on sale. Violet loved junk food and immediately started to decide what she was going to eat.

"Amazing! So many yummy looking sandwiches. Wait, should I take the pastries instead? Or maybe I'll take both with some juice," Bell said, looking at the glass case filled with food.

"Violet, come here!" Ruby ordered.

Oh boy! I hope I'm not in trouble, Violet thought as she walked over to Ruby.

"Help me to join these five to six tables so that we can sit here and eat," Ruby yelled.

"Okay," Violet said.

"Psst. Sarah," Andrea whispered in Sarah's ear.

"What?" Sarah whispered back.

"Can I talk to you in private?" Andrea asked.

"Um, sure, come on, let's talk in that bathroom," Sarah whispered.

"Um, er, that's a bit odd," Andrea said, then she took a deep breath and said, "Okay, let's go."

"Hey, Ruby!" Sarah yelled. "I gotta use the bathroom."

"Hm? Okay," Ruby answered.

"Me too," Andrea said.

"Okay, okay. Don't ask me for permission. No need," Ruby said.

"Okay." Andrea followed Sarah into one of the bathroom stalls.

"Yeah, so what happen—?" Sarah began asking. Butshe stopped when Andrea put her hand on her mouth.

"Someone's here, shh. We will need to whisper," Andrea whispered angrily.

"Okay. So, what happened?" Sarah asked.

"Do you have any idea of what happened to Ruby?"

"Seriously. That's all? Come on. You could have asked me that when we were sitting. And how would I know?"

"I'm sorry, it's just that you are Ruby's favourite learner, so I thought that you would know." Her voice trailed off.

"Hmm, I'm sorry for getting angry at you, now, let's go."

Sarah crept out of the stall and a minute later, even Andrea came out. Soon, everyone finished their food and left the cafe to continue their journey to the speed-o-matic.

***

At almost the same time, the Freeup were walking towards the speed-o-matic, after Hilary had booked tickets for recliner seats.

"Do we have to wait in a line?" Mary asked.

"I think so," Hilary said.

"I hope it won't take too long to get the tickets," Pat said. "How does the ticket thingy work, anyway?"

"It's simple. The guards are the kind people who you can't lie to," Hilary said. "I just have to tell them my name and tell them that I'm taking y'all to Mid-Mart, and we're allowed to go."

"Nice," Mia said. "Explains why the line is moving so fast." She took a step forward to cover the empty area in front of her.

"Wait. But what if someone lies?" Emma began asking.

Hilary understood what she was asking and cut in, "The guards are a kind of magic people who you can't lie to. Their power is like truth spells. So, if they ask you something, their power—" She stopped because the person in front of them had gone.

"Now, it's our chance," Hilary cried.

"Hello," the guard said. "Name and people."

"I'm Hilary," Hilary said. "14 people, including me."

"Have you done booking? And if so, what kind of seats?" the guard asked.

"Yes, I've done the booking. And I booked recliner seats," Hilary answered.

"Go ahead," the guard commanded.

"C'mon," Hilary said. She walked inside the train.

"Whoa," Pat said, "it's amazing!"

The train was huge, and there were doors every ten feet at each side. Each door was a different colour. There was music in the hall, and it felt like a palace. There were balloons and windows wherever there weren't any doors.

"THIS IS SOO COOL!" Mia yelled.

"Yeah," Nora said. "Just as I remember." Her voice trailed off.

"Bad memory? Or an emotional one?" Pat asked.

"Uh, it was good, but I came on the speed-o-matic with my uncle," Nora said. Her voice became shaky. "After my parents died."

"Hush, it's okay. Come on, let's go," Pat said gently.

They arrived in a corridor. There were a lot of doors. Some were labelled as 'bed' or 'recliner' or 'normal' with numbers on them.

Hilary walked into a room which said 'RECLINER TWENTY-TWO'. The coach was as big as the Freeup's bedroom (the learners'), which is to say, huge. It may well have been bigger than that. There was a crystal chandelier in the centre of the room. There were fifteen recliner seats in black, each with a cosy-looking attached pillow.

There was a small TV at the back of every seat and the distance between each of the seats was as much as a single bed! All of them gasped in amazement. It was wonderful and even had a mini fridge with a small counter beside it. There was a bathroom with a bathtub in it. Probably for the people who took the speed-o-matic in the evenings, so that they could take a bath in the morning before they arrived.

The mirror in the bathroom was cool, the outer border made from real gold. *This must have cost Hilary a fortune! I'll ask her about it later, I need to see what else is in here*, Mia thought as she wandered around. There was also a shower head made of pure silver.

"This must have cost you a fortune, Hilary. It's so good. And real gold. OMG!" Mia exclaimed.

"Honestly, it cost some money. But not too much," Hilary replied.

"Hm. How many Magisos did—?" Mia began.

"Ahhh," Sia said, relaxing on the recliner. She had just switched on the massage button.

"It cost five thousand Magisos in total," Hilary said.

"Now, it's time for a recliner party," Sophie cried.

"Uh, sure," Nora said, still a little glum.

"Yeah," Pat said enthusiastically. "This is going to be so much fun," and she threw herself on a seat.

"Wow! Oh my!" Nora had just found the massage button. She found it very cool and relaxing.

They all relaxed and enjoyed themselves.

22. The Paths Cross Again

The Ruleup had boarded another speed-o-matic, the one which went from their village. They had a narrow escape because the guards were all sympathetic to Freeup's cause and had very nearly kicked them out. But Ruby was telling them the truth about going to Mid-Mart for supplies, not destruction. The guards, as per their ethical standards, had to allow the Ruleup to enter.

"Argh! The silly Freeup has got basically everyone on their side," Ruby yelled in frustration once they had reached their normal seats room on the speed-o-matic. On the way, everyone had given them bad looks. Clearly, they were all on the Freeup's side.

"Well, at least we were let in, that's good," Sarah said. "Right, guys? Guys?"

Everyone else was too busy angrily muttering under their breaths about Ruby giving them normal seats instead of recliners to answer Sarah.

"Huh? Oh yeah," Ava said.

The Ruleup's room in the speed-o-matic wasn't as good as the Freeup's. There were fifteen seats. The normal seats were made of wood, with no cushioning or covers.

"What! I am no way sitting on the wooden couch. There are sixteen of us. They should have—" Sarah started yelling.

But Ruby cut her off, "The wooden sofa can be removed. Because the seats can be turned from wooden couch to normal seats. They probably forgot to change it."

"Oh, sorry," Sarah said in a small voice, feeling ashamed. *Why didn't I think of it? Argh! Now, I made a complete fool of myself*, Sarah thought angrily.

The entire room was as small as an office meeting room. The chairs were in two rows, eight chairs in each. Each chair was a dull grey colour, unless you made it into a wooden couch and pressed a TV button that would make a small TV appear in front of you. The bathroom had a normal mirror without a boundary and a normal shower. Everyone started complaining.

"Be quiet," Ruby snapped, even though she agreed with the girls. "Be happy with what you get. When I was small, we never—"

"I don't care. You are always going on and on about yourself," Lily interrupted angrily. "Making yourself the victim of everything, so that you can get pity."

Everyone was surprised. Lily hardly ever spoke.

"I was just explaining to you that you should be happy with what you get," Ruby said. As much as Ruby wanted to tell Lily off, she didn't. Because Lily was good at magic, and she had once nearly gone into the Freeup. If Ruby displeased her, she worried that Lily may switch sides. And right now, Ruby only had Lily who was almost as good as Jane. She just always hid it. Jane had already shifted sides plus, Luna had been Lily's best friend.

"Fine," Lily said, in a tone that somehow sounded like, 'yeah right!'

Ruby sat down on a chair and cried out in pain. She got up instantly, as if the chair had been electrified.

"What happened?" Sarah asked.

Daisy came over. "You got up like it had a high voltage."

"It did," Ruby stammered, staring at the chair. "It had a high voltage." They stared at her.

"Um, Ruby? My chair is not like that, mind if I try yours?" Sarah asked.

"Ahhhhh!" Sarah yelled in pain. "Your chair is the only chair which seems to be electrified."

"Uh-huh," Ruby said, in some kind of dream. She quickly closed the curtains of the window she was looking out of. "Wait, what? The chair isn't electrified anymore. Yay!"

"Uh, Ruby? Are you feeling good?"

"Hm, yeah. Just nothing. I thought I saw—" Ruby's voice trailed off.

"Ruby, you are seeing random things today. Come and rest for a while," Sarah said.

"No, I am not seeing things. What I saw was very real—" Ruby protested.

"Ruby, it's okay. You are probably stressed out from our war and because of that, you are seeing things which are not really there," Sarah cut her off.

"But—" Ruby took a deep breath. "You're probably right. I am seeing things."

Just then, "Argh, Ruby! You needed to pay for TV. Great. No TV. Now, what will we do for ten hours?" Lily yelled angrily.

"Lily," Sarah hissed. "Ruby is not feeling well, and you are—"

"It's okay—" Ruby began.

"How is it okay?" Sarah yelled.

"—because I'll go and speak to the guards and ask them for a recliner room. Okay? Any objections?" Ruby continued.

"Yay, please do it," Sarah yelled happily.

Everyone else yelled, "Yeah!" Or, "Definitely!"

Ruby just nodded and left the room. *Oh, I just hope the guards allow us to change rooms*, Ruby prayed. She reached the 'Help' counter.

"Hello, I am Luciana! What would you like help with?" the lady at the counter asked.

"Hello Luciana, I want to change my room."

"Hm, okay. May I have your name, please?"

"Uh yeah. Ruby."

"Okay, Ruby. And where are you currently seated?"

"Normal seats."

"Okay, and what kind of seats do you want to switch to?"

"I want to switch from normal to recliner."

"Okay. Before I check if a recliner room is available, I need to ask, are there any more people with you? And if so, how many?"

"There are sixteen people including me."

"Okay. Now, let me check if any recliner rooms are available."

Ruby patiently waited as Luciana murmured a spell to check the empty areas in the train and started to look for available recliner coaches.

"Okay. So, there is one recliner coach available which I can give you! But—"

"But what?"

"I will have to give you four extra seats since I can't give you a fifteen-seater. We have a twenty-seater, which will be expensive considering you might want food access and television access."

"Oh, I want all those luxuries but um, please give me a fifteen-seater. Can you just add another seat?"

"Hm. Okay, I can. I'll ask the builders to nail another recliner seat. And you will have to pay extra for that." Ruby paid and got the Ruleup to be ready for the transfer.

There was a knock at the door and Luciana came in and said, "Um. Miss Ruby? Your recliner room is ready and—" She stopped speaking because the train had suddenly started going faster and then returned to its normal speed.

"Um. Yeah, we're ready," Ruby said, motioning for her learners to follow Luciana, who was waiting patiently at the door.

The recliner room was the same as the Freeup's one except it had an extra recliner.

***

At the same time, when Ruby had seen something out the window, so had Nora. And Sarah was wrong; what Ruby saw was not a dream. Just as they were entering the recliner room, Ruby had seen Nora and Nora, Ruby.

"What! Not possible. No way," Nora yelled when she saw Ruby in the speed-o-matic next to them. There were two trains on side-by-side lanes. Some of the Freeup were watching TV on their personal foldable TV while others were reading magazines or relaxing. Quickly, Ruby closed the curtains. Nora did the same.

Pat, who was sitting in the recliner seat next to Nora, asked, "What happened?"

"I saw Ruby pass in the train next to us!" Nora exclaimed.

"What? No way. You were probably just dreaming," Pat replied.

"Uh, yeah. Probably," Nora said, still a little unsure.

"Come on. Stop thinking about that. Watch this very funny show with me," Pat said, laughing.

"What's the show name?" Nora asked, dismissing all her thoughts.

"*Circus Pircus*," Pat replied.

Nora looked a bit taken aback. "Uh, the circus which came into town nine years ago?" She asked.

"Yeah, wait, you said you travelled in the speed-o-matic with your Uncle James after you arrived on Magisis, so—" Pat said.

"I used the speed-o-matic to visit the *Circus Pircus* which came to Jafrer," finished Nora.

"Oh, I'm sorry. You probably don't want to watch this anymore," Pat said uneasily, turning off the TV and folding it.

Just as she was about to finish folding it, Nora stopped her and said, "It was pretty funny. It might help to take my mind off things, so let's watch it."

A smile spread across Pat's face. She switched it back on. She searched for *Circus Pircus* and started the show. After ten hours, the speed-o-matic arrived in Jafrer. Everyone in the Freeup's room was sleeping.

As the train stopped with a jolt, Hilary woke up and yelled, "Ah! Oh, the train's stopped." She went and shook everyone. "Wakey wakey, time to go to Mid-Mart."

"Oh! It's time to wake up. Already? Aw. I wished I could sleep more." Sia yawned.

At nearly the same time, the Ruleup walked out of the second speed-o-matic but luckily, the two groups didn't see each other because there was a humongous crowd. The Speed-o-matic was located behind, but right next to Mid-Mart. Hilary and Ruby were going nuts trying to keep track of their learners.

Since there was a lot of noise, the two groups didn't hear each other. And that was good, otherwise Nora would have declared war on Ruby right there. The doorway to Mid-Mart was so big that it could fit at least fifty people at once. The building had 15 floors and the cashiers were outside the building in a shade. There were thirty cashiers in all, two for each floor.

Nora picked up a newspaper and started reading an article about why the Mid-Mart branches had all reduced the number of cashiers.

Written By—Reporter Selena Sawer 12-10-3021

The speed-o-matic makes a deal with Mid-Mart!

The owners of the speed-o-matic have recently made a deal with Mid-Mart. When asked why they did so, Mr Alex West, the owner of the speed-o-matic, said, "Our speed-o-matic is mostly used to go to Mid-Mart, so why not partner with them? Now, you can use our speed-o-magic for payments in Mid-Mart branches all over the planet. It is working wonderfully, and the Mid-Mart people thank us for it."

With this deal, even the Mid-Mart quality has improved. Our reporters found out that Mr Alex West and Mr Ron Sandry, the owner of Mid-Mart, were childhood friends. Their old relationship was one more reason that such a deal could happen. The new updates to Mid-Mart are wonderful and people just love it. Now, they don't have to wait in lines all day long.

Mr Sandry has revealed that a whole new floor of wonderful things is going to come up in Mid-Mart but he won't say what it will have. Everyone is bursting with excitement—what is this amazing new floor? And will it be as awesome as all the other floors? Our reporters have been searching for information but sadly, have found none. Watch out for more updates about this deal.

For exciting news like this, you can use the reading spell and think of the number 8209137465.

"Whoa! Hilary, read this," Nora said, after she finished reading the newspaper. She handed it to Hilary.

"Huh? Oh yeah! I already read that on the train, I meant to tell you all but forgot," Hilary said, shrugging and handing the newspaper back to Nora.

The entrance was made of glass doors. Two guards stood at each end of the doors. They were opening the door for everyone. Inside were two more guards who were checking if the person had the bill with them. The building had a lot of windows, which sparkled in the morning sun. The mart had a helpdesk and some more guards. There was a glass lift which had a view of the mountains and the speed-o-matic. Just ahead of the mountains, there was the speed-o-matic waiting area.

The second floor had pots and pans. Third floor was full of candy. It was any toddler's dream come true. On the fourth floor, there were a lot of toys. There were soft toys and all other kinds of toys one could imagine. The fifth floor was filled with things for home—beds, kitchen counters, closets, etc.

There were all kinds of furniture too. The whole of sixth floor was a gift shop while the seventh floor was a huge flower shop. The flowers were grown there itself and sold. Eight floor was a stationery shop. It also had bags and things like fidget spinners and quills. Floors nine, ten and eleven were filled with clothes, hats and shoes.

There was also a photo booth on all of the floors. Twelfth floor was dedicated to makeup with a corner for kids, filled with colouring and story books. There were also some crayons. The thirteenth floor was a book shop with sections for toddlers, kids, teenagers and adults. The building was at least two miles wide.

This meant that the bookshop and everything else was huge. On the fourteenth floor, there were cleaning supplies and on the fifteenth, lots and lots of food. There was possibly everything edible you could imagine in there. There were stacks of cans and bottles in racks. There was a freezer with ice-creams and cold drinks.

There were lots of fruits and veggies. Each floor had at least six to seven guards. Both, the Freeup and the Ruleup, were headed there. But thankfully, there were five lifts, so the Freeup got inside one and the Ruleup in another.

23. MID-MART

It was a good thing that the Freeup and the Ruleup didn't meet. But of course, good things don't last long.

"Wow! Just look at these wonderful stacks of food," Nora exclaimed, as they walked by a rack full of fast food.

"You kids can make groups of fours or fives and go to any part of Mid-Mart you like. You all have my number memorised, so just call me up on the talk spell. We will head home in two hours. Is that clear?" Hilary announced.

"Yes. Yay! Thanks, Hilary," everyone yelled together.

Nora, Pat, Emma and Mary set off together. The four of them went to the eighth floor. Ruby had done the exact same thing with her learners. Sarah and Andrea were on the eighth floor with Ruby, exactly where Nora, Pat, Emma and Mary were headed.

"Hey, Ruby?" Andrea asked.

"Yeah?" Ruby said.

"There are like sooo many people just on the eighth floor!" Andrea exclaimed.

"Argh!" Ruby said, now she looked up in the air. "What am I going to do with her?" Ruby then looked at Andrea and said, "Silly, Mid-Mart is very famous. It's obvious that there will be 'sooo' many people on every single floor. Ugh!"

Nora and Pat walked out of one of the elevators. There were a lot of people with them, so when Ruby glanced up as the lift doors opened, she didn't make them out. Almost a minute later, another lift reached the eighth floor. This time, Emma and Mary walked out with a family of six in front of them. The Ruleup had their backs turned to the lift, so they didn't see Emma and Mary come out either.

"Hey! What took you so long?" Nora asked, when Emma and Mary reached them.

"Sorry, we couldn't fit in the elevator you went in, so we took another one," Emma apologised.

"That's fine. But just don't tell Hilary, she'll start yelling at us about how we should have all gone into one elevator instead of splitting up because we could get lost and all of that, okay?" Pat said, rolling her eyes when she reached the part about Hilary telling them off.

"Yeah, yeah, of course we won't. Did you think that we liked getting shouted at by Hilary, eh?" Mary replied.

"Ha-ha. Now, come on. Let's shop." Nora laughed.

Nora headed straight to the keychain section. There was another rack right behind the keychain rack and Pat headed there. It was full of small toys for fidgeting. Emma and Mary went next to Pat because she was looking stunned.

"Hey! You okay? You're looking—" Mary tapped Pat on the shoulder and began asking.

"Nora was right, what she saw was true," Pat interrupted, still looking and sounding stunned.

Pat had told Emma and Mary about what Nora thought she saw out the window of the speed-o-matic.

"What? How can you be so sure? Seems even you are seeing things. This whole Ruby business has got stuck in your head," Emma said.

"No! Look, there's Ruby," Pat said in a hollow voice, pointing to where Ruby was talking to Sarah about something or the other.

"No, not possible!" Emma exclaimed.

"Guys! Let's think about this coincidence later. We need to make sure Nora doesn't see Ruby," Pat exclaimed.

"You need to make sure I don't see who?" Nora asked.

Pat wheeled around. Nora was there. She was close, close enough to hear very clearly what they were talking about!

Now, Pat's mind was running with thoughts—*did Nora hear everything they said? And if so, what if she declared war on Ruby right now? What would happen then? She didn't want to fight right now!*

"You all need to make sure I don't see who?" Nora demanded once again, when the other three were facing her, getting impatient minute by minute.

"Uh, we were, er, um, uh—" Pat stammered.

Fortunately, Mary interrupted her and said, "We need to make sure you don't see the *Circus Pircus* show again. Uh, um because Pat still thinks that you didn't enjoy it because it brought back bad memories."

"Hmm, okay, but let me tell you this; it doesn't bring back bad memories. It's just that I was lost in my thoughts. But I really enjoy that show," Nora said.

Though she said so, Nora had actually heard everything the three of them were talking about. *OMG! Ruby. I knew I didn't just dream it up. She was really there. Argh! I'll get revenge on her, but I can't fight her in a public place. I'll try my best not to think about it. First, her dad killed my parents and then she killed Rita. I'm not sure I can't think about it, but I'll have to try my best,* Nora thought angrily. But she pretended to be clueless and wait things out.

"Okay, let's, um, continue shopping now," Pat said.

Pat motioned for Mary and Emma to follow her. Emma and Mary started following Pat to a corner of the floor, which was away from Nora and Ruby.

"Phew! That so close," Pat exclaimed.

"Yeah! But let's not let our guard down. Nora already suspects us," Emma said.

"Let's all try to act normal, okay?" Mary said.

"Let's continue shopping but remember, Ruby shouldn't see us and Nora and Nora shouldn't see Ruby," Mary said.

"But what does it matter if Ruby sees us?" Emma asked.

"Because then *she* will declare war on us. Did you forget that Ruby is very keen on defeating us? She wants to rule over Magisis as soon as possible," Mary replied, slapping her forehead.

"Oh yeah, you're right. Maybe we should change floors?" Emma said.

"Yeah! We'll do it as soon as Nora is finished searching for whatever she wants," Pat said.

But Nora had different plans; she wanted to follow Ruby everywhere in Mid-Mart so that once Ruby was done shopping, she could declare war on her. It had been half an hour since the Freeup had come. Nora had snuck near Ruby and heard her saying that they were planning on leaving in an hour and a half.

Nora was anxious to fight Ruby and was grinning widely as she thought about what great luck she had had.

"Hey Nora? Have you found what you were looking for?" Emma asked, tapping Nora on the shoulder.

"Huh? Oh, um, yeah! This pretty, glittery heart keychain. I'll just find a suitable case for me to put it in and we'll go to the thirteenth floor. We'll get some books. That fine with y'all?" Nora asked.

"Yeah, sure!" Emma said. "I love books. Let's go there."

"Phew! I mean, yes, let's go," Nora said. She wanted to head to the bookshop because she saw Ruby, Sarah and Andrea go into a lift. They were the only ones in it, so Nora guessed that they went to the book shop because that was where the lift had stopped.

"Okay, let's go, guys," Pat said, eyeing Nora suspiciously.

The four of them walked silently to the lift and went to the thirteenth floor.

"Guys! I'm heading off to the teenager's section, y'all go wherever you want. But if you wanna come, just come," Nora announced when they reached the thirteenth floor.

"Yeah, we'll come with you," Emma said; even she had spotted Ruby. She went along with Nora as a precaution. "Guys, you coming?" she asked through gritted teeth.

Pat and Mary understood and followed Emma and Nora.

"Hm, hm, hm, hm," Nora hummed.

"Nice tune. Where did you hear it?" Emma asked.

"Huh? Oh, um, me and my father used to skip in a park and hum this tune together. I just remembered it," Nora said, her voice cracking.

"I'm sorry I asked. I'm really sorry. I think I'll head off to the, um, washroom. Excuse me," Emma said, guilty. She hurried away from her friends.

"Emma, wait! I didn't mean to—" Nora began. But Emma was gone.

What on Magisis is my problem? This is the second time I asked something which made Nora feel sad. Oh my! I can't even stay with her anymore without feeling guilty, Emma thought. She felt a mixture of emotions—sad, angry at herself and guilty.

Emma quickly went into a bathroom stall. She put the lid down of the toilet seat and sat there and started to think of what she could do to help Nora not feel so sad and painful whenever her parents were brought up in a conversation.

"It's impossible. She won't be able to recover from it. It's too much of a deep pain," Emma yelled in frustration, throwing her hands up in the air.

Emma immediately wished she hadn't yelled because a few other people started groaning angrily and muttering bad comments under their breaths. *Uh-oh, gotta go*, Emma thought. She quietly snuck out of the bathroom stall and ran quickly to the teenagers section. She heard some argument and so hurried on. On reaching closer, she heard Nora yelling something and Pat's voice in the background.

24. Nora Loses Control

What had really happened was that Nora had been a bit too keen on keeping track of Ruby. She was looking at Ruby and just then, Pat came up behind her.

Pat gasped. "Nora, how did you—?" Her voice trailed off.

Nora was caught off guard. *Humph! Well, leave fighting Ruby for later. Pat has found me looking at Ruby, and I can't make any excuse 'cause Ruby is looking at a poster. That too on a teeny-tiny blank wall,* Nora thought angrily.

"You knew Ruby was here, didn't you? And you never told me," Nora yelled at Pat.

"'Cause you would declare war on Ruby, and this is a public place, so you—" Pat began protesting.

But she was interrupted by Emma coming towards them. "Pat! Did Nora—?" she asked.

"Yeah, she knows now," Pat said.

"I didn't find out now, I knew it all along," Nora said.

"What? How!" Mary exclaimed. "How do you know all this?"

"Well, well, well. It looks as if the three of you were keeping a secret from me," Nora said, ignoring Mary's question.

"We had no choice. Now, will you please tell us how you know this already?" Emma said.

A few moments later, Nora yelled, "Fine!" And explained them. She, of course, didn't explain her plan. Otherwise, Pat would try to stop her or go and tell Hilary.

"Hm, now let's get off this floor," Pat said, after Nora was done explaining.

"Hey! Wait, I need to, er, take a book. That's why I came on this floor," Nora lied.

"I know you very well, Nora. And you simply won't ignore Ruby like that. I know what you are planning to do," Pat said coldly.

"You do? I mean, uh, what plan are you talking about?" Nora said. "I'm not planning anything. Why would I plan anything?" Nora gave a nervous laugh.

"Mary, Emma? Can I talk to you in private?" Pat asked in a low voice, turning her head a bit.

Mary and Emma were standing behind Pat, listening intently.

"Um, er, yeah, sure," Mary stammered. "Um, Nora, you can look for your book."

It'll give me more time to look at Ruby, Nora thought. *I can let them talk.*

"Fine," Pat said. She turned around. "I know Nora very well and she won't just drop the subject of her parents' death like that. She will probably find a way to kill Ruby ASAP. I think I know her plan but before that, I really need to inform Hilary," Pat whispered.

"Okay, let's find her?" Emma asked.

"How will we? I mean, we don't know where she is," Pat whispered.

"Why can't we just use a talking spell?" Emma asked.

"Nora will hear us," Pat answered.

"She was on the fifteenth floor when we left. So now, she is probably on the fourteenth floor because only one hour is left for us to go home and she wanted to get something from there," Mary replied.

"Yeah! Smart thinking, Mary," Pat exclaimed softly.

"Thanks! But now let's go," Mary said. "Hopefully, Nora has found her imaginary book."

Pat and Emma laughed while Mary just grinned.

Suddenly, Nora called out to them, "Hey guys. What's so funny? Tell me the joke too."

"Nothing, though are you done searching for your book?" Pat asked.

"Yeah," Nora said.

"Okay, let's go to the fourteenth floor, I broke my toothbrush, so I need to get a new one," Mary lied.

"Okay, and I need a new tube of toothpaste. I didn't exactly like the one Hilary provided us with," Nora said. She actually needed one.

"Okay, so let's go," Pat said, heading towards the elevator.

The rest of them followed. A minute later, the elevator reached the fourteenth floor. The door opened with a 'ding'. Nora and Mary went to the bathroom supplies area. Pat and Emma found Hilary near the cleaning supplies area and rushed to her. They told her everything. Pat also told her about what she thought Nora's plan was—to fight Ruby once their time at Mid-Mart was over.

Hilary dropped the supplies she was holding onto the floor. Her mouth fell open and was left hanging there. Recovering, she finally closed her mouth and screamed, "What? Oh no! We must stop Nora this instant."

"Shh! You don't want Nora to know this, do you?" Pat said. "That I figured out her plan?"

"No, no, I don't but—" Hilary's voice trailed off. "Okay, let's stop Nora." She ran towards the elevator.

"Um, too late. She's gone. And that elevator just reached the ground floor," Mary squeaked. "And that is exactly where Ruby is now. I saw her leave Mid-Mart. I saw her through the window."

"OMG!" Hilary yelled. A lot of annoyed people stared at Hilary, though she didn't care. She had a war to stop. She ran to the elevator and took one to the ground floor. Pat, Emma and Mary followed her. They reached the ground floor and found the whole Freeup coming out of different lifts. Two hours were up. Nora was going to attack Ruby.

"Nora, don't!" Hilary yelled.

"Don't what?" Nora asked, confused.

"Um," Hilary began stammering.

"What are you doing here anyway? I thought you were getting a new tube of toothpaste?" Pat asked, coming to Hilary's rescue.

"Oh yeah, sorry. I actually got one and was about to pay for it," Nora replied, shrugging.

"Okay, let's go and check out our stuff," Hilary said with a nervous smile.

Everyone in the Freeup paid for their things. The Ruleup had already done so. There was a waiting area for everyone using the Speed-o-matic. Unfortunately, it was empty. The Ruleup and the Freeup were the only ones there. The sitting area was near a field. Pat was about to tell Nora not to attack but she couldn't.

Nora couldn't hold it back anymore. She yelled, "*Minuo!*" And pointed her finger at Ruby.

The Ruleup were lazing in a field near the waiting area. Ruby barely had time to blink before Nora's spell hit her. Ruby screamed in agony. She fell backwards out of her chair, her eyes screwed up in pain. She was covered in blood. She screamed again. Nora's spell was a bleeding spell, one of the worst spells that a magic person could use.

In a haze of pain, Ruby croaked, "Help!"

Sarah leaned over Ruby to help her, and the others prepared to face the Freeup.

"HOW DARE YOU HIT RUBY LIKE THAT!" Lily yelled. She attacked Nora with a killing spell. Nora deflected it. She sent another bleeding spell at Lily, but she stepped aside. Others joined the fight. Jane was fighting three people at once.

Lily yelled, "You cannot defeat me."

"Oh, but I can," Nora said. She sent a torture spell straight at Lily's face before she could understand what Nora was about to do. Lily's eyes widened in terror. When the spell hit her, she screamed and fell backwards. Her expression froze—like one's would when they die.

Lily died because she was born with a disease called Kolimosmarte, a peculiar and a very bad disease. If you had it and somebody used a torture spell on you, you would instantly die because the disease made your heart weak. Nora seemed to understand that she'd killed Lily. She gasped in horror and fell to her knees when she realised this.

"Nora!" Hilary cried. "What—?"

"I don't know, I don't know," Nora sobbed.

Pat knew Nora wouldn't be able to fight after killing someone. She cried, "*Volant!*" And indicated Nora to the area behind the Freeup, so that there would be less chances for Nora to get hit with a spell. Meanwhile, Sarah had managed to heal Ruby. Ruby had seen Nora kill Lily. She roared in anger and charged.

The Ruleup will feel the same way we had, Nora thought. *The same way we had when Ruby killed Rita*. She was right.

The Ruleup became much more ferocious. The Freeup started to lose. *Yes! Now I will be able to take over Magisis. The Freeup are losing. I am so happy,* Ruby thought happily. Still, one of her learners had died under her protection. Just when she was about to send a torture spell at Hilary, the man in black appeared. He was around 15ft tall. Ruby's eyes shone with pure hate and sent the torture spell at him instead.

Jane tilted her head and met Luna's gaze. Both of them were thinking the same thing. *Why is Ruby attacking her dad? Why would she hate him?* Nora's anger returned when she saw the man in black. He had short, black hair and small dark blue eyes. She charged forwards. But Hilary and Pat caught her.

"Nora, don't," Pat yelled.

Ruby also charged. Sarah and Andrea caught her.

"What are you doing?" Sarah asked.

Both Nora and Ruby shouted together, "He killed my parents!"

They paused. As much as they hated each other, they hated the man more. They looked at each other, *let's do it*, and charged.

"I will not be tortured!" the man roared. He uprooted a tree and threw it at Ruby. Ruby ducked. But he hadn't noticed Nora. She shot her bleeding spell again. It hit the man on his back. He shrieked, but it did not impact him like it had impacted Ruby.

He turned around. "Who—oh it's you," he snarled. "You're going to pay for what your Uncle James did."

"No," Nora said. "*You* are going to pay for what *you* did." She tried to shoot the bleeding spell at him again, but this time, he was ready. He deflected it easily.

"And you," the man said, turning to Ruby. "Your parents were weak."

"Don't you dare start," Ruby snarled.

"Still, they wanted to rule," the man continued.

Ruby lost it. She clenched her fists. "My parents weren't weak." She leapt up and punched him on his face. It shouldn't have made a difference. Instead of breaking her wrist against the man's hand, the air exploded when Ruby touched him.

"Do not use your spells against me." He started growing even more. Trees went flying everywhere. The Freeup and Ruleup tried to stop him, but they couldn't.

"I am the JABEZ! You cannot defeat me," the man, Jabez, yelled.

"Uh, seriously? Jabez? Great name you got there, Jabez." Hilary snickered.

"I am the bringer of sorrow. Beware!" With this, Jabez threw a tree at Hilary. She screamed and started to run. The Freeup started to run behind her, and the Ruleup behind Ruby. The Freeup ran for miles.

Finally, Hilary said, "We need to use a different way to go back to the headquarters."

"How about teleporting?" Nora suggested.

"Good idea," Hilary said. "*Languae Magicae!*"

The Freeup found themselves in their headquarters.

"What do we do now?" Mia asked.

"We need to rest," Hilary said. She fell backwards into the dining table.

"Yeah, sure," Pat said, panting like mad. She sat on a chair and fell asleep. Everyone else did the same.

At about 2 am, Hilary got up all of a sudden, her back aching from the weird angle she was sleeping at and the sharp corners of the table. She felt like her magic was weak. She felt like she had no powers. "What's happening?" Hilary asked herself.

25. Weakness Comes to Magisis

Hilary didn't want to disturb her learners in the middle of the night since the previous day had been so tiring, but then, this was really important. She decided to wake only Pat and Nora at first.

Nora stretched her arms and yawned. "Has it been a very long time since we were sleeping?" she asked anxiously.

"No," Hilary said. "Come to the grounds, I want— I need to talk to you." She was not going to tell them what she felt in front of the younger ones.

"Okay," Pat said slowly, getting up. She and Nora shared a look. *What's going on?*

They walked to the ground in silence.

"I feel," Hilary hesitated, "weak. Powerless. With very little magic."

"But we don't feel that way," Pat said, confused. Worry lines appeared all over her face. *What was happening? Why did Hilary feel this way?* Pat was so worried for her.

"Maybe I'm imagining it," Hilary said hopefully. But there was very little hope in her. She felt so powerless, as if someone had drained all her powers and energy. Like she was a small insect that someone had crushed with their boot, and she was in the process of dying.

"Have you ever felt like this before?" Nora asked.

"No, I haven't," Hilary said.

"Let's do a test, then," Nora said.

"What?" Hilary asked.

"You should do a spell and see how well it works," Nora said.

"Okay," Hilary said nervously. She had no idea what was wrong. But something was, and she was afraid to find out. "*Cresceret*!" She pointed at a rock that was around one foot tall and one foot wide. Instead of becoming double its size like it should have, it became a mere half inch taller and wider.

Hilary was horrified. “No! How is this possible? I’m not—no. I refuse to believe this happened.” She was very taken aback. How could this be happening? It just wasn’t possible. She couldn’t.

“But,” Nora said, “should we try doing it too?”

“Yes,” Hilary said.

Both of them tried, and both of them succeeded.

“Hilary, let’s think about this in the morning and rest for now,” Pat said.

Hilary looked on the verge of tears, but she said, “You go ahead. I’ll join you soon.”

“Okay,” Nora said.

The two girls walked back into the headquarters. Hilary sat down on a bench, trying to understand what was happening and gazing at the starry sky. Suddenly, a bird flew towards the headquarters. The protection barriers should’ve kept it out, but it only twitched slightly when it passed the barriers and crashed into the headquarters.

The bird was small, so it didn’t do anything to the headquarters. But Hilary understood that her magic was not as powerful as it should have been. The protection barriers had gone weak. Hilary stared at the sky, too terrified to move. She was exhausted and dozed off.

The next day, when the Freeup got up, they were shocked that Hilary wasn’t there with them.

“Where’s Hilary?” Mary asked anxiously.

“Oh no, maybe she fell asleep outside,” Nora said.

“Outside?” Mary said. “What would she be doing outside?”

“Just come on,” Nora said. She found Hilary sleeping on a bench. “Uh, Hilary?” Nora said, shaking her.

Hilary got up. “Where—oh,” she said. She realized that she’d fallen asleep outside. *How could I?* Hilary asked herself. *It is so dangerous since the barriers are weak.* “I need to tell you guys something.” She explained everything to them. “So, when I was sitting outside, a bird banged into our headquarters—”

“Wait WHAT?” Nora asked. “How is that possible? A bird would be stopped by our protection.”

“They are weak,” Hilary said. “The protections are weak.”

“How do we find out what’s happening?” Sia asked.

“How about we check if there is anything in the news?” Nora said. “Wait, how do we get a newspaper?”

"Someone will have to think about newspapers," Hilary said.

"I'll do it," Mary said. She thought about newspapers and a newspaper appeared on the bench Hilary was sitting on.

"I'll read it," Hilary said.

Everyone gathered around her. Hilary began reading

Written By—Reporter Selena Sawer 13-10-3021

The Freeup and the Ruleup, bad or good?

There was a large giant invader at Mid-Mart. The Freeup and Ruleup were fighting there and have unleashed the giant. There have been many complaints from the locals stating: "I lost two of my four children in that battle. All because the Freeup and the Ruleup fought. I used to support the Freeup, but now I think they're terrible," Mrs Emily Johnson said.

"I will not allow my child to stay in the Ruleup. They're dangerous," Mrs Diana Smith said.

The Freeup and the Ruleup are not to be supported. Many people have felt weak, their magic has failed them. The magical powers of Magisis are draining, only the people who have shared the power of another person can still do their magic. The mysterious giant named 'Jabez' has caused havoc and ruined our lives.

Something must be done, but it seems like this is a battle lost well before our time. Keep hope, stay strong. Watch out for more updates. Use the reading spell and think of the number 8209137465.

"This battle has turned our followers against us, and the Ruleup's followers against them. But we are not the people who called Jabez. He came here because he wanted to rule," Hilary said gravely. "Diana Smith is Tina's mom, the Ruleup is in for a very hard time. At least your parents believe in us. Girls, I, too, am one of those losing their powers."

By teaching her learners, Hilary was sharing part of herself, her magic, to them. By trusting them and keeping less secrets, she was sharing her magic with all her learners. Like a mother would share her magic with her children and so on.

"That's what's happening," Nora said.

"Hilary, we need to stop this," Jane cried. "We need to go there and stop this draining, or we'll never be able to stop Jabez."

"But how?" Hilary asked.

"We need to find the machine or gadget or whatever he may be using, to let the magic flow back," Jane said.

"But what if it isn't a machine? We have no evidence that there is a machine," Hilary wondered.

"Jane is right," Nora said. "We need to try, even if it is dangerous. We need to destroy the power, magic, machine whatever."

"If there is one," Sia reminded them.

"No choice," Jane said with a stubborn light in her eyes. "We need to try."

"We'll all go—" Hilary began.

"No, not all," Luna said. "We'll take some people with us, and the others will stay back to protect the headquarters."

"Okay," Hilary said. "So, the ones who will be going are Nora, Pat, Jane, Luna, Mary and Emma. Oh, and Sia and Mia, I am not sure if I should send you or not."

"Hey! We are going to come too. We are good at magic," Sia and Mia said together.

"You should leave as soon as possible. I'm sorry but I can't come. But don't worry. I will be sharing my power," Hilary said.

***

"Ruby! Ruby! I can't believe this is happening. Please stop her," Tina said, crying.

Ruby gasped. "What happened? Who should I stop?"

"Read today's newspaper," Tina said, wiping her tears.

Ruby took it and once she had read. "You want me to stop your mother from taking you home?" Ruby asked, looking very serious.

"Yeah, please stop her. I don't want to leave. Ruby please," Tina cried.

"I'll try, let her come into our headquarters first, then we'll see what to do," Ruby said sternly.

The rest of the Ruleup had been near when Tina was crying. Soon, all of them had newspapers in their hands.

"Hey! Mrs Smith can't take Tina away," Hannah yelled angrily.

"Yeah, she can't," Lucy agreed.

"Sisters! She can take Tina away, she is her mother," Bell said.

"As much as I hate to admit it, Bell's right," Ruby said.

"But I want to stay here and fight," Tina yelled.

"I am your mother, so I can take you away, you don't have a say in this," Mrs Smith said, suddenly appearing in front of them.

"Mrs Smith, how did you—?" Ruby's voice trailed off.

"The last time I came here, you had allowed teleportation for me. It seems you forgot to disable it," Mrs Smith said coldly.

"Mom! Please don't take me away. I don't want to—" Tina protested.

"Enough, I am taking you," Mrs Smith yelled.

"Okay, Mrs Smith. You can take Tina," Ruby said. "C'mon. Let's go, Tina. I will escort you and Mrs Smith outside. Andrea! You and Ava go fetch some drinks from the kitchen, we need to give Tina and Mrs Smith a nice farewell before they leave forever."

"Ruby, w—?" Tina began protesting.

Ruby gave Tina a look that said, *be quiet, or else you will really be out of the Ruleup!* Ruby had come up with a plan to make Tina stay in the Ruleup. She had quietly made a paper and quill appear in her hand, wrote something and passed the note to Sarah. The note read:

Sarah! I have a plan to make Tina stay in the Ruleup. Quickly go to the top floor. Over there, you need to say the spell 'inactivare'. Point the spell at the big panel-like thing in the small room. That will disable the teleportation in our headquarters. Hurry up. I know what to do next. One more thing. Burn this note once you've read it.

Sarah nodded her head after reading the letter and said, "Going to the restroom."

"Okay," Ava said.

Thankfully, she and anyone else didn't read the letter or even see it since as soon as Ruby passed the note, she had gone to the back of the group to read it. Sarah hurried to the top floor of the headquarters and did exactly what Ruby had instructed. When she came down, no one was there. Everyone was outside in the front yard.

"Thank goodness! I thought you guys had disappeared," Sarah cried, joining everybody in the front yard.

"Sarah," Tina said in a hollow voice, "something is happening, my mother is feeling weak as if her powers are gone."

"What? She needs to try a spell to be sure," Sarah said.

Mrs Smith tried the mass destruction spell on a random rock. It didn't work.

"I know why this is happening. Remember what was said in the newspaper? That Jabez guy is draining Magisis' power," Lucy yelled.

"Oh yeah! But then why isn't Ruby feeling weak?" Violet asked.

"Because, because I think he wants me to—" Ruby hesitated. "Tell you later."

She then glared at all of her members with a look, saying, *don't you dare question me!* Ruby was very good at giving looks and none of her learners questioned what she said.

"Okay," Mrs Smith said, getting impatient. "Can we go now? If you are done with your so-called giving us a 'nice time.'"

"Yes, sure," Ruby said.

As soon as Tina stepped out of the headquarters with Mrs Smith, Ruby yelled, "Tina, you forgot your belongings."

"Uh, yeah, I did," Tina said.

"C'mon, I will help you pack. Mrs Smith, you don't need to come," Ruby said, dragging Tina inside and closing the doors on Mrs Smith.

"Okay. Now, we need to ignore her," Ruby said, as soon as she locked and bolted the doors with magic.

"Hey! This is against the law. You can't separate me from my daughter. Open these doors right now, Ruby," Mrs Smith yelled, banging on the door.

"Ruby, I love you," Tina cried, hugging Ruby hard. "But will my mom be okay? I feel bad abandoning her. Dad is visiting another planet for his job, news-reporting."

"She'll be fine," Ruby said, awkwardly returning Tina's hug.

Sarah felt jealousy burning inside her.

Why was Ruby being so motherly to Tina? She can only be motherly to me and no one else, Sarah thought. And then, when Sarah couldn't bear it anymore, she excused herself. The Ruleup were celebrating because they had managed to keep Tina to themselves.

Sarah was sulking. She was lying down under her bed covers and started to cry loudly to get Ruby's attention. But the Ruleup were playing loud music and totally forgot about Sarah.

Sarah started to really cry now. "WHY? WHY IS THIS HAPPENING TO ME?"

Of course, nobody heard her. They were too busy celebrating.

"Oh yeah! Uh-huh, Tina's not going. Tina's not going," Andrea yelled, dancing.

"Guys, stop partying already," Sarah yelled. "The power of Magisis is being drained." She had come out of the bedroom.

"Sarah, don't be such a spoilsport. Come party with us," Tina said.

"You! And you just shut up. I was talking to my friends. Not you Ms I-think-I'm-So-Perfect," Sarah snapped, turning around to face Tina.

"Girls! Stop arguing already. Tina is right. Jabez's power isn't affecting us, right? So just leave it," Ruby said. "And Sarah." Ruby's voice softened. "Come dance with us, don't be such a spoilsport. Enjoy Tina's party. After all, she is such a good student, she got us five more wonderful learners."

Sarah clenched her fists. *How dare Tina steal my rank?* Sarah thought angrily. *Especially after I saved her from being removed from the Ruleup.* Of course, her thinking wasn't exactly right. Tina wasn't being removed from the Ruleup. She was just leaving because of her mother. Sarah glared at the table as if it was all Tina's fault. She thought, *I'm going to take revenge on Tina.*

26. The Surrender

Jabez stomped on the streets of Jafrer, now 25 feet tall. He was uprooting trees and yelling, "Surrender to me, I am your ruler." The people of Jafrer were running in fright, some trying to fight him, but it was useless. His power seemed endless.

"We will not be ruled over," a very brave—or a very stupid villager said. He tried to roll under Jabez's legs and stab him, but Jabez kicked the villager dead. Some others tried to teleport away, but the power of Magisis was draining.

Finally, when many people were dead, the remaining villagers spoke as one, "We surrender. Please don't kill us."

Jabez smiled cruelly and lowered a tree he was holding. "I am your rightful king!" He boomed, his voice echoing everywhere. "Bow to me!"

All of the villagers bowed in unison.

***

"Are you guys ready?" Hilary asked.

"Yes," Pat said nervously.

They walked out of the headquarters. And found themselves facing 30 extremely strong-looking guards. *Great.* Just when they'd started getting their courage back.

"What do we do now?" Luna asked softly.

"Fight them," Jane said grimly.

They tried, but their spells had no effect on the guards and simply rebounded. Jane and Nora fell unconscious. Luna and Pat could barely keep their eyes open; they were feeling very weak and drowsy since they had sent weakness and sleeping spells at the guards. Mia, Sia, Mary and Emma were wounded badly. Somehow, they made their way back into their headquarters, and promptly collapsed with the effort.

"What happened?" Hilary cried.

"We need to heal them," Olivia said, "with Salve."

"But it won't heal them at once, we will need to take them to the Healing Room. We will need to feed them lots of healthy food and use

Salve on them every day. It will take at least a week for them to heal," Scarlett said.

Sophie was staring at Scarlett.

"What? I read a lot of books," Scarlett said.

Chloe and Sophie looked at each other and shrugged.

"Let's take them now," Scarlett said. "They need urgent medication."

"Okay, me, Amber, Sally and Hazel will take care of Hilary since she is struggling to stay conscious. Her powers are draining, and she is also trying to keep our headquarters' borders safe," Olivia said.

"Okay, we will take care of them but can at least two of you come with us to help carry them or drag them? These elder learners are very heavy. I don't know how much they eat," Scarlett said, panting as she tried to drag Nora.

"Okay, we will help you with that," Hazel said.

Hazel, Sally, Scarlett, Chloe and Sophia dragged the eight learners to the Healing Room and put them in beds. There were at least fifteen beds in the Healing Room. Hazel and Sally went back to Hilary but before going, they left some sandwiches for the eight learners.

Scarlett, Chloe and Sophia started using Salve on the eight learners. Sophie then went up to the kitchen and made some food. Amber came along and told them that she would help in taking care of the learners.

"Hey guys. Amber is helping us to take care of these elder learners," Scarlett yelled as she entered the Healing Room.

"Shh! They've just started sleeping. We gave them the sandwiches," Chloe hissed softly. "It was very hard to make them sleep. I don't know how my mom used to put me to bed."

Scarlett giggled and said, "Okay, we won't make noise."

Amber gave a smile and nodded in agreement. Soon, they got bored, so Amber went down and got some books for them all. But shortly, all the eight learners woke up. Nora yawned loudly, which scared Amber.

"Ah—oh, it's only you, I got scared. Give a warning next time please," Amber said.

"Are we in the Healing Room?" Mary asked. "Why am I bleeding?"

"You guys are hurt! The spells which you put on the guards rebounded and affected you instead," Sophia exclaimed.

"But we should be better in no time with Salve!" Mary exclaimed.

"No. You guys are badly wounded. Some of you even fainted," Scarlett said. "So, you guys need to be in bed for a week."

"What!" the eight learners yelled together.

"Impossible!" Sia yelled.

"Yeah!" Mia yelled in agreement.

"Hey! Watch it, guys. Scarlett here knows a lot about medical stuff," Amber said.

"Yeah," Scarlett said, shrugging. "I have read a lot of medical books. When I grow up and after we defeat the Ruleup, I might even work as a doctor in a hospital."

"Yeah, yeah, cool, but seriously, a week in bed?" Emma said.

"Yeah! A whole week in bed, and I might make it two if you guys try to get up and pull any stunts," Scarlett threatened.

"Whoa! Okay okay, we won't get out of bed," Mary said.

"Good! Now time for yucky medicine," Amber teased.

"Hey," Nora said.

"Guys. Cut it out. Amber, do we get to eat, or is that something else we can't do? 'Cause I'm hungry," Pat said.

"Oh yeah, me and Amber made some food for y'all," Scarlett said.

After a few minutes, all the girls had finished eating.

"Now what? Will you guys do a play or something to entertain us? Because I am bored," Mia asked.

"What? No way," Chloe said.

"Ugh! You won't have to do one," Scarlett said, slapping her forehead. "Because they need to sleep now."

"Hey! No way. I am not sleeping now," Jane protested.

"First, we will use Salve on you. Then, you have to sleep. So yes, you aren't sleeping now," Sophie said.

"Fine," Nora said, rolling her eyes.

The younger girls quickly used Salve on the other girls and then sat on armchairs near the beds.

"Are y'all gonna sleep here too?" Pat asked.

"Let me go ask Hilary," Sophie said. She was out of her seat in a flash.

A minute later, she came back and said, "Hilary said yes, we can sleep near y'all. She said that there are some foldable beds and a few of us can just sleep on the armchairs if we like."

"Oh," Pat said sadly.

"You guys wanted to get out of bed, didn't you? When we would be away," Sophie said.

And by the looks on their faces, she knew she had struck the truth.

"Uh, what? No, um, er, why would we want to, um—" Luna stammered.

Sophie cut her off and said, laughing, "Ha-ha. I knew it. And the learners older than us are supposed to set an example for us, not do something that they're told not to do."

The eight girls immediately pretended to be asleep to avoid the shame. The other girls just shook their heads playfully and started lazing around. After a while, they did, truly, fall asleep.

***

The Ruleup's party continued for two hours.

"I'm bored of this party now," Sophia said. "How about we party outside?"

"Are you CRAZY?" Ruby yelled. "What if Tina's mom is still there?"

"Um, we can check if she's still there," Sophia said, like it was obvious.

Ruby snorted. "Okay. Okay, fine."

The Ruleup followed Ruby out of the room. Just when Ruby was about to use the invisibility spell on herself, Andrea said, "Look. There is a slot in the door, and a note."

"Huh?" Ruby said. "Omg, what is this?" She pulled out the note.

Dear Ruleup,

My magic is nearly gone. I used up the last of it to write this note. I won't come to take Tina because I think she will be safer with you now after that man in black showed up. I am going back to my house. I also made a slot in your door if you don't mind. And there are some weird guards outside your headquarters, I hope everything is ok?

Everything else on it was smudged. Mrs Smith was feeling very weak now. Then, suddenly, she remembered something she'd read in the newspaper. *Jabez is draining the Magic of Magisis*, Mrs Smith thought. But the Ruleup weren't affected by it. Perhaps, just perhaps, Tina would be safer with the Ruleup. She had used the last of her magic to write the note and pass it on. She had no idea how she was going to get back home—suddenly, a large hand grabbed her and the world turned black.

"Yay! Now I can stay here with no problem." *But what about Mom? I'm worried,* Tina thought. *Did I abandon her? What if something happens? What if—TINA! Don't think negatively. Deep breaths.*

"Yup," Ruby said happily.

"Wait," Ava said. "'I also made a slot in your door if you don't mind and'? She wrote something else also."

"Maybe she did it by mistake—" Ruby gasped. "The rest of this is smudged."

There was silence.

"It's probably just nothing," Sarah said, breaking the tension. "Let's go out and party."

"You're right," Ruby said. "Now, we go out and party!" She opened the door and marched out. It was pretty windy and pleasant there.

"We party here?" Daisy asked.

"Yes," Ruby said. She walked to the post box where a poster was sticking out. "OMG!"

"What?" Sarah asked.

"There's a curfew!" Ruby exclaimed.

"Oh no," Sarah said.

"Let's just party," Tina said to appear cool, though she was very worried. *How will Mom get home?* She kept thinking.

They walked until they were at the end of the front yard.

"Hey, who are you guys?" Ruby asked.

Two people looking like guards turned.

The older looking one said, "We are Jabez's guards. We are guarding all the places so that people don't come out during the curfew. Jabez is the new ruler of Magisis."

Ruby's expression was beyond hatred. "He took over Magisis? How dare he! Get out of my way unless you want death."

"You can try and use your spells on us," the head guard said calmly. "The Freeup tried too. Your spells will just rebound on you. The Freeup sent horrible spells at us and got hit with the effects of their own spells."

"I don't believe you," Ruby said.

"Try it, then," he said.

Ruby hesitated. "Fine," she snapped. She sent an unconsciousness spell at him. But the guard was speaking the truth. The spell rebounded and Ruby fell down, unconscious.

The guard smiled. "I warned her," he said. "Now, go back inside. And take this."

Sarah glared at him. Then she yanked the paper out of his hands, grabbed Ruby and pulled her back inside. Others just followed her, giving dirty looks to the guards. Tina went forward to help Sarah, but she pulled Ruby out of Tina's reach. Andrea went to help, and Sarah did the same thing.

Better do this to everybody, otherwise I will be suspected, Sarah thought. She made some cold water appear by magic and then splashed it all over Ruby's face.

Ruby gasped and got up. "Where—?"

"The guard wasn't lying," Sarah said. "The spell rebounded."

"Oh," Ruby said. She got up. "Now, what do we do?"

"He also gave me this," Sarah said, handing Ruby the paper.

"Jabez's Ruling. Rule one: Always inform my guards why you are stepping out and where you are going. If disobeyed, you will be sent to the dungeons of my castle. More rules coming soon," Ruby read out loud. "Wait, there's more. 'New rules to be applied after the curfew is over. The curfew will be for a month.'"

"One month curfew. I'm dead," Alice said. She crashed into the sofa behind her.

Ruby rolled her eyes. *So dramatic*, she thought. "Now, training."

୨ ୨ ୨

27. A Rule a Day

Every day, a new set of rules started coming in through the slot. The guards had made a slot in every single door of Magisis. Jabez first started to rule over the biggest continent of Magisis, Anlemiss. He also took advantage of the Freeup and Ruleup living there as a way to signal to others to avoid any resistance.

Day 2

Jabez's Ruling. Rule 2: Since you can't communicate with each other anymore in absence of your magic, I am taking pity on you and giving you this thing called 'technology' to call each other. I will send a manual later today. The technology item is called 'Zekop'. You can only call up to five family members and three friends.

PS: I will be adding more 'technology'.

The whole of Anlemiss gasped after they read this while a few children danced about in joy. This new thing would be so much fun! Hilary was very angry. "What? How dare he! First, he drains the power of Anlemiss and then he wants to replace it with some silly thing called 'technology'? Argh!" she yelled.

"Hush, Hilary. Once the eight girls feel better, we will kick Jabez and his technology off this planet," Hazel said. She started kicking the air as if to show Hilary what exactly they would do.

"We'll see," Hilary said grumpily.

"Pfft," Ruby said. "We don't need this rubbish. Let's just keep it near the window," when she read the note.

Day 3

Jabez's Ruling. Rule 3: Your supermarket will now be controlled by me, and I will add whatever I want. If the owners have any problem, I will duel with them. It is certain that they will lose and then, well, they will be kept as my prisoners.

PS: I'm taking over the Mid-Mart and the speed-o-matic first.

Hilary read it and sighed. "Why does he have to make such silly rules?" she asked herself.

"Don't know," Olivia said, appearing from the shadows.

"Ah! Stop doing that," Hilary screamed.

"Okay, okay," Olivia said. "Don't lose concentration on your work."

Hilary rolled her eyes.

"Who cares? We have enough supplies. The guards also gave some food with the letter so whatever," Ruby said.

Day 4

Jabez's Ruling. Rule 4: Hello! No rule for today.

PS: I might give a double rule tomorrow.

Hilary was relieved and Ruby didn't care.

Day 5

Jabez's Ruling. Rule 5: Manual book has been sent with this. Read the whole book at least two times. Once done, my guards will install the Zekop for you. This is compulsory. At 2pm sharp, guards will come for installation.

PS: You're in luck. There is no Rule 4 at all.

Hilary was annoyed and so was Ruby. The guards came and did as mentioned. Nora (Hilary was struggling to share her powers with her learners) and Ruby nearly fell asleep reading the manual.

Day 6

Jabez's Ruling. Rule 6: Every day at sharp 8am, you all need to sing a song. The words of the song are attached. Memorise it and sing it to my guards.

"Now, this is just plain dumb!" Ruby exclaimed.

Hilary was so tired that she just nodded her head and returned to her work.

The same day, the eight learners finally got out of bed. Scarlett and the other girls had decided to leave the eight girls by themselves. But as soon as they tried to get out, everybody's legs turned into jelly. They all fell down and hurt themselves, some banging into tables. Amber walked in at the same moment and found them.

"Guys! Come here this instant," Amber yelled.

Scarlett, Sophie and Chloe rushed into the room. When they saw what was happening, their mouths fell open. They recovered quickly and helped the eight learners into bed.

"One more week in bed for y'all. I can't believe you did this," Scarlett yelled, throwing her hands up in the air in frustration.

"We just thought that—" Mary muttered, looking at the floor.

"I don't care what you thought. Now, you guys are all bloody and weak again. We cannot leave them alone again," Amber yelled. "And that too just when you were all getting healed. THIS IS SO—"

"Let's go," Scarlett said.

"But—" Amber protested.

Scarlett gave her a look that said, *seriously, girl, do not mess with me!* Amber grumbled something and went out of the room, followed by the other three.

"Aw man!" Emma said after the younger girls had left. "I cannot believe we got into trouble with 11-year-olds."

"I know," Mary agreed.

Pat and Nora looked at each other, both of their expressions saying, *seriously, these guys are just 13.* Pat and Nora snuggled back in bed. They were not bleeding since the younger girls had used salve on them again. Sia and Mia thought of some pranks to play on the younger ones, once they were fully healed.

Luna and Jane followed Pat and Nora and slept. After a while, everyone was asleep. It was ten in the night and Hilary was also sleeping. The magical barriers were still there because Hilary was still using her power in her sleep. A week later, the eight learners were fully healed since they didn't try to go adventuring again.

Sia sighed, relaxed. "Finally! We are fully healed. What a long two weeks we had, staying in bed."

"Yeah, yeah, except that no more relaxing for y'all," Amber said.

"What? Why not?" Sia asked.

"Y'all need to train now. To defeat Jabez," Amber said, rolling her eyes.

The younger girls had gotten extremely bossy over the elder girls in the two weeks but the older girls didn't mind.

"Oh no, I totally forgot," Mary yelled.

Amber went out of the room, shaking her head. Suddenly, a yell was heard from below. Then they heard Scarlett calling out to them. They all scrambled downstairs and found Hazel lying unconscious on the floor, her leg bleeding and her head had a brutal bruise. Scarlett was looking over Hazel anxiously. She made a sign as if to call them closer.

28. An Accident

"How did this happen?" Jane asked anxiously.

"I'm not sure," Scarlett admitted. "But from the looks of it, I guess the wind made the door swing open suddenly and Hazel's head banged into it. About the leg, I don't know since there is nothing that explains that."

"Oh, let's take her to the Healing Room," Jane said. She first used Salve on Hazel to stop the bleeding and then took Hazel in her arms, carrying her to the Healing Room.

"Psst! Nora, Pat," Scarlett whispered.

Pat and Nora looked at Scarlett and she asked them to follow her. Scarlett reached the bedroom, Nora and Pat came in behind her. Then she locked the door.

"Why did you lock the door?" Pat asked.

"Because I think that Hazel is very badly injured," Scarlett said.

Nora and Pat sat down on their beds.

"Ok, but why couldn't you tell us this in front of everyone?" Nora asked.

"Because—" Scarlett's voice trailed off.

Nora was getting impatient now. "Because what?" she asked.

"Because I think that Hazel's bruise might have an effect on her brain," Scarlett said in a hollow voice.

"What? This can't be—" Nora protested.

"Actually, Scarlett knows a lot about medical stuff, so this can be true," Pat interrupted. *I hate to think she might be right,* Pat thought. An empty sort of feeling spread through her body.

"This is really serious, Scarlett. Are you sure about this?" Nora said.

"Yes, I am very sure," Scarlett said. "Because when I reached downstairs, I was reading and then Hazel yelled. I threw the book down and rushed to her. By the time I reached her, she was unconscious. But before that, she was acting as if she couldn't see anything properly."

Nora and Pat didn't know what to say. This could be very serious.

"Are you sure?" Nora asked again.

"Yes, yes, I am sure," Scarlett said.

Nora let this sink in, then she said, "Okay." Nora started pacing the floor.

"Can you please leave me and Nora alone for a while? You know, to process what you just said and discuss it?" Pat asked. "Only for a while."

"Okay, I will be in the Healing Room if you need me," Scarlett said, unlocking the door and walking out.

Pat closed the door and locked it.

"Now what? I mean, this is really serious. What if Hazel lost her memory, or something?" Pat said.

"Or *something*," Nora said, still pacing the floor.

After a few minutes, Nora said, "Maybe, maybe it was just a small thing? Maybe she couldn't see anything because pain blacked her vision? There is still a chance that Scarlett was just hallucinating. Maybe because she had been reading so much about medical stuff that she remembered something that had the same symptoms and got confused with something else?"

"So many maybes," Pat muttered.

"I know, but—" Nora said.

She was interrupted by a knock on the door.

"Who is it?" Pat asked impatiently.

"It's me, Amber," a muffled voice came.

"I just wanted to ask if you know where the extra first-aid supplies are. Because I think we will need more, Hazel's leg is still bleeding. And Salve is having only a minor effect," Amber said.

"Oh no! I think Hilary keeps them somewhere. We'll help you find it," Pat said.

Amber nodded. Pat came to the Healing Room with Nora and Amber.

"Luna, Jane. What happened? Isn't Salve working?" Pat asked.

"No! I don't know why, but it isn't," Luna said.

"It must be here somewhere," Nora muttered, as she was searching the storage shelves of the Healing Room.

"Hey! Look, there it is. Next to the door," Pat exclaimed, pointing next to the Healing Room storage door.

Nora looked there and then pressed a keyhole. Suddenly, another door, which was the colour of the wall (completely invisible) opened to reveal a cupboard. Nora quickly grabbed a bottle of liquid and rushed to Hazel's side.

"Here. This should reduce the bleeding," Nora said.

Luna took the bottle, poured the liquid onto a piece of cotton and gently dabbed it on Hazel's leg. After a few minutes, the bleeding reduced. Luna did the same thing again and the bleeding stopped. The younger girls went upstairs to be with Hilary. She was getting very weak. Amber handed her some food. Hilary took it and started eating it quickly.

"Now that her blood loss has stopped," Nora said, "should we sit here and wait for her to regain her consciousness?"

"I think so," Pat said.

They sat down. Nora started reading a book about healing and Pat started going through the secret cupboard. After half an hour, Hazel got up. She looked around and tried to speak but was too weak.

"Pat, Hazel's awake," Nora cried.

Both of them ran to her side.

"Hazel, what do you remember?" Pat asked.

Hazel tried to say, 'We were going to Mid-Mart, why—?' But her vocal cords seemed to have forgotten how to work.

"She is very weak," Nora said. "Pat, get some food."

Pat took a plate of food and handed it over to Hazel. "Eat this."

Hazel did. Once she was done, she tried to speak. "What happened?" Her voice sounded very small and insignificant.

Nora frowned. "Don't you remember getting hurt?"

Hazel blinked. "No. I remember going to Mid-Mart."

Pat gasped. "That means she really lost her memory," she said in a very low voice.

"We need to talk to Scarlett," Nora cried.

"Why?" Hazel asked, her voice getting softer. Then she lost consciousness again.

"We have to talk to Scarlett," Nora said again. She sped out of the room. Pat followed her. "Scarlett, where are you?" Nora yelled.

Scarlett yelled back, "Here, in the kitchen."

Pat and Nora rushed into the kitchen and closed the door.

"Scarlett, you were right. Hazel has lost her memory. She only remembers going to Mid-Mart. Absolutely nothing after that," Pat cried.

"Yeah," Nora said, nodding her head so fast that one might feel it will break off.

"Oh no," Scarlett said.

"Will we be able to help her?" Pat asked anxiously.

"Maybe. Maybe not," Scarlett said.

Nora and Pat just stared at her silently.

"We need a proper answer to help Hazel," Nora said angrily.

"We might need to make a spell to help her. If Scarlett doesn't have a plan," Pat said.

"You can try but there isn't much to think about to carry out the spell, and what if it goes wrong? You can't try it on anyone," Nora said.

"I'll think about how to help her. I am going to the library to find ways to help Hazel. Maybe there is something I missed while reading," Scarlett said. She got up and went to the library.

Nora and Pat looked at each other, like, *what just happened?*

"Maybe Scarlett is nervous?" Pat suggested.

"Yeah, that could be it," Nora said.

The eight learners were sitting next to Hazel in the Healing Room.

"Hazel? What exactly do you remember? I mean, what happened after Mid-Mart?" Pat asked Hazel for the hundredth time in a week.

"I told you, I don't know. I just remember we left Mid-Mart and then I am blank. When I regained consciousness, I was here in the Healing Room, feeling weak and my voice was not working," Hazel yelled angrily.

"Okay. Fine. But come on, anything? Do you remember anything at Mid-Mart at all?" Pat asked.

"Guys, I know how we can heal Hazel!" Scarlett yelled, bursting into the room.

"Really? Tell us," Luna said.

Everybody was looking at her, expecting her to begin.

"There is this potion which can heal every single thing. Of course, not bring back the dead. But it can be highly risky for the person taking the potion," Scarlett explained.

"Okay. Do we have this potion? Because it has been a bit more than a week and Hazel still doesn't remember anything," Jane said.

"Yeah! I asked Hilary and she told me that we have it in the secret cupboard, but she also told me that if you put more than a drop in Hazel's mouth, she might die," Scarlett said.

"Oh my gosh!" Sia exclaimed. "We need to be very careful."

"Yeah! Hilary said that the bottle is very hard to find since it is very small," Scarlett said.

"Oh, great! Just great," Mia yelled.

"What's the big deal?" Nora asked. "We can just use a summoning spell."

"Yeah, but it is very small, remember? So—" Jane started saying.

"I know, I know," Nora cut her off, "But it will appear in my hand, so we can easily give Hazel the liquid and then she'll be fine. It's as easy as that." Nora rolled her eyes.

"Actually, it's not. A ton of things could go wrong," Jane said. "What if you felt itchy on your palm right after you summoned the bottle? Then you would crush the bottle. And remember the liquid is really harmful, so—"

Nora threw up her hands in protest. "Nothing will happen. Think positive."

"Fine," Jane said, rolling her eyes.

"Nora, will you begin already? Do you even know the state Hilary is in? As soon as Hazel is fixed, we really need to fight Jabez," Pat said.

"Okay, okay," Nora said, not taking offence. "*Convocar!*"

Nora expected to feel a pinch or something like that in her hand, but nothing of the sort happened.

"Um, guys?" Nora said anxiously.

"Yeah? Did you feel anything when the bottle appeared?" Luna asked.

"Uh, that's exactly the problem. I can't feel anything! But I did see a sparkle appear for a second which means that I did summon it," Nora explained.

"Oh no! That probably means that the bottle is somewhere on the floor. Everybody, get on the beds! We don't want to crush the bottle," Sia said.

They took about ten minutes to find the bottle all thanks to Luna inventing a spell to find things. It was easy since she thought of the times she found her lost things, which was quite often.

The small bottle appeared in Luna's hand. She cried out in joy, "I have the bottle. I have the bottle."

Everybody looked at her as Luna went over to Hazel and very carefully, put a single drop of the liquid into her mouth. Hazel gulped the drop and frowned. She clenched her fists as if holding back pain. Then, after a few moments, she stopped frowning and unclenched her fists.

"Hazel? Now, do you remember?" Nora asked.

"Jabez! He has been ruling over us for three weeks at least, and Hilary's magic is draining," Hazel said, a bit dazed.

"You remember," Mia said. She started dancing.

Everyone else cheered happily and noisily. The younger learners were called, and everyone took the party downstairs. Hilary smiled weakly.

"Hey! Let's give Hilary some of this stuff," Amber suggested.

Nora nodded. "Good idea!" She went over to Hilary. She did what Luna did, carefully putting one drop of the liquid in Hilary's mouth.

Hilary gasped. She then blinked her eyes very fast. "I feel better," she said.

"Awesome!" The Freeup cried.

The next day, the eight girls started to train and plan how they were going to defeat Jabez. The younger girls started to focus more on Hilary though sometimes, they too went to help the eight learners.

"Hilary, we aren't ready yet," Nora said. "Is it okay that we delay it a bit?"

Hilary hesitated. Suddenly, a note came through the slot.

It said:

Jabez's Ruling. Rule 22: The water supplies are cut off for one week. No water will come through your non-magic water supplier. And if any of you try to protest against this, I will cut the water supply for two to three more weeks. You are powerless against me, and you have to realise you only thrive because I let you.

Nora and Hilary stared at the note, trying to digest Jabez's cruelness.

29. Jabez's Headquarters

The Freeup were nearly ready to go and fight Jabez. Except that they didn't know where his headquarter was.

"But how would he have built a headquarter in just a month?" Jane asked for the tenth time.

"Maybe he hasn't built one," Luna suggested. "And that'll just be better for us." She shrugged.

"That is not possible since he has mentioned his HQ in his rules," Jane yelled.

"Luna! Jane! Stop arguing! Remember Jabez adding something called 'technology'? Maybe his HQ is technology?" Pat said.

"But—" Jane protested.

"We are going to find his HQ and that is final," Pat interrupted.

"I never said that I don't want to find his HQ," Jane yelled.

The eight learners were carrying so much stress that they kept arguing with each other. It was all the younger ones could do to try and keep them from starting a fight among themselves. And sometimes, even when the younger ones tried, they got yelled at. There was a lot of tension building between them.

***

Meanwhile at Jabez's Headquarters

"Guards! Come here now," Jabez ordered, looking high and mighty on his throne.

Jabez's throne was completely black, just like all his clothes; one could almost feel they were one and the same.

"Yes, Your Majesty?" one of the two guards asked.

"I called you here to do some work," Jabez said.

"But, Your Majesty, we are guarding other things," the second guard said.

"Enough! Do you want to get fired, Daniel?" Jabez said.

"No, Your Majesty," the second guard, Daniel, said.

"Good! Go get me a piece of paper with a lotlit. And you, Jim, put stronger security for the draining machine," Jabez commanded.

A lotlit was like a pen except that it could write anything you wanted in any kind of handwriting. Jim and Daniel hurried out of the room. After a few minutes, Daniel came back in.

"What took you so long? You just needed to get a lotlit and a piece of paper," Jabez yelled furiously.

"Sorry, Your Majesty, very sorry," Daniel stammered.

Daniel handed him the things.

"Guards!" Jabez yelled. "Come here!" Ten guards came rushing in. "Guard my throne!" Jabez ordered. He then left the throne room. His cloak swept the floors majestically. All the guards who met him, bowed.

Ah, this is life! When everyone respects me. Earlier, my stupid guards had started to become lazy because I hadn't started ruling over a planet yet. But now, they don't act lazy anymore. This is truly life, Jabez thought, as he reached his bedroom.

Jabez's bed was also completely black. His bed covers were black, like everything else in his room. His closet was shiny black with dull silver curly door handles. He opened his closet. "Hm, which outfit should I wear when the Ruleup comes here?" he asked himself.

His closet was full of black colour clothes. He even had black pyjamas. His bed was right in front of a black-stained floor-to-ceiling window. Two shiny silver curtains were positioned in front of it. His desk was a bit away from his bed with a window in front. All the window frames were black.

The desk had a silver open container. In the container were some lotlits. Next to the container was a light hovering a few inches from the table. There was a drawer in the desk with papers. The desk also had a stack of books placed on it untidily. A few papers were already on the desk, on them were some half-written rules.

In the bedroom, there was a recliner sofa with a small table in front. Jabez sat down on the chair. He took a paper with some shiny gold boundary on it and started to write with a lotlit. Every few minutes, he would chew on the back of his lotlit, thinking of what to write next. After half an hour (and a nearly-chewed-up lotlit), Jabez was done. The paper read:

Dear Ruleup,

I am inviting you to my headquarters. I am having a party. A celebration for a month of my ruling. But you see, I have a special offer to make to you. The party starts at 6pm sharp. The offer is really exciting plus today, my guards are going to capture the Freeup. They are very weak and even their magic barriers are down. I have given you enough information for now. The rest will be told at my party. Also, by the time you arrive, the Freeup would have been captured and put down in my dungeon prison. By the way, the curfew is lifted.

Sincerely,
Jabez.

Jabez read it again and smiled to himself. There was no party, but there soon will be, when the Ruleup would be ruling with him (but *he* would be ordering *them* to do things) and the Freeup his prisoners. He got up, took the paper in his hand and left the room.

The corridors near Jabez's rooms had large life-size pictures and portraits of him on the walls. The wallpaper was dark maroon. The floor had a dark red rug. The corridors away from Jabez's rooms either had pictures of him or his family members. The picture frames were, yes, black. The corridors had dim lights on the ceiling.

He entered a room that had two guards on the door. Each of them was holding a shiny silver pointy spear.

"Hello, Your Majesty," Martin said, bowing.

The guard next to him, Cal, also bowed. Cal and Martin were Jabez's favourite guards. They were brothers and had been working for Jabez the longest. They were also his eldest guards.

"Hello, Your Majesty," Cal said. He bowed.

Jabez went inside the room. It was his control area. He could contact all of his guards outside the headquarters from here. He contacted the guards near the Freeup by pressing a button. A thick mist formed in front of him and in that, a guard appeared.

"Hey! Sammy. Ready to capture the Freeup? And why is your armour off? Your power is in the armour, not in you, you know that, right?" Jabez asked. Jabez's guards were all non-magic people. He had chosen the strongest of them and given them armour which contained magic. That was how the guards got power.

Sammy was the leader of the group guarding the Freeup. Jabez could see the inside of the tent and Sammy while Sammy could see Jabez and the control room.

"We know, we have only taken it out for a few minutes, Your Majesty," Sammy said. "It is a littl—"

"Nonsense! Wear it back immediately. Any updates?" Jabez said and muttered, "Silly non-magic people."

"According to our spies, Hilary is getting weaker by the minute. The potion thing which she took has already worn off. And the older girls are arguing a lot, Your Majesty," Sammy said.

"Good, that means you and your guards can capture them easily," Jabez said happily. *My plan is forming beautifully.*

"Yes, we will," Sammy agreed.

"In a few minutes, get ready to capture the Freeup. It's nearing five-fifteen." Jabez waved his hand and the mist disappeared.

Jabez pressed another button, and the thick fog came again, this time showing another guard.

"William. Any updates?" Jabez asked.

"Yeah. Tons. The Tina girl? Remember her, Your Majesty?" William said.

"Yeah, I remember her," Jabez said.

"Well, she was crying for her mother in the bedroom by herself. She was worried a lot. If you want to carry out the plan of making the Ruleup work for you, you will need to free her mother, Your Majesty," William explained.

"Don't tell me what to do and what not to do," Jabez snapped.

"Sorry, Your Majesty," William said meekly.

"I'll find a way to do it. Anything else?" Jabez asked.

"Yeah. The Ruleup are pretty happy. They didn't care about the rules until now, when you started with the evil ones. We did as you told us to do, we added a PS saying that it didn't apply to them, Your Majesty," William said.

"Okay, fine, send a guard at HQ, I need to give the party invitation," Jabez said.

William nodded and then said, "Sure, Your Majesty. The guard will arrive in a minute's time. He is coming by the speed-o-magic you gave us. Also, the Ruleup has started to train in their dark magic again."

"Fine," Jabez said. He waved his hand in the thick mist and the call ended. He left the control room.

"Hey Martin? Is Adam at the dungeons?" Jabez asked.

"Yes, Your Majesty," Martin said.

Jabez went to the left and took a corridor to the right. The corridor ended into a staircase leading down to the dungeons.

"Adam, where's Mrs Smith? Did you shift her to prison no 12?" Jabez asked.

"Yes, Your Majesty," Adam said.

Jabez nodded his head and went to prison no 12.

Tina's mom was lying on the bottom bunk there, looking very pale. The prison had a steel bunk bed with a thin mattress. The bunk bed was on the right side of the prison. The prison had no lights. There was only a weak lamp on a small table next to the bottom bunk. On the left, there was a shelf with two books about Jabez's evil doings.

The walls were made of cold stone. Below the shelf, there was a wooden chair. There was a spell to stop any magic from working in the prison. This spell worked only in small spaces. The bars were made out of metal and there was a barrier so that prisoners couldn't stick their hands to do any magic.

Diana Smith got up the moment she saw Jabez. "Let me go, please, what have I ever done?" she pleaded.

Jabez ignored the question and said, "Your daughter is coming soon. Then, I will decide whether to let you go, or make you stay here."

"What? Why? Is she alright?" Diana asked, scared.

"Yes, she is fine, hopefully. Anyways, it all depends on Ruby. If she does what I want, you will be out of here. If not, you and your daughter will be stuck in this prison," Jabez said coldly.

Diana looked really anxious and hungry, so Jabez decided to be generous. He took a plate of food from a shelf, opened the door, put the plate inside and then locked it again. The food was horrible but Diana Smith didn't know that.

"Eat it," Jabez commanded. "And don't think I'm being kind."

He didn't wait for a response and went away.

"Adam," Jabez yelled.

Adam came out from a room.

"Remove Diana Smith from prison no 12. Lock her in one of the guard rooms. The Ruleup don't need to see her," Jabez commanded.

"Yes, Your Majesty," Adam said.

"Hey, Oliver! Come with me. Need to move Ms Smith again," Adam said.

Oliver and Adam went to Diana. They took her plate of food and put it on the shelf again.

"Come with us," Oliver said.

"I am being let go?" Diana asked weakly.

"In your dreams." Oliver laughed.

Oliver and Adam took each arm of Diana's and dragged her to a guard room. Diana tried to eat the food they gave her back. It was horrible. In the end, she put the plate on the desk and slept on the bed, trying to ignore her hunger.

30. An Invitation

As soon as Jabez left the dungeons, he went to the guard who was waiting patiently. Jabez gave him the invitation and left. The guard carefully put the letter in a golden embroidered envelope and set off.

Jabez headed to his bedroom. He started writing more rules. After a few minutes, a guard came and told him that the message had been delivered, and that the Ruleup had agreed to come to the party.

***

"Whoa!" Tina cried when the message came in through the slot. "Jabez's inviting us to his party."

"What?" Ruby asked. She ran forwards to see the letter. "OMG! I don't believe this."

"Please, can we go and make this right?" Everyone shouted almost together. They were all very tired of the curfew.

Ruby gasped suddenly. "Yes, we're going." *The Freeup as prisoners?* Ruby thought, shuddering.

One month of curfew and endless terrible rules had changed the Ruleup. Now that they knew how it felt like being ruled, they too longed for freedom and understood the need for it. Ruby would never do something this terrible, even if it was what her parents wanted to do. She had started realising she didn't want to live only for power. She didn't yearn for the exact same thing Jabez did.

"Yup, we'll go change our outfits," Andrea said.

When they went to get their clothes, they started whispering loudly.

"Need to save the—"

"Long for freedom—"

"Cannot let anyone rule—"

Sarah stared at them. *They've turned into good people. I'm gonna betray them to Ruby. Then they'll see,* she thought, horrified.

Sarah took Ruby aside.

"Hey Ruby, see our dresses," Sarah said. She yanked Ruby into the room.

"Nice dresses. Though we aren't going to a grand ball, it's only that silly Jabez," Ruby said.

Then she heard them. Instead of yelling at them, she smiled. "You too? Good! Now, I won't have to force you. We'll go there to save the Freeup instead of trying to rule."

They cheered. Sarah couldn't believe what was happening. *How can Ruby turn good?* But she didn't say anything and appeared to agree with them, all the while thinking what to do.

***

Nora was spying on Jabez's guards, hiding in a bush. The guards were sitting in a large tent with their armours off. One guard stepped out of the tent and looked around. Nora turned her hair into a dagger and jumped out of her hiding place. She lunged at the guard and pinned him to the floor, pressing the dagger to his throat.

"Tell me the location of Jabez's headquarters if you care for your life. If you don't, you die here on this spot," Nora said threateningly. "Don't even try to yell. Otherwise, I really will kill you."

The guard got really scared. "It's right in front of Mid-Mart. You don't know because of the curfew. Can I go now?" He looked at her pleadingly.

In reply, Nora cried, "*Memoria Damnum!*" With this spell, Nora removed the guard's memory from the moment he had come outside. She quickly dashed back into the bush. Just in time.

"What am I doing here?" he murmured. He ducked back into the tent.

"Let's go, guys," Nora whispered.

The seven other learners popped up from bushes.

"Hold hands," Nora whispered. She teleported them all to Mid-Mart.

They saw Jabez's palace. It was a large black castle with five towers. Four at each corner were the watchtowers. The fifth tower was wider and taller than the rest. It was right in the middle of the castle. It was like a viewing area, just a place to take in the view. There were guards just about everywhere. The castle had a huge brown wooden door. All the guards had shiny silver pointy spears. There were flags on all the five towers. These were completely black, with Jabez's symbol on it.

"Hey, how about Jane and Luna go to find and destroy the machine while we fight the guards?" Pat suggested.

"Okay," Luna said.

Jane nodded.

"Hey, we didn't elect a leader. Let's choose one now," Mia said.

The others nodded.

"Okay, at the count of three, let's say who we want as the leader," Nora said.

The others nodded.

"One, two, three," Nora said.

"Nora," everyone, except Nora, whispered at the same time.

"Pat," Nora whispered. She was taken totally by surprise. "What?" she shrieked. "Why me?"

"Because Jabez is more of an enemy to you than to any of us," Pat said.

Everyone nodded.

Nora tried to digest this. "Okay," she said slowly.

"So, what's our plan?" Emma asked.

"I didn't know until now that I was the leader. I thought Pat was. I never bothered to think of one," Nora snapped. "Hold on."

The Freeup had made no plan since Hilary was very weak. They had just set off, without thinking of what they'd do once they learnt about Jabez's headquarters.

After a long and boring thirty minutes, Nora whispered, "I have a plan."

"What is it? What is it?" Everyone asked.

The plan was to sneak inside the headquarters by hiding in bushes and climbing inside from an open window. Then, they would go to the middle of the castle to the fifth tower and destroy the machine. They guessed that the machine would be in the middle tower since most of the guards seemed to be hovering around there.

"Nice plan. But do we have a backup pla—?" Luna whispered.

Nora quickly put a finger on her lips and pulled Luna down into the bushes to hide from an oncoming guard. After a few minutes, when the guard had returned, the eight girls popped their heads out.

"Let's go," Nora whispered.

She kept hiding in bushes or behind trees whenever a guard came in sight and others followed her lead. They reached the door, which was black and made of iron. Next to the door, were the boundary walls of the palace. Beyond that, there was a stone footpath and another door, which was set in the middle of the walls of Jabez's headquarters.

Nora quickly went through the doors since the guards there had fallen asleep. The guards at the entrance were chatting with each other and didn't notice Nora. The other seven girls wished themselves luck and did what Nora did. None of the guards saw them too, thankfully. But as soon as the girls were out of sight, both the guards got up and whispered something into some devices they were holding.

"Look, an open window. No one seems to be around here. Let's climb in," Nora whispered.

She sent the others in first and then she, Luna and Jane climbed in. They found no guards on their way until they reached the corridor near the middle tower.

"Hey, you! Stop!" a guard yelled. The six girls turned around, Jane and Luna hiding behind them. "Stop or we will kill you all," the guard yelled.

"Jane, Luna. The door is right next to you, we'll keep them off, you go there," Nora whispered.

Jane and Luna nearly went inside but another storm of guards came through the door, pushing the eight girls behind.

"Charge!" A guard yelled.

Everyone started to fight. Taking advantage of the fight, Jane and Luna quickly sneaked into the middle tower. It was completely empty. There was a floating platform which led upstairs. They went on it and pressed a button which said 'UP'. The platform shot up. It stopped suddenly when it had crossed at least eight floors.

"Whoa! I am not doing that again," Jane said.

Luna nodded. They saw a huge, eight floor tall machine. It had a bunch of pipes going around in different directions. They were transparent in colour. The pipes had some liquid flowing through them. At the top of the machine, there were three antenna-like structures.

"Okay, how on Magisis do we destroy such a tall machine?" Jane said in frustration.

Luna said nothing for a minute. "Using *Destrucmasa*," she said grimly. "There's no other way."

Jane sighed. "You're right. We'll have to."

"Three, two, one, *Destrucmasa!*" Jane and Luna cried together.

"One more time," Luna said.

"*Destrucmasa!*" they cried.

"Two to three more times, I think," Jane said.

"Destruc—" They began.

Someone grabbed their hands. They screamed and tried to throw them off.

"Oh, you aren't going anywhere," Martin snarled. "Not from Jabez's favourite guards. Our power lies in our armour, and we're not stupid enough to remove it."

"Now, you both go to Jabez's prison," Cal said, smirking.

"Let go of me," Luna said, struggling.

"I'm not dumb enough to do that," Cal said, who was holding Luna's arms back.

"Oh, so you are dumb. Just not a lot?" Luna mocked.

"Come on Cal, let's get Luna and Jane to prison no 17," Martin said.

"How do you know our names?" Jane squeaked.

"We have our ways," Martin said. He gripped Jane's hands tighter.

"Stop that! Are you sure you want your master to see us bedraggled?" Jane said, trying to say something to save herself. She continued to struggle.

"Oh, he won't mind. In fact, he'll love it. Now, let's get you both to your prison," Cal said.

Martin and Cal went down on the floating platform, pushing Jane and Luna in front. The platform went to the bottom and came to the corridor where the others were fighting. As soon as the other guards saw that Jane and Luna had been captured, they started yelling in joy.

"Now, do you want to get captured like your friends or do you want to go back to your house?" Martin asked. But he knew the answer.

The others stood speechless, frozen in horror.

31. Little Ruby

"We'll leave," Nora stammered. This was after Luna and Jane had pleaded all of them to go.

"Good," Martin cried. He and Cal went to the corridor leading into the dungeons. While leaving, he made a circle with two of his fingers though nobody noticed it since he had kept the gesture hidden. The windows in the other corridors closed with a small thud. He nodded towards Cal, Cal understood, whispering instructions for more guards to stay hidden near all the entrances.

"Let's tell the guards we are leaving, and then we'll sneak around here instead of leaving," Nora quickly whispered this to everyone, making sure the guards did not hear them. Everyone nodded. "We'll leave. We can find our way by ourselves, thank you," Nora said, turning around to face the guards.

"You have five minutes to leave the castle. If you don't leave by then, the consequences will be severe," one of the guards warned.

The guards went into the machine room while four near the door stood there, guarding it. Nora and the others went out of the corridor.

***

"Why are you capturing us anyway? What good will come from keeping us?" Jane asked.

"Shut up!" Martin ordered.

Jane opened her mouth to speak but then decided against it. They soon reached prison no 17. Martin and Cal pushed both the girls inside.

"Enjoy rotting down here forever," Martin said.

"Ta-ta," Cal said, smirking. He high-fived Martin. They locked the door and went off.

"Your Majesty, we have sent more guards to the control room and have captured two members of the Freeup, Luna and Jane. We will take duty there if you like," Cal said, bowing to Jabez in his throne room.

"Okay," Jabez said. "The Ruleup will be here soon. I don't want them to feel disappointed that only two were caught. Sammy failed in catching the

Freeup, their armour disappeared. They will try again tomorrow. I assume the plan is working?"

"Yes, Your Majesty. They don't suspect a thing," Martin said.

"Oh, and one more thing. Don't let anyone tell the Ruleup there was no curfew, I mean, they can't have so many disappointments at once. I'll convince them later that for their own good, I had kept them locked in their HQ for a month," Jabez said.

"Okay, Your Majesty," Cal and Martin said together. They bowed and exited through a back door.

Ruby was horrified. The Ruleup had arrived a few minutes ago and had reached the throne room. Jabez seemed to be busy, so she had eavesdropped on this conversation. She, of course, didn't tell the others for her own reasons.

"Let's go guys, it's 6:05," Ruby said.

The others nodded. Ruby pushed open the throne room door and went inside.

"Well, well, well! If it isn't the famed Ruby and Ruleup," Jabez said. "Come in! Come in! I don't know why my guards didn't escort you in."

"It's fine," Ruby said cheerfully.

They were pretending to be good to Jabez so that they weren't suspected. Jabez snapped his fingers and a lot of armchairs popped up out of nowhere.

"Sit here," Jabez said.

"Thanks, this is all so nice," Ruby cried, sitting on an armchair.

Jabez stared at her suspiciously, but then his expression quickly dissolved into a smile. The others also sat on the armchairs.

"I wanted to invite you all to rule with me," Jabez said, getting straight to the point.

"What? Wow! That's amazing," Ruby said. *What? What's wrong with him? Why would we want to rule with him?* Ruby thought. *He's gone completely mad!*

"So, do you accept it?" Jabez asked excitedly. Of course, he was shocked Ruby was so happy.

Ruby said, "Guys? Can you leave us to discuss this matter?"

The other groaned but got up and left the throne room.

"So, do you accept? I mean, won't your learners also want to have a say in this because—" Jabez began saying.

"Leave me to decide that, Jabez," Ruby said coldly.

"Hey, hey. It's fine really. And I'm sorry for what I did to your parents but really, they were so scared and—"

"Enough, I'm going. And never even try to get me back here. Because I don't accept your offer," Ruby interrupted angrily. "And I NEVER will."

"But Ruby, I'm just telling you the truth! For how long will you hide from it?" Jabez exclaimed, getting up.

The thing about the truth hit Ruby hard, really hard.

"What do you mean? I don't know what you're talking about," Ruby stammered.

Aha! I've got her around my thumb now, Jabez thought smugly.

"Guards! Out! And lock the door!" Jabez ordered.

The guards obeyed.

"Why are you doing this? You can't blackmail me into ruling with you," Ruby yelled.

"Oh, I won't. I'll just read your past," Jabez said. "And then, you'll have to rule with me. I can just wipe your memory of this ever happening, so you will remain loyal to me, always."

For the second time in her life, Ruby's fear showed on her face. Usually, she managed to hide it but not this time. She was really frightened. She knew that Jabez could read minds and tried to put random memories to stop him from finding her secret.

"Don't resist. I'll scan your whole brain now. Wait a minute!" Jabez exclaimed, so lost in his thoughts that he forgot that he was speaking.

Ruby suddenly got an idea. She put a bad memory in front of her mind, a memory that she knew was painful for her. But that was what Jabez wanted, she just needed to make him feel overconfident, pretending to be frightened and obeying him.

"Aha! There's a memory. Now, let me play it. Just a second, the memory will play, and you—" Jabez began.

"What? How did you—?" Ruby gasped, pretending to be surprised. It was weird how she could lure Jabez into a trap when he was reading her mind, but it worked anyway.

"Shh, it's starting," Jabez cried.

Suddenly, Ruby could see something that had happened in her past but as if she was a spectator. Jabez could see her past too, almost as if it was a movie. A long and wide mist appeared in front of Jabez. Ruby turned around so that her back was facing Jabez. Her past came into view.

A six-year-old Ruby was creeping down the steps of her house.

Liam (Ruby's dad) and Heather (her mom) were in the living room. It was around 7 in the evening. Liam and Heather were looking scared.

Liam was tall and had blue eyes. His hair was a dark shade of black. He looked friendly and it was hard to believe that he was evil. Heather was a bit shorter than Liam. She had green eyes and Ruby's hair. She also looked friendly. Both of them were thin. Liam was wearing a brown t-shirt and white pants. Heather was wearing a blue top and a long green skirt that reached her legs.

"Mom? Dad?" Little Ruby asked. "What happened? What's wrong?"

"Huh? Oh, um, nothing darling," Heather stammered. "How about you go upstairs to your room and read a book? You needed to study for your, um, exam, right? So, go study."

Little Ruby instantly knew something was wrong. Her mother never told her to study for exams. She always studied a bit right before the day of the exam and always copied from the kid sitting next to her, who was always the smartest.

"Mom, you never tell me to study," Little Ruby protested.

"Honey, what I meant was go read the book of dark magic. Your teacher told me that you needed more practice in the mass destruction spell. Go practice! You need to earn the name of the Best Dark Kid ever," Heather said.

"Yeah, okay," Little Ruby said. "But can I at least get a hug?"

"Of course, honey," Heather said.

She quickly climbed down the rest of the steps and hugged her mother.

"Don't I get one too?" Liam asked.

"Oh Dad! As if I was ever going to forget you," Little Ruby said. Then she hugged her father. "Family hug time."

All three hugged each other. With this, Little Ruby went up the stairs and closed her bedroom door with a bang. But she stood just at the door.

"I need to find out what's wrong," Little Ruby said to herself.

She quietly opened the door and snuck back down the stairs but this time, went only halfway down.

"What do we do? Jabez is going to tell everyone you-know-what," Liam asked.

"The first thing we need to do is protect Ruby. What if Jabez does something to her? We need to protect her," Heather said with force.

"I know, but we'll have to tell her that we're scared. We'll have to tell her the truth of us having doubts upon our ruling," Liam said. "We are not any more powerful than the others on Magisis. If we try to rule, they might as well put us in prison or something."

"Hush! Not so loud. I know that Ruby's room is far away but if you yell so loudly, she will hear us," Heather said.

Little Ruby had to climb down further since Liam and Heather had started talking in lower voices.

"Jabez is going to arrive soon. We need to get Ruby and run away from him, we need to—" Heather began whispering.

"Mom! Look. A large man in black is outside," Little Ruby yelled.

"Ruby? You heard us?" Heather asked.

"Yes," Ruby said.

"It's Jabez! Heather, it's too late," Liam exclaimed.

"Yeah, that's right! It's too late," Jabez said. He came bursting through the door.

"Mommy, save me!" Little Ruby exclaimed.

"You poor little girl, you don't even know what is about to happen to you," Jabez said.

"What do you mean?" Little Ruby asked, shaking with fear.

"Well! Looks like your parents haven't told you of my threat?" Jabez asked.

"No! Don't do it. Please spare us," Heather protested.

"Mom! What's wrong? What is Jabez's threat? Mom! Dad! Why won't somebody tell me?" Little Ruby asked, looking from her mother to her father.

"Well, let me tell you then, little girl! My threat is—" Jabez said.

"No! Don't tell her," Liam begged.

"Oh, I will tell her! And you both won't be able to stop me," Jabez yelled. "I'm going to tell everyone that your parents are very weak."

"No," Heather yelled.

Before they could do anything, Jabez pointed at Heather and made a very violent crushing gesture. Heather fell down dead, the sound of her last breath echoing in their ears. Liam and Little Ruby screamed.

Jabez smiled cruelly. "Nothing can stop me." He made the crushing gesture towards Liam too.

Liam fell down dead, his mouth forming some last words towards Ruby, "I love you."

"Dad! Mom! No!" Little Ruby said.

"I have an offer for you," Jabez said. "You can rule with me. Your parents were weak. But you have a lot of potential."

"I don't care. I don't want anything to do with you."

This angered Jabez. "What did you say, little girl? I'll kill you too. Enjoy a place in hell with your parents."

Jabez pointed at Little Ruby. But before he could make any gesture, Little Ruby yelled, trying to point at Jabez. But she was shaking, her aim went wrong, and she pointed at the house instead, "*Destrucmasa!*"

The entire house crashed upon them. Jabez screamed and started to turn really big. Ruby ran as fast as she could, dodging pieces of falling debris.

"I'll be back, Mom and Dad!" she yelled. Little Ruby wiped tears from her face, she was alone now and knew she had to be strong.

After a few minutes of running, Little Ruby reached a farmhouse. She slept on the hay the whole night.

"Hey, you! What are you doing here? Kid, get up," the farmer yelled in the morning, poking Ruby with a stick.

"Ouch! Hey. Stop. I'm not a thief. I'll leave," Little Ruby yelled, rubbing her eyes.

"Get out now!" the farmer yelled.

She left the farmhouse.

"I need to find Mom and Dad's bodies and bury them," Little Ruby said to herself, tears pouring down her face.

She reached her broken down house and moved debris with a spell. Ruby soon found her parents, dead, under a fallen wall. She pulled them from under the pile.

"A sorry sight, isn't it?" Jabez said menacingly.

"What have you come here for? To kill me?" Little Ruby asked, no longer feeling afraid. Only angry, raging.

"No, as much as I want to, I won't. You're impressive at dark magic, join me. And rule with me. If you don't want to, well, then just remember what a good offer you turned down," Jabez said.

"Well, I decline. Get out," Little Ruby yelled.

Jabez shook his head and then vanished into thin air. Little Ruby wiped her nose on her sleeve. She dragged her parents to the burial grounds and buried them. She then went to a florist shop.

"I want burial flowers please," Little Ruby said to the shopkeeper. Little Ruby took the flowers and started to cry as she went back to the burial grounds. "I wish I had someone to hug, someone to share my pain with. I'm going to be alone forever, why did you leave me, Mom and Dad?" Little Ruby said to herself and started to cry again.

"Rest in peace, Mom and Dad," Little Ruby said softly. From that day onwards, Ruby was set on continuing her parents' dream. That day was when Jabez had sparked anger and regret in Little Ruby, which started her days of evil.

Suddenly, the memory stopped.

"Now, do you want to join me, *little girl*?" Jabez asked smugly.

32. Sneaking Around

"I would like a tour before joining you," Ruby stammered fearfully.

"Fine, a tour it is then," Jabez said. "Guards, unlock the door!"

The door unlocked from outside. Ruby quickly wiped her tears so that the guards wouldn't see them. She nodded her head towards them and took a corridor to the right. Jabez had given her a map of his headquarters and according to it, Ruby was heading towards the kitchen. Suddenly, she stopped. She heard a voice muttering something. It was coming from an empty room next to the kitchen. Ruby stood next to the door, listening.

"Ugh! I can't believe it," the voice muttered.

Oh my gosh! Ruby thought. *It's Sarah!*

"I so need to betray Ruby to Jabez. I cannot believe that they all turned good. Just like the silly Freeup. I can't believe that even Ruby has turned good," Sarah muttered. "Now, it's up to me to stop the Freeup and the Ruleup uniting. It's a good thing that at least Jane and Luna got captured. Though I need to tell Jabez about the rest of the Ruleup turning good. Then, I'll help him capture the Freeup."

Ruby was about to go inside and kick Sarah out of the Ruleup, kill her, whatever, but a thought hit her. What if she pretended to be on Sarah's side and fooled her? Then she could avoid gain an upper hand.

"Though I wonder how—" Sarah muttered.

"Sarah," Ruby said sharply, entering the empty room.

"Oh, Ruby! What are you doing here?" Sarah asked nervously. *Oh my gosh! What if Ruby heard me? What if my cover is blown?* Sarah thought.

"I heard what you said," Ruby said coldly.

"Really? I mean, what are you talking about, Ruby?" Sarah stammered.

"No need to lie, Sarah." Ruby paused. "Because I'm on your side."

"What? Really?"

"Yeah. I actually pretended to be on the other side because I didn't need the rest of the Ruleup to go to the Freeup and tell them. Even though it will take them ages and ages to convince the Freeup, I couldn't risk it, y'know."

"Yeah, true. Though now what?" Sarah asked.

"You know what? I'll be back in a while after I take a whole tour of this place and then we'll discuss it. You sit here and think of a plan till them; and *stay here*. By the way, where are the others?"

"The others are in the living room, next to Jabez's throne room," Sarah replied happily.

"Okay," Ruby said. She waved and left the room. Ruby headed straight to the living room. "Guys, listen to me," Ruby said sharply, entering the living room.

"Oh, hey Ruby! What happened?" Andrea asked.

"We can't trust Sarah," Ruby said plainly.

"What? Why?" Anne asked.

"Let me tell you why," and explained everything. She also told them about her chat with Sarah.

"OMG! I don't believe it," Ava yelled after Ruby was done.

"But I do. Sarah was looking horrified when we said we turned good. She thought nobody saw her, but I did," Andrea yelled. Everyone was very surprised at this. They had expected Andrea to have faith in Sarah.

"Oh no! That means that she didn't turn good," Hannah yelled.

"Yeah, but we can't let her know that we have found out her secret," Lucy said.

"Yeah, duh!" Alice said. She rolled her eyes.

Hannah opened her mouth to say something, but she was interrupted by the door opening and Jabez entering the room.

"Hey, Ruby! I thought you were taking a tour of my palace, not gossiping with your learners," Jabez asked.

"Jabez, I just came here to tell them the good news," Ruby replied, gritting her teeth. *Don't send a killing spell at him*, she told herself. *It won't kill him. It'll just get everyone into trouble. DON'T!*

"Okay, fine," Jabez said. He left the room and closed the door, which was good, because if he'd stayed there a second more, she would've attacked.

"Phew! That was a close one," Ruby said.

"Yeah, but what's the good news?" Daisy asked.

"Oh yeah! About that," Ruby said.

Everyone silently waited for Ruby.

"I, um, accepted Jabez's offer for ruling with him," Ruby said.

Everyone's jaw dropped open.

"You did what!" Alice exclaimed, breaking the silence.

"Why did you do it?" Ava asked furiously.

"I had to," Ruby yelled, "because—" Ruby's voice trailed off.

"Because what?" Everyone asked eagerly.

"I can't tell you," Ruby said, turning her back to her learners.

"You have to tell us," Anne yelled.

"I can't," Ruby stammered.

"Why?" Everyone asked.

"I just can't, okay," Ruby yelled. Everyone was taken aback. "I'm sorry I yelled," Ruby said.

"Hey, it's okay. Just, please tell us when you can, okay?" Andrea said softly. Patting Ruby on the back slowly.

"I think you deserve to know," Ruby said. She gulped.

Ruby told them about the memory which Jabez had shown her in the throne room. Her voice cracked as she came to the part of her parents' death.

"Oh Ruby. We're so sorry," everyone said together. They all got up and went to give Ruby a big and comforting hug.

Jabez came into the room at the same moment and saw them hugging. The others let go of Ruby as Jabez entered, glaring at him like he was some very nasty piece of dirt. Ruby managed to give Jabez a faint smile and ran out of the room. She found a room with a lot of boxes in it. She went in there and closed the door behind her. Ruby started to sob silently, leaning on the door.

"I wish I had someone to hug, someone to share my pain with," Ruby said, repeating the words she had said sixteen years ago at the burial grounds. She felt like she was six again, grieving on her parent's dead bodies.

Finally, she straightened, her entire body shaking with silent sobs. "I have to keep on going," she told herself. "I need to make this worth it."

Ruby wiped her tears. She opened the door and left the room. She arrived in the dungeons. Ruby asked a guard where Jane and Luna were being kept and who they were guarded by. The guard didn't get suspicious of her and told her to go to prison no 17. He was very talkative and told Ruby all the details freely. She went to the prison to free them and explain what had happened.

***

"Shh. Look, a guard," Nora whispered.

The guard went in the other direction.

"Now what? Should we all try to rescue Jane and Luna?" Mary asked.

"I wish we could," Nora said. "But the dungeons will obviously be filled with guards."

"Can we at least try?" Mia asked.

Just then, five big, strong guards appeared.

"Hey! Didn't you guys leave?" a guard yelled, faking his surprise. *Not that I expected you all to get away. It's Jabez's castle, escape is impossible when you're the enemy.*

"Run," Nora yelled.

The six of them ran to the other side. But five more guards came from that way. They ran to another side but ten more guards came from there. Five guards appeared from the remaining side. Now, they were cornered and outnumbered by at least twenty-five guards.

"Uh, hey guys? How about we leave and y'all think this never happened?" Nora asked nervously.

"Nuh-huh, now we'll just capture you. Y'all lost your chance to escape. Guards. Charge," a guard said who was obviously the leader.

***

"Martin and Cal," Ruby called when she reached prison no 17.

The two guards turned around.

"How do you know our names?" Martin snarled.

"Another guard told me," Ruby replied plainly. "Now, come on. Bow to me," Ruby barked.

"Why would we do that?" Cal snapped. "You are—"

"Because I am now ruling with Jabez. So, I am your mistress. Bow," Ruby barked.

"Oh! We didn't know. Please forgive us, mistress." Cal and Martin bowed.

"That's better," Ruby said. "Now, clear off! I need to have a little chit-chat with these prisoners." Ruby gave her most evil grin.

It seemed to do the trick. "Yes mistress," Martin and Cal said and left. Before leaving, Martin gave Ruby permission to open the prison no 17 with magic.

"How on Magisis did you guys end up here?" Ruby asked, unlocking the door.

Ruby slid in quickly and shut the door.

"And why would we tell you?" Jane asked furiously.

Luna glared at Ruby and sat next to Jane as if she was protecting her. Ruby had seriously no idea what to say.

"Guys, I've turned good," she said.

"We so believe you," Luna said sarcastically. "We're happy that kind, generous Ruby has come to rescue us. Have you *any idea* how *lame* that sounds?" She glared at Ruby even more.

"Hey," Ruby said. "I'm telling the truth."

"And how do we know you're not lying?" Jane asked.

Suddenly, Jabez walked up to the prison. *Was he following her or something? Why did he have to poke around everywhere?* He grinned. "Good that you're taking a head start in your duties of ruling with me."

Ruby glared at him fiercely. "Get out!"

Her anger was boiling on the surface, she didn't care if Jabez could hurt her back or that he was powerful. He had killed her parents. Jabez shrugged and walked away.

"You," Jane snapped, "how can you expect us to trust you? You horrible, nasty, terrible LIAR!"

Ruby looked down, miserable. "I—"

Jane got up so suddenly that Ruby stopped. "I'm not going to listen to anything you say," Jane snarled. "Get out! I don't care if you can hurt me with magic."

Jane thought so much like Ruby. Ruby liked the girl.

"Jane, wait," Luna said. "Let's see what Ruby has to say." She pulled Jane down.

"I won't," Jane yelled. She tried to tug her arm free, but Luna's grip was too strong. She sighed in frustration. "Fine."

Ruby didn't want to repeat what had happened when she was six, but she had to gain their trust. She told them how she felt at being ruled over, how she too longed for freedom and understood the pain. She explained to them about how Jabez had invited them to come to his palace while the Freeup were kept prisoners.

That was the only reason she was even here. She told them about being asked to rule over with Jabez but then, she lost motivation to go on by the time she came to the part where Jabez had forced her to rule with him.

But now, even Jane wanted to know what happened. "What happened? How did he convince you? I thought he killed your parents."

"I'll explain it to you briefly," Ruby said. "I had the plan to make him feel overconfident. He has the power to read minds so I put a memory in which he killed my parents." Ruby looked down, afraid to see their reactions. "Also, my parents were scared. They had power, but no more than anyone else on Magisis."

Jane and Luna gasped at her. Jane felt a bit more convinced now that Ruby had changed sides. Why else would she tell them her weakness? Ruby forced herself to continue. Finally, she got excited when she came to the part of finding out that Sarah was still evil.

"Then I heard a voice," Ruby was saying. "It was Sarah. She was talking about betraying the former-Ruleup, trying to think of a plan. I wanted to kick her out at that moment, but I thought that I should pretend to be on her side. Now, she's thinking about an imaginary plan to help me defeat the good 'Ruleup.'"

"Wait a second, why do you keep saying Ruleup like it's an insult?" Jane asked.

"Tell you later," Ruby said, "when everyone else is there."

"Ruby? Let us discuss what we want to do, please can you leave for a few minutes?" Luna asked.

"Okay," Ruby said. She got up and left the prison, locking the door behind her.

"Jane—" Luna began.

But Jane cut her off, saying, "I believe Ruby has turned. If she hasn't, then, well, we're dead. But I think it's worth risking that."

"Yeah," Luna agreed. "Now, how're we supposed to call her?"

"I have an idea," Jane said. Then at full volume, she yelled, "I AM TIRED IN THIS PRISON. RELEASE ME!"

Ruby heard her and went running back to prison no 17. Cal and Martin followed her.

"Cal, Martin, I can handle this on my own. Get out," Ruby said.

They nodded and left Ruby alone. Ruby muttered something which made the door open. She went inside and closed the door. "What did you decide?"

"We have decided to come with you," Jane said, as if the words had a bitter taste.

Ruby smiled. "Come out with me and put the invisibility spell on yourselves. And please, grant me permission to see you."

Jane and Luna walked out of the prison after Ruby opened it. Instantly, Ruby pointed her finger at Jane. "*Factice*!"

Instead of making Jane explode into dust, another Jane appeared at Jane's shoulder. Jane breathed a sigh of relief silently. *I can trust her this far*, she thought. "Uh, what is this?" she asked.

"Making a dummy," Ruby said. "So that the guards think that you're still there."

"Smart," Luna said admiringly.

Ruby pointed at Luna too. "*Factice*!" She took the dummy Luna and dummy Jane and put them in the top and bottom bunks.

Meanwhile, Jane and Luna made themselves invisible. Ruby turned, and instantly gasped. Since Jane and Luna were invisible and let Ruby see them, they looked a bit lighter in colour, slightly see-through, and a bit ghostly. She knew they would look like that, but it still threw her off balance.

"First, we need to destroy the machine which is draining Magisis' power," Jane said.

Ruby opened the map and checked the way to the machine room. "Follow me."

Soon, they reached the room and met ten guards.

"Move!" Ruby ordered, in a scary, evil tone, making an angry face. It wasn't hard. She just had to channel her anger towards Jabez and having been evil for so many years. "I am your new mistress."

"Yes, my mistress," they stammered, opened the door and let them in. These guards hadn't got their armour with the power of seeing invisible people, so they couldn't detect Jane and Luna.

Ruby climbed on the floating platform, Jane and Luna hurried behind her. Once they had reached the area with the machine, Ruby pretended to look at it and admire it to ensure the guards didn't get suspicions about Ruby fiddling with the machine, leave alone destroying it.

"You destroy the machine and hit some random targets, so I can pretend to be confused and scared," Ruby whispered to Jane and Luna.

"Okay," they whispered. "*Destrucmasa*."

Their first shot was random, cracks appeared on the ceiling and some chunks fell down.

"Ah!" Ruby screamed and ran.

"*Destrucmasa,*" they whispered again, this time aiming at the machine.

A mighty boom shook the room, and the side that faced Jane and Luna cracked a bit.

"*Destrucmasa,*" they whispered.

"*Destrucmasa,*" they whispered again.

"*Destrucmasa,*" they whispered again, this time concentrating super hard. They thought about everything that had happened because of Jabez, they thought of Ruby and Nora's lost parents, they thought of how Jabez took a part of everyone away for himself. The entire machine exploded.

"*Supernatet*!" Ruby cried. Some of the rocks started floating, she didn't have enough energy to make all of them float. Ruby ran to the floating platform, Jane and Luna behind her.

Using the spell was tiring, so as soon as Ruby reached the ground, she stopped levitating the rocks. The rock rockets rained down with unbelievable speed.

"*Salvare*!" Ruby cried. A shield expanded above her.

"*Protegerus*," Jane and Luna whispered. An invisible shield protected both of them too.

"Run," Ruby hissed.

***

"Hey guys! How are you?" Hilary asked her learners cheerfully as she entered the room they were sitting in.

"Whoa, Hilary! How are you—?" Amber's voice trailed off.

"Something's happening," Hilary cried.

Scarlett frowned. "What?"

"I think they broke the power-draining machine. I can feel my power coming back," Hilary cried.

33. Invisible Help

Jane, Luna and Ruby ran for five minutes and then stopped to catch their breath.

"Now what?" Jane asked.

"How about—?" Luna said.

She was interrupted by the sound of war up ahead and Ruby gasping.

"Nora, Pat, Emma, Mary, Sia and Mia!" Luna exclaimed.

"Who was that, my mistress?" a guard asked. "I heard someone speaking?"

"What? No! There was nobody," Ruby said.

"But—" The guard protested.

"Shut up and listen to me," Ruby yelled. "Get—"

"My mistress, you must listen. These kids didn't leave. We need to imprison them," the guard protested.

"*You!* What's your name?" Ruby yelled in a murderous voice.

"My name? It's Albert."

"Okay, *Albert*," Ruby said. "First of all, *never* interrupt me. Second, *always* listen to me. Third, don't even *think* about interrupting me."

"Yes, my mistress," Albert stammered. He bowed.

"Good," Ruby said.

"One more thing, my mistress. Let us just make them weak. Then we'll leave them to you," Albert said.

"No," Ruby said before she could stop herself.

"But why, my mistress?" Albert asked. He raised his eyebrow suspiciously.

"Because I can manage," Ruby said. *Oh no! They're suspicious of me,* she thought.

"Just let us help, my mistress," Albert said.

Ruby groaned. What was she going to do? Albert looked at her, waiting for a response. The Freeup decided to stop staring at them blankly and attacked. One of Jabez's guards got knocked down.

"I'm sorry, my mistress," Albert yelled. He plunged into battle with the Freeup.

Ruby groaned and started to walk away.

"Ruby," Luna hissed urgently. "Where are you going?"

"You help the Freeup," Ruby said.

"But—" Jane said.

Ruby slipped away, her footsteps echoing down the hallway. Jane and Luna stared after her. The wise thing would have been to go after her but they simply did what Ruby asked them to do. Help the Freeup.

Yes! Mistress is probably going to get more guards, Albert thought happily as he saw Ruby walk away.

"*Funem Ignis,*" Jane whispered. Ropes of fire shot out of her hands, wrapping themselves around the guards. The guards screamed in pain, and they got burns on their body.

"Which one of you—ah—foolish people try to hurt us," Albert yelled, wincing in pain.

"It's not any of us, that's all I know."

"Emma. Stop talking and attack," Nora hissed.

"Wh—oh yeah. Oops." Emma turned around to attack

The guards surrounded them in a circle. Five more guards joined the battle against the eight girls.

"You're outnumbered, even if we're bruised and burnt," a guard said, "there are too many of us. Surrender! A—"

"*Ahogo,*" Luna whispered. The guard who was speaking, choked.

"We're never going to surrender," Nora said. "And it looks like one of your guards was so scared that he fainted." Nora knew he had choked, but still said 'fainted' in case the guards were stupid enough to believe her.

"Shut up," Albert said. "We aren't stupid. He choked because of your invisible friends." *Also known as our prisoners, I have the armour which can see invisible people,* he thought.

"What? If you mean Jane and Luna, you captured them yourselves!" Mia exclaimed.

"No, Albert may be referring to your *other* friends," another guard said. This one didn't have any invisible people seeing armour. The only reason Albert had the special armour was because he was part of the group that guarded the Ruleup's headquarters and had come here. Albert smirked, but he didn't tell anyone what he knew, it would take too long.

***

Sarah was still sitting in the empty room where Ruby had left her, legs folded, back straight and eyes closed. She looked like she was meditating but actually, she was thinking hard of a plan. Until now, she had had none except going to Jabez and betraying the Ruleup. But Ruby was on her side, and she had told her not to betray the Ruleup. Sarah was now trying to improvise.

"Why can't I think of—?" Sarah muttered.

Sarah was interrupted by a woman coming in.

"Who are you?" the woman asked, clearly frightened to see Sarah sitting there.

"Who are *you*?" Sarah asked.

The woman gulped. "I'm one of His Majesty's maids."

"Why are you here?" Sarah asked.

"This is the kitchen storage, why else would I be here?" the maid asked.

Sarah snorted. "Yeah, right! As if I'm gonna believe you. This room is empty."

"His Majesty told us to empty it because he saw a rat. Now the rat is dead, so I need to get the boxes and everything back inside," the maid said.

Sarah scowled and left the room. She started to walk down a corridor. Little did she know that she was about to walk right in the middle of the war between the Freeup and Jabez's guards!

34. The Saveup!

The Freeup were losing the battle, even with Jane and Luna fighting invisibly. Mia and Emma were unconscious. Suddenly, the guards stopped attacking.

"Surrender," one of them said. "You have lost."

Nora held her breath, hoping to think of a way out. But the only thing she could think of was surrendering. "Fine," she said very reluctantly. "We surrender."

The guards cried in triumph but their victory was just a moment too soon. Just then, the door burst open and the Ruleup came charging in.

"Oh, thank you, my mistress!" Albert exclaimed. "You have come to help us, though we are winning."

"Shut up," Ruby cried. She plucked a strand of her hair, turned it into a dagger and threw it at Albert.

He screamed and dropped. "Charge!"

The Ruleup charged—but not at the Freeup. They charged at the guards, knocking them down with unconsciousness or injury spells. The guards stumbled, and tried to fight, but they were outmatched. Just as they were winning, Sarah came in.

An expression of horror, shock, disbelief and anger came on her face. "Ruby—" Sarah said. Before she could say anymore, Jane, who was standing nearby, hit her with a spell and Sarah fell down, unconscious. In five minutes, the Ruleup, with the help of the Freeup, had defeated all the guards.

"Ruby," Pat said, "you changed sides?"

"Yes," Ruby said, smiling. "And my group with me. Except Sarah." She threw Sarah a look of hatred.

"What about the invisible friends?" Pat asked.

"About them." Ruby gestured to Jane and Luna to show themselves.

Jane and Luna made themselves visible again, smiling widely.

Sia gasped. "Jane? Luna?"

"Ruby, let us out," Jane said.

Mary was about to say something, but they heard a lot of footsteps nearing them.

"More guards," Ava said. "They're coming. We have to go."

All the Freeup and Ruleup made themselves invisible, opened a window with much difficulty and jumped out. Then they levitated each other and reached the ground safely. They ran, in an attempt to get out of the area where they couldn't teleport from. Soon, Ruby was able to teleport them all to the Freeup headquarters. The Freeup could enter but the Ruleup couldn't.

"Hilary, let them in," Nora cried.

"No! What's gotten into you, Nora?" Hilary said. "Are you crazy?"

"Hilary, they turned good. The Ruleup turned good," Mary cried.

"Except Sarah," Mary added.

"What is wrong with all of you?" Hilary yelled.

"Hilary, you can use the spell on us. The spell which detects if we are good or not," Ruby said calmly.

"Fine," Hilary said. She came outside and performed the spell on Ruby. "*Bonum!*"

A few seconds passed before Hilary asked, "You turned good?"

"Yeah," Ruby said.

"Well, in that case, let's make a HQ where both the groups will live in."

"Nice idea!" Ruby exclaimed.

"Hey, hey! Not now. We need to defeat Jabez first," Nora yelled.

Everyone laughed.

"True, for now, Ruby and the Ruleu—" Hilary said.

"Former-Ruleup," Ruby corrected.

"Okay, for now Ruby and the former-Ruleup will live with us," Hilary said. "It will take me about an hour to add more rooms and extend our headquarters to fit the former-Ruleup."

Soon, the Freeup and former-Ruleup learners had rooms side-by-side. Hilary and Ruby together upgraded the protection. Hilary and Ruby shared a bedroom. The library was now taking up most of the third floor. Bedrooms were on the second floor. On the fourth floor was the Healing Room and also a few empty rooms for the learners to practice spells in.

Third floor had a gym. On the first floor (the ground floor), there was the living room and kitchen. The dining area was also on the ground floor.

The outdoor area now had a swimming pool. The main practice area was at the back of the property just next to the pool. On the fifth floor, there was a meeting room.

The rest of the floor was just filled with old boxes having old things. There was also a storage room on the fifth floor. The building had a staircase, and a lift-like thing called a 'Frolite'. You just needed to say the floor you needed to go on and the Frolite would take you there.

Hilary went inside the Frolite and said, "Fifth floor, Frolite." Ruby and Hilary had called for a joint meeting of the Freeup and former-Ruleup.

"So, you all are wondering why we have called you here," Ruby said.

"Yeah?" Everyone said.

"We are going to disband our groups and create a new one. The Saveup," Hilary said.

"The Saveup! The Saveup!" Everyone cheered.

Hilary and Ruby waited for the cheers to die down.

"Now, we need to get down to planning," Hilary said.

"Can we have a break for a while?" Nora asked.

Hilary and Ruby sighed. "Fine, but only for two days," they said in unison.

"Woohoo! We have a break for two whole days," everyone yelled.

"Enjoy! Meeting over. So Ruby, let's have a talk and catch up?" Hilary asked.

Both of them climbed onto the Frolite and went to the second floor. Everyone started doing whatever they wanted.

"LUNCH TIME," Ruby yelled.

Ruby and Hilary had added some communication spells on every floor, even in the outdoor area so they could be heard everywhere. Everyone rushed to the dining room.

"What's for food?" Ava asked.

"Here comes pancakes," Hilary said, carrying two trays with plates.

"Yum!" Hannah exclaimed.

"I'm making more, someone help me carry them here," Hilary said.

"Right, I'll help," Lucy said. She got up and went inside the kitchen with Hilary.

Soon, lunch was over. Pat made her way to the second floor.

"Sleepy already?" Nora asked, grinning.

Pat glared at her and snapped, "What I do is none of your business. Anyways, just because I'm going to my bedroom doesn't mean I'm going to sleep." And with that, she stalked off to the second floor.

Nora looked hurt and surprised. *Pat's never behaved like this, what has happened to her?* She wondered.

"Hey, it's okay. She's probably just a bit tired," Hilary said, putting an arm around her shoulders.

Nora nodded. "Yeah, it's fine. I want to go read."

"Go enjoy yourselves. Why are you standing here? These two days will be the last for a while. After that, only practice and planning," Hilary teased.

"Maybe even cleaning the HQ," Ruby suggested.

"Oh yes," Hilary said.

They laughed.

"Why would Pat be so mean?" Nora muttered, sitting alone in the library, pretending to read something.

Pat entered, clearing her throat.

"Oh Pat," Nora said. She tried to hug her.

Pat pushed her away. "Don't touch me!"

"But—" Nora said.

"Why are you being so affectionate anyway?" Pat snapped.

"Because I thought we were friends," Nora blurted.

"Ha! Well, you are wrong. Excuse me but I need to read something," Pat said.

"This isn't the Pat I know," Nora cried indignantly.

"Pfft! And don't even think of touching me again," Pat warned. "Otherwise, I'll hit you."

Nora looked hurt and ran out of the library.

"Baby," Pat muttered, loud enough for Nora to hear. She continued to search for the book.

"Second floor, Frolite," Nora said as she entered the Frolite.

Nora went to her bedroom, which she shared with Mia and Sia. Mia and Sia were down in the swimming pool, so she was alone. She *wanted* to be alone. She wanted to think of a reason for Pat's behaviour. Just then, Sia and Mia entered.

"It was so much fun. And then—whoa! What's this?" Sia said. "Why're you so sad?"

"Oh, it's nothing. I was just worried about my uncle. I'm sure it's fine." Nora managed a smile.

Sia nodded, unconvinced. They took turns in the bathroom to change.

"Nora, are you sure you're okay?" Mia asked, drying her hair with a towel.

"I'm fine," Nora said.

"Wait a sec, is that the book you packed on Tachél? I mean, you seem to read it all the time," Mia asked.

"This? Yeah, my dad used to read it to me in bed every night. And this is from Magisis, Mom had bought it while she was pregnant."

Mia made her way to hug Nora but Nora mumbled, "I have to go," and rushed out of the room.

"What's up with her?" Sia asked Mia as she came out of the bathroom.

"I don't know but she's been behaving oddly," Mia replied, scratching her chin as she always did when she was confused.

"We must find out what's wrong," Sia said.

Suddenly, Luna and Jane came in.

"Guys. Do you know what's up with Pat? She's been acting sooo weird lately," Jane said.

"Really? So has Nora," Sia said.

"Huh," Jane said.

"Pat is with you and Jane in your room right, Luna?" Mia asked.

"Yeah," Luna said.

"Hey! Let's team up, the four of us, and then let's try to find out what's going on with both of them," Sia suggested.

Jane and Luna nodded.

"So—" Sia began.

She was interrupted by the communication spells.

"MEETING, NOW!" Hilary's voice screamed.

"What now," Jane groaned.

"NOW!" Hilary's voice boomed again.

The four girls rushed to the Frolite, which was already crowded.

"Well finally, y'all came here," Hilary said. She was standing with her arms crossed over her chest in the meeting room. Ruby, in the exact same pose as her.

"What happened?" everyone asked.

“Ha! How can you all pretend to not know what happened?” Ruby snapped.

“What do you mean?” Tina asked.

“Don’t pretend to be all innocent,” Hilary barked.

“Okay Hilary, seriously? What is going on? None of us know. Care to explain what she is going on about?” Ava asked.

“Hmph! Fine. We’ll explain it even if you know what happened,” Ruby growled.

“Me and Ruby were sitting in the meeting room, studying the map of Jabez’s HQ and making plans of how to enter through the secret hideouts, fool the guards’, etcetera. We had made a few lists and locked them in a box, which would open only by mine or Ruby’s voice. The list had all the things about Jabez’s HQ we know but was only half done when we heard a loud crash from the pool.

“Both of us hurried downstairs, leaving the important papers out in the open. There was nothing major but when we returned, tons of ink had been splashed on the map! And the important list of things was stolen! We searched everywhere but couldn’t find it. Hence this meeting,” Hilary explained.

“It would appear that one of you broke the glass statues near the pool and then, while we were busy attending to it, did all this,” Ruby said.

“Who all were at the pool when the things broke?” Emma asked.

“Sia, Mia, Hannah, Bell, Tina and Sophie,” Ruby said.

“It has to be one of them,” Mary suggested.

“Actually, no. I think that someone else must have sneaked there and broke the things to cause a diversion,” Hilary said.

“Whoa, you do know right, that you’re basically saying one of us is a criminal?” Mia asked.

“Yes, and this is a serious matter. If this was a prank, it was a very cruel one and whoever did it, should come out now. That HQ map will never be retrieved. Jabez obviously doesn’t trust Ruby anymore,” Hilary said.

“We give you all time till Wednesday, which is three days from now. Own up. Would you rather lose our freedom over saving yourself from embarrassment of a bad prank? Don’t make the wrong decision. Whoever did this, please speak up by Wednesday,” Ruby said.

"Dismissed," Hilary said. She and Ruby stayed back while the others left the meeting room.

"Who do you think did it?" Ruby asked Hilary. "Nobody seems suspicious to me."

"Oh, but Ruby dear, you missed out the most suspicious person of all," Hilary said.

"Who are we talking about exactly?" Ruby asked.

"Nora. She's been in a bad mood today and acting oddly," Hilary replied.

"What? No! Nora hates Jabez. Why would she be in his favour? And Nora has been behaving oddly because Pat was mean to her. I can't believe that you haven't noticed that Pat and Nora were practically best friends. And Jabez killed Nora's parents!" Ruby exclaimed.

"True, I just focused on one point, but still. Nora is strong, Pat's words couldn't have affected her so badly," Hilary said.

Ruby took a deep breath and said, "Let's discuss this a while later with a fresh mind."

"Time for bed," Hilary's voice came from the communication spells in the night.

Everybody groaned but still got into bed. Soon, everyone fell asleep except Nora. At around 11 o'clock, she threw back her covers, got up, put on her fluffy slippers and headed off to the library.

"It'll do me good to read something," Nora mumbled.

She walked slowly and passed Pat's room. Each room had names of all the three girls living in it. The names were written on a steel plate stuck to the door. Nora absently read:

Pat, Jane and Luna.

She was tempted to open the door and peek inside to see how Pat was doing but stopped herself. She soon arrived at the library and as soon as she opened the door, shivered. *The library looks and feels so creepy in the dark. Maybe I should head back and just try to sleep—huh? What's that strange noise?* Nora thought. She felt as if someone was moving.

The whole library was dark. Only one spot, near a window, had some light. There was a figure with its back to Nora, leaning over something. It appeared to be sitting near the window, only slightly visible. The figure turned around to face Nora. It was Pat.

"Don't stare like you're stunned that I'm in the library," Pat snapped. *Ugh! Great. Why did she have to come snooping around here?* Pat thought, annoyed to see Nora.

But it wasn't Pat who Nora was staring at. It was what Pat was holding in her hands.

୭ ୭ ୭

35. Betrayal

The map of Jabez's headquarters shone like a light in Pat's hands. She kept it down, not even trying to hide it.

"You stole the map." Nora couldn't believe her best friend doing something like this.

"Yeah, fine. I stole the map, so what? You gonna sneak on me?" Pat said smugly. But her voice shook slightly. *Very* slightly.

Nora just stood there, speechless. *What should I do? My best friend stole the map. At least she's not completely sure of it as her voice is shaking a bit. Maybe I can use that to my advantage, bring her back to reality?* Nora thought.

"Pat," Nora said. "You can't do this. Jabez killed my parents."

"I don't care." Pat stood up. "He didn't kill *my* parents, so I don't care. I'm tired of being on the losing side."

"We are not on the losing side. Jabez will soon be on the losing side as what he is doing is wrong," Nora said. "Your parents won't be proud of what you're doing."

Pat rolled her eyes. "You know that this is not going to make a difference, right?"

"Pat, you *can't*," Nora said.

"I can." Pat's eyes blazed. "You can't stop me from doing anything. I can do enough to confuse even Hilary. I used *Destrucmasa* spell to make the glass statues fall."

"Pat, please. We need your help. Don't betray us. Not here. Not now. Please," Nora cried. Her expression was beyond anxiety. She was horrified, scared and felt completely betrayed.

Pat snorted. Nora knew this wouldn't work, she would have to change tactics and reach right down into Pat's heart.

"Pat, think about all the fun times we have had together. How you tried your best to stop me from doing something stupid. I *know* you wanted to be friends with me. It isn't too late to turn back. Turn good again, Pat. Be the happy and fun Pat I know. Please don't betray us," Nora said.

Pat seemed to hesitate for a bit but then she said, "You cannot, ever, stop me. *Memoria Damnum!*"

Nora realised just in time. "*Protegerus!*" Nora cried. "*Nesciusement!*"

Pat also made a shield around herself while attacking. "*Minuo!*"

Nora too made a shield, but it wasn't strong enough and didn't do more than soften the spell. The spell still hit her, and she gasped as she started to bleed a bit. But Nora knew that she couldn't let Pat escape or remove the memory of this incident.

She sighed, knowing she would have to do this the hard way. Nora got a burst of courage from somewhere inside her that helped her focus on the main thing: *Fight Pat*. She didn't bother using Salve and instead glared at Pat.

"Do not underestimate me. I'm sorry you didn't turn good again. Now, there's nothing I can do to help you. You've turned evil, I'm still good. And evil and good always fight at one point in time. This is the time when I fight you," Nora said.

Pat snorted. "Never thought you had any courage, huh. I know you're still the stupid little girl crying over me. And what's with the 'good and evil' speech? It doesn't even sound heroic."

"*Minuo!*" Nora cried.

Pat dodged just in time.

"Horrified, eh? Well don't be, I was telling the truth. It's time to leave the past in the past," Nora said. She kept sending minuos on Pat. Pat made a shield around her, but it couldn't stand Nora's fury for much longer.

Pat hissed in annoyance and moved closer to the window behind her. She turned to give Nora one last look; *another time*. She flung the window open and leapt out of it, seeming to dissolve in the darkness of the night. The last thing Nora saw Pat do was slam the window so hard that the room seemed to shake.

And Pat flew, free in the open air, till she reached the boundaries and teleported away.

"Pat," Nora called after her. But Pat was gone.

Nora was totally exhausted. She couldn't face everyone yet, maybe it was all just a bad dream. She headed absentmindedly to bed. The next day, she woke up with a start by Hilary's booming voice coming from the communication spells.

"WAKE UP, SLEEPY HEADS!" Hilary was yelling.

"AHH!" Every girl agonised.

Mia groaned, "Why does Hilary have to yell so loudly?"

"I don't know. I wish I could sleep a bit longer, but Hilary's second wake-up call is coming any minute n—" Sia said.

She was interrupted by Hilary's second wake-up call, "GET UP! STOP LAZYING AROUND!"

Nora yawned, got up and went to her bedroom. Their bedroom had light blue painted walls. The floor was a wooden-planked floor. Three single beds were lined up against the wall. The first bed, which was on the right side of the bedroom door, had 'Sia' written on the front of it. The second bed, right in front of the bedroom door, had 'Mia' and the third bed, which was a bit far from the bathroom door, had 'Nora' written on it.

The names were written on a golden coloured steel nameplate in black. Next to each bed was a bedside table. Nora's bedside table had a small light floating a few inches above it. There was also a small book kept on the bedside table with a small bottle of perfume.

The book was Nora's personal diary. There was also a purple mug which said 'Nora'. In the purple mug were a few lotlits. Nora's blanket was purple too, with a few pink and blue flowers on it. This was the same blanket Nora had slept with every night she was in Tachél. In her bedside table, there was a drawer where she kept a book from when she was small, a small blue bunny (her favourite soft toy from Tachél) and a few other knick-knacks.

Mia's bedside table had a few books, lotlits and a floating light on it. In her drawer, she had really random things like pieces of paper, strings, coins, a small pouch and much more. It was rumoured that Mia wanted to become an inventor. In Sia's drawers were a bunch of things personal to her. Each of them had a locker-like cupboard in one corner of the room.

Nora's cupboard was all purple, Mia's was all teal and Sia's all pink. There was a colour theme to everything. For some reason, all of Nora's things were in purple and white, Mia's in teal and white and Sia's in pink and white. Every single room was colour-coded like this, depending on the colour chosen by the occupants.

"Hey Sia, will you accompany me to the crafts shop today? Hilary won't let anybody go anywhere alone," Mia said.

"Sure, though I'm out of pocket money. Can I borrow some of yours? I'll pay you back," Sia said.

"Okay, but why?" Mia asked.

"'Cause even I need to get some stuff," Sia said, like it was obvious.

"Whatever," Mia said, shrugging.

"COME DOWN FOR BREAKFAST IN FIVE MINUTES, QUICKLY!" Hilary yelled through the communication spells.

The three friends looked at each other. *Let's go.*

On their way downstairs, Nora asked Sia and Mia if she could go with them to the crafts shop. Sia and Mia nodded.

"It seems like Hilary and Ruby had a bad night," Nora whispered.

"Yeah. Both of them look so grumpy. They won't even stand next to each other," Mia whispered back.

"Well, of course they had a bad night," Sia whispered. "Their notes on Jabez's HQ had just been stolen."

"That doesn't explain why both of them are standing so far apart," Mia argued, keeping her voice low.

"Everybody, have a seat. There will be a one more day extension to your holiday. For food, there is pancake," Hilary announced before Sia could reply.

"YAY!" Someone yelled.

"Thanks, Hilary and Ruby. You guys are the best," someone else yelled.

Hilary and Ruby looked very uneasy. The previous night, Hilary and Ruby had been sitting on their beds, researching something from books.

"Who do you think did it?" Ruby asked Hilary.

"If you mean the map thing, I think Nora did it," Hilary said.

"How many times do I need to tell you that Nora is innocent?" Ruby cried. "Pat is the one who has been acting weirdly, not Nora."

"Why do you think that?" Hilary asked, getting annoyed.

"Because Nora would never support Jabez. Jabez killed her parents," Ruby said.

"Jabez can manipulate people," Hilary yelled.

"Nora would never, ever, ever fall for it. She's strong. She'd fight it."

"No, she wouldn't. Whenever it comes to her parents, she's always really weak. She would never be able to fight it. And Pat knows that. So, she's keeping far from Nora. And Nora's acting to be all sad and teary-eyed. It's all a big act."

"It's not! Why do you have such a grudge against Nora anyway?"

"I don't."

"Yes, you do."

"You're just supporting her because Jabez killed her parents, and he killed yours too."

Ruby stared at Hilary. "You don't know what it is like to lose your parents. You have both. If you knew how it was, we would never fight about this." Ruby's voice cracked. She looked away.

Hilary realised she'd gone too far. But she couldn't step down now.

"You think she's like you, so you like her and don't want her to be evil," Hilary argued, but deep down, she knew she was wrong. She just wasn't ready to accept it.

Ruby turned around hard, her eyes blazing. "One day, Hilary, you will realise that you're wrong. Maybe Pat's not guilty, but Nora definitely isn't. Good night." Ruby stormed from the room and closed the door with a bang. She went to one of the guest bedrooms and slept there.

Hilary sat on her bed, feeling worse than before. "Yeah, I suppose," she said. "Good night."

***

"Uh, yeah, sure. Let's just eat now," Ruby said.

Hilary sat at one end of the table while Ruby sat at the other. Ruby glared at Hilary, but Hilary looked down. She didn't feel like it was worth fighting anymore. Nora scanned the table for Pat. She was sitting there, looking completely normal and joking with Jane and Luna. Weird.

It must've been a dream, Nora thought. *Pat left the Saveup HQ. I saw her.*

Then she thought—*what about the Minuo spell?* In her nightmare or whatever happened last night, she was scratched on her hand. She checked if there was anything. No. She didn't remember doing any Salve. So, it must've been a dream.

"What happened?" Sia asked.

"Nothing," Nora said.

"Why're you turning your hand around like that and checking?" Sia asked.

"Um," Nora said. "I had, like, um, made a mark on myself by mistake while drawing with a sketch pen." She managed a smile. "Just checking if it is gone yet. And it is."

Sia looked at her suspiciously. She could tell Nora was hiding something but decided to drop it.

Nora sighed. *What happened last night? Was it a dream or not?* She couldn't make out.

"Hey, why so low?" Hannah asked.

"Huh? Oh, um, nothing. I was just thinking about my nightmare last night. It seemed pretty real," Nora said with a nervous laugh.

"They always do. I've had my share of them too," Hannah said.

"Where's your twin, Lucy?" Nora asked.

"She's just hanging out with Pat now. I guess she's just a bit uncomfy here, so she's seeking help from Pat," Hannah said.

"Oh, it must be sad to be separated from your twin," Nora said.

"Yeah," Hannah admitted, "it is sad."

"Well then, you can be my friend from now on," Nora suggested.

"Sure, I would love to!" Hannah exclaimed.

"Hey, Nora! Coming to the craft store with us?" Mia asked.

"Yeah, can Hannah come too?" Nora pleaded.

"Sure, that'll be fun!" Sia exclaimed.

"Yup! The more the merrier. But we still need to ask Hilary," Mia said.

"I'll ask her," Sia said. She knew how to convince Hilary very well and slipped off to Hilary's and Ruby's bedroom.

"Come in," Ruby's voice came when Sia knocked urgently.

"Where's Hilary?" Sia asked as she entered.

"She's downstairs, at the pool," Ruby said.

"Hey, can I, Mia, Hannah and Nora go to the crafts store?" Sia asked.

"I'll come with you. But you should probably also take Hilary's permission," Ruby said.

"Okay," Sia said.

She left the room and told her friends what had happened. The four of them then went downstairs to the pool.

"Hilary! Can Nora, Hannah, Mia and I go to the crafts store?" Sia asked once she spotted Hilary.

"I'm busy, so I can't take you. Sorry," Hilary said.

"But—" Sia began.

"Who else will take you guys?" Hilary asked.

"I will," Ruby said coldly. She had just come to the pool and heard Sia and Hilary's conversation.

"Oh, yeah. I forgot about you," Hilary said gruffly.

Ruby gave a cold laugh and said, "How kind of you to forget. Now, I'm going to take our learners to the crafts store."

"Fine," Hilary said, a bit too loudly.

"You have thirty minutes only," Ruby said. "Use them wisely. I'm gonna come inside with you."

"All clear. Thank goodness this shop hasn't been taken over by Jabez yet," Ruby said. "But it might be taken over soon. The surrounding shops have been taken over. I'm sorry but now you guys only have fifteen minutes. Quickly shop for whatever you want."

Hannah, Sia, Mia and Nora quickly went inside, Ruby following closely. There was a teenage boy at the cashier. Sia smiled at him, and he smiled back.

"Hello! Customers at last. Nobody has come here for a long while," the boy said. "I'm Dan." He winked.

"Hello Dan. Sorry but we're in a bit of a hurry. I would caution you to close your shop as soon as we leave," Ruby said.

"Okay," was what Dan could manage.

The four girls quickly bought a few things and paid for it.

"Thanks a lot. I can't say how—" Dan said. He was interrupted by a loud boom.

Dan stood petrified. He was looking straight ahead of him, at the doors. Everyone turned around to see Jabez and his guards at the door.

"*You!* Wasn't last time enough satisfaction for you?" Ruby growled.

"Hmm. This is amazing, I have so many important members of the Saveup in my clutches. Today's my lucky day." Jabez chuckled. "I can't believe you were so dumb to come here."

"How do you know we're the Saveup?" Hannah asked, surprised.

"Tut-tut tut-tut. Do you really think I wouldn't send my spies on you? I'm not dumb like you," Jabez said.

"Why are you hurting so many innocent people?" Nora demanded, trying to keep Jabez's attention to herself.

"Nice try, little girl. But you can't keep me occupied with talking. Did you think I wouldn't notice that you're trying to keep all the attention to yourself while your friends try to attack me?" Jabez sneered. He tilted his head in challenge. Because they didn't react, he sent a blast of fire towards the Saveup. They dodged.

A full-scale battle started. Stuff from shelves was flying everywhere and things were scattered on the floor.

"Dan, run," Sia whispered to Dan. "Please."

"But—" Dan began.

"Just go, I don't want you to get hurt," Sia whispered.

"I don't want you to get hurt either," Dan whispered.

"Please," Sia whispered, her eyes watering.

"Okay. Take care of yourself, Nina," Dan whispered, he put his hand on her cheek. "Bye." He got up and started to quickly creep away.

"No, you don't," Jabez yelled. He pointed at Dan. Dan crumpled to the floor, screaming in pain.

Sia gasped, tears forming in her eyes. "No."

Ruby attacked from behind and stabbed Jabez in the back using a dagger (a strand of her hair which was turned into one). Jabez yelled in agony. But the pain made him more relentless. He hurled a shelf at Ruby's head. She barely escaped it.

"Please, Nora. Help Dan. I'm terrible at healing magic," Sia whispered to Nora.

Nora nodded. She knew this was important to her friend, and she had to do it. While everyone was fighting, Nora was trying to heal Dan. Salve wasn't working and Nora was getting really worried.

The battle was obviously not going too well for Saveup. Mia collapsed against a wall. Ruby was trying to keep Jabez's attention to herself while Sia tried to take advantage and attack. Hannah was trying to stop the entire place from collapsing.

A tornado of shelves and other stuff surrounded Jabez. Nora pointed at Jabez and yelled, "*Minuo!*" It didn't do much to Jabez, but it did distract him.

Jabez roared. He attacked Nora with fireballs, poison, and debris. Nora couldn't protect herself when Jabez's attention was completely directed towards her. With a sound like breaking glass, her shield collapsed. She dodged a fireball, and it made a huge hole in the wall behind her. Jabez sent another fireball and Nora dodged that too, but it hit Dan instead.

"Stay safe, Nina," those were his last words and he stopped breathing.

"NO!" Sia yelled, angry tears burning her eyes. She glared at Jabez. A spell was burning in her throat. She didn't want to say it but couldn't hold back any longer. "*Tuer*."

A huge red line formed on Sia's index finger, it shot out and it headed towards Jabez. And the spell hit Jabez right in his heart. Jabez roared in pain and dropped to his knees. He couldn't attack Sia, not right now. But he could still take a hostage. Nora was distracted and didn't see it coming. Jabez pointed at her, and she collapsed. Then he left, for once soundlessly.

Sia took a deep breath. Mia really wanted to ask what had happened, but now wasn't the time. Groaning, she got up.

"We *need* to save Nora quickly. But we need to get out of here first," Ruby said. Everyone held hands and Ruby teleported herself and the learners to the Saveup headquarters.

Hilary came running out at the sight of them arriving.

"What happened? Why is everyone looking so dirty and tattered?" She asked.

Ruby took a deep breath. "We just lost Nora."

36. The Spy and the Betrayer

"You did what?" Hilary asked furiously.

"Let's sit down for this. I'll explain everything," Ruby said.

Hilary glared at Ruby. "What do you mean you lost her? Did she—?" Hilary's voice cracked.

"No, I'll explain everything. Let's sit down," Ruby said reassuringly.

"Girls, you go on and freshen up. Don't tell anybody anything," Ruby told Sia, Mia and Hannah.

They nodded. As soon as Sia and Mia reached their bedroom, they started talking.

"Why would Jabez want Nora?" Sia asked.

"I don't know. Maybe because she's more powerful than most of us?" Mia suggested.

"No. That's not it," Sia said.

"Y'know, it's a shame we lost that shop. It was a nice shop. It had great quality products, and they were cheap too!" Mia exclaimed.

"Yeah. I'm gonna miss that shop," Sia sighed, "and its keeper."

"What?" Mia asked.

"Nothing," Sia said quickly.

Meanwhile, Hannah was in her bedroom. Nobody else was there. She took a quick bath and changed into a fresh pair of clothes. Just as she finished wearing her clothes, there was a knock on the door.

"Come in," Hannah said.

Lucy walked into the room.

"Hi," Hannah said.

"Hi," Lucy said plainly. Lucy took something from her bedside table and went back out. When Lucy was at the door, she stopped and turned to look at Hannah. "By the way, you should wash your face. It has *a lot* of dirt on it," and then she went out.

Hannah blinked. "Well that definitely wasn't mean," she muttered sarcastically and kicked the wall as if that was going to help. *Lucy was mean to her. Her new friend had been captured. Why was everything going so wrong?* She kicked the wall again. Then she sat down on her bed and lay down, sobbing.

Meanwhile, Hilary and Ruby were in their bedroom, arguing. Ruby had just finished telling what had happened at the crafts store.

"It is all your fault," Hilary yelled. "If you wouldn't have taken the girls to the store, Nora wouldn't have been captured."

"Firstly, it isn't my fault. Secondly, why are you worried about Nora all of a sudden, eh?" Ruby yelled back.

"I've always cared about her," Hilary argued.

"Just a few hours ago, *you* were making *her* responsible for what happened with our notes," Ruby countered.

"FINE! But Nora was acting suspicious. *Very* suspicious."

"No, she wasn't." Ruby took a deep breath. "Let's just make the announcement of what happened at the shop and discuss this later."

"Fine."

Ruby went to the top floor while Hilary made the announcement.

"EVERYONE, COME TO THE MEETING ROOM AT ONCE!" Hilary announced.

After five minutes, everyone had arrived.

"Why are we having this meeting, Hilary?" Alice asked.

Hilary ignored Alice and began speaking, "We are holding this meeting because we have just lost Nora. She got captured by Jabez. Some of you here know the story. But most don't. Ruby will tell y'all what happened."

After Ruby finished, everyone had a *lot* to say. Everyone had different opinions, and everyone was yelling loudly.

"Shouldn't have taken them."

"Jabez wants Nora?"

"Hope Nora is okay."

"Ruby's fault."

"Poor Nora."

"A trap."

"The shopkeeper?"

"Enough," Hilary yelled. "Let's decide on what to do next."

After a lot of arguing and discussing, the Saveup decided on ending their break and making rescue plans for Nora.

"I doubt we can do anything. We don't even have the headquarters map," Bell said.

"Nope. I remember Hilary and Ruby giving everyone turns to look at the map. I remember the entire headquarters map from memory. I can conjure it from my imagination. *Obtestor!*" Lucy said.

Jabez's headquarters map appeared in front of Lucy. She gave it to Ruby.

"Wonderful, Lucy! That was amazing. Thanks to you, we might rescue Nora after all," Ruby exclaimed.

Everyone cheered for Lucy. She had saved the day.

"Everyone, let's meet in the living room in an hour to share your ideas about how to rescue Nora. Dismissed," Hilary said. Everyone left.

***

After Jabez had dragged Nora away.

"Albert, I've got her," Jabez said.

"Great news! Where do we keep her, Your Majesty?" Albert asked.

"In one of our cells. How about cell no 28?"

"Okay, Your Majesty."

Albert opened cell no 28 and Jabez threw Nora in it.

"She'll wake up soon. When she does, call me. I need to spread the news and then attend to my new employee," Jabez ordered.

"Okay, Your Majesty."

Albert locked the door of the cell and went away.

"Cal, Martin! I got Nora. Now, the Saveup will take this bait and come straight into my headquarters where I will make them all prisoners and rule Magisis forever," Jabez said gleefully to Cal and Martin.

"This is absolutely amazing, Your Majesty! We are so happy for you," Cal exclaimed.

"Yeah," Martin agreed.

"Your Majesty. The girl, Nora, is waking up." Albert came rushing after about an hour.

Jabez immediately teleported himself in front of cell no 28. He watched Nora slowly get up as his strong unconsciousness spell wore out. She was confused and dazed. *Where was she?* Then she spotted Jabez.

"Well, well, well. How are you feeling, little girl?" Jabez asked.

"Shut up. I'm not little anymore. I'm 17 years old," Nora spat.

"Keep control over your temper. You are in *my* prison, under *my* control. I can hurt you and you won't be able to hurt me back. Choose your next words very carefully," Jabez said.

Nora gritted her teeth. She was *so* angry right now. She felt like punching Jabez. But it wouldn't matter. She couldn't hurt him. Jabez was right.

"Good choice to keep your mouth shut. I'll see you later. Now, I need to attend to my new employee. Excuse me," Jabez said. He teleported somewhere else.

"Ah. My new little betrayer," Jabez said.

There was a girl about Nora's age standing in front of Jabez. She was wearing a black cape with her hood up, which made it hard to see her face.

"First of all. I'm not going to call you *Your Majesty,*" the girl snapped. "Second—"

"*First* of all. You will do as *I* say. I do not tolerate disobedience. If you don't want to end up in a prison like your friend, I would advise that you obey me," Jabez interrupted.

"She is not my friend. And fine," the girl grunted grudgingly.

"Uh-uh. You're forgetting something," Jabez said.

The girl rolled her eyes. "Fine. I'll obey you, *Your Majesty.*"

"Good. You have been hired. Go do what you want. I'll tell you when I want something from you," Jabez said. "Take this map to guide you everywhere in the headquarters."

The girl nodded and headed out of the empty room. Before she could leave, Jabez appeared right in front of her.

"Our spy has some news. Let's meet her." Jabez grabbed the girl's hands and teleported them away.

"How dare you!" the girl protested. "You—" but she stopped, remembering what Jabez had said earlier.

Jabez ignored her and instead, looked at the other girl. The other girl was wearing a grey cloak. Her hood was also up.

"I'm going to call you," Jabez pointed at the girl with a grey cape, "Spy. And I'm going to call you," Jabez pointed at the girl with a black cape, "Betrayer."

"Whatever." Both of them shrugged.

"Mission successful. They took the bait. They're making plans to save Nora," Spy said.

Jabez scowled. "Great job, Spy! You better get back to Saveup headquarters or they'll realise you're missing," he said.

Spy nodded and tried to teleport away. It didn't work.

"Forgot to give you both permissions to teleport without me," Jabez said.

He pointed at Spy and muttered something. Spy was able to teleport. Then he pointed at Betrayer and muttered something.

"I'm going to go see Nora," Betrayer said.

"I don't think so. I know you're going to reveal your identity. It's better if our enemies are kept in the dark about you," Jabez said. "After all, you're our secret weapon."

Betrayer gave a cold laugh. "But Nora can't escape. She's going to be the heaviest guarded prisoner you have. How can she escape? Anyways, once she knows it's real, she'll be heartbroken, it will be torture for her to think about how *I* betrayed her."

"Hmm, you do have a point. Fine. You will be responsible for torturing Nora, hurting her, mocking her and all that. I need you to prove that you are actually loyal to me unlike that stupid Ruby," Jabez said. "Today at 7 in the evening, come to me."

She looked at the map for directions and started walking away. The map had a charm on it that made the particular person holding the map see where they were. Jabez teleported himself into his control centre. He pressed a button, and a thick mist surrounded him. He closed his eyes and replayed his memories over the thick mist.

Then, he opened his eyes and stopped at one memory. It was the day Uncle James had made him unconscious. *How had he done that?* Jabez was so powerful. Just then, it hit him. That day, he hadn't been as powerful as he was today. He had only taken over two planets until then. And that was his third one. Jabez couldn't believe that Uncle James was so powerful.

It would have taken five people with strong magic to make him unconscious even then. But Uncle James had done it all by himself. He had underestimated Uncle James. Uncle James was Jabez's new target. He decided to torture Nora by telling her how her uncle, her only family, was about to be attacked. He tracked Betrayer with his powers and teleported there. Betrayer was checking out the kitchen for snacks.

"Ahhhhhh!" she yelled when Jabez teleported right in front of her, dropping her bag of chips. "Will you stop doing that?"

"You can't tell me what to do, so keep quiet. Anyways, I've decided to attack Nora's uncle, James," Jabez said. "I'm going to tell her that 'cause it will be pure torture for her to know that her only remaining family will die. Then I'll leave. You come a minute later and give her your news. Come with me to the dungeons now. You can stay a few cells away and when you see me walking away, go meet her. Got that?"

"Yes, Your Majesty," Betrayer said. "Let's go."

Nora was sitting on the first bunk of the bed, thinking. She looked up when Jabez approached.

"What do you want?" Her anger uncontrollable. She had failed her friends. She'd lost so much. *How could it get any worse?*

Jabez opened the door with a flick of his hand, went inside, and closed it with another flick.

"I'm going to attack your Uncle James," Jabez said gleefully.

"No!" Nora screamed. "Please, no. He's the only family I have left."

"That just makes it better, doesn't it?" Jabez said. "Well, I've got other places to be," and he teleported out.

Nora was trembling. How much worse could her day get? Just then, she heard footsteps again. Betrayer opened the door and came inside. She closed it again. She carelessly threw back her hood. Nora knew that it was not just a nightmare but still couldn't believe it. It was *Pat.*

37. SaveUp Ideas

"NO!" Nora's voice came out forcefully, full of anger. But inside, she felt betrayed, horrified and very sad. She had held onto a hope that the duel with Pat was just a dream, but now, there was doubt.

"Yes! Yes! Yes! I *have* betrayed you! I *have* joined Jabez! It wasn't just a dream last night. I have done it all," Pat said. "You seriously thought that you had a bad nightmare? *Seriously?*"

"I was so confused when I got up. I just wished it to be a nightmare so badly to save our friendship," Nora said. Now that Pat was saying it, Nora couldn't believe that she thought that it was just a dream. How could she have?

Pat snorted. "Seriously, *no one* can be as daft as you are."

Nora looked away as tears welled up in her eyes. It was all over. Pat had betrayed her, not just by joining Jabez but also by betraying their friendship. And now, Jabez wanted to kill her uncle. Clearly, her uncle stood no chance. Nora had seen Jabez destroy that shop without even making an effort, which reminded her.

"How did Jabez capture me anyway? And now that you've joined Jabez, you should know *all* about what he has done. How he has destroyed planets. Killed people," Nora said bitterly.

"He just put a very strong unconscious spell on you, and you crumpled to the ground. Easy. Once Sarah heard about it, she had such a laugh," Pat said.

"Sarah? Oh right. I forgot she's working with Jabez," Nora said.

"Tomorrow sharp 3 am, I'll come back to see you. Or maybe not, you're not that important," Pat said. She left the cell.

Why will she want to see me so early in the morning? Nora wondered.

Meanwhile, as Pat was strolling in the corridors, suddenly, Jabez teleported right in front of her.

"Now that the little girl knows, there's no point in trying to keep it secret. I'll let all my guards know that you are Pat," Jabez said.

"You have to stop doing that," Pat snarled.

"You don't talk like that to your king. And don't forget to add *Your Majesty* at the end of every sentence," Jabez said. He started to walk away.

"I'm not one of your guards, you know. I'm not gonna call you that," Pat yelled after him. She was very mad right now. She didn't know why. But she just was.

"I would think hard about that if I were you," Jabez said. He snapped his fingers and disappeared.

Pat walked ahead, thinking about Jabez the whole time. She was so absorbed in her thoughts that she didn't see ahead of her and crashed straight into Sarah, making her cloak fly off. Sarah could see who the girl in the black cloak (Pat) was.

"Who? Oh, it's you," Sarah said.

"Yes, it's me," Pat snapped.

"What are you doing here?" Sarah asked, holding up her hands, ready to attack.

"I'm the new employee," Pat said.

"*You*? Ugh. Well, I hope you're not sharing *my* bedroom," Sarah said.

"Wha—? Oh wait, I totally forgot. Where am I supposed to stay? I'll just go and ask Jabez," Pat said. She quickly walked away. Sarah stared after her. She couldn't believe that someone from the Freeup had come to Jabez's side. No. Not the Freeup. It was the Saveup now. Sarah went off in the same direction as Pat. That was the way to her bedroom.

She quickly took out her map muttering, "Really, Jabez's castle is so big, one could get lost in it for ages." She was observing other parts of the castle on the map when she crashed into somebody. It was Jabez.

"Sorry," Sarah said, and bowed.

"And this is how one should behave. You can stop bowing, Sarah," Jabez said. He and Pat were standing there.

"I am *not* going to bow to you every time I meet you," Pat said.

"Really?" Jabez asked, his voice rising dangerously. "Are you one hundred percent sure of that?"

"I—yes," Pat snapped.

"I would obey me if I were you. I'm pretty sure that you don't want to be punished," Jabez said, his voice rising. He was totally done with this stupid Pat and her attitude.

Pat understood and quickly gave a graceful bow. "I'm sorry." While she was bowing, she rolled her eyes. She hated these rules so much.

"That's more like it. Anyways, you should get back to Saveup headquarters," Jabez said. He vanished. Sarah vanished with him.

Bet Jabez dragged her away with him, Pat thought. *But what would Jabez want with Sarah? Anyways, I better keep my cool with Jabez. It's terrible but I'll get used to him soon, I guess.*

Pat sighed. She closed her eyes and vanished from Jabez's headquarters.

***

Pat teleported outside Saveup headquarters. She levitated, put on an invisibility spell and flew straight into the library. After going behind a shelf, she reappeared. Just then, Ava walked into the section where Pat was.

"Pat, where did you come from?" Ava shrieked.

"I have been here for a very long time, Ava. I can't believe you didn't see me in this part of the library," Pat said.

Ava stared at Pat. She didn't know what to say. Pat coolly walked out of the library. When she walked by Lucy's room, she stopped. The door was a bit open. She peered inside and saw Hannah was on her bed, crying. Pat pushed open the door and went inside.

"Hey," Pat said.

Hannah looked up. "Go away."

"What happened?" Pat asked.

"Nothing. Just go away," Hannah said.

"Is it Nora? Look, Hannah. We're all sad here. But that doesn't mean you have to cry. We'll get her back, okay?" Pat said.

"It's more than that. You won't understand," Hannah said.

"I will only if you tell me," Pat said.

"Just leave, okay? I don't want to talk to you. Get out," Hannah said rudely.

Pat said nothing. She was thinking of what to say. *Keep your cool. Don't blow your cover*, Pat kept thinking. She was already in a bad mood and now this?

"I'm sorry, but I just need some time to myself," Hannah blurted out.

"I understand," Pat said. She got up and left. Pat went back in the direction of the library, hoping to find Lucy there.

In the meantime, Hannah finally stopped crying and wiped her tears. Crying won't do. The meeting was in twenty minutes. But Hannah couldn't come up with any ideas of how to save Nora. After ten minutes, Hannah decided to go to the meeting room. She was one of the first there but Pat and Lucy were already there. They were chatting away merrily.

"Hannah. Come join me and Pat," Lucy called out.

Hannah nodded, thrilled. Her twin didn't hate her after all. Maybe Lucy had just been a little grumpy when she had abused Hannah. She got up and sat next to Lucy. More people kept coming in until the entire room was full. Hilary and Ruby entered after five minutes.

"Now, who has ideas?" Hilary said at once.

A few hands shot up.

"Sally, how about you go first?" Ruby asked.

"I don't know why I didn't think of this first. You could just do the repairing spell on your spoilt lists," Sally suggested. "Then you can use that to make plans."

"No!" Pat blurted. She couldn't control it. What if it worked? And Jabez lost?

Everyone stared at her.

"I mean that it won't work. And a few pieces of the lists have gotten lost," Pat said.

"How do you know that? We never told anyone if anything was lost," Ruby asked.

"I did my research," Pat countered, her mind racing.

"I suppose," Ruby said, eyeing Pat suspiciously. "But why did you yell 'No!' like that?"

"Because it's a waste of energy," Pat lied, her voice still a bit high.

"Pat's right," Hilary said.

Ruby looked like she wanted to say something. In fact, she looked so angry that a few people thought she might burst but somehow controlled herself.

"Have you got anything else to say, Sally?" Ruby asked.

"No," Sally said.

"Who's next?" Hilary asked.

"We could send someone to pretend that they are on Jabez's side. Then that person can get information, maybe even the map and then we can plan our attack," Luna suggested.

"We already have the map Lucy conjured from her memories," Hilary said.

"Yeah, but I remember the map was a bit different. There were way more markings on the original and it also showed the power-draining machine in the centre. But in Lucy's map, many markings are missing and the power-draining machine is in the corner," Luna objected.

Ruby quickly took a look at the map. "Luna is right. The power-draining machine is indeed in the corner. Lucy, explain yourself."

"Um. Er. Maybe the spell went wrong?" Lucy suggested.

"Lucy, we cannot afford to go wrong," Hilary said.

"Yeah, we were counting on you," Ruby said. "You need to learn to be responsible."

Ruby and Hilary glanced at each other. After their argument, it was the first time they had agreed.

"Well, I'm sorry," Lucy said, exasperated.

Everyone glared at Lucy except her sisters.

"It's not Lucy's fault," Bell cried.

"It definitely wasn't my sister's fault," Violet cried.

"How can you blame Lucy? Anyone can make mistakes," Anne yelled.

"You guys should at least have had a backup plan. How can you blame Lucy for that?" Hannah shouted.

"Hannah is right. Don't tell me you guys put all of your trust in Lucy's map?" Tina asked.

Ruby and Hilary looked at the floor. They had indeed forgotten to think of a backup. They had now made the same mistake twice.

"Well?" Tina asked. "Did you?"

"Yeah, we did. And we're sorry. But Lucy should have double-checked," Hilary said.

Hilary sighed. Everything was going wrong.

"Let's stay focused, guys. Anybody else has any other ideas?" Ruby asked. Everyone shook their heads. "Then this meeting has come to an end. Work on more ideas and give them to me or Hilary any time. Dismissed," Ruby said.

Hannah and Lucy headed off to Anne, Violet and Bell's room. Hannah took a seat on Anne's bed.

"Lucy, don't feel guilty, okay? Everyone makes mistakes. Mistakes can be forgiven," Bell said.

"Not this one," Lucy murmured.

"Lucy, don't be so hard on yourself. It's all right," Hannah said.

"I feel so guilty. I should have made sure that the spell worked correctly," Lucy said.

"I'm sure Hilary and Ruby will forgive you," Anne said reassuringly.

"Yeah. Even if they don't, we're here for you," Violet said.

"I'm the luckiest girl on the planet to have four such wonderful sisters," Lucy said, tears of happiness falling from her eyes.

The five sisters had a group hug.

"Now that's enough of your crying," Hannah said. She wiped Lucy's tears.

***

Jabez sat down on his bed. He was thinking hard of ways to attack Uncle James. Obviously, James would have put protection spells and more. Jabez didn't even have his master card anymore. The power-draining machine. It was destroyed! It would take at least twelve months to get it back to its full strength. He got up and started pacing the room. Suddenly, he remembered that he was going to meet Pat at 7 o'clock on the same day.

I guess I'll research about mind protection spells these Magisis people have. I'll need to find a way to break them, if Pat is using any. I also need to assign her a bedroom. As he was going to the library, Cal called out.

"What? I'm in a bit of a hurry," Jabez asked.

"You wanted to attack another shop today, remember? You told us to be ready, Your Majesty," Martin, who was sitting next to Cal, said.

"Oh. I forgot about that. We'll do it tomorrow; today, I have a lot of other things to do already," Jabez said.

Jabez soon reached a wide door. He pushed it open and went inside his grand library. It had at least fifteen dozen bookshelves that reached from the floor to the ceiling. The bookshelves were a dark colour of magenta and were filled with thin, fat, small and big books. There were also numerous beanbags scattered around, some tables and chairs. Wide windows, directly in front of the wall with the door, were placed after every three bookshelves. Jabez went to one of the empty bookshelves close to the windows.

"I want books about mind protection spells of Magisis, and anything related to it," Jabez said out loud.

As if the bookshelf had heard him, about fifty books appeared on the middle shelf. He made the stack of books fly over and land near one of the beanbags and started reading. After a while, Albert came rushing in.

"Where are your manners, Albert?" Jabez asked, exasperated. He looked up from his book.

"Sorry, Your Majesty. I just wanted to inform you that both of your new employees have arrived with news," Albert said.

"Send them here."

After ten minutes, Albert came in. Pushing Pat and Spy inside. Pat's cloak's hood was up, so was Spy's.

"Ouch! Don't push," Spy hissed. She walked forward, Pat next to her.

Jabez looked up.

"What is it that you have interrupted my reading for?" Jabez asked.

"Well, about the fake map—" Spy said.

"What happened to it?" Jabez asked, suddenly interested.

"That stupid Luna guessed it was fake. She noticed that the ex-power-draining machine was in the corner, instead of the middle," Pat explained.

"Of course! Why didn't I think of that?" Jabez muttered. "That back-stabbing Ruby had rescued Jane and Luna."

"I'm sorry, Your Majesty. We should have noticed it before. We are very sorry, Your Majesty. We—" Spy began.

She was interrupted by Sarah flinging open the doors of the library and running inside towards Jabez. On the way, she bumped into Spy and this time, the Spy's cloak flew off her head.

"Argh!" Spy said. She quickly tried to put it back on, but it was too late.

"*Lucy*," Sarah gasped.

38. The Neighbours

"Lucy?" Sarah said again. "No way! It was you this whole time? Thankfully, someone from the ex-Ruleup." Sarah flung her arms around Lucy. "Cal and Martin got hurt," Sarah said. "Really badly."

"How?" Jabez asked, getting up.

"Well, they were trying to clear the debris of the ex-power-draining machine. It seems some leftover radioactive substance from the machine made their powers go haywire. Instead of clearing the debris, the debris fell on them," Sarah explained. She didn't know what radioactive substance was because she wasn't interested in science.

"When did this happen?" Jabez asked.

"Just before I came here, I was passing by and saw everything. I didn't know what to do, so I ran here instead," Sarah said.

"You saw what was happening and didn't even try to help," Jabez yelled angrily.

"My powers went haywire too, Your Majesty. Some kind of force pinned me to the wall," Sarah said, trembling.

Jabez seemed to calm down. "All right," he said. Then he turned to Lucy and Pat. "Both of you, I need to see you today. Midnight, be there."

"But I plan to go to Nora at 3 am!" Pat exclaimed. "What about sleep?"

"My dear Pat, what is more important? Sleep or your duties?" Jabez asked, pinning her with a glare.

"My duties, Your Majesty," Pat stammered.

"Good," Jabez said. Sarah, Lucy and Pat followed Jabez to the ex-power-draining machine room. The place was a total mess with debris everywhere. Cal and Martin were lying unconscious on the floor. They were completely soaked in blood and were still bleeding.

Jabez knelt on one knee next to them, put his hand over their bodies and closed his eyes. Cal and Martin's wounds healed, and they stopped bleeding.

"That should do it for now," Jabez said. "Sarah, take them to the infirmary."

"How?" Sarah asked.

"Use a levitation spell and get it over with," Jabez snapped.

"Okay, Your Majesty," Sarah said, and bowed. She muttered a levitation spell and Cal, followed by Martin, flew up a few inches in the air. Sarah left, guiding the floating bodies.

"Both of you, quickly get back to the Saveup. Make an excuse to be out till tomorrow 7 o'clock in the morning," Jabez said.

"Why till 7 o'clock?" Pat asked.

"Stop asking questions and do as you're told. Be back in an hour," Jabez snapped. He was really angry.

"Yes, Your Majesty," Pat said.

"Sorry, Your Majesty," Lucy said.

"Albert will show you your rooms," Jabez said. "I have some reading to finish." He strode out of the room.

"Do you have any idea where Albert is?" Lucy asked.

"Well, I think they have guard quarters. We'll ask the first guard we meet. C'mon," Pat said. She and Lucy walked out.

A guard named Sammy led them through the corridors. After a while, the corridor sloped downwards and became wider. At the bottom of the slope was a gate. On the gate was written:

GUARDS' QUARTERS

Sammy opened the door to a huge room, the size of a ballroom. On each side of the room, were more rooms, each with the name of the guard who was living there. At the far end, there were a few empty rows without rooms. There were loads of tables and chairs and a huge thin table on which there were empty food plates and utensils.

"Albert should be in here. If he isn't, just look in your map, I have work to do." Sammy pointed to a door and walked away.

On it was written:

ROOM 23, ALBERT

Lucy knocked on the door.

"Come in," Albert said.

"Ah, are you here for your rooms? Come with me, I'll show you," Albert said.

Albert walked for a little while before stopping. It seemed like they were in the corridor next to the Guards' Quarters. The corridor sloped downwards and there was a normal wood door. On the wood door, there was a steel plate on which was written:

ALLY QUARTERS 1

Albert pushed open the door and went inside. The room was about half the size of the one they had just come from. The left and right sides of the room were divided into three parts with doors. On each door, there was a name plate and a room number. The first room on the left side was labelled:

SARAH CHORRO, 1.

The next room was labelled:

PAT KAWSE, 2.

And the last room read:

LUCY DOXON, 3.

On the right side, the labels read:

GONGER FAUST, 4.

KOMMY LOCKS, 5.

JORNY CLOY AND WESTIE CLOY, 6.

"I assume you know what your rooms are," Albert said.

"Why would Sarah think I'm sharing her room?" Pat whispered to Lucy.

"Maybe because Jorny Cloy and Westie Cloy have to share too," Lucy whispered back.

"These rooms are only for emergency use since you both live with the Saveup," Albert said.

Lucy nodded. "Okay."

Albert nodded back and left, closing the door with a bang behind him, making Lucy and Pat jump.

"Argh, I hate that guy," Lucy grumbled.

"Tell me about it," Pat murmured.

Pat waved goodbye to Lucy and entered her room. She looked around. The room wasn't too big, nor too small—just the perfect size. In front of the right wall was the bed. Next to the bed was a tiny side table with a hovering light. Above the bed, a window let in some natural light. There was also a table and chair. On the wall, just in front of the table, hung a soft board. On the desk were some basic stationery, a few lotlits, two erasers, and a scale. A stack of white ruled paper sat nearby.

"What does Jabez expect me to do with these papers?" Pat grumbled. She opened the drawer in the desk. In the drawer were a few maps and red markers. Pat scanned the maps and realised they were of Magisis and the planets surrounding it. She put the maps back in the drawer and decided to go meet her neighbours. She found some keys on the desk and locked the door when she left. She knocked on the door of room number six.

"Who is it?" a soft voice asked.

"Hi! I'm your neighbour from room number two. Can I come in?" Pat said.

"Nobody lives in room number two," another voice said.

"I just moved in," Pat said.

"All right. Come in," the second voice said.

Pat pushed open the door. The room was just like hers except that it had a bunk bed and there were two cupboards with two desks. There was a girl and a boy sitting in the room. Both of them had dark green hair and downturned olive-green eyes. The girl had shoulder-length hair and the boy had normal size hair.

"I'm Westie and that is my twin brother, Jorny," the girl said. She had a soft voice.

"Hi! I'm Pat," Pat said.

"Where do you come from?" Westie asked.

"Magisis, what about you?" Pat asked.

"We come from Negofer," Westie said. "Why did you join Jabez?"

Pat explained everything.

"Wow. That is quite a story," Jorny said.

"What's yours?" Pat asked.

Before anyone could speak, Lucy came bursting into the room. "Pat, we need to get back now, it's already late." She grabbed Pat's hand and led her out of the room. "We need to give excuses to the Saveup, remember. C'mon," Lucy said. She teleported herself and Pat to the Saveup headquarters boundaries. They both flew into the library window and found Ruby there.

"Hey Ruby, me and Lucy are going to turn in early. Feeling tired. We were up all night, thinking of ways to save Nora," Pat said.

Lucy and Pat went out of the library into their respective rooms. They created dummies of themselves, tucked those in their beds and then met outside in the hallway. They flew out of an open window and teleported back to the Ally Quarters 1 in Jabez's castle. Lucy went to her room while Pat went back to meet Westie and Jorny's.

"So, where were we?" Westie asked.

"You were about to tell your story of how you guys ended up working with Jabez," Pat said.

"Ah, yes," Jorny said.

"Where is everyone?" Mrs Cloy called out, entering the living room where Westie, Jorny and Mr Cloy were sitting. 10-year-old Westie was drawing and Jorny was playing with cards.

"Come on. We need to pack up. We're moving, remember?" Mrs Cloy said.

"Let the kids relax for a while, Aller," Mr Cloy said.

"But we need to move tomorrow, and you know that the other people are moving in the day after, Wollow!" Mrs Cloy exclaimed.

"Okay, okay," Mr Cloy said.

Everyone set to work. They emptied out the house and travelled by train. On the way, the train shook as if it was about to topple but got steady in a couple of minutes. Once they reached their new house, they unloaded all of their stuff. Just as they were about to enter: *BANG! BANG!*

A man landed in front of them. He had green eyes and brown hair. He also had a brown moustache. He had a darkish skin colour.

"Well, well. The only family on Negofer who knows where the magic flower is. Give me the location or I'll have to kill your poor children," the man growled menacingly. His name was Lisve. He was from the same planet as Jabez. He and Jabez were enemies, and they were racing to get more magic than the other. Lisve snapped and Westie and Jorny were suddenly next to him in a cage.

"No," Mrs Cloy cried out.

"Yes, Aller. Now, tell me the location or I kill your children," Lisve said.

"But—" Mrs Cloy said.

"The location, or your children. Choose. Which is more important?"

Mr Cloy took a deep breath. "Sausty Falls. Just behind the waterfall, the flower is growing. It will give you the magic," he said.

"It better be true or I'll kill all of you," Lisve said in a threatening voice. He snapped and the cage around Westie and Jorny broke. Then he flew away.

"My sweethearts. Are you okay?" Mrs Cloy asked. She ran to them and hugged them.

The same night, the Cloy family was sitting in the living room, and they heard another huge bang. There were more bangs and then finally, the front door broke down. Lisve stepped over it and entered the living room, his face red with anger.

"You liars! You will die," Lisve yelled. "You gave me the wrong location."

"Hide," Mr Cloy whispered to Westie and Jorny.

Both of them quickly hid behind the sofa while Lisve was yelling.

"You will pay for what you did," Lisve yelled. He pointed at Mrs Cloy and yelled something in another language. It sounded like 'Wasty Klopy Iop'. Mrs Cloy froze and fell to the ground.

"Mom!" Westie yelled.

"Shh," Jorny whispered.

Next, Lisve pointed at Mr Cloy and said the same thing again. Mr Cloy too froze just as he opened his mouth and fell to the ground. Sparkles flowed out from Mr and Mrs Cloy. Lisve inhaled loudly. All the sparkles flowed towards him and entered him. That was him consuming Mr and Mrs Cloy's magic.

Lisve eyed the sofa suspiciously and walked over to it. He thought he had heard a small whimper from behind it. He went behind and found the twins. "Aha!"

Westie and Jorny ran for their lives. They ran out the front door and out into the garden. Lisve ran after them. He created a force-field around the entire house. "You're trapped. Now, tell me the location, or I'll just have to kill you and take the memory," he said.

"The flower is there, right behind that bush. It's in a transparent container." Westie pointed to a huge bush. Jorny was frozen in fear and Westie had literally been dragging him around. She knew her dad had not lied but perhaps someone had taken the flower before Lisve got there.

BANG! BANG! BANG!

Jabez came flying outside of the force-field. "Seriously, Lisve? Hurting a bunch of ten-year olds?" He broke the force-field and then pointed at Lisve. A lightning bolt struck Lisve. He fell to the ground and forgot the location of the flower. He still remembered that they had told him the location but forgot the actual location because of Jabez's power. Jabez went over to the bush and inhaled. Then he took out a knife and killed the plant.

"Come with me, I can save you. Lisve will have his strength back soon," Jabez offered.

"Okay," Westie stammered. She and Jorny went into the house. They came back ten minutes later, carrying a suitcase between themselves. They were also wearing backpacks.

"Don't be afraid, I won't hurt you," Jabez said kindly.

Westie took a deep breath. "We're not five-year-olds," she snapped.

Jabez took her hand and then flew up into the sky. After a while, they saw a huge spaceship. Jabez landed right in front of it and entered it. "Come on."

After that, Jabez told Westie and Jorny the truth. Slowly, he started manipulating them, though they didn't realise because he had removed any memory of him manipulating them.

"I'm sorry, guys," said Pat. "But what magic flower?"

"Can I trust her?" Jorny asked Westie.

Westie nodded. Jorny took a deep breath. "Every planet has got magic in its own way. But Magisis has got a lot of it. We at Negofer guard the secret of our magic closely. Negofer's magic came from one single flower. You had to inhale its fumes to get the magic. If you killed the person with the flower's magic, the murderer would get the magic if he inhaled sparkles coming out of the dead body.

"Our magic was very unique. Once people found out that our family had the magic, everyone wanted to have it. You would have thought people would attack but Negofer doesn't have war. But we knew that if other planets found out, they would want it too and so, we told nobody.

The magic was strong, if you inhaled it all, you would get the power of ten combined. Promise us you will tell nobody," Jorny said. "All the people of Negofer also have power over plants, but that's not much."

"I promise," Pat said. "I can't believe it. How do Negofer people bear with all the boasting from a few people on Magisis?"

"We never lived there long enough to find out," Westie said.

Pat looked around. The soft board on the wall was filled with markings on the maps and notes. "What's this?" she asked.

"Jabez tells us to make plans and find weak spots for attacking planets. We do that and mostly stay in here. Except for meals," Westie said.

"Wait a second, you stay in this room all day?" Pat asked.

"Yeah," Jorny said.

"You don't even go to the library?" Pat asked.

"No," Jorny said.

"That's terrible!" Pat exclaimed.

"We know. Hey, we need to do some work, so come back later," Westie said.

"Okay," Pat said. She left the room and decided to go see Kommy Locks. She knocked on the door. No answer. She knocked again. Still no answer. She knocked once again. This time, the door opened. A girl's head peeked out.

"Sorry, I was in the washroom, come in."

Kommy Locks had silky shoulder-length purple hair with streaks of pink and blue. Her cheeks were chubby, and she had shiny emerald-green eyes.

The room was just like Pat's except Kommy had decorated it better. Her desk was filled with things and her bed had more pillows. She had a plant on the floor. Her soft board was pinned with pictures, maps and much more. She had two stools put neatly in the corner. It looked like Kommy had grown up in this room.

"Hey! I'm your new neighbour from room number two, thought I'd just pop in for a greeting," Pat said.

"Okay. Hi," Kommy said plainly.

"So, how'd you end up working for Jabez?" Pat asked, taking a stool and sitting on it.

"I am from a planet called Lepromin. I was five years old when an attack happened in my city. My parents were against Jabez's cause. You could say that I was the school bully. My parents tried to stop me but couldn't. When they were distracted by someone getting hurt, I packed my things and ran away.

"On the way, I saw Jabez. He had attacked my city. I agreed with Jabez's cause, and he took me in as his own. I have lived in this room for eleven years and am eighteen now. I don't know what happened to my parents, but I don't care. You should listen to Gonger's story, it is totally bizarre," Kommy said, her eyes becoming dreamy. Kommy got up and went to her desk. She took some papers in her hands and straightened them.

Out of the corner of her eye, Pat was sure she saw a statue on the desk move its head towards Kommy.

It's just my imagination, Pat thought. *Statues don't move.*

"Look, I need to report to P—Jabez. I'll talk to you later," Kommy said, she gave a nervous laugh, got up and led Pat out of the room. Then, she slammed the door on Pat's face.

Pat looked shocked and angry. She decided to go see Gonger. But before she could knock on his door, it opened. A boy peeked out.

"What do you want?" the boy, Gonger, asked.

"I just wanted to—" Pat said.

"Get in or get out," Gonger said in a dangerous voice.

"Okay, okay," Pat said. "No need to yell."

Gonger rolled his eyes and pulled Pat inside.

"Hey!" Pat exclaimed.

"What do you want?" Gonger asked, clearly bored.

"I wanted to get to know all of my neighbours," Pat said.

"Okay. I'm Gonger Faust, twenty years old," Gonger said. He paused and then said, "Slayer of Leslie and Barry Faust."

39. Pat Stands Up

"Sorry, who?" Pat asked. "I must have heard the surnames wrong."

Gonger looked out the window. "No, you heard it right." He took a shaky breath. "I killed my parents."

Pat gasped. Now, her mind was racing with questions. *Why did Gonger kill his own parents? How was he acting so calm about that? What was his story?* And in no connection to this all, *how did he know she was coming before she knocked on the door?*

"You killed your own parents? Why?" Pat asked.

"I'll tell you my story," Gonger said, ignoring Pat's questions.

"It was just a normal day in my town, Assley on Lepromin. I was sitting in my bedroom and reading. My parents came to me. My mom said, 'Gonger, darling. We just got an alert from headquarters that some very powerful being is trying to attack our city. This man, Jabez, says that he will destroy the city and then rebuild it as his own. We need to go help the others defend Assley.'

"She kissed my forehead and went away with my dad. My parents worked with the Protectors of Assley. They were basically the police of our town. I was really angry with them. They were never home and even if they were, they never spent time with me. They were like strangers to me. I decided to run away. I was in such a hurry that I forgot to tell Kommy of my plans.

"Kommy and I used to have a lot of fun bullying together in the neighbourhood. Like her, I too agreed with Jabez's cause. I headed off towards the border of Assley. There, I saw my parents and a few other powerful people trying to fight off Jabez. Suddenly, I got an idea. I could zap some sound waves on the barrier and break them to let Jabez in.

"That would teach my parents. With just a few zaps, the barrier gave away. Jabez stormed in and killed everyone except my parents. My mom had the power to make herself invisible and my dad had camouflage. They could hide until Jabez was out of reach. They set off the invader alarm to alert everyone.

"I came out of my hiding spot and faced them. 'Gonger, darling! What are you doing here?' My mom asked. 'Don't call me darling. You barely know me. You and Dad are always so busy that you never had time for me. You are a total stranger to me. And I'm so happy that the invader will destroy this city. I hate living here,' I yelled at my mom.

"Then, I blasted very loud sound waves at my parents, which killed them. I followed rows and rows of burned down houses and finally spotted Jabez. He was burning houses and killing people who were begging for mercy. 'HEY, YOU!' I called out. Jabez turned his head towards me. He was about to kill me when I said, 'Need help? I know where the strongest people live.'

"Jabez thought for two seconds then said, 'Lead me.' I led him around town, telling him where the weakest and the strongest lived. Jabez kept on burning houses and his zombies did the same. Once the entire town was burned down, I spotted Kommy. 'Kommy!' I yelled. She came running towards me. 'There you are! Mr Invader, can I join you? If I heard correctly, you want to rebuild the town of Assley and rule it?' Kommy said.

"Jabez nodded, amused. 'Join me, little ones. My name is Jabez. Gonger, you know where my spaceship is. Go there. I will come there later with Kommy.' I nodded and ran away. We camped out for a month in another town Jabez had rebuilt. After that, we went back to Assley where Jabez's guards were roaming around, and people were living in newly built houses.

"The entire town had a cloud of gloom on it. 'Welcome to Rewado Assley,' Jabez said. He took out a small model of his castle, pressed one place and the castle grew to normal size. We stayed there for at least two months before going to attack other cities," Gonger said.

"Wait a second, magic, sound waves?" Pat asked, confused.

"Lepromin also has magic. But one person has only one kind of magic, like a power. I have the power of sound and Kommy has animation. She can bring non-living things to life and control them," Gonger said.

"Oh. Okay," Pat said.

"Now, tell me *your* story," Gonger said.

Pat told Gonger everything.

"Hmm. I will be keeping an eye on you, Kawse. You could be just another betrayer, like Ruby," Gonger said, eyeing her suspiciously.

"I'm fully loyal to Jabez," Pat said plainly.

"Anyways, I have to do some work. Bye," Gonger said. He grabbed Pat's hand, dragged her outside and slammed the door shut.

"THANKS!" Pat yelled, really annoyed. She knocked on Lucy's bedroom door.

"Come in," Lucy called out.

Pat pushed open the door. "Thank goodness you're not busy," Pat cried out as soon as she had entered.

Lucy's bedroom was just as empty as Pat's bedroom.

"What happened?" Lucy asked.

Pat quickly told Lucy everything about Cloys', Kommy's and Gonger's stories.

"Wait, so all these people suddenly got busy when they were done with their stories?" Lucy asked.

"Yes! What am I doing wrong, Lucy?" Pat asked, sitting beside Lucy on the bed.

"I don't know. But the Cloys seemed to be *actually* busy. I guess Kommy and Gonger are just bad-tempered people," Lucy said.

"Yeah, I guess it makes sense," Pat said.

Suddenly, Jabez stormed in.

"Both of you. Go to the Saveup. Cause trouble," Jabez barked.

"Yes, Your Majesty," Lucy said, and bowed. She slid her hand into Pat's and teleported them outside Saveup headquarters.

"What was that about?" Pat asked.

"I have no idea, but Jabez seemed angry. It's best we follow the plan," Lucy said. She levitated herself and Pat up into the air until they reached the window of Lucy's bedroom and flew inside.

"Let's go break some stuff," Pat said. She made herself invisible and went to her room. She quickly removed the dummy and went back to Lucy's room. Lucy had just finished removing the dummy by the time Pat arrived.

"Hmm," Lucy said. "So, what should we break?"

"I guess Hilary and Ruby seemed pretty angry at each other. Maybe something that'll make them angrier?"

"Ooh, yes," said Lucy. "Let's go in their room and see."

They turned invisible and went into Hilary and Ruby's room. No one was there, but they stayed invisible just in case.

"How about that picture of Ruby and her family?" Pat asked.

"All right," Lucy said. "Do you know the level 5 separation spell?"

The level 5 separation spell was the most advanced separation spell. Something broken by it couldn't be repaired, with or without magic. The broken pieces were like opposite sides of magnets that always repelled.

"Level 5 spells are chants, Lucy," Pat said. "Have you not learnt that? And yes, I kind of know it."

"But I only know the English version and the chant is in Latin, like all the other level 5 spells."

"Not a problem. I know Latin. Tell me the chant, I'll do it."

Pat nodded, relieved. She told her the words.

Lucy nodded. "Here goes nothing." She closed her eyes and focused on the picture.

Separatum et numquam iungere
Separatum et numquam iungere
Conteram illud in unfixable pieces
repellere in aeternum
removere praeteritum identitatem.

The image shattered, right next to Hilary's bed, in such a way that it looked like Hilary broke it.

"Perfect," Pat said. "Now, let's get out of here before anyone notices."

"Now what?" Pat asked, once they were safely in Lucy's room.

"How about we break a few more things and then go back?" Lucy suggested.

"Sure," Pat said.

"But when Hilary and Ruby find out about all the broken things, won't they do the truthfulness spell on everyone and find out we're working for Jabez?"

"We'll have to talk to *him* about it," Pat said.

"We will keep everyone distracted and busy. They won't notice the broken things until the next day. We will go to Jabez's place at night," Pat said.

"Let's make them all play Find-the-Tag. We'll say it's for keeping everybody's mind off the stress of making plans!" Lucy exclaimed.

"Awesome idea! It'll be so much fun." Pat's smile faded. "Something we haven't had in a long time."

"Don't worry, once we defeat the Saveup, you'll have loads of fun. Now c'mon," Lucy said.

Pat and Lucy headed off in different directions. They both went to the learners' bedrooms and broke a few things, messed things up, etcetera. After thirty minutes, they both met up outside Pat's bedroom.

"Meet you later?" Lucy asked.

"Sure, bye," Pat said. She waved and then pushed open her bedroom door.

"Pat. There you are," Luna said sharply, as Pat entered the room.

"What happened?" Pat asked.

"Ruby told us that you had gone to sleep early today, so we came to look for you and you weren't here," Jane said.

"Yeah, I woke up. Then I was just hanging out with Lucy," Pat said.

"There's no time to 'hang out'. You should be making plans," Jane yelled.

"Stop treating me like I'm a two-year-old. I'm your age. I know what I need to do, I was just taking a bit of rest to keep my mind off stressful things," Pat yelled.

"Both of you, calm down. Pat, we wanted to discuss something with you," Luna said, standing in between Jane and Pat.

Pat folded her arms. "Go on."

"We wanted to make plans with you because we know what Jabez's prisons are like. And you are—*were* close to Nora," Luna said.

"Right. What do you want from me?" Pat asked.

"We—" Jane said. She was interrupted by Hilary's voice coming through the communication spells.

"Come down to the living room, everyone!" Hilary yelled.

Pat, Luna and Jane went to the living room.

"This meeting is about plans for Nora's rescue," Ruby said.

"And more importantly, how to win the battle with Jabez," Hilary said.

"Everyone who has encountered Jabez's magic should take a moment to remember what it was like. We need to know what kind of spells he uses," Ruby said.

"He doesn't use dark magic. That much I know. Because my past experience using dark magic is nothing like Jabez's," Hannah said.

"Are you sure it's not just an advanced version of it? Because if it isn't, we're in *huge* trouble," Mia said.

"I've encountered Jabez's magic," Ruby said. "And it's not an advanced version of dark magic." her voice cracked. "It's way worse."

"I'm pretty sure that Jabez isn't from this galaxy. I've heard of attacks on other planets like Lepromin, Negofer, and," Jane cleared her throat, "Tachél. People have been quoted as having seen Jabez, zombies, men, a huge-hooded figure."

"It has to be Jabez. But that means we're dealing with something we've never seen before. A whole new type of magic," Ruby said.

"I guess it's true. Because Jabez doesn't use spells, he just points or focuses, and magic happens. He's strong, I don't think I wanna see him in battle. It gives me shivers just thinking about it," Scarlett said.

"That little fight at the shop will be enough to give you nightmares," Sia said.

"Stop scaring Scarlett, Sia," Hilary said. "We need to be strong in these times."

"It's not my problem that Scarlett is a scaredy cat," Sia snapped.

"What happened to you, Sia?" Hilary asked kindly.

"None of your business," Sia said, annoyed.

"Sia, what happened?" Mia asked.

"We came to this meeting for a reason. Get back to that," Sia yelled.

"The meeting can wait, the well-being of our learners is important too," Ruby said. "I'm sure Hilary agrees."

"I do," Hilary admitted. "Sia, you look like you haven't slept in a long time."

Sia's dark purple eyes looked tired and weary, there were also dark shadows underneath them.

"Sia, please. Tell us what happened. Tell me if not everyone," Mia pleaded.

Sia's voice cracked. "No, I can't."

"Sia, has it got something to do with that Dan person?" Hannah asked, her mind wandering off to the shop attack.

"Don't call him that," Sia snapped, getting up. "He is a lot more dignified than that."

"Sia, calm down. Just tell us what happened," Mia said, pulling Sia back down.

Sia's anger evaporated and there were tears in her eyes. "I can't."

"Please," Mia pleaded. "There has to be a reason why you used the killing spell on Jabez."

"Can't I avenge somebody's death?" Sia whispered.

"But you did it more in an affectionate way," Mia said. "Please, Sia. I need to know."

Sia took a deep breath and without warning, started speaking, "Dan was my brother. Elder brother. We kept it a secret. He had brought disgrace to my family, but it wasn't even his fault. He got expelled from school because of a nasty trick someone else played and blamed on him. He was really smart and started inventing spells and making things.

"He opened his own shop and started selling whatever he invented. I loved him. We used to spend the weekends together before I joined the Freeup. Then, that day at the shop, he died. We always had a special bond. Whenever we fought, he would always come to me and say sorry. He would hug me and lift me in the air. He called me Nina," Sia said, tears formed in her eyes. They fell and kept falling. Sia embraced Mia.

"I'm sorry," Mia said, hugging Sia tighter.

"It wasn't your fault," Sia said, sniffing.

"I'm sorry, it was all my fault. I never should've taken you guys to the store," Ruby said.

"No, it wasn't your fault. Jabez would've attacked the store anyways. And then, all his fury would have been on Dan. It's good that we went," Sia's voice cracked. "I got to see him one last time."

"I know but it seems like Jabez came there because we were there," Ruby said.

"Don't blame yourself," Sia said. She smiled. "Me and Mia would have found a way to get out anyway."

Ruby smiled back, "Well *that* is true."

Hilary broke in, "Should we continue the meeting now?"

"Yes, where were we?" Jane asked.

"We were talking about Jabez in battle," Luna reminded her.

"Ah, yes. But I doubt Jabez will do any fighting. He'll just let his guards do all the work," Jane said.

"Yes. But when we get Nora back and fight him, he'll have to fight back and use his powers," Ava argued.

"I guess. We have to come up with *major* protection spells. And how are we supposed to beat Jabez!" Jane exclaimed.

"Slow down. We should take one problem at a time. First, some of us should focus on Nora and the rest, on coming up with strong spells. We don't have all the time in the world and have no idea what Jabez could be doing to Nora," Hilary said.

"That's true. If you guys need help from others, take it. We really need to hurry. We need to end this," Ruby said.

Everyone nodded.

"Um, can I say something?" Lucy asked.

"Go ahead," Hilary said.

"I was thinking, we're all really stressed out right now. So, why don't we play a game for the rest of the evening? It'll help us take our minds off things. Tomorrow, we'll be able to think better with a clearer head," Lucy said. "We can play Find-the-Tag."

"That's perfect! After playing, we'll get tired and will have an awesome sleep. And if we have an awesome sleep, we'll be able to think better the next day," Emma exclaimed.

"I guess, but it's nearly dinner time," Hilary said.

"Please, Hilary," everyone begged.

Hilary smiled. "All right. We can have food *after* playing the game."

In Find-the-Tag, there were five seekers who had to find everyone else. The game had only three rules.

Rule Number. 1: No spells that can keep you away from the seekers, aka separation spells.

Rule Number 2: You can use magic.

Rule Number 3: Have fun.

Once the seekers found a person, that person and all those found out, needed to distract and confuse the seekers. Once everyone was caught, whichever seeker had caught the most people would win. The seeker always chose a colour and then put a mark of that colour on the person who they caught. The game lasted for an immense amount of time but it was a lot of fun.

"I'll be a seeker," Ruby said.

"Me too," Lucy, Ava, Pat and Mia said.

They went on till around 11 o'clock in the night. Everyone was very tired. Hilary and Ruby quickly made some food. Everyone gobbled it up and instantly went to bed. Soon, Pat and Lucy got up to go. They both could've gone out from the window, but there were no windows in the corridor and all the other windows had girls sleeping near them, so they didn't want to risk it.

They decided to go to a window without a girl sleeping near it, which was on the floor below. They met up in the corridor and decided to use the staircase. To go there, they had to cross Hilary and Ruby's bedroom door. But Lucy tripped on a broken tile. Her elbow crashed into the bedroom door and her leg kicked a vase nearby.

"Darn," Lucy muttered.

"Are you okay?" Pat asked.

"I'm fine," Lucy said. "But it made too much noise. They will come to see. Let's get outta here."

Right on cue, the door opened, and Pat and Lucy scampered away. When Ruby looked, all she saw was the end of Lucy's cloak.

I'm just imagining things. And if the noise would have been real, Hilary would have woken up too. She's a light sleeper, Ruby thought. But Hilary was actually a very heavy sleeper, Ruby just didn't know that. Ruby went back inside the room, not noticing the broken picture near Hilary's bed, and went straight to bed.

***

Pat and Lucy teleported into Lucy's room.

"I guess we both should get some rest too before Jabez comes?" Pat suggested.

"Yeah, see you later," Lucy said.

Just as Pat closed the door and turned around, a horrible sight met her eyes. The bedsheets were all in a messy heap, there were papers on the floor, bed and the desk. The chair in the room had fallen down, the drawers were all open. Stationery and papers were scattered messily inside the drawers. The window was shattered.

Pat was very angry, *who had done this to her room? And why?* Sure, she could just fix it with a spell. But all this meant that someone either hated her or wanted to get her kicked out.

"Ugh!" Pat yelled. She didn't bother to clean up the room. Instead, she went over to the window and looked down. Jabez was in the courtyard and looked like he'd just done a lot of crazy stuff. Looking at him made her feel that Jabez had searched her room and messed it up. Pat felt anger clouding her brain. She threw open the window and climbed onto the windowsill. She flew down to the courtyard and landed right in front of Jabez.

"*You*!" Pat spat. Her eyes were blood red with anger. "You messed up my room, you ruined it. You searched it. YOU STILL DON'T BELIEVE ME, SO YOU HAD TO COME AND SEARCH MY ROOM. WHAT KIND OF A MASTER ARE YOU? YOU STUPID, STUPID—"

"Careful how you speak to your master," Jabez said dangerously. "*I* am the one in charge here."

"CAREFUL HOW YOU SPEAK TO YOUR ALLIES!" Pat yelled. She softened her tone. "You don't want me to leave, do you? Or should I say, do you want me to leave? 'Cause I might. I think you want—"

"That's enough. I can very well mind-control you into working for me. And my magic is very different, it leaves a lasting impact. Or perhaps I should just kill you and get it over with it?" Jabez said dangerously. Obviously, he was lying. His magic didn't work like that. Jabez couldn't control Pat's mind forever. Sure (once he stopped controlling her mind), it would make Pat's brain give her tiny tugs to be loyal to Jabez, but it wasn't that strong. Pat was strong, she could fight that.

"Ha!" Pat cried. "As if. If you could control people that easily, you would. You could control Ruby into joining you. You could control any enemy and make them kill themselves. And if you kill me now, Lucy will leave too. And if you kill her, there will be no Saveup spies left. I swear, no one else is going to join anytime soon."

"I have many spies you don't know about. How do you think I found out about Ruby, Nora, Hannah, Sia and Mia going to the crafts store? How do you think I knew that Dan was Sia's brother? How do you think I know so much, Pat Kawse? Do you think that I just go into my library and search everything up?" Jabez asked, his voice rising. "That is not how it works. And if your useless brain can't process that, it isn't my fault. Now, get out of my way!" Jabez looked really threatening.

Pat threw her head back and laughed. "Sure, you may know some stuff. But the truth is, your spies can't get in everywhere. They don't know where Hilary and Ruby keep important stuff. You can't just ask questions and get answers. We can. That's why you need us. Go ahead. I'm not afraid of you." She looked him in the eye to prove it.

Jabez looked her back in the eye. "You think that you are not afraid? Even you know that deep down, you are afraid. Very afraid, as you should be. You're afraid I'll take your home, just like I took Nora's. You're afraid that I will kill your family, just like I did for many. You're afraid of many things which I can do.

"Deep down, you know it. This act of confidence doesn't fool me. I can do many things you can't even dream about. I have power, and I know how to use it. I know how to bend rules to my will. I can do so much. I have power and I will rule the universe with it," Jabez yelled.

"Sure, you will," Pat said sarcastically. Jabez was right, of course. She was afraid. But she had to make sure she didn't show it. "But then how did someone aim a killing spell at your heart? How much pain were you in? Didn't Nora's uncle knock you unconscious? Is that all-powerful, huh? *Is it?*"

"We all have our own moments of weakness. But I guess someone as self-absorbed as you wouldn't know. I know that you worry I'll kill your father, grandma, little brother and sister. I know that your mother died, but you hid it. I know how she died; you don't know that. I know that you want to spend every night in your bedroom, crying for everything you have suffered.

"I know that your heart breaks every time your little sister cries. And you know that I know all about you. I know your personal interests, I know everything. You could be completely loyal to me, Pat. You could join me forever. You could become my daughter," Jabez said. He tucked a strand of Pat's hair behind her ear.

"No," Pat said, trembling. She backed away from Jabez. "No, never. You can't. I won't. I'm leaving." She backed away a couple more steps and stumbled.

"My dear Pat. You aren't going anywhere." He pulled his hands towards his chest and Pat was pulled by an invisible force back to face Jabez. "I know you could be my daughter. Join me forever, become—"

"NO!" Pat yelled. She closed her eyes and took deep breaths. "You can't blackmail me into this. I refuse. Besides, this has side-tracked us from our main topic. If you search my room like that, why should I not leave? So that I can be your daughter after you kill my family? Really? That's your plan?"

"Who said anything about killing your family? I was just offering you a better life. Did your parents ever ask you how was your day while you were working for the Freeup? Did they ever even send a letter to ask how you were doing?" Jabez asked. "You can leave if you want. But I'm afraid you'd be on the *losing* side then."

"Better than being with *you* anyway." She turned around and stormed across the courtyard.

Jabez rolled his eyes and again pulled his hand towards his chest. Once again, Pat was pulled back to her old position. "Fine, what do you want me to do?"

Pat looked satisfied. "Clean my room up and never come inside it again."

"I will clean the room and I can come in it with *your* permission. Deal?" Jabez said. He said the word 'permission' like it was dirt.

"Okay," Pat said.

Jabez strode out of the courtyard. He went up to Pat's bedroom and with a flick of his hand, the entire room was straightened up and the window repaired itself.

Pat laughed so hard that she doubled over. "I can't believe it. You actually did it. You fixed—"

"Shut up," Jabez snapped, completely annoyed. He opened the door and stormed off.

Pat doubled over with laughter and happy tears fell from her eyes. She didn't remember the last time she had laughed so much. Suddenly, Jabez swung open the door. He grabbed Pat's hand and teleported both of them to the dungeons, in front of prison no 47.

"Hey!" Pat protested. "We had a *deal.* You can't enter my room without my permission."

"Shut up! I'm the boss, you can't boss me around. Anyways, look who's in here," Jabez said, pointing to the cell in front of them.

Pat didn't want to follow any of Jabez's orders but she glanced there in spite of herself. She gasped and wriggled out of Jabez's grip and looked again to see if what she was seeing was right. It was. All her anger towards Jabez about breaking the deal evaporated. In the prison, lying unconscious, was her sister. Crystal.

40. The Daughters of Jabez

Pat stared in shock. She felt anger boiling inside her. Jabez had done this to her sister. *Younger* sister. She was only *seven*. He had promised not to hurt her family. Lies. Jabez had promised so much. They. All. Were. Lies. Crystal wasn't even moving in her sleep, something she never did. All Jabez's fault.

Her sister was in a mess. Jabez's fault. Pat felt so much anger that she had never felt before. She wanted to ruin Jabez's life, just as he had ruined hers. She was *done*. She was going to take Crystal out of here and leave Jabez. She was gonna betray Jabez. She was going to save Nora too, to prove to the Saveup that she had left Jabez.

This was it. Jabez had gone too far this time. Pat's shock had evaporated and turned into pure rage. She put her hand on the lock, expecting it to open by her will. Instead, her hand got a slight shock. She withdrew her hand.

"Really? Did you think I would let you save your sister so easily? No, my dear Pat. No. I prefer to keep my hostage far out of reach. I know what's going on in your mind," Jabez said. "You don't need your family, Pat. They never talked to you. They never took you seriously. They removed you from their house and threw you into the Freeup. I will not be like that, Pat. You still have the choice. You can still be my daughter."

Pat stayed silent. The deal *was* convincing. Her mind started arguing with itself. But she couldn't let her sister stay like that.

But she was only sleeping.
Who knows how long Jabez had kept her here?
She was only sleeping, no harm in that?
But what about all the pain he must have caused while taking Crystal away?
Crystal's mind would have blank spots for the days she was captured.
Jabez was better than her own family.

What if Jabez never let her go?

Did it really matter that much? Her family didn't care. Crystal was only sleeping.

Finally, the side of her mind which wanted to become Jabez's daughter won. Pat took a deep breath. She nodded—just once. Barely a nod at all.

"Hi, Dad," Pat said, and hugged Jabez.

Jabez didn't hug her back. He was too shocked to process what had happened. Had Pat really agreed to become his daughter? Slowly, he wrapped his arms around her, too.

"Hi, daughter," Jabez said, his voice thick.

Pat hugged Jabez tighter. She felt good. She felt loyal to Jabez. She felt connected to him. Albert walked around the corner, whistling. He spotted Jabez and Pat hugging.

"Uh," Albert said. He slowly inched away from the scene. Then, once he had turned a corner, he ran like his life depended on it. Jabez let go of Pat and cleared his throat.

"Um, we should get down to business," Jabez said. "I think I have a session with you and Lucy."

"Uh, yes. We do," Pat said, and gave a nervous laugh. She smiled and ran to Lucy's room.

***

Lucy was sitting on her desk, reading the map of Magisis when Pat flung open the door. "Come on. Jabez wants to see us," Pat said.

"Oh yeah," Lucy said. She folded the map and put it on the desk. "Let's go."

Lucy followed Pat to the library.

"Daughter and Lucy," Jabez said.

"*Daughter*!" Lucy yelled.

Pat nodded and explained everything to Lucy.

"Oh. So, she's your daughter now?" Lucy said, her eyes narrowing and nodding. "Okay."

"Jealous, hmm?" Pat asked, smirking.

"Now, now. That's enough, Pat and Lucy," Jabez said, standing between them.

"What have you brought us here for? I have better things to do than spend time with *her*." Lucy pointed and glared at Pat with an extremely sour expression.

Pat felt hurt. It wasn't like she *loved* being Jabez's daughter, but it sure had some advantages.

"I have brought my wonderful daughter and her *friend* here so that I can read your minds. I'm so sorry, Pat dear. But I'm not sure if I can trust you both yet, y'know," Jabez said.

"Aha! You're giving *her* special attention so that she won't leave you," Lucy cried. "But that doesn't mean *I* won't."

"Now, now," Jabez said in a very sweet voice. "Okay. Let's begin the mind-reading. Albert, have you enabled the force-field and locked the doors?"

From somewhere nearby, Albert cried, "Yes, Your Majesty."

Jabez nodded. He motioned for Pat and Lucy to take a seat. Pat and Lucy each took a bean bag and sat in front of Jabez's bean bag.

"Now, I'm going to read each of your minds, one by one. There will be a sharp pain in your head, I recommend you don't try to fight it. If you do, it will cause more pain."

Pat and Lucy nodded.

"Let's start with Lucy." Jabez closed his eyes and entered Lucy's mind.

Lucy's head started spinning. She wanted to fight it, but whenever she tried to do so, the pain became more intense. She choked and shuddered. All of her memories started replaying like a video in her head. Her vision clouded and she couldn't see Jabez anymore. She could only see her memories. They kept replaying.

Whatever she thought, was heard as if she was saying it out loud. All her memories, since she joined Jabez and before that, the fake map, Lucy and Pat escaping from the Saveup, breaking the picture. All of them. And her thoughts were like loud-speakers, playing in sync with the memories. She moved her head backwards. It was all she could do to stop screaming.

Jabez opened his eyes abruptly and Lucy's pain slowly faded away. He smiled. "How was the experience?"

"Horrible," Lucy cried. "My memories—they like—"

"Nuh-uh. Don't spoil the surprise for dear Pat," Jabez said, smirking.

Jabez closed his eyes again and this time, Pat's head started to throb.

She tried to stop the pain. Whenever she got closer, it pained harder. She wanted to yell in pain. It was too much. Then, suddenly, her vision blurred. Jabez's figure disappeared and her memories started playing. She was walking alone, thinking bad thoughts about Jabez. What was worse, was that she was insulting Jabez and her thoughts were loud. She shivered and tried not to cry.

The pain was too much, Pat needed it to stop. Her head pained like never before. She wanted to fight it, stop her memories from playing. Stop the thoughts, stop the pain. Pat yelled out loud in pain. She fell out of her seat. But the pain only got worse. Her chest felt like it was going to close up on itself. She wasn't breathing anymore. Suddenly, the pain stopped, and she blacked out.

"Pat," Lucy yelled. She slapped the unconscious Pat.

"Ah!" Pat yelled. She got up. "What happened?"

Jabez explained, "The mind-reading suddenly stopped. I think your brain somehow fought it, but the price was to black out. I should probably do some research about it."

Lucy scowled. Jabez had told Pat about Lucy slapping Pat. This was horrible, it would have been awesome if Pat hadn't known. Pat looked angry and opened her mouth to yell at Lucy. Lucy balled her fists, ready to back herself up.

"Both of you, off to your rooms. You need to return to the Saveup tomorrow," Jabez said, before Pat could start yelling.

They stormed off to their rooms.

***

Lucy closed her bedroom door with a bang and started thinking. How had she ended up in this mess in the first place? Pat, she had convinced her. About the power that Lucy would have if she worked for Jabez. Lucy's mind was racing. Why had Pat chosen her? And there was *no* power in being with Jabez. Jabez just kicked you around and made you do jobs for him. But still, she was on the winning side. That was all that mattered.

Anyways, she was just curious and never wanted to leave Jabez. She had never dreamt about it and never would. She had promised herself to be fully committed to Jabez. After all, you can't win without problems arising. Lucy smiled. It wasn't that bad that Pat was Jabez's daughter. Lucy could give requests to Jabez as Pat's 'best friend'. Hopefully.

Jabez paced his room. He was going to attack Uncle James today. He had triple-checked his work but was still worried.

"What am I missing?" Jabez murmured to himself. He picked up his plans and notes, everything related to the attack. He examined the map his spy had drawn for him. Apparently, it showed the layout of Uncle James' house, including where his protections were. His spy had not been back for several days, which was a good sign. The Spy, Indsey, had just returned two days back. But Jabez was worried, he couldn't miss anything. The plan needed to go well. He needed to succeed.

"I'm way behind on my daily work. So many rules haven't been posted, shops haven't been attacked. People haven't been caught," Jabez said out loud. He went over to his bed and took out his map. He could see where everyone was and what they were doing. If he tapped on somebody's black dot and close his eyes, he could look through that person's eyes. He tapped on Indsey's dot and closed his eyes. Indsey was in her bedroom, reaching her hand out to switch off the bedroom light.

"Indsey, my room. Right now," Jabez said. His voice could be heard only in Indsey's brain. Indsey groaned and teleported herself to outside Jabez's door. Jabez opened the door before she could knock. "Indsey, I need you," Jabez said.

"Yeah, yeah. Tell me, Daddy. What happened?" Indsey asked, she sat down on an empty chair in the room. Indsey was the only person who didn't need to respect Jabez since she was born with magic (unlike the guards and spies present in the castle). Just like him. While his guards, cooks, maids, cleaners, zombies, etc. had to respect him, she was his Head of Spies.

All of the spies were Indsey's troops from her planet. They were all magic but still had to respect Jabez. Indsey and Jabez had a special bond. She stared at Jabez with her golden eyes and rolled a bit of her rainbow hair on her finger. Her hair was originally white but she had coloured dark rainbow streaks everywhere on her hair, like someone had thrown paint on her hair and then it had spread out and become a really cool hair colour. Her hair was straight.

"Sweetie, I need help. I feel like I've missed something in my plans," Jabez said. Indsey was his daughter, real daughter. Jabez had been visiting a planet from his galaxy and had fallen in love with and married a girl, Thea Opal. Thea hadn't been very bad to begin with but Jabez had convinced her.

Thea had given birth to a baby, but had died protecting Jabez when Indsey was five. Jabez was attacking a city and some other powerful being was threatening him. To protect him, Thea came in the way and took a horrible spell that killed her.

"Wait a second, are you telling me that you don't trust my plans?" Indsey asked in a dangerous voice that said: *I'm offended. Curse you!*

"I'm not doing that. I just feel like we may have missed something, sweetie," Jabez said.

Indsey snorted. "Have my plans ever failed you, Daddy? Like Sia's brother's plan and—"

"I know, I know. But this guy, James, is really powerful. He's like the strongest on this planet. And I'm so behind on work. So many rules haven't been posted and people haven't been caught. I haven't destroyed and rebuilt shops or houses," Jabez interrupted.

"Okay, calm down," Indsey said, rolling her eyes. "Dad, you gotta chill. Take one thing at a time."

Jabez took deep breaths. "I'll triple-check the plan again while you can tell me how James' house looks and about the protections."

Indsey told Jabez whatever she remembered about James' house once again. "Oh, and there was this protection spell on the door so that only people who James wanted to let in, could ring the doorbell. Until then, time slows down so that the person won't know that there is a spell," Indsey explained. "I know because I used a large scanner spell that gave me a detailed report without setting off alarms," Indsey added, seeing the look of amazement on Jabez's face.

Jabez stayed silent.

"Look, I know I forgot to tell you this scanner spell but *don't* give me the silent treatment," Indsey said.

"No, it's just that we've underestimated James. He can slow down time and bend it to his will," Jabez said quietly.

"Oh my gosh! You think he can do that?" Indsey asked, getting up.

"The spell means he can. I never knew a spell can slow down time and bend it to the spell-caster's will. This means James has that kind of power, that kind of pure determination to make such a spell," Jabez said quietly.

"Dad, I think your enemies are getting stronger. Now, forget what I said and take two things at a time. If you can't handle the plan for the attack right now, make more rules. Show 'em who's the boss," Indsey said. She walked over to Jabez and helped him to his feet.

Jabez nodded. "Time to make some rules. Oh, and Lindsey? I'm sorry for keeping you here till so late."

"No problemo, daddio," Indsey said, she walked over to the door and teleported herself back to her bedroom.

Jabez sighed and straightened up his papers. He turned and a weird sight met his eyes. Pat and Lucy were apparently frozen in the middle of a physical fight.

"Get off each other!" Jabez barked at them. Pat and Lucy quickly got off each other and straightened up. "What are you doing here?" Jabez yelled.

Pat opened her mouth, but Lucy spoke first, "We came to tell you that," she continued on to tell Jabez about breaking the picture and many other things and playing Find-the-Tag to keep everyone distracted.

"Obviously, they're gonna search everyone's memories now, they're not gonna risk their lives. I know what to do," Jabez said.

***

Indsey reached her room and instantly collapsed on the bed. Her room was large and there was a four-poster bed in the middle of it. Right behind the bed, was a floor-to-ceiling wall with pearly white curtains. On the wall, in front of her bed, was a large desk. It was really long and had dozens of papers, stationery, knick-knacks and a large soft board pinned up to the wall.

On the soft board, there were maps, notes, pictures and a large red thread connecting a few papers and maps. Next to the door, there were a few posters and shelves. The shelves had tiny statues or some jewellery in them. On the opposite wall with the door, there was a large walk-in closet and next to it, another large ceiling to floor window with pearly white curtains. There was a chest next to Indsey's bed that had toys from her childhood and other things important to her.

"Dad isn't telling me something, I know it," Indsey said to herself. She sulked for a while and then got up. She went over to the chest next to her bed and took out a picture of a woman with straight hair and the same hair colour as hers. The woman was not too tall and not too short, she was wearing a magenta tank top and black shorts. At the bottom of the picture, Indsey had drawn a small red heart.

"So cute," a voice behind Indsey said.

Indsey turned and saw Kommy. "*You*."

"Yes, *me*," Kommy said, scoffing.

"What do you want? It's not as if you can ruin my life anymore. I mean, you already stole my dad, my life," Indsey said, glaring.

"Shut up. The whole world doesn't revolve around you," Kommy said.

"Learn to respect me, I'm older than you. I have stronger magic. The only thing you can do is make non-living things do things like living things. That power is awesome, but not on you. I could stop your stupid 'animation' with just a flick of my hand. As I grow older, my power grows stronger. *My* dad, mind you, has very strong magic. And my mom was also pretty strong," Indsey said. "And both of their powers mixed together creates a very strong being."

"Yeah, yeah. Whatever, I really don't care," Kommy said, rolling her eyes. "And he's my dad too."

"Oh, really? I don't think so, Locks. Because you see, my dad didn't marry your mom. And I have had enough. Ever since I was ten, you have come in between me and my dad. You have ruined my life," Indsey took a deep breath, "and your mom didn't die for my dad. Oh wait, I forgot. You don't even know what became of your parents. They could be dead or rotting away in a prison right now." Indsey smirked.

"What do you mean?" Kommy asked, raising an eyebrow. Her heartbeat fast. *What trash was this Indsey saying?*

"Oh, nothing. And I'm *so* happy that you aren't angry, because you act like a total brat when you're angry," Indsey said.

Kommy balled her fists, ready to attack. Indsey held up her hand, ready to defend.

"Stop," a voice said with authority.

"Jorny?" Indsey gasped.

"How did *you* have enough courage to come here and talk to," Kommy nodded towards Indsey, "*Her Majesty*?"

"Ah, finally. I'm earning some respect here," Indsey said, smirking.

"I came here to tell you, something weird is happening with the newbies," Jorny said.

"The newbies?" Indsey asked.

"Pat and Lucy, the new enrolments," Jorny said.

"That disgusting Pat, I don't care what happens to her. I like Lucy though," Kommy said.

Jorny looked shocked. "She's not so bad," he mumbled.

"Oh, *those* guys. What happened to them?" Indsey asked.

"I don't know. His Majesty was smiling evilly and then he did something. They fainted or something, I don't remember. I was really sleepy but then, what caught my attention was that they disappeared. So, I came running here," Jorny said, frowning.

***

"What do you mean?" Pat asked, kind of scared.

"Oh, nothing serious. I'll just remove your memories of betraying the Saveup and store them in a closed box and then, I'll teleport you both back to your beds at the Saveup. When they will read your minds, you won't get caught. I will keep a tab on you and when the time is right, I'll teleport you back here, unconsciously in case you try to hurt me. And then, when you both wake up, I'll open the box so that your memories flood back into your brains," Jabez explained. "And don't worry, the wrong memories won't come to the wrong person."

"Okay," Lucy said slowly. She didn't want to trust Jabez but if she didn't want to get caught, she had to do what was necessary. She took a deep breath. "I'm ready."

Jabez nodded. He looked at Pat. By her expression, she wasn't ready. That was good, she wouldn't try to resist or panic. Then, without warning, he made some hand movements and pointed at Lucy and Pat in turn. They both crumpled to the floor in a heap. Jabez lifted his hand and Lucy and Pat disappeared.

They were now going to be back at the Saveup, sleeping soundly in their beds. He smiled, but his smile faded as he saw that the door was slightly open. And an end of a certain green cloak had just turned the corner. There was only one person who wore that shade of green.

41. A Question of Loyalty

"Jorny Cloy," Jabez said softly. "Trouble awaits you." Jabez was sitting on a chair in his bedroom and Jorny was sitting in another, looking pale-faced. Kommy and Indsey were standing silently in the corner.

"Can you call Westie?" Jorny asked, looking scared.

Jabez raised an eyebrow. But he still made some weird movements with his hand. Westie appeared in the room. She was drinking water. When she saw the scene before her, she threw the paper cup at the side, which then hit Kommy who got splashed with water on her face.

"Hey!" Kommy yelled. She wiped her face with one hand and glared at Westie. "You're gonna regret that, Cloy."

Indsey snickered.

"I'm sorry, I didn't mean to," Westie apologised. *Ha! She deserved it. Stupid, stuck-up brat,* she thought. *Oh wait, what if His Majesty is reading my mind? Um, I didn't mean it.*

"Sit," Jabez ordered. He snapped and Westie was sitting in a chair next to Jorny.

Westie and Jorny shared a look. It meant: *Oops.*

"So, let's decide your punishment, shall we?" Jabez said, smirking.

"Punishment? Why?" Westie said, raising an eyebrow. She wasn't going to deflate like a balloon, she had courage.

"Because your twin was snooping around and then he had the courage to go and interrupt my daughters—" Jabez bellowed.

"Daughter," Indsey corrected.

"And you, Westie Cloy, obviously sent him to do the snooping around because Jorny Cloy has no courage of his own," Jabez yelled, clearly annoyed.

"I wasn't snooping around, and I do have courage," Jorny cried. Why did everyone *always* think he was the shy and scared twin? WHY?

Jabez stared at Jorny coldly. "And your punishment will be that you twins won't be able to see each other for two weeks."

"What!" Jorny yelled.

"You're not our parent. You can't do that," Westie yelled.

"Don't rebel against me. It won't end well for you or your brother," Jabez said.

"You can't separate us," Westie said.

"I can do whatever I want," Jabez said.

"I think you're being a bit too harsh, Daddy," Indsey said.

"I don't think you're not right, Dad. The Cloys' deserve it," Kommy said.

"Nobody asked you," Indsey barked.

"Stop. Indsey, Kommy's right. Go back to your room," Jabez said. "Same for you, Kommy. Don't smile too much, I'm in a bad mood," he added sternly.

"I don't work on your orders," Indsey said in a low threatening voice. She looked Jabez in the eyes. Then she put up the hood of her blood red cloak and teleported away to the courtyard.

"That stupid, stuck-up—" Kommy said.

"Enough. She's my daughter, learn to respect her. And I told you to leave," Jabez said, his voice rising.

Kommy shrugged and teleported away.

"Now, let's think of an arrangement, shall we?" Jabez asked, giving a mischievous smile.

Westie kept her mouth shut, looking angrily anywhere but at Jabez.

He got up and raised his hands, they were all teleported to the Cloy twins' room. Jabez waved his hands, and the room became double the size it was before. He made movements with his hands again and a wall separated the room into two halves. All of Jorny's stuff flew through the wall to the other side while Westie's stuff stayed where it was. "I think I should make the barrier soundproof." Jabez smiled evilly.

"Don't even think about it," Westie yelled.

"Watch me." Jabez smirked.

Jabez did so and also made a protection around the wall so any magic that would hit the wall would repel and go back at the magic-caster.

Jorny, don't worry, Westie thought. *We still have our special connection.*

From where they came from, twins were a very rare thing. But whenever twins *were* born, they had a very special mind connection in which they could think of the name of the other twin and then they could hear each other's thoughts. It was very hard to separate them. The twins would rebel until they were together again.

I know, Jorny thought. *But Jabez could be eavesdropping, so we need to be careful.*

It wasn't good enough. They hated being separated, and already missed being together. The mind connection improved things, but it wasn't enough. They wanted to be together.

Try to sleep, Westie told Jorny through her thoughts. *I know it'll be hard, but you can't not sleep. Good night.*

Good night to you too, Westie.

They tried to sleep, but they knew sleep was coming hard tonight.

***

Indsey glared at the grass of the courtyard. It was pitch black, perfect for her grim mood. She should probably go to sleep, but she didn't want to. She felt as if her life was being ripped apart slowly. The more time Indsey was away from Jabez, the closer Kommy could be getting to Jabez. But the one happy thought that stayed with her was that she had gotten payback on Kommy Locks by ruining her life.

"She deserved it," Indsey said to herself. But deep down, she knew it was wrong. She just couldn't get herself to do it. It would cause planning, time, explanations, anger and embarrassment. "If Daddy found out, I'd be dead." But he couldn't find out. She wouldn't let him. It was too big of a confession to make.

Indsey felt really tired. Even before she could teleport to her room, she collapsed on the grass with exhaustion. Luckily, her head didn't hit the grass too hard. The grass was really soft, surprisingly.

***

The next day, when Pat woke up, she was in her bedroom at the Saveup. She felt confused, her memory of what she did after dinner, blank. Then, her memory just told her of getting in bed. *Maybe I was just really tired and imagined things*, Pat wondered. She shook her head clear of annoying or unwanted thoughts.

"You good?" Jane asked.

"Uh, yeah. Just my head's aching a bit," Pat said, frowning at herself.

"Water," Jane said, as she passed Pat a glass of water.

"Thanks," Pat said, she took the glass and drank the water. "I feel better."

Pat then yawned loudly and got up from her bed. She freshened up and went downstairs. On the way, she heard some shouting noises coming from Hilary and Ruby's bedroom. "Are they at it again?" She wondered out loud.

"Yes, they are. Come on, let's go before they come downstairs," Luna said, passing by.

Pat followed Luna to the dining room. Something seemed to be wrong. Everyone was sharing angry thoughts and frowning.

"Everything okay?" Pat asked, taking a seat between Jane and Luna.

"Not really. It seems like there was a break-in. Most people are talking about their stuff being broken, stolen, hidden and that kind of stuff," Luna explained. "Ava says that while she was walking by Hilary and Ruby's room, she heard Ruby accusing Hilary of something. When I passed by, they seemed very angry."

"Shame really," Jane said. "This all had to happen just when Hilary and Ruby seemed to start agreeing with each other."

"Yeah. Anything of yours broken or something like that?" Pat asked both of them.

"No, except that the body lotion jar was broken. Nothing important," Luna said. *It was a bit expensive and rare though,* she thought sadly.

"Shh. Hilary and Ruby are coming. Everyone, quiet," Jane called out softly.

Instantly, everyone stopped talking and soon, only the sound of footsteps approaching was heard. Hilary entered the dining hall and faced the Saveup. "We are going to have a very important meeting after breakfast. Everyone *has* to come. No excuses. It is a compulsory meeting, and NOTHING is more important than this meeting. Understand?" Hilary yelled.

"Yes, Hilary," everyone muttered.

Ruby entered the room, her eyes red. She took a seat next to Hannah and pulled a plate towards her. She started eating, buried in her thoughts.

Hilary ignored Ruby. "You can all start eating. I will be back in thirty minutes, by then y'all should be done with your food." Hilary took a plate and then left the room.

Everyone pulled their plates towards themselves and started eating. As soon as Hilary left, chatter broke out.

"Meeting about?"

"Think happened between them?"

"Ruby!"

"Hilary's mad."

"Looks sad."

"So weird!"

"Interlinked?"

Hilary walked in after a while with her right-hand index finger wrapped in a bandage. "Everyone, put your dishes in the sink and then come up to the meeting room."

"If Hilary got hurt, why wouldn't she just use Salve?" Pat whispered to Hannah.

"You tell me. You're the elder one here. You're supposed to have more knowledge," Hannah whispered, getting up.

Pat got up too. "You're what, twelve?"

"Fourteen. But still, you have more knowledge," Hannah countered.

"Whatever. I remember reading about how some strong Level-Five Spells can kind of block some easier and common spells," Pat said.

"Right. I guess we could make a better guess on why Salve did not work only if we get more information."

"Hold on. Don't get all detective-y right now. We have more things to focus on." Pat started walking up the stairs, Hannah beside her.

After a while, Hannah said, "Do you mind if I ask something?"

"Go on."

"I thought you are hanging out with Lucy nowadays, am I right?"

"Not really. I was just discussing some ideas with her, I guess. My memory has been sorta blurry."

"That happens loads of times with me. If I think something isn't important, I just forget it after a while. Then, I get busy and have other things to focus on—you get the point."

In the meeting room, Hilary was sitting at the head of the table with Ruby standing near the desk in the corner, writing something on a piece of paper. Everyone filled into the room and took seats.

"Today's meeting is something which everyone surely knows about," Hilary said.

"To be clearer, we want to discuss the matter of the stolen/broken possessions," Ruby said, turning around to face the room.

"Ruby has prepared a paper on which we are going to write what happened with whose possessions and try to find a connection that can lead us to the thief," Hilary said. "And we are sorry but if we can't find a connection fast, then we will have to read everybody's memories to see how loyal everyone *actually* is."

"Privacy?"

"Unfair!"

"To find loyalty?"

"Jabez would do—"

"Silence!" Ruby yelled.

Slowly, everyone stopped talking.

"One by one please. Just raise your hand," Ruby said.

A dozen hands shot up into the air. Ruby pointed to Sia.

"What if we have personal secrets? Not related to our loyalty to the Saveup. What about our privacy?" Sia asked, getting up.

Hilary and Ruby shared an awkward look: *Um.*

"We could just glimpse at a memory and see if it is personal and then move away from it," Hilary said, deep in thought.

"See, we're already getting new ideas," Ruby said.

Andrea, who had been very silent for the past few days, raised her hand.

"You would still see a part of that memory, be it personal or not," Andrea said, her voice barely a whisper.

"Well—" Hilary's voice trailed off.

"I'm not saying there is something wrong with this. I'm just saying you could do it some other, better way," Andrea said, speaking a bit louder than before.

Ruby and Hilary stayed silent, not knowing what to say. Ruby opened her mouth to speak but shut it again.

"Hold on, hold on," Emma said.

Every head turned to her direction.

"Can't you just use a level five truth spell on us? 'Cause I heard that the truth is drawn straight from our memories. And then, you could just have a vote on whether you guys should use the truth spell or check our memories," Emma explained.

"That's an awesome idea," Ruby said, her face lighting up. She got up and ran to the desk at the corner of the room. She got out a cardboard box and wrote something on it. She waved her hands and then, the box was suddenly painted and decorated. She waved her hands again and one single lotlitt and loads of pieces of paper appeared.

"Here you go," Ruby said as she levitated the box, lotlitt and papers and dumped them at the head of the meeting table. "Everyone can now write what they vote for."

Hilary looked stunned but quickly recovered.

"Do you guys get to vote too?" Sia asked, tilting her head.

"We are fine with anything. Even if we have our own opinions, they don't apply," Ruby said formally. The atmosphere in the room seemed to change. Everybody went silent. "Sorry," Ruby said. "Did I do something wrong?"

"Not really. It's just that we all treat each other like friends and family," Hilary explained.

"Oh," Ruby said, not sure what to say.

"It's fine, really. I mean, we both are leaders of this situation. And the situation is pretty serious. So, it's fine to be formal now and then," Hilary said.

"Right," Ruby said, releasing the breath she'd been holding. She felt relieved.

"Okay. We would usually say 'no pressure' but now, we simply CANNOT say that because this is really urgent. The thief could strike again," Hilary said. "So, how about fifteen minutes to think it over? What do you say, Ruby?"

"Fifteen sounds fine," Ruby said.

"Okay. Everyone, think it over and then we will start the voting," Hilary said.

Everyone shifted in their seats and started discussing.

Ruby went over to Hilary. "What would you have voted for, if you had the chance?" she asked stiffly. Ruby was still very mad at Hilary for the incident earlier in the morning. The incident was just too unforgivable. Ruby didn't even have any words to describe it.

"Well, probably for the truth spell. Though we will have to use the level five truth spell. And it is a chant. This needs strong focus, energy and most of all, purpose. And doing it on so many kids at once," Hilary shook her head, "I can't even imagine."

"Yeah. Well, I'll just go around and see what these people are thinking," Ruby said. She started taking rounds of the room. Stopping now and again to see and ask some kids about what they were planning.

Hilary stared sadly at the horizon. All her anger against Ruby had drained away. She felt sad for her instead. Hilary wished she hadn't yelled at Ruby. It must be so hard for her. Still, she was strong and kept her steady. Hilary admired her. "Hey, Ruby. Come here for a second? Please?" she asked.

"Uh, okay—" Ruby's voice trailed off. Not sure what was happening, she slowly and carefully walked over to Hilary.

The room turned silent. Hillary gave them all a silent look: *Continue your conversations*. Everyone took their eyes off Hilary and Ruby and immediately, the talking restarted.

"What happened?" Ruby asked, once she had reached Hilary.

"I just wanted to say sorry. About today morning," Hilary said, choosing her words carefully. She winced, expecting some explosion to happen.

But Ruby was keeping her cool. Yet, she kept silent. Not a word. Not an expression on her face. Nothing. Nothing at all to give Hilary a hint of her emotions. Hilary didn't know what to say. What to do. This was awkward. Rage filled Ruby's eyes so fast that Hilary stumbled back.

"After what you did, you think that SORRY WILL MAKE UP FOR IT?" Ruby gave a cold laugh. "No, Hilary. Sorry will never make up for what you did. You probably think it was just a stupid old picture, it doesn't even matter. But you will never know what it feels like. Because you, Hilary, have two living parents. You won't ever know the pain. The loneliness. You can't even imagine what it was like to survive on my own at such a young age.

"I took care of young girls who hated me. And I know that they secretly still do. What you did will never be forgiven." Ruby's eyes filled with tears of anger and sadness. "You have a life where people care about you. Guardians who love you. Me? I have nothing. Nobody."

Ruby ran out of the room. She had kept steady for so many years. Burying her pain, sadness and loneliness with better, happier memories. She had kept strong, reminding herself it was okay. But it wasn't okay anymore. She couldn't stay strong. She ran and ran. She reached a bathroom, ran into it and shut the door. She stared at the sink and cried. She was broken.

42. The Vote

Ruby had woken up early in the morning earlier that day. She just couldn't sleep anymore. She was feeling a bit puzzled, because of the noise in the night. It was bothering her still. She wanted to let it go but it was still itching at the back of her mind. Ruby yawned and stretched out her arms.

Just as she was about to get out of bed, she glanced at her bedside and her jaw fell open. Her picture wasn't here. She untangled herself from her blanket and immediately rummaged in her bedside table drawer. Hilary yawned and raised a sleepy head.

"What happened?" she asked.

"I can't find something precious. It's my—" Ruby turned to look at Hilary. Her eyes drifted to the bottom of Hilary's bed. "PICTURE!"

"Okay, so what about it?" Hilary said, confused.

Ruby ran to Hilary's bed with a mixture of angry and sad tears in her eyes. "My picture," she whispered. She held up a frame from which, broken pieces of glass and her picture were sticking out. One shard of glass scratched her hand. Ruby winced as pain shot up her hand. She dropped the frame.

"Are you okay?" Hilary asked. She got up from her bed and sat next to Ruby. She tore a part of her bedsheet and started wrapping it around Ruby's hand.

"Don't," Ruby said. She removed the cloth. "How could you? You did this, didn't you? You broke my picture."

"I—what?" Hilary asked, even more confused.

Ruby gave a cold laugh. "Don't pretend you don't know. Just accept it and prevent a lot of drama," she said. "Go on, accept it."

Hilary inhaled a sharp breath. Her anger rising above the surface, slowly and steadily breaking her resistance against it. "Just stop. I did nothing," she yelled. She didn't even know what to say. This was so absurd. "How can you even think I did it?" Her eyes shot to the picture. Realisation hit her. "Oh." The picture was right near her bed, almost as if Hilary had taken the picture and destroyed it near her bed.

"See? There is clear PROOF," Ruby said, her anger uncontrollable.

Hilary's temper slowly came back into play. "You are just so dumb. Can't you see? Even if I had broken the picture, I would NEVER EVER make it so obvious," she yelled.

"Aha! So you did break the picture," Ruby cried.

"I—no!" Hilary stamped her foot. "Clearly, the actual criminal wanted to make it look like I broke it, when I didn't."

Ruby stayed silent. "You could have been sleepy. Or maybe I came in. All I know is that you broke my picture. And you will pay," she yelled, after skipping a beat.

"It's like you *want* me to be the thief," Hilary yelled.

Ruby bit her lip. "I—" her voice trailed off. She tried to think of how to explain what was up. But it was just so crazy indeed.

Hilary eyed Ruby suspiciously. "What?" Her eyes softened as she looked deeper into Ruby's eyes. Hilary saw pain, sadness and regret in them. Her anger softened. She started to put an arm around Ruby.

"Don't," Ruby said. She turned away. She just couldn't let Hilary know. She just couldn't.

***

Back in the meeting room, as soon as Ruby left, everyone started whispering. Hilary only caught a few words but knew they weren't supporting her.

"—lary's fault."

"Problem?"

"Ruby."

"Should feel bad."

"Poor Ruby!"

"Not good."

Hilary muttered, "I'll announce when we meet next. Dismissed." She quickly ran out before anyone could say anything else. She ran into one of the practice rooms and shut the door behind her. Hilary took deep breaths as she leaned against the door. She never should've brought up the topic at all. This was all her fault.

It was like the Saveup was going to shatter. Once more, there were going to be two different groups. Their future was even foggier. Hilary put her head back and cursed silently. She couldn't let this break her. She had to be strong. For herself. For her learners. For Ruby.

***

Indsey woke up to loud noises. She instantly groaned.

"Ugh! Pa, look at this girl. She's pretending to be hurt so she can get your attention," Kommy yelled.

"Shut up," Indsey yelled. She felt very energetic. She got up suddenly and kicked Kommy in the stomach.

Kommy groaned in pain and clutched her stomach. "Oof."

"Serves you right," Indsey yelled.

Jabez walked in. "SHUT UP, BOTH OF YOU! INDSEY, APOLOGISE AT ONCE!"

"No, I won't. What will you do? Huh," Indsey yelled. She was *so* done with Jabez supporting Kommy all the time. "Am I not your real daughter? Or is this stupid lost idiot only your daughter?"

Jabez looked like he was ready to explode. "You—*YOU*—"

"What you? My name is Indsey Opal. Daughter of Thea Opal," Indsey yelled. "And you didn't care about her enough. You only care for your power. She *died* for you. And this is how you remember her?"

"I—" Jabez's voice trailed off.

"Don't listen to her. She is just trying to manipulate you," Kommy said, folding her hands.

"Don't listen to *her*," Indsey said. "She doesn't even know what happened. Yet, she's *always* poking her nose. No, not nose. HER ENTIRE FACE IS ALWAYS IN MY BUSINESS."

"Uh—" Jabez said, confused.

Indsey and Kommy both started yelling.

Jabez clutched his ears. "SHUT UP! Both of you," he yelled. "You both are bickering like two-year-olds."

"I don't care anymore," Indsey said, lowering her voice dangerously. "I simply have no care in the world if you are my father. I am done with Kommy and her tantrums. I'm done with your bossiness. I am leaving."

"You can't just leave," Jabez said, barely able to get the words out. He was so shocked, horrified and scared. What had he done? Was taking Kommy in really such a big mistake?

"She's trying to make you feel bad and kick me out. Pa. Look here," Kommy said, trying to get Jabez's attention.

Jabez didn't look at Kommy. He felt *weak*. As if someone had taken away the purpose of life. He *cared* about Indsey. He cared about his only real daughter.

***

Ruby tried to stop the tears. She just couldn't. *What have I done to myself?* She thought. She tried to think straight or at least try and get a hold of herself but found it impossible. It was such a heavy blow that had hit her; even worse, it had hit home. Ruby felt as if someone had broken her life by just doing one thing. There had always been a flaw in her carefully built sanity, and all it needed was the right trigger, and boom. She was a mess. *Get a hold of yourself,* a voice in her mind said.

I can't, Ruby's brain replied.

You need to.

I'm trying.

Try harder.

It's impossible. I'm trying, okay?

Try, please. For your parents?

That last thought helped her try and build a steadiness in herself. She had to do it for her parents. She had to make them proud. She had to make their deaths worth it.

"I'm ready to fight," Ruby said boldly and loudly. Hearing herself, her energy and determination were back in full force. She knew Hilary hadn't done the deed but she would have to tell her why she blamed Hilary.

***

Hilary was feeling terrible. She could have just messed up their only chance to save Magisis. She was not only guilty, but also scared. *What would happen now? Was this really the end? Could this really be the reason their world would be lost?* Suddenly, Hilary found it hard to breathe. The room was closing in. She was feeling dizzy. Just then, the door burst open. Ruby ran towards Hilary and hugged her. Hilary found it easy to breathe again and the walls parted. She regained steadiness.

"Who knew a hug could have so much power, huh?" Ruby said in her usual voice.

"Yeah," Hilary said, and smiled. She put her forehead on Ruby's shoulder, sighing.

"I know. I'm sorry," Ruby said.

"I should be too," Hilary said.

"Am I forgiven?" They both asked and started laughing.

"Yes!" Hilary and Ruby said together. They both laughed again.

"I blamed you even when I knew you weren't the criminal. I wanted to make it you because I couldn't bring myself to believe that anyone else had such spite against me. I wanted to make it you because I trusted you. It was easier to believe you did it. I wanted to believe it was just a mistake you made. It was easier to forgive it but then, my mind adapted to the thought that you did it. And then, it was just pure anger," Ruby said.

"It's okay," Hilary said softly. Wiping a tear on Ruby's face. "Don't cry."

"I know," Ruby said, sighing. "I'm stronger now. I have a stronger purpose to be strong and keep sane."

"I think I know what it is," Hilary said.

"Yeah," Ruby said, forcing a smile.

Hilary and Ruby went out together. All the learners were still in the meeting room. Hilary led Ruby there.

"Ruby," someone yelled. Instantly, everyone got out of their seats and hugged her.

"I'm fine now," Ruby said, smiling for real this time.

"You sure?" Alice asked.

"Yes," Ruby said reassuringly.

Ruby and Hilary explained everything. Everyone listened carefully, mindful not to interrupt. They admired Ruby for the courage to speak her heart out, especially in this matter. She had shared so much and was starting to share her power with them.

"I'm glad you told us this, Ruby. It shows we can trust you. Not that we had any doubt of it before," Jane said. She unexpectedly hugged Ruby. Ever since the two groups became one, Jane had still felt uncomfortable around Ruby, considering their past experience. But now, she felt she was more trustworthy.

"Thanks," Ruby said, smiling. She felt like Jane had forgiven her. As if some past awkwardness was gone. "To be honest, I feel good sharing this with y'all." Ruby laughed. "I'm becoming like Hilary, with her 'y'all's,'" she said, rolling her eyes.

Everyone joined in the laughter.

"Hate to ruin the mood, but we should get down to business," Hazel said.

"Yes, we should," Ruby said, taking a deep breath.

"I think we should give our votes, because we need to really speed things up," Jane said. "Like—things are happening to our planet. We can't just sit and—and well—"

Ruby nodded. "We should. The thing is, we don't really have much time. You guys should take only a minute or two to think about your opinion and then vote quickly."

"Okay, but what were the options again? Sorry, my memory has been kinda weird and so many important things have happened since then," Pat said, her voice getting more panicky with each word.

"It's okay," Hilary said kindly. "I'll tell you what two options were there. Having your mind being read by me and Ruby or a truth spell to see if you betrayed us or not."

"Oh, yeah," Pat said. "Thanks so much, Hilary."

Hilary smiled. Ruby was thinking. Pat seemed very kind and innocent. But just a few days ago, she'd been so mean to Nora. Ever since Nora had been captured, Pat had been very worried and concerned about Nora. But was it all just an act? Now, finally, Ruby's mind would be at rest. Whatever option Pat chose, Ruby would still get to know if she was a traitor or not. She would get her answers. Unless Pat had a way to deflect it; she didn't dwell on the thought too much though.

Ruby cleared her throat. "I hate to admit it, but Hilary and I do have a few doubts about some of you. I'm not going to take any names though," she said and somehow managed not to glance at Pat.

Tension formed in the room. Everyone moved uncomfortably in their seats and whispers started.

"It's okay. Really. None of you need to worry, okay?" Ruby said reassuringly. She bit her tongue and looked away. She tried not to shake. She was afraid, afraid who'd betrayed them.

Hilary checked everyone's votes. "Most of you have voted for the truth spell. We'll be starting from eldest to youngest. Everyone ready?"

Everyone nodded.

"Um, Pat, Jane, and Luna? Who's the eldest among you three?" Ruby asked.

"I am," Pat said. "Jane second."

Ruby's heart hammered against her chest. Now was the moment she had been waiting for. The truth was going to be revealed about Pat.

***

"Are you mad!" Jabez yelled. Jabez's sorrow was turning into pure rage. He felt like shaking Indsey from top to bottom.

"No, I'm not, thanks for asking," Indsey said, her voice steady and bored, not crackly or sad.

Jabez let out a sharp breath. "You're not leaving," his voice rang out clear and loud.

"Yes, I am. And you can't do anything about it," Indsey said in a challenging voice. Her tone was rising slowly.

Jabez let out a cold laugh. "You underestimate me, Indsey. Oh, you don't know how much you underestimate me."

"No, Mr Jabez. I don't. I'm your daughter, and I have all your power plus more."

"Mr Jabez? Ooh, so you finally decline him as your dad? Yes!" Kommy yelled. Jabez and Indsey glared at her. "Ok, I'll just keep shut," Kommy muttered, avoiding Jabez's gaze.

"Oh, how I wished to hear those words from your mouth since the first time I set eyes on you," Indsey said. "Being without parents who cared about you really taught you something, didn't it?" she sneered.

"Don't you get started on my parents, you—" Kommy said, her eyes narrowing and her lips pursing.

"Enough. Apologise to Kommy now, Indsey," Jabez said.

"Neve—" Indsey began.

"NOW!" Jabez yelled.

Indsey inched closer to him. "If I ever used my full powers, I could weaken *you*. But I don't. I keep limits to myself unlike some people." Her tone was soft and dangerous. Indsey moved her head up and eyed Jabez. "And now, I'm leaving, with my people. Including all the spies." The last sentence Indsey said was barely a whisper.

"No," Jabez said. "They're my people, your mother was the queen of them. And being her husband, I'm their king. They will obey me over their princess."

"But their princess is kinder to them," she said. "They will obey me." Indsey smiled.

"Oh, yeah? Will they? What if I take away important people from them?" Jabez said.

"You wouldn't. I won't let you take hostages of the innocent," Indsey yelled in her father's face.

Jabez snapped numerous times in a pattern. "Zombies are on their way right now."

"I'm not handling this nonsense anymore. I'll be back soon, to take back *my* people." Indsey drew her cloak around herself. "I wish you had died instead of Mother," and disappeared with a whoosh, leaving flames where she had been standing.

43. Indsey's Travels

Kommy scoffed and cupped her hands around her mouth. "Show-off," she yelled.

Jabez glared at her and felt like slapping her but didn't. Kommy gulped. She'd crossed enough boundaries for one day. She felt very uneasy. *Would this cause her trouble?* She was very worried. Maybe if she just said sorry? *I'll have to give it a try,* Kommy thought to herself. "I'm sorry. I didn't mean it," she said.

Jabez stared at the flames one last time. "You better not," and with that, left the courtyard.

Kommy sighed. Her Pa always thought *so much* about Indsey. There was nothing special about that girl. She went to her own room and brooded for a while.

***

Indsey was really angry. And her anger took her to Lepromin. A town named Assley to be more precise. She strolled through the roads. On a whim, she decided that today, she would free the innocent souls of this town. She knew her father had left guards here to keep everything under control. He'd even made one of his guards the mayor; Mayor Gérdy. He was one of Jabez's most trusted guards.

Indsey put the hood of her cloak up. It was just past noon. She nodded her head towards the guards outside Gérdy's house. They knew her, of course. They trusted her. The guards nodded back and opened the door. Indsey felt relieved. *Dad hadn't raised the alarm yet, huh?* Better for her. She walked inside.

Inside, there was a reception and a clerk. Indsey walked towards the clerk. "Hi, I want to meet Mayor Gérdy."

"Do you have an appointment?" the clerk asked.

"No," Indsey said.

"Then I can't give you permission to see him."

"Are you new? Because I don't think you know who I am," Indsey said, stepping up a bit.

"And who are you?"

"Indsey Opal. See it in your records if you don't believe me. There will be a picture of me."

The clerk did something on the cloud hovering in front of him. "Um, not really. I can't find anything in first names."

Indsey sighed. "Try Jabez's daughter."

"Uh—I—" The clerk stuttered. He quickly fumbled on the cloud and then said, "You may enter, Your Majesty."

Indsey smiled reluctantly. She always hated it when her father hired new people. They *always* wanted to know who she was and to them, she was nothing more than 'Jabez's daughter'. It annoyed her to no end, but she could do nothing about it. She walked straight in the passageway then turned left and reached a room marked 'Mayor Gérdy's Workroom'. She knocked on the door a few times, in a pattern.

"Come in," a voice called out.

Indsey pushed open the door.

Mayor Gérdy was sitting on a chair placed behind a desk. "What pleasure do I have to meet the Indsey Opal?" He said, giving a full-toothed smiling that looked fake.

Indsey sat on the chair in front of him. "I wouldn't give myself such a high title."

"You wouldn't come here unless you had business."

"Ah, as a matter of fact, I do." Indsey shifted in her seat.

"Well, what is it?" Gérdy asked politely.

"I want you to let me be on the news today in five minutes. *Everyone* in the *entire* town should see it. I want none of your guards, or you, to be listening to that news. In fact, I want you to patrol the borders." Indsey leaned closer. "I have a feeling an attack is about to happen at the border of your town at a very certain time."

Gérdy narrowed his eyes. "Right. As you wish." He got up. "The recording room is right in front of this office." Then he left the room.

Indsey smiled to herself, her plan was going well. She teleported to the borders. Her head felt dizzy, and she felt a bit weak. That always happened when she teleported; it drained her energy. But Indsey shook her head and felt as good as new. She set up some attacks at the border and also set a timer.

The exploding fire, timed. The illusions, timed. Her magic was unique that way. She could think about doing the spell and then, a single word would release it. It was a secret though. Nobody knew she could do that. Then, Indsey teleported to the recording room. She drank some water from a bottle kept there for her.

A guard knocked on the door of the recording room and said, "Everyone in the town is ready to see you."

Indsey said, "Okay. Now get lost." She heard his footsteps leaving. Indsey took a deep breath, then clicked on a button to open the Misty Call.

"Hello, Assley. I'm Indsey, Jabez's daughter. I know what you think, I'm evil. But just today, I have realised my mistakes. I have found the better side. I will burn Assley down and rebuild it as it once was. Using the same foundations, I will build you all, your dream homes. After Assley burns, *my* people, mind you, not my father's, will come and help you rebuild your homes as they once were. You can also tell them to build how you'd like your dream homes to be.

"I'm not doing this because I pity you. I'm doing this because I know my father's mistakes. I won't let them define me. I will make my own moves. I won't stay under his command. Please believe me. You all are strong people but afraid that the guards will hurt the people you love. I have created a distraction; they won't be harming you. You can burn down this New Assley yourselves and win back your loving old town. You are all free," Indsey said.

Just as she finished speaking, loud explosions were heard. The mayor's house was somewhat near to the border. Indsey smiled to herself. Her work here was done. She would send a few of her planet's most expert builders. But the work to be done after here was harder. Indsey would have to face some very grim past mistakes and correct them. She would have to face shame and embarrassment. But right now, her own life was more important.

As the mayor's house shook and cracks appeared in the walls, Indsey jumped out of the window and teleported mid-air.

***

As time was passing by, Indsey was feeling more and more ashamed of herself. She didn't want to face her past. It was too horrible. Now that she thought about it, it seemed like a very stupid and dumb thing to have done. She felt like her father was right. She had behaved like a two-year-old. But back then, she was mad and driven by power. *Just like Daddy*, Indsey fumed.

"Why? Why did I do so?" Indsey asked out loud and started crying. She was feeling very lonely. She wanted someone to lean on, someone to share her pain with. Like, maybe a sister or a brother? But not a fake sibling like Kommy. Even thinking about her made her sick. It made her feel like she was a mad monster trying to turn good but her past kept pulling her back, making her that monster again.

"No! No, no. No," she said between sobs. After having cried for a while, she felt a bit better. She looked up at the sign of 'Welcome to Haertop'. Indsey had returned to the cruel town of Haertop, finally. Enough was enough. She wasn't going to treat Mr and Mrs Locks like this anymore. She was going to get them out of this horrible village.

They didn't deserve this. This was the worst way to take revenge. She didn't care if they hated her or thought her to be the cruellest person in the world. She *would* free them, and she'd think about what'd happen next later.

This was the worst town on Lepromin. And it was very brutal too. Most of the people here had very less money and all the criminals lived here. Plus, its prison, the Sauel Prison was the toughest and most brutal prison in the whole *galaxy*. It had many things like torture chambers, lock-ups and harsh prison life.

It was horrible and Indsey couldn't understand why she had thought of this place. What made her feel a little better about her mistake was the fact that she had mentioned to the manager not to use any weapons or any other torture devices on Mr and Mrs Locks. They were to be left alone in one of the apartment-like places. But they were supposed to be updated on everything Jabez and Kommy did. Especially what horrible things Kommy did.

The location changes every single week; heavily guarded prison indeed. Well, I'll have to sign them out and do all the paperwork. But it will be worth it, Indsey thought. She was formulating a plan in her mind as she waited at the bus stop.

After a few minutes, the bus arrived. Indsey got in. She didn't want to teleport and feel her head spinning at the moment.

"Next, Greepop Lane," the conductor announced.

Indsey sat on a seat and dived deep into her thoughts.

***

Soon, she arrived. There was a lot of paperwork and confirmation to do, but finally, she got the permission to get into the house that doubled up as a prison. Indsey walked up to the door and knocked.

"Can I come in?" she called out, unsure of what to do.

A man who looked around forty with shabby dusty rose-coloured hair came to the door. His emerald-green monolid eyes looked tired and had wrinkles around them. There were also dark spots underneath his eyes. "Of course," he said with an expression of confusion. She stepped into the room. "Follow me," the man said.

He turned at a bend in the hallway and the thin passageway opened up into a small living room, which only had two sofas and a coffee table. There was a little shelf cabinet in a corner filled with books, two or three plants and a mini canvas. On the wall, there was a nice abstract art painting signed as 'Jaz Locks'.

When Indsey entered the living room, she realised the passageway was so thin because there was more to the living room. There were a few steps and a small open kitchen facing it. Over there, cooking something, was a lady who looked about forty and had dark purple hair. She had grey eyes with dark spots underneath them and wrinkles around them.

"Who is it now, Tommy? Another guard?" the lady asked, sighing. "I've told them specifically where they can find pancake batter, the healthy ones. Yet, they always get the wrong ones."

"I don't know either," the man said. "Who are you?" He turned to Indsey.

"I'm Indsey. Indsey Opal," Indsey said.

"Yes, okay. I'm Tommy and that is Jaz. What do you want?" the man asked, still not understanding.

Indsey gulped. Now came the hard part. "I'm," she took a deep breath, "the one who imprisoned you both." She sank to her knees and sobbed.

Tommy looked shaken. "I—" He didn't know what to say. How could he react to something like this? Sure, he would be expected to be angry. But this girl looked only about twenty years old, and he and Jaz had been here for ten years. This meant that Indsey had carried the burden of this secret since she was only ten years old.

Jaz dropped her spatula. She looked shocked. She too wondered how this girl could have done it. "Indsey, darling, you don't have to lie. Who forced you to tell this horrible truth?" Jaz asked.

"Nobody did," Indsey said, between sobs. "I did it."

Jaz walked towards Indsey and sat beside her. "But why?"

Tommy went towards the kitchen and took a glass of water. "Here."

Indsey took the glass and drank. Once she was calm, she continued, "Your daughter, Kommy. My father rescued her. She took my place. I was always second after her. And before I knew it, Kommy was my father's favourite daughter. I hated her for that and I wanted revenge. At that time, I was pure evil, like my father. I was so wrapped up in hate that I never thought about what I did. But afterwards, I began regretting it. Yet, I didn't know how to correct my mistakes and I was scared a little. So, I just kept quiet and soon, got busy with other things and well—"

"We understand, sweetie. I know how hard it can be to carry secrets like this. It's okay. I don't mean to be rude, but now that the damage has been done, why have you come here?" Jaz said.

Indsey wiped her tears and stood up. "Yes, I was coming to that. I've come here to free you. I've realised my mistakes and now I'm against everything Jabez does. And I have the courage to finally accept my mistakes."

"Thank you, we appreciate it," Tommy said. "But, what about Kommy? What has become of her? Is she doing well?"

"Yes, what about Kommy?" Jaz asked.

Indsey gulped. "Well, she's not exactly my favourite." She started explaining her feelings towards Kommy and how Kommy always behaved, every single detail Indsey had observed about Kommy.

Tommy clenched his fists. He got that Indsey was really depressed and everything but how could she just come up to somebody's parents who she had imprisoned and explain why they hated their child? "I don't believe a single word. My daughter is nothing like what you said," Tommy shouted. Sure, Kommy had betrayed them, but still.

"Tommy, stay calm," Jaz said. "It's hard for me too, but that doesn't mean you let out your anger and pain on Indsey."

"Whatever. But she can't just walk up to us and talk about how she hates our daughter," Tommy yelled.

"I'm sorry. I shouldn't have. I just came here to tell you that you will be free in a few hours. I should go now," Indsey waved, and then left.

44. Jabez's Sorrows

Pat walked forward. She didn't look afraid. Ruby wondered if she was wrong about suspecting her. Ruby cleared her throat. "Let's start?" she asked.

"I'm ready," Pat said. But from the inside, she was VERY nervous. What if something went wrong and hurt her somehow?

"Right." Ruby started chanting. She drew all her energy in her words. All her feelings. She used the determination she had to figure out the thief. She used all the power she had in her, and the spell worked. But as soon as the chant was over, Ruby lost all her energy and collapsed.

Someone splashed ice cold water on Ruby. "Huh?" Ruby said. She rubbed her eyes, but her vision was very blurry. She felt someone open her mouth and stuff food in it. Finally, the blurred shapes became Hilary, Pat and Scarlett. "What happened?" Ruby asked.

"Ask the expert," Pat said.

"You collapsed because you used too much of your energy. The chant; it is very powerful and dangerous," Scarlett said.

"But, good news. Pat is innocent," Hilary said.

"Wow!" Ruby's face lit up. "That's great." Her mind was finally at rest. So, Pat wasn't the thief after all.

The spells continued. Both Hilary and Ruby were very worried when the time for the last person came. Since nobody else had been found guilty, all eyes were on Olivia as she stepped forward for her turn.

"I can't believe it. It's *you*," Hilary said.

"It doesn't have to be," Ruby said. But she didn't believe herself either.

Olivia opened her mouth and shut it again. How could she respond to this? Ruby started chanting. Once the spell was over, it turned out Olivia too was innocent.

"But who can it be then? If it isn't someone from the Saveup? Nobody else has access to our headquarters," Hilary cried.

"Maybe the spells went wrong?" Jane suggested.

"No. That's not possible," Ruby declared.

"Let's all just sleep over it, I suppose," Luna suggested.

"Luna is right. Everyone, rest. Night approaches. Me and Ruby will come back to this matter tomorrow," Hilary said.

***

As soon as Pat slipped into her sleep, lightning flashed in her dreams, and she was suddenly standing in front of Jabez. Pat pinched herself to see if it was real. It was. Standing next to her was Lucy. Pat was scared to death. What the heck was happening?

"What?" Pat cried. "How am I here? With Lucy?"

"I summoned you," Jabez said.

"Why would you summon us?" Lucy asked. She too was frightened but did a good job of not showing it. "We both, of all the people. Who has no relation at all?"

"Because I need to return your memories. Duh," Jabez said. Before they could speak, Jabez started speaking some gibberish in another language and doing weird hand movements. Wind started howling, lightning flashed. Weird symbols floated around the room and suddenly, Pat and Lucy were thrown back.

"What was that?" Pat asked. A sudden flashback of her lost memories came into focus. The betrayal, Nora. Jabez. Kommy. Gonger. The Cloys', everything. She got up. Pat turned to Lucy. "Did you—?"

"Yeah. I did," Lucy said, trying to remain calm. She gulped.

"Okay, now I have tasks for both of you. Lucy, I sent some paperwork to your room. I need you to track some stuff for my next attack. And Pat, go and check on Nora."

***

Pat walked through the lonely, dull corridors. The only light was from a few fire torches here and there. The only people she saw were Jabez's guards. She opened the door to Nora's cell and sat in front of her.

"Wake up," she rolled her eyes, "I have news about your uncle." No response. "Fine. You wanna keep pretending like you're not awake," Pat screamed. She pointed to Nora with her finger. "I'm warning you."

Not a sound. Pat muttered a spell. All her anger turned into electricity and shot out of her finger. Nora gasped and got up. She felt jumpy as if electricity was running in her. But she didn't say anything about it.

"I warned you," Pat said.

Nora rolled her eyes. "That didn't even hurt."

"It woke you up, though. And that's what I meant to do."

"Well, so tell me why you're here."

"No reason. Just to check on you. To make sure you haven't escaped."

"I *will* escape." She didn't know why, but she lunged at Pat and grabbed her hand. Pat screamed and tried to pull away as electricity surged into her. But Nora's grip was too strong.

"Stop it," Pat cried. She knew what was happening. Every single time she had met Nora, she had hurt her with electricity. Nora's body had somehow absorbed all of that energy and stored it. It appeared that in her extreme need, Nora could use all of that energy, which had multiplied over time.

Nora knew she could end up killing Pat because of all the energy she was forcing into Pat's body. Somehow, she managed to leave Pat and instead, touched the doors of her prison. The energy crackled and sizzled, spreading through the door. Nora retracted her hand and as soon as she did, the door exploded into ashes.

Nora looked at the scared expression on Pat's face, it made her want to stay and comfort Pat. But she reminded herself that Pat wasn't who she thought she was. Nora ran out of the cell and didn't stop, not when she saw the guards, not when they raised their spears, not when they spread the alarm.

She just kept running and running and running. Whenever a guard tried to stop her, she threw electricity at them and kept running. Soon, she found an unguarded back gate from which she ran out. Once out, she teleported but ended up in some random forest and collapsed. All her energy was finally drained, and she could do nothing to keep awake.

***

"WHAT!" Jabez bellowed. Pat had just told him the story of Nora's escape. "HOW COULD YOU LET THIS HAPPEN? YOU WEAK, STUPID GIRL!"

"Excuse me!" Pat cried. "How is this my fault? *Her* body somehow stored that much energy. *She* nearly killed me. *I* did *nothing wrong*. It is not *my* fault."

"Blah blah blah. That's all I heard you say. Anyways, I'm deciding your punishment now," Jabez said, smirking.

"I didn't do *anything*. How was I supposed to know the energy would pile up? Punish the guards. They had a lot of time to stop her from escaping."

"But she blasted them all with her stupid electric thingy that apparently you gave her." Jabez got up from his throne, his voice rising. "Do you have *any* idea of how many soldiers I have lost today? Or how many soldiers are in need of extreme medication?"

Suddenly, a guard came running into the room. It was Albert. "Sir—"

"Manners!" Jabez screeched.

"Sorry, Your Majesty. But I have really important news. It's about Indsey. We've received a report and recording from one of your spies on Assley. You know, the ones you hired, not the ones Miss Thea brought," Albert mumbled.

"What? News about my daughter? Show me the recording right now."

Albert opened a sort of box and mist filled the room as a crackly recording was projected onto it. The recording was about what Indsey had said to the townspeople of New Assley, how she had set the spells and destroyed everything.

"My soldiers, everything. Ruined."

"I'm sorry." Albert put his head down and excused himself.

Jabez's anger was uncontrollable, so was his pain. His very *own* daughter did this to him. Just because of an argument and a wrong decision Jabez had made about Kommy. This was absolute nonsense. If she didn't agree with his cause, why didn't she just go into hiding or something? Why did she have to interfere and make things worse for him? He decided to pay a visit to New Assley.

***

Nora woke up to the sound of birds chirping. Where was she? Oh right, some forest. She slowly got up and stretched her legs. She had to find her way out of here but before that, she had to keep warm.

"*Flammae*," Nora whispered, she pointed to a dry part of the forest floor so the entire forest wouldn't catch on fire. She put stones around the fire and then summoned some sand. She kept the sand near the fire in case she needed to put it out or control the fire.

Nora sighed. She opened her mouth and hummed to the tune of the birds. She was so tired. While she hummed, Nora wandered near some fruit trees and berry bushes. She picked them, took them to her fire and started cutting the fruits and berries with a sharp piece of wood. After a while, she roasted the food over the fire and ate it. Her stomach full, Nora fell asleep right there. When she woke up again, her fire was already out. And what Nora saw next shook her from top to bottom.

45. MEETING IN THE WOODS

Pat was standing right in front of her. "Well, well, well, look who's here," she said.

Nora sighed. "Just because your stupid, stuck-up master captured me, doesn't mean I don't have power against *you*. I mean, just take a look at yourself, Pat. So weak. So dependent on Jabez. Don't you think it's time to switch back to the right side?" she argued, though not with conviction.

"Don't think your words will *ever* convince me to turn back. Because your words mean to me the same as what trash does. I don't care about what you have to say. I'm just here to take you back to the place you belong. Jabez's dungeons."

"Ha! As if I would *ever* let that happen. Keep dreaming, Pat. I'm not coming back. I'm not letting myself be taken away. You wanna fight me? Sure."

Pat hesitated.

"I don't know why you joined Jabez, but he's never going to give you what you want. Stop working with him," Nora yelled. Her heartbeat fast in her ears. Would Pat really believe her?

Pat swallowed. They didn't say anything for five minutes. Then Pat finally muttered, "I guess."

"No." Nora gave a cold laugh. "Don't think I will fall for your tricks. After all this while, a bit of yelling was all it needed to take you back, is it? No."

Pat glared at Nora. "Fine, then. I'll fight you, if that's what you want. You aren't more powerful than me."

"That's not what I want," Nora cried. "I'll do it, but only if it comes to that. You should go back and tell your *awesome master* that you couldn't find me."

Pat kept quiet, thinking of what to say. Then, softening her tone, she said, "For your family?"

"How do you know that?" Pat yelled.

"I figured there was going to be some kind of bargain. That if you don't join Jabez, he'll kill your family?"

"You—"

"Pat, listen to me. You have felt more at home at the Saveup than you have ever felt at Jabez's headquarters. You have friends and family. Think about your family, your parents, your siblings, your friends, cousins; so many people who have loved you and made you feel at home. So, just because of power, why would you betray all that? Just for having the upper hand? People still don't know it was you, do they? Think of how they will feel when they find out. Think of how they will feel when they know that their awesome Pat has betrayed them?"

"But he has Crystal," Pat's voice barely came out as a whisper. Nora looked at Pat, confused. "My little sister. She's only seven."

"How would she feel if she finds out her elder sister works for the person who has captured her?"

"But then she'll die," Pat yelled. "I can't let that happen."

"So be a spy," Nora said. "Don't let anyone know. Spy on Jabez for us instead of spying on us for Jabez."

"How?" Pat asked. "He can read minds."

"Don't let him, then," Nora cried. "Crystal won't want you to fight on the wrong side." Pat couldn't think of anything to say to that. She didn't respond. "Please, Pat," Nora said. "Don't do this."

Pat looked down. "Are you going to tell everyone?"

"I have to," Nora said. "But I'll tell everyone that you're not on his side anymore. I promise."

Pat didn't do anything for a while. Suddenly, she hugged Nora tightly. "I'm sorry," she said.

Nora smiled and teleported away.

"Hey guys!" Nora yelled, running into the Saveup headquarters. "I'm back."

"NORA?" Jane yelled.

"NORA!" someone else yelled. Soon, everyone was hugging her and laughing.

Hilary smiled at Nora. "I'm so glad you're back. How did you escape?"

Nora sighed. "Long story."

***

"PAT AND LUCY?" everyone yelled when Nora told them who'd betrayed them.

"I *told* you it was Pat," Ruby cried.

"No, not Lucy," Hannah and her siblings shouted.

"CALM DOWN!" Hilary yelled. "Nora isn't done."

"Pat isn't evil anymore. Jabez was threatening to kill her little sister. That's partly the reason she stayed with him. But I've convinced her to be our spy."

"She can be tricking you," Ruby said.

"I don't think so. She wouldn't have let me go if she was," Nora countered.

"We should deny Pat and Lucy's access to our HQ," Sia said.

Hilary nodded and started muttering a chant under her breath. Nora glanced at everyone. The Wells sisters were crying. Everyone else looked on the verge of tears or shocked.

"It can't be," Bell whispered. "*I* was the one who taught Lucy a lot, this is mostly my fault for letting her turn."

"No, it's not," Hannah said fiercely. "Those were her decisions entirely. It had nothing to do with you or your teachings. It was *my* fault. I should have seen the hints earlier. She's my *twin*, for god's sake."

"It's not *anyone's* fault," Ruby said. "They made their own decisions. And they hid it well. But I must ask. Nora, do you know how they hid from the truth spell?"

Nora shook her head. "Wait, what truth spell? About what?"

"Oh, um, yeah. We forgot to catch you up about what's been happening here. Well, I'll tell you now," Ruby said. She told Nora about everything that had happened since she had left.

"Oh, okay. No, Pat never mentioned anything like that. Nor did I ask her because I had no idea. Sorry," Nora said.

"No, no. It's fine. We'll just ask them when they next come to HQ. I mean, they don't know that we've caught them, right?" Hilary asked.

"Hopefully not. I trust Pat not to betray us. Jabez might send them here for more spying business."

"I knew Pat was suspicious, guys. The other day in the library, I just walked past a shelf I had walked by a minute ago and there she was. Sitting there reading a book as if it was so normal," Ava yelled.

"Then why didn't you tell us, Ava?" Ruby asked.

"Must have forgotten, I'm terribly sorry really," Ava said, looking at her feet.

Nora had a flashback to the 'dream' she'd had. It was real, obviously.

"It's fine, Ava. Pat and Lucy have tricked us all. We don't blame you," Ruby said.

"Now, what do we do? Sit around and wait for them to show up?" Jane asked.

"I have a better idea. Let's open the tracking system for HQ. And let's set an alarm for when Lucy/Pat enter the HQ. *But* let the alarm be silent and only ring in mine and Ruby's ears. Meanwhile, y'all can just continue with practice, reading, learning and everything you do. Though, do remember, the battle planning meeting is still scheduled for today.

"Nora, if you can, get Pat to give us a map of Jabez's HQ," Hilary said. "Everyone, start working. Oh, and I will just allow Pat and Lucy's access to HQ for today, we need them to arrive today."

Everyone nodded and set off in different directions. Few to the library, few to the practice rooms, few to their bedrooms. There was not a place in the building which was not filled with people. Nora headed off to her own room. She opened a book and started scribbling some ideas in it. She thought of every single piece of information she knew about Jabez and his headquarters. She noted down everything she could remember and made diagrams.

"Hey," Sia said, entering the room. "It's been three hours and you're still writing in your book? Come on, come to the library with me. Mia's there too. We thought of reading some books together. Maybe we can compare notes too."

"Cool idea, but how about you get some books from the library here and do it?" Nora asked.

"Cool, I'll do it right now." Sia quickly left the room.

Mia and Sia both came into the room after fifteen minutes. Both of them held huge stacks of books. And they started planning.

Hilary paced the room while Ruby was sitting. "I don't believe it. How could they?"

"This is the tenth time you've said it, Hilary," Ruby said. She was growing tired of it.

"But still. I put my *trust* in Pat. I *trusted* her, and she betrayed me."

"She betrayed all of us."

"I stood up for her, and look at how she repaid me."

"You do know, right, that she is a spy for us now?"

"You yourself said she could be tricking us."

"Hilary, calm down. I know this is hard for you but it's hard for me too."

"Okay, let's think straight. Now, the battle planning meeting is scheduled for five in the evening. But if Pat and Lucy arrive just a little earlier, we might have to cancel it. And another thing, how will we tackle them? Just say, 'Hey guys! We know you are evil and work for Jabez.'?"

"They might just try to get away, you know. We have no plan whatsoever for this. How about we just let *them* confess. We will be cold and ignorant to them, until they break."

"Yeah, I bet you have a lot of experience of that." Hilary snorted. "Look, I can't just do that, knowing that they betrayed us. I can't. Sorry, I can't."

"I don't know what else we *can* do."

"We'll just confront her and tell her to explain herself. Of course, we can't trap her because then, the longer she stays here, the more secrets she has of ours. We can't put up a shield either. The only other thing we *can* do is give them all of their stuff and kick them out maybe." Hilary sighed. "I have no idea."

"It's a good plan actually, I like it. Even if it *does* seem like we are doing absolutely nothing, we can't do anything else now, can we?"

"Yeah. I'm sure the girls will understand."

"So, let's go tell them?" Ruby asked.

Hilary went to the control room where all the headquarter barriers, water supply, trackers, and everything else was. She spoke into the communication mic, "GIRLS, LISTEN UP! WE HAVE A PLAN TO TACKLE PAT AND LUCY. MEETING ROOM. NOW."

All the girls rushed to the meeting room.

Hilary started explaining what the idea was, "And then, we deny their access to headquarters, so they are immediately thrown out."

"I like it," Jane said. "And it's the only thing we can do."

"But I told you guys, Pat is on our side," Nora yelled, annoyed.

"Nora, I'm sorry. But we can't trust her, she could be tricking you. Working as a triple agent. We don't know enough to trust her. I'm sorry," Ruby apologised.

Nora looked tired. "Fine."

"Does anyone have any other ideas?" Hilary asked.

Everyone shook their heads.

"Okay, then," Ruby said. "Meeting dismissed."

***

Pat teleported back to Jabez's headquarters. Now, she had to spy on Jabez. What if he read her mind? Then what would he do to Crystal? She faced him in the throne room.

"You're back," Jabez said.

"I couldn't find her, Your Majesty," Pat said. "I'd expected that. Why would she stay in the woods? She's gone to the Saveup headquarters, obviously."

"Is there any solid evidence she's at the headquarters?"

"No," Pat lied.

"Then you should go and check."

"What about Lucy?"

"Take her with you."

Pat nodded and bowed. She left the room and went to search for Lucy.

"Hey, Lucy," Pat said, walking into Lucy's room.

Lucy scowled. "Hi."

"Um, so Nora escaped," Pat said, not sure how to break the news.

Lucy jumped to her feet. "WHAT?"

"Yeah," Pat said.

"How?"

Pat told Lucy about the lightning thing. Lucy was convinced that it was all Pat's fault. Pat barely managed to keep her cool.

"Jabez has asked us to go to the Saveup HQ and check," Pat finished.

"But what if Nora *is* there?" Lucy asked.

"Then we teleport back here and stay here."

Lucy glared at Pat. "Fine," she said. "Let's go."

The two of them teleported away.

46. The Thieves

When the two entered the Saveup headquarters, everything seemed perfectly normal. Until Ruby and Hilary pounced on them.

"We know you both are the traitors," Ruby said bitterly. As soon as the alarm had rung in her and Hilary's ears, they'd called the entire Saveup. And when she finished speaking, the rest of the Saveup gathered behind her and Ruby.

"What—" Lucy started. *How could they have known? Was Nora back already?* If so, she had to act quickly. She glanced at Pat. Pat nodded. They moved back a couple steps so it would be easier to make a run for it.

"Don't try to run. We're not going to hurt you. We just want to talk. Want to know why you turned," Ruby said.

"Does Hannah know?" Lucy whispered, her heart turning cold with fear.

"They all know," Hilary said.

"No," Lucy whispered. It couldn't be, this just couldn't be happening.

"There's always a price for your actions, Lucy," Ruby said. "Always."

"So, she's back, is she?" Pat asked.

"Nora? Yes. She's back all right," Hilary said.

Lucy's heart sank. All her sisters knew. She was a disappointment to them now. But she didn't regret it. They had never liked her anyway, had they? Still, there was something at the bottom of her heart, a tiny tug. The love for her sisters. *Stop it, Lucy. They don't love you,* she thought.

"Have our families been told?" Pat asked, her voice barely a whisper. Now, she was actually worried.

Ruby shared a look with Hilary. "Not yet."

"Do you want us to?" Hilary asked, though she already knew the answer.

"No!" Lucy and Pat yelled together.

Ruby slipped into the crowd behind. She found Nora and whispered to her, "Is Pat just a really good actor or has she actually betrayed us?"

"I don't believe that she'd betray me. Not again. Not after what she told me."

"I guess, but she's really acting well. I didn't believe at all that she's turned good again. Stuff like that; it just doesn't happen."

"Yeah, you better go back now. Otherwise, they'll get suspicious."

"Are you gonna let us stay? We have nowhere else to go," Lucy cried.

"Of course not," Hannah said, coming to the front. "I can't believe it, Lucy, you're my twin. My sister."

"We can't let you stay here. It would be foolish. You would just give more of our secrets to Jabez. It's obvious you're spying on us. Now, I understand what the mysterious disappearances were about," Hilary said calmly.

"Besides," Nora said, "you can stay at Jabez's palace. I'm sure he would welcome you both with open arms."

"We've already packed all of your stuff, with the help of your roommates. We will deny your access to headquarters. Forever," Ruby said.

"But before that, we have decided to give you both time to say goodbye and have a little chat with your family and friends," Hilary said.

Hannah stepped out of the crowd and pulled Lucy towards all the Wells sisters.

"How could you, Lucy? We stood up for you when you were in trouble. But that was also a plan to throw the Saveup off, wasn't it? You were following orders, not making mistakes. That map," Bell yelled.

"Don't touch me," Lucy yelled. "You're no family of mine. You were all always mean and rude. And now you're my enemy."

"Lucy!" Bell screamed.

"I can't believe it. You're supposed to be my twin. And now look at you. I thought we were friends. And now you call me your enemy? Just forget it," Hannah said. She ran away, unable to stop her tears. Unable to face Lucy.

"Yes, it was part of the plan," Lucy said. "You stood up for me when I was already working for Jabez, not before that. Not when I needed it."

"We are your sisters. We always stood up for you," Violet screeched.

"Look at what you've done. We'll have to tell Mother and Father about this. You've broken the family. It will never be the same," Bell said.

"Who even cares?" Lucy raged. "It doesn't matter. It never did." She turned away and left. She went over to where her belongings were kept and sat in a corner with them.

Pat rushed forward. "You know I was just acting, right?" she whispered.

"You seemed very convincing," Ruby said.

"Thank you?" Pat said.

"We can't trust you," Hilary said. "I hope you understand."

Pat looked down. "Yeah," she said. "Yeah, I understand." She knew she should have expected this, but she still felt pretty sad. She felt like she was a disappointment to everybody. To be honest, she was, wasn't she? She had just betrayed them all to Jabez.

"Pat, you idiot," Jane cried. She ran up to Pat and punched her arm. "How dare you. I trusted you. I helped you. I thought we were friends."

"I'm sorry," Pat cried. "I really am. I made the wrong decision, I know. Jabez won't give me anything I need or want."

"I know you're supposed to be good and all now, but really? How could you?" Luna said, careful to make sure her voice didn't reach Lucy.

"I wanted more power," Pat said. "And I needed to protect my family after what happened to my mother." Her voice cracked. *No, you can't break down now. Not here, not in front of everyone*, Pat steeled herself.

"What happened to her?" Luna whispered.

Pat shook her head. "Not now. No time." She was shaking.

"Take your stuff and go back with Lucy. If you ever need to communicate, come outside our HQ and touch the boundaries, just your fingertips. And we'll know it's you," Ruby said. "Bye now."

Pat nodded. She took her stuff and walked over to Lucy. "Let's go," she said. Lucy got up. The two of them walked out of the boundaries and teleported away.

Nora watched as the two figures of Pat and Lucy disappeared into thin air. She turned and fled to her room. She ran up the stairs and went to her room. She needed some time alone. Some time to think.

***

"This is bad," Jabez said. He was trying to calm down, but it didn't work. He threw a chair at a bookshelf in the library. "THIS IS HORRIBLE. IT'S ALL YOUR FAULT, KAWSE. This would have never happened if you hadn't let her escape."

"It wasn't my fault," Pat cried. "You told me to use the lightning. I didn't do it on purpose."

"Shut up!" Jabez yelled. "Don't try to make excuses. You can't do anything good anyway. Both of you have no use to me anymore. Go to your rooms and don't come out unless I need you. My guards will provide food. Out! Now!"

Lucy put her head down. "Let's go, Pat," she mumbled.

"No, Lucy. We don't have to be all weak," Pat said. "Don't let him crush you."

Lucy nodded. "I guess," she said and dragged Pat away to her room.

When they left, Jabez headed to his room. He was in a rage of destroying things. This planet had rebelled against him too much. *Time to show them how powerful their ruler actually was.*

Pat was in her room in Jabez's headquarters when a guard came and informed her she had some work to do. Jabez had sent some papers with instructions. Battle ideas against Saveup. She put down her lotlit and thought. She felt very guilty, being a double agent was so hard. She knew the Saveup's weaknesses and how to plot against them.

But if she had to keep the other side of her identity safe, she had to give the ideas too. Though now that she was loyal to the Saveup, she couldn't betray them either. Then again, her little sister's life was on the line against an entire planet's.

"Ugh! I can't do this," Pat yelled, frustrated. She threw her lotlit.

"Can't do what?" a voice asked. The door burst open.

Pat jumped and turned. She gulped. It was Jabez. "Uh—I—"

"Tell me now," Jabez demanded.

"I can't think of battle ideas," Pat lied.

"Really?" Jabez asked, and eyed Pat suspiciously.

"Yes."

"Well, then. Only one thing left to do. I'll have to put you with Westie and Jorny for now. You can go and get some ideas and inspiration from them. But I trust all you need to do is think hard, because if you are truly loyal to me, you should know everything about the Saveup. Westie and Jorny have many good ideas. Go team up with them for now."

Jabez twirled one of his hands. "Oh, and tell them they have to throw something at the barrier and it will break because I lifted the charm. Are you sure you can't do this on your own?"

A sudden thought struck Pat. Jabez had manipulated the Cloy twins. That meant she might be able to turn them good. "Uh, yes. I'll go and talk to them."

"Okay then." Jabez disappeared.

Pat quickly gathered her lotlit, papers and all the other stationery and went to the Cloys' room. She knocked on the door. "Guys, open up. It's me, Pat."

Silence. Pat knocked again. This time, a scared Jorny opened the door and poked his head out.

"It's okay. Jabez sent me here. I'm supposed to tell you to throw something at the barrier so it will break because Jabez lifted the charm."

"Okay," Jorny said. He closed the door. He threw something and then opened the door again. "Hi, come on in."

Pat nodded and slipped inside the room. She looked around the room. Slowly, two rooms were merging into the same old cramped up room Pat had seen the last time she was here. She kept her things on one of the desks. "I know this is none of my business, but why did Jabez punish you guys like this?" she asked.

Westie quickly explained to Pat what had happened, "And then, he got all angry and bossy and put us in this situation as a punishment."

"Oh, I'll tell you my side of the story," Pat said. She too shared what Jabez had done. Then she complained how Jabez had told her and Lucy not to come out of their rooms because of the Nora incident.

"Yeah. I did hear that Nora escaped. Though no one told us the whole story," Westie said.

Jorny wasn't listening to what everybody was saying. He was looking down, his face bearing an expression of pain.

"Hey," Pat said, nudging Jorny. "What happened?"

"Nothing," Jorny murmured, not looking up.

Westie sighed. "He's been like this ever since Jabez punished us. He thinks it was all his fault that he went and interrupted Indsey and Kommy. Really, Jorny. It wasn't your fault."

"It was," Jorny muttered.

"Hey, don't be all like that, Jorny. And what if it was? Jabez's problem. Am I right?" Pat glanced at Westie.

"Yeah, Pat's right, Jorny. Cheer up," Westie said.

"Okay, okay. By the way, why'd you come here?" Jorny asked.

"Oh! Um, Jabez wanted me to brainstorm some battle ideas with you guys. But I also wanted to just have a chat," Pat stuttered. Now came the tough part, turning Westie and Jorny to the good side.

"Right," Westie said, eyeing Pat suspiciously.

"Look, Jabez just sent me here because I need to inspire myself to get ideas, blah blah blah. So, can you help me?" Pat asked.

"Yeah, sure," Jorny said.

"Hey, don't you ever think about how sad the families of the people Jabez kills would feel?" Pat asked. She was diving in too deep waters, she knew it. Not only because it was suspicious but also because she was risking her own secrets. She had to go slow but couldn't. "Like what if someday he did that to your family?"

"Well, except our parents; we did have this aunt and two small cousins. I don't know what I'd do if they too—" Jorny said.

"I know this is none of my business, but why didn't you refuse Jabez's offer and go search for your family instead?" Pat asked.

Westie went silent. Jorny looked at his feet.

"Sorry, I didn't mean to—" Pat apologised.

"No, it's okay. Well, I just thought that at the moment, Jabez was the only one who could protect us. I was scared. I had to protect Jorny," Westie confessed.

Pat whispered, "Do you ever wish you never worked for Jabez?"

Westie looked taken aback. "Uh, hey, is that the time? We should start battle planning." She glanced nervously at Jorny. Westie got up and went to one of the desks. She opened the drawer and got out some papers and stationery. "Here, Pat, you can sit on one of these desks with us. I'll just summon another chair." Westie muttered a spell, and a chair was suddenly in front of her.

Pat nodded slowly and sat on the chair. She put it near a desk and set up her things. Jorny did the same.

"We should start with what we would do if the Saveup did a surprise attack on us," Westie said.

Westie, Pat and Jorny discussed ideas, noted them down and spent a few hours on it.

Ugh, now I have to go. And I haven't even turned them to the good side even a bit. Though why was Westie suddenly so jumpy and scared when I mentioned not working for Jabez? There's some mystery here all right, Pat thought to herself as she left the Cloys' room. She went to her own room.

The next day, the Cloys came to visit Pat.

"Hey," Pat said, smiling. "What's up?"

"Nothing much," Jorny said.

"Um, we thought of what you said yesterday," Westie said nervously.

Pat stopped smiling. "Uh. Yeah?"

"I understand what you were saying," Westie said. "But why did you ask? Did *you* ever think about changing sides?" Her eyes narrowed suspiciously.

"No," Pat cried, a little too loudly.

"Right, definitely not suspicious," Westie said.

"No, I mean, it's just that I'm Jabez's daughter and all right now; so why would I ever want to betray him? Betray all this power?" Pat lied. After a minute, she sighed. "The thing is, he *has* attacked my family."

"What!" Jorny and Westie yelled at the same time.

"Maybe 'attacked' is a bit of an exaggeration, but he captured my little sister Crystal," Pat said.

Jorny looked horrified.

"Why would he do that?" Westie asked.

"To have leverage over me," Pat said, unable to hide her anger. "So that I don't leave his cause. She's just SEVEN."

"What? Why?" Jorny said. "That's terrible."

"Seven," Pat yelled again. "That's how young she is."

No one said anything as Pat calmed down.

"I just wanted to know if he's been doing anything against you guys. I think that separating two of his followers is pretty cruel."

"Do you, now?" someone from the door said. All three of them jumped back.

"Yes, I do," Pat screamed.

"You really think your little talk will turn the Cloys out of my service? You think I would just leave you unguarded after you let Nora escape?" Jabez asked.

"I don't care. I'm leaving now," Pat shouted. "*Languae—*"

"But have you forgotten about Crystal?" Jabez asked, smirking.

Pat stood there, frozen in shock. Suddenly, a mighty *BOOM* shook the castle.

A guard ran into the room. "Your Majesty!" he shouted. "The Saveup has attacked."

47. More Than Saveup

Jabez barked at the guard, "Take the zombies and every single resource we have and fight back. Defend the headquarters. Evacuate everyone and tell them to help."

The guard nodded and ran away.

"I have a deal, Pat. If you fight by my side in this war, I might just consider letting your sister go," Jabez said.

Pat gasped. She hesitated. She couldn't just let her sister die. She just couldn't. "Okay," is all she could manage.

"Well then, come on. We need to fight back," Jabez yelled. He ran, the others at his tail.

***

When Jabez arrived on the scene, there seemed to be more than just the Saveup. There seemed to be the entire Anlemiss. They had splashes of different colours all over their armour. There was MAGISIS written in sparkly white letters on their abdomen. Jabez sprang into action. His rage was a force in itself.

He drew himself to the height of twenty-five feet, made weird actions, said spells; every single piece of magic he knew, he used. He was sure he couldn't lose. His guards and zombies outnumbered the Anlemissians, the people of Anlemiss.

More and more Anlemissians fell dead or unconscious. There were too many people on Jabez's side, and they knew it. But they didn't stop fighting back. This was their home. And they would fight to the death for it. For their children, family, friends. It wasn't like Jabez's army wasn't facing any losses. They had been heavily affected too. But since there were more of them, they had the upper hand.

Nora fought back with all her might. Every time she moved, she looked for where Pat was. She tried to find out if Pat was harming Jabez's army from inside. But she couldn't see her anywhere. No one created chaos in the middle of the zombies and armoured guards. Her hopes slowly thinned. What if Pat had really just lied to her and had betrayed them again?

Pat sneaked back into the headquarters. Jabez didn't notice her. He was too busy fighting and laughing and raging evil. Pat knew this was right. She had to do it, take the risks. She ran to her sister's prison. "Crystal," she whispered.

"Pat? Save me." Crystal sobbed.

"I'm sorry. I don't have access to this door. I'll put a protection spell on you, but I will have to destroy this prison. This entire place," Pat whispered. After muttering a protection spell on Crystal, she shouted, "*Destrucmasa!*" Pointing to the prison.

The tiny room in which Crystal was, exploded. But the bars remained intact. "Crystal. The roof. Climb up your bunk bed and escape. You know basic magic. Help others. Use the spell I used and tell others to use it too. As soon as you can, run home and alert Dad. Tell him that I told you guys to flee," Pat cried.

"No, I can't leave you here," Crystal screamed.

"You'll have to. But I will come back and find you," Pat promised. "Leave now. I'm going to try exploding the entire headquarters,"

Crystal sobbed. She couldn't do anything else. It was her only option. She wiped her tears and nodded. She escaped her prison. Pat used Destrucmasa to destroy random rooms. She ran and ran, kept exploding rooms. She told all the maids and other workers to run and save themselves. She had to keep her promises. Had to make her family proud.

But the more spells she used, the more her energy drained. Still, she kept going. She didn't stop. After the last explosion, she levitated herself out the window and landed in the battle. She glanced back, the headquarters was in ruins.

The people of Anlemiss were even lesser now. They needed help. And fast. But there was no one coming. No magical saviour entering the battle. They couldn't keep going. They'd be wiped out. They had to change their strategy.

"*You!*" Jabez shouted at Pat. "I still have your sister. And I will kill her, your family, your friends. I will leave nobody you care about alive."

"I released her. And she and your prisoners have fled. You'll never *ever* again harm those who I love," Pat screamed. "This is for Magisis." Pat turned a strand of her hair into a large missile and threw it at Jabez.

Jabez dodged. He was about to attack Pat. But he got distracted by something in the sky. The sky darkened as fifty large dark shapes crossed the sun. Everyone stopped fighting and looked up to check what was happening.

Then, the people of Anlemiss started cheering. Pat squinted at them as they got closer, trying to make out what they were. Were they spaceships? The spaceships were GINORMOUS. It looked like someone had rounded up everyone from the solar system and had brought them to Magisis. Because they had. One very bold—and powerful—person had.

Jabez roared in rage and yelled, "Attack the spaceships!"

Almost everyone from his army concentrated their magic or weapons on the ships. But its metal was strong, and nothing happened to them. The Anlemissians used it as a distraction and started aiming their worst spells at the army, knocking them down in large amounts. Jabez's army was forced to point their attention away from the ships.

The ships opened and thousands of people wearing jetpacks floated down. They all were wearing some kind of armour. The people with creepy dark brown, maroon and red armour had TACHÉL embroidered on the sides of their helmets. Those who had a half-open helmet and armour, with a mixture of peaceful shades of blue and green with spots of white that looked like clouds, had NEGOFER written on their jetpacks.

People with heavy neon yellow and orange armour had LEPROMIN written on their thigh armours. There were some people even from Magisis. The rest of the gang had flashy purple and dark grey armour with SELPLY embroidered in silver on their chests.

Pat was *amazed.* The Saveup had called for reinforcements from other planets. Now, they had so many people on their side. But Jabez's army was as large as ever. What if they couldn't defeat Jabez? Pat was losing hope. What could she do? She jumped into battle, attacking Jabez's army. Now at least, her side stood a chance.

Somewhere else, Hilary was defending herself against three guards at once. And in another corner stood Jane and Luna, fighting ten zombies together. And right in the middle of the war, stood Jabez. He was yelling and shooting spells at everyone around him. Whoever dared fight Jabez, ended up dead or critically injured.

Near Jabez was Gonger. He was fighting Ruby and losing terribly. Suddenly, one spaceship which hadn't opened up yet, zoomed right above their heads. It turned and a figure jumped out of it, levitating in mid-air. It was Uncle James.

48. Kommy

Nora ran towards her uncle and lifted up in the air. She crushed him with a hug. "Uncle!" she cried.

"My sweet Nora," Uncle James said. He hugged her back. "I will keep you safe," and then jumped into the battle.

Jabez quickly recovered from the sight of Uncle James and continued with the battle. The Saveup had set up camp not too far from the battle. Thankfully, it was hidden from Jabez. Over there, all the wounded were being healed and those not fighting, like small children, were taking refuge. When the other planets arrived, those at camp expanded it.

The war continued into the next day. But in the middle, people would slip away, and others would replace them. The fight didn't end in the night, it just kept going on and on. Everyone rested now and then but neither of the sides gave up. At midnight, while Pat was busy fighting off a horde of zombies, Nora approached her.

"Go to the camp and take some rest. I'll fight off these zombies," Nora cried, aiming a spell at a few zombies.

"I can't," Pat cried.

"Your family's come to visit you, go," Nora said.

Pat froze in place. She quickly nodded and ran off. Some healers took Pat to a bed in the camp. She had cuts everywhere and was limping. Crystal spotted Pat. Her light grey eyes twinkled. Her dark blue hair with streaks of very light grey was braided. Crystal ran towards Pat and hugged her.

"We were so worried about you. Dad and Jayden were about to go and search for you." Jayden was Pat's twelve-year-old younger brother.

"What?" Pat croaked.

"Yeah," Crystal said. "Wait, there they are. DAD! JAYDEN! PAT'S HERE!"

A man who looked in late thirties turned to Crystal. He ran and hugged her. "Don't you dare worry us again like that. When the Saveup set camp over here, they told me you were spying on Jabez from the inside. Do you have any idea how dangerous that was?" The man scolded Pat. He was Mr Kawse.

"Sorry, Dad," Pat cried.

"Anyway, guys, listen to me. I mixed some chemicals and made a potion that can blow up stuff. I should go try it on somebody." Jayden beamed enthusiastically. He looked very similar to Pat except he had blue-green hair.

"Jayden, we have a spell for that," Mr Kawse said.

"Yeah, but this can explode people and go through armour," Jayden said.

"Guys, you can't go out there. Wait, where's Gran?" Pat asked.

"Sleeping, it's midnight, sweet pea!" Mr Kawse exclaimed.

Suddenly, Hilary ran to Pat. "Pat, we need you outside. ASAP!"

Pat ran after Hilary. They were struggling. Nora was trying to defend herself from ten guards. Alice and Daisy were trying to confuse five zombies by disappearing and reappearing in different places. At least forty people from Tachél were winning against twenty zombies. Jane was trying her best to defend herself but was losing strength.

"Jane, go back to camp. I'll fight these zombies. Go," Pat cried. She jumped in front of Jane. "*Vaporizar!*" Instantly, the zombies turned into zombie soup.

Sally was shouting insults at all the guards and zombies while running from them. Andrea was battling against Sarah. "*Nesciusement!*" Andrea yelled. *Don't think about it. She isn't your friend, it's okay to fight here*, she repeatedly reminded herself.

Sarah deflected the spell by making a force-field.

"*Flammae!*" Ruby cried, pointing at zombies.

The zombies caught fire and then turned to dust. Ruby summoned water and put out the fire on the grass.

"Surrender now, citizens of Magisis and other planets. Or more of you will die for no reason. How much ever you fight against me, it will not matter. I am undefeatable," Jabez bellowed. He made some movement with his hand and forty people who were battling against him froze and dropped dead to the ground.

But no one gave up. The people of Magisis weren't letting Jabez stomp on their freedom and magic. Those from other planets weren't letting him get away with all the damage he'd done to their respective planets either. No matter how strong he was, he was still the destroyer of many lives.

Nora was tired as she had fought through the night. She wanted to take a break but at the same time, wanted to keep going. Jabez had killed her parents. And she was going to make him pay.

Sia wanted to run over to where Jabez towered and throw killing spells at him until he died. He'd dared to kill her brother. But she didn't. She held her ground and had to fight off the waves of zombies and guards first.

Westie hesitated as the battle raged around her. She couldn't believe Jabez had captured Pat's sister. How could he do that to someone so young? And how could she fight for him once she knew how cruel he could actually be? Separating her from Jorny wasn't the nicest thing in the world either. He'd done a lot of evil. She looked at Jorny and knew he understood her. They would fight against Jabez. As Westie charged into battle, she knew she was doing the right thing.

Hannah felt heartbroken as she saw her twin sister fighting for the enemy. There was nothing more she wanted to do than run to her and hug her. The best she could hope for was that she wouldn't have to fight Lucy, because she wasn't sure if she'd be able to face her.

Lucy wasn't thinking of what she was doing. Her mind was set on one thing. Destroy the enemy. She didn't care who she was fighting. If the person wasn't on her side, she was going to kill them. Days passed. The war kept going.

Gonger was using sound waves to leave the enemy stumbling and disoriented. He laughed as a group of five people stumbled to their knees and begged him for mercy.

Kommy was sitting in Jabez's camp. She was drawing all sorts of horrible creatures and then bringing them to life to defeat the Saveup. Everyone gasped as a huge dragon blowing flames rose from Jabez's camp. It flew over to where the people of Magisis were and started blowing flames everywhere. Suddenly, it swooped into the ground and crushed many people with its sharp claws.

"*Encogerse!*" Ava yelled, pointing to the dragon. The dragon shrank by an inch. Maybe more.

"*Hacer Tinta!*" Rose shouted, pointing her finger and moving it in random places. The dragon got splashed with so much ink, it stumbled.

Other people also started shouting spells at the dragon. The people from Selply zoomed up and started hitting the dragon with their weapons. But more creatures rose from Jabez's camp, and more people were forced to shift their focus away from Jabez's army on the ground. Hilary went back to the camp and called for reinforcements.

"*Minuo!*" Jane yelled, pointing her fingers at different creatures at once. They at once got cuts and bruises and started to bleed.

"*Ecoutroler!*" Andrea yelled at the dragon. She concentrated as she controlled the dragon's mind to hurt itself.

After taking a lot of damage, the dragon finally fell. But more creatures came from Jabez's camp.

"We need to disable Kommy. Stop her from making these creatures," Pat cried.

"Leave that to me," Indsey said, flying towards Pat. "I'm on your side now, I'll go kill Kommy."

"Wha—" Pat began. But she was interrupted as guards attacked her.

Indsey snuck into Jabez's tent, going into stealth mode. She slipped into the room where Kommy was and used a spell to make all of her paper and pencils disappear.

"WHAT?" Kommy screamed, turning around. "*You!*"

Indsey used a spell and threw Kommy backwards. "Oops." Indsey smirked.

"Oh, you will regret that," Kommy yelled.

"Ha-ha, what *can* you do, Locks? Draw something?" Indsey gave a cold laugh. "Sorry, darling. You're powerless against me."

"I can make other non-living things come to life. Just watch. I'll make you pay for all the misery you have made me face."

Indsey ignored her and used another spell to make Kommy bang her head into the wall continuously.

"Make! That! STOP!" Kommy screamed. She twirled her hand and whispered to a chunk in the wall to keep hitting Indsey until she was dead.

But Indsey exploded the piece of wall.

"Table, keep charging at Indsey until she is so weak, she can't even stand," Kommy said this so suddenly, Indsey didn't have time to register and the table charged straight at Indsey.

Indsey clutched her stomach as pain shot through her body. Through gritted teeth, she muttered a spell that made Kommy slap herself. Kommy somehow resisted for a second, while she whispered to the chair to fly to Indsey's head and crash over it.

Indsey dodged the chair but accidentally came in the path of the table. As she stood there, the table charged at Indsey. It did so many more times before Indsey could do anything. Indsey crumpled to the floor.

"Ha! Who's weak now?" Kommy cried.

Indsey slowly got up, trying to ignore the pain. The table had stopped charging at her. Indsey felt anger like she had never felt before. It was boiling inside her. "You are going to pay." Indsey twirled her hand.

Kommy let out an ear-piercing scream. She felt like someone had stabbed her in the gut. Blood soaked her clothes. She wasn't going to give up now. "Every single object in this room, come to life. Do not rest until you have destroyed Inds—"

Indsey quickly shot a spell at Kommy, which made her vocal cords stop working. Kommy opened and closed her mouth like a goldfish, no words coming out. But the spell wasn't strong enough as it was used in haste. Kommy used all her energy to fight the spell and finally spoke, "Indsey Opal, I swear on my life, I will not rest until I kill you." She ran at Indsey.

Indsey moved out of the way as Kommy ran into the wall. "Give up, Kommy. Don't force me to kill you." *Even though I want to.* "I'm no longer that kind of person. Kommy, please."

"No, I will kill *you*!" Kommy roared.

Indsey had no other choice. She whispered a spell at Kommy. Kommy froze. She swayed and fell to the ground, breathing her last.

49. Twins

Indsey sobbed. She couldn't help it. "I used to like annoying you. You were like a sister to me. Except, we always fought. Oh, Kommy." Indsey buried her face in her hands. She fell to her knees and sobbed over Kommy.

Everyone was glad that the creatures had stopped coming. But Jabez wasn't. Why had Kommy stopped? He sent a guard to check what had happened. Indsey looked up as a guard entered. "Please, don't tell Dad," she whispered.

As the guard turned to leave, Indsey made the guard faint. She put him in a corner and left. But she took Kommy's body to the Saveup's camp. The healers there agreed to bury Kommy. Indsey left the tent to go back into the battle. Fighting against Jabez's guards even though she was battered and bruised.

"Indsey, you need to rest. Get changed, get some armour. Rest. You're bleeding everywhere. Indsey, please," Westie cried.

Indsey regretfully left the battle. Even though she knew they were losing, she had to get healed. Nora, Jane and Luna were outnumbered in battle against many guards.

"Stop this," Jane cried. "Don't you all have a family too? Stop working for Jabez and help us. Think what your families would feel when they figured you were evil."

The guards hesitated. Three out of five guards froze. Nora had aimed unconscious spells at the other two. The remaining conscious guards ran off and miraculously fought against a few zombies.

"Guys, try to turn the guards to our side. Ask the people at camp to try and get more people. We're outnumbered and we can't let people die like this," Nora whispered. "If you can, get the entire Saveup in the battle. Whoever is resting, if they can, get them here."

Jane and Luna nodded. Jane ran towards camp and Luna went to convince more guards. A few people from the planet Selply were fighting against Jabez's guards. They had no magic but were naturally very strong.

Super-strength was their power. They had weapons and more cool things to fight. One of the guys punched Jabez's guard so hard that his jaw broke.

It seemed to go on forever. But the people against Jabez *were* slowly convincing guards against him. It was working. Slowly, but steadily, the people fighting for freedom leaned towards getting the upper hand. But they were all very tired and had to take shifts fighting while Jabez's zombies didn't. Which was why the losses continued.

Emma and Mary were fighting Jabez's army, standing back-to-back. They kept rotating because they were surrounded by at least a dozen guards. Suddenly, when Emma had just turned, hardly any time to register that Jabez, who was near her, was sending a spell at her, Emma froze. Mary glanced back at her best friend. Emma stopped moving and then crumpled to the ground, the sound of her last breath echoing in Mary's ears.

Mary screamed in rage. She tried to make her way towards Jabez, but a couple of people in blue and green armour landed in front of her. The people of Negofer. They were trying to *stop* her from attacking Jabez after he'd killed her best friend.

A couple of large trees shot up in between Jabez and Mary. The people of Negofer were using their power over nature. Jabez started uprooting them immediately. One of them grabbed her, the other grabbed Emma and they shot into the air.

"No!" Mary yelled, trying to twist out of their grasp. "He killed Emma."

"You can't charge at Jabez," one of them said kindly. "We've been trying to keep as many people away from him as we can. We don't really fight. Protection comes naturally to us, though."

"But—" Mary began.

"I am so sorry for your friend," said the one holding Emma. "We'll get you to safety in the camp."

Mary wanted to argue, but deep down, she knew that they were right. She didn't stand a chance against Jabez alone. They let Mary carry Emma's body inside the camp. Mary was very angry but as quickly as it came, it vanished. As she put Emma down, she sobbed, thinking about all the happy memories they had ever shared. She sank to her knees and cried, hugging the lifeless shape of Emma. Mary slowly got up and took Emma to the healers. The healers took one glance at her and knew what had happened.

"Purple burial flowers," Mary whispered to them.

Now, she understood what Nora felt. After a while, she returned to the war, but this time with anger burning in her veins.

Jayden was getting very worried about Pat. She'd been fighting for so long with hardly any break. He wanted to make sure she was alright. He'd begged his dad to let him help them and Pat. But his dad had said that he was too young. He couldn't rest while there was a war. He h'ad to do something. Jayden got up slowly and glanced at Crystal. She was sleeping.

"I'll be back soon," he said to her. He sneaked out of the camp's back entrance. The night was cold, and colours of battle flashed to his right. He could hear the sounds of people yelling spells and other war cries. The trees to his left seemed eerie. He shivered and kept going.

Jayden felt nervous as he stepped into the battlefield. A cold feeling went up his spine. *You can do it, don't back out now. This is for Mom, this is for Pat*, he willed himself on, overcoming his fear. He used all the spells he knew which could do damage. Jayden approached a person from Selply losing against two guards.

He instantly took down one of the guards and then, turned his attention to another battle. As he glanced to his right, he saw the large shape of Jabez. He tried to run but he was too slow. He tripped and fell on his face. Jayden tried to get up, but his leg had twisted. He raised his hands to say a spell, but it was too late.

"This is because of what your sister did," Jabez boomed. He pointed at Jayden.

Jayden felt pain shoot through his entire body. It was too much to bear, he tried to hang on but couldn't. He said one last spell, which was pointed at Jabez. "*Exitium Extrema*," he whispered. And those were his last words. He closed his eyes, letting himself feel that he'd made a difference.

A large explosion boomed at Jabez's feet. Then, a person from Negofer swooped in, grabbed Jayden and took him back to the shelter of the camp.

Crystal was sitting on a bed near the entrance of camp. She was waiting for Pat or her dad to come back. Jayden had disappeared and she was worried sick. She glanced up as a person from Negofer entered. She glanced at the body in the person's hands. "Jayden!" She sobbed and ran.

The person holding Jayden gently put the body down on the ground.

Crystal knelt next to Jayden. "What have you done to yourself?" she cried. "Dad told you not to leave. But you never listened." She closed her eyes and sobbed. She didn't know how long she sat there, crying. Sometime later, she took Jayden inside, getting blue burial flowers and sitting by his side. She fell asleep but was awoken by a voice.

"Jayden!" Pat screamed. She ran towards Crystal. "What happened?"

"I was sitting there. Waiting for you or Dad to come, Jayden had disappeared while I was sleeping. Then I looked up and a person from Negofer came in. Holding Jayden." Crystal's voice cracked.

Mr Kawse came in later and everything was explained to him. He stumbled to a chair, shocked. Why did this keep happening to him? First his wife, now his son. Mr Kawse buried his face in his hands.

Uncle James was winning in battle. He was swift, clever and powerful. He tried his level-best and didn't give up. Seldom would he take a break. He kept fighting, determination running through his body. He had a goal—protect Magisis from Jabez. Keep Nora alive. He had had years of training and loads of magic.

But this wasn't enough. He seemed to be failing at his goal. As his energy drained, it was getting harder to keep fighting. Uncle James got weaker and weaker. Finally, someone managed to get him to the camp and forced him to rest.

Soon however, he was back in the battle. As he fought off many zombies and guards, he slowly neared Jabez. He knew he couldn't win against Jabez but he could at least try. He wasn't going to run. Uncle James fought, using his own size against Jabez. He slipped underneath Jabez's feet, used tricks to confuse him and hit him with spells.

But it was very tiring because Jabez had just come back from a break while Uncle James had been fighting for long. Using all the remaining energy he had, Uncle James slashed at Jabez with a sword and hit him with spells continuously. But it didn't work. Jabez hit Uncle James with the spell of death. He stumbled, as his vision blurred and noticed Nora near him.

Nora ran to him. "No. Uncle, stay awake. Please, don't leave me," she sobbed.

Uncle James fell to the ground, but Nora caught him. He held her hand tightly. "I love you, Nora. Save Magisis for me." And that was the last thing he ever said. But he died in peace, knowing they would win. Even if they didn't, he knew he had made a difference.

Something poked Nora's hand, a paper? She just stuffed it in her pocket as she shakily got up. Nora felt her rage returning. She'd never felt so angry in her life. Jabez had killed the only family she had left. She yelled in rage and charged at Jabez. He was just standing there, smirking. She was going to rip the smirk off his face with her bare hands if she had to.

Then she banged into something. Nora looked up and realised someone had put a force-field around her and Uncle James. It was Pat. She levitated herself into the force-field. "Nora, you'll kill yourself if you run at Jabez like that. Please, get a hold of yourself. I know how you feel, I lost my mother and my brother too. Please, Nora." Pat kept herself steady for Nora. She had to support her best friend.

Nora lifted Uncle James.

Pat held Nora's hand and then flew into the sky using the Volant spell. She landed inside camp. "I'm sorry," she said, her voice barely a whisper. Pat looked away from the body of Uncle James. She went and got everything Nora needed. "Rest, Nora. You need it."

"No, I cannot rest. No, oh, wait, Uncle James left me a piece of paper," Nora mumbled, she emptied her pocket and took out the paper. On it was a note:

Dear Nora,

If you are reading this, I am already dead. You know that our power comes from Magisis, from our bloodline. But I was different, I was gifted. So, I could choose to give my power to the heir of our name and, I chose you. Once I am gone forever, my magic will be transferred to you. I cannot tell you how and when you will get it. But I only hope that when it's time, you would know. You must find a way.

I love you. Stay strong.
Uncle James.

Nora didn't feel any different. She tried her best to summon this extra magic, this was as good a time as any to really need it. But she had nothing, only exhaustion, frustration, anger and she wanted to destroy everything, everyone. The anger just kept building inside of her.

Meanwhile, on the battlefield, Hannah had just killed four zombies when she saw Lucy. Lucy was facing many people from Negofer at once. And by the look on her face, Hannah knew Lucy was about to kill them all.

"No!" Hannah cried, running towards her. "Lucy, don't."

The people of Negofer suspected something was up but they still gave Hannah her space. They left Lucy and Hannah alone. Instead, they fought off other people.

"You can't tell me what to do and what not to do. You're my enemy, I'm yours. So, let me do the mass killing spell or die yourself. I'm fine with either," Lucy hissed.

"Lucy, please. You were never like this. I beg you, don't do it. You're my twin. I know that deep down, somewhere in there, you're just a normal girl like me and wish for the safety of your family. Lucy, I know you think power is everything right now, but just imagine. Violet, Bell, Anne, Mom and Dad. Everyone who loves you. What will they think? What will they do without you? What will I do? Think about all the happy times we have shared. The mischief we got into together. Please, don't make me do it, Lucy. Don't."

"You don't decide what I do," Lucy yelled. "You never cared about me in the first place."

"That's not true," Hannah cried. "I cared about you the most."

"Well, now you don't," Lucy shouted back. "I'm here for power. You always thought I was your powerless sister. I'm here to prove you wrong."

"I never doubted you for a *single second*," Hannah screamed.

"*Salvare!*" Lucy hissed. Then she started to chant.

Hannah gasped, horrified. "You can't," she cried. "You're not the kind of person who causes mass killing. You'd never."

Lucy smiled through the chant; her message clear: *Watch me.*

Hannah looked around at all the people surrounding her. If she let Lucy finish, she'd die along with all the others fighting for freedom. She couldn't let Lucy do this. She had to face her fears and fight her twin.

"*Nesciusement!*" Hannah cried. But her spell rebounded off Lucy's force-field.

Hannah tried some other spells, hoping they would go through the force-field or weaken it. But with every spell, Lucy came closer to finishing her chant. There was only one way she could stop her. But it was the last thing she wanted to do. Yet, it was necessary. She collected all her courage and pointed a finger in the direction of her twin.

"*Tuer.*"

50. Victory or Not?

Lucy froze as she realised the spell was directed towards her. It was the only spell that could break through the force-field and actually *work*. Even before she could digest this, the spell hit her. Pain shot through her body. She fell to the ground.

Hannah ran to Lucy. "Lucy, Lucy, stay awake. Fight the spell." She sobbed.

"I love you," Lucy tried to say. She still loved Hannah and her other sisters, deep down, the whole time. And she knew they loved her. But she'd wanted power so badly that she'd let Pat convince her otherwise. Was this really what she was planning to do to others—just because she wanted power?

"Shh, don't. Don't speak, I know what you mean," Hannah whispered. She levitated herself, holding Lucy. She reached the camp and sank to her knees. "I'm sorry, Lucy."

Lucy smiled, she let her eyes close, knowing it was the right thing. She would always love Hannah. She couldn't stop the spell and let herself go. Let herself die in peace. Hannah sobbed for hours. Just sitting there with Lucy in her lap. She had no sense of time. She didn't move until her sisters found her. They took the twins inside and Hannah managed to explain what had happened in between sobs. And then, the sisters all mourned for Lucy.

But the deaths didn't stop there. More people gave their lives to protect their galaxy from Jabez. The war continued for days. One day, the Saveup had a meeting.

"We have lost many good people, Emma, Ava, Clara, Mila, Jayden, Dan, Lucy, Uncle James and many more people I cannot even remember," Hilary said. "But today, Ruby and I have a plan to defeat Jabez once and for all."

"The day Sia used the killing spell on Jabez, it hurt him. What if many of us directed the spell on him at once? It is worth trying. Me, Hilary and five more will approach Jabez and use the spell. The rest of you will keep his guards and zombies distracted from us," Ruby explained.

"We thought it over and decided it is best that the people who want to kill Jabez the most do this."

After discussing, it was decided that Nora, Pat, Sia, Mary and Hannah were going to go with Ruby and Hilary.

"So, when do we put this plan to action?" Rose asked.

"We all need to recover and be fully prepared, so I suggest we take a break to freshen up and rest. After that, we go and kill Jabez. Today," Ruby said.

Hilary nodded. After the break, the entire Saveup set off into the battlefield together. They made their way through to the middle, where Jabez was.

Jabez laughed. "Oh! Look at this. The entire Saveup is here. And they think they can defeat me by charging on me all at once. Ha-ha."

Nora growled. She bit back a snappy comment.

"Hold it strong, Nora. Don't react. Don't let him get to you. Focus," Hilary whispered.

"Oh, look. Their leader is so scared she can only whisper. No courage to speak. Ha-ha, I get it. I know I'm super awesome and super great," Jabez boasted. "Now—"

Suddenly, the rest of the Saveup charged. They hit him with spells non-stop. Jabez roared and hit back with even more powerful spells. Hilary, Ruby, Nora, Pat and the others all readied their positions.

In the background, Nora could hear the groans of pain coming from her friends. They needed her to do this. She channelled all her hatred for Jabez, every single thing he had done to innocent lives, everything he had done to her family. She took a deep breath and readied her position.

Pat's hands trembled as she lifted them, ready to aim a spell at Jabez. This was it. This was the end. She could finally make him pay for everything. Hilary was shaking from head to toe. But she gathered her courage and reminded herself why she needed to do this. For her parents, family and friends. For everyone around her.

Ruby had no hesitations. She was ready to attack. Though deep inside her heart, she did feel like the scared little girl she was the day Jabez had invaded her home. But she didn't let that feeling overcome her. She stayed strong.

Sia thought of her brother as she turned to Jabez. She knew this was the right thing. But wasn't she no different than Jabez if she was too committing murder? *He deserves it. For all the bad he did*, she reminded herself. She raised her hand, tasting the words of the evilest spell ever that she had already used once before.

Hannah was trembling. She couldn't do this again. But she had to. She knew it. She thought of Lucy. Lucy would know this was the right thing. Hannah took a deep breath and channelled all the strength left in her, ready to say this horrible spell one last time.

Mary's eyes blazed with anger. She was going to kill Jabez, even if it cost her sanity, her life. But she was going to give Jabez a taste of his own medicine. Mary was going to avenge Emma. Anger burned through her body.

"GO!" Hilary yelled.

Ruby had been right. Jabez *was* overconfident. He wouldn't ever even *dream* that the Saveup could stop him. He let himself enjoy fighting the others, as seven of them spoke the spell at the same time.

"*TUER*!" They yelled.

Jabez gasped as the spell hit him. They couldn't stop him. He was right. Jabez was terribly weakened, but that could be fixed. "You'll never win against me. Your idea was smart, but not smart enough," he screamed. He sent waves of magic at them, overpowering them.

They fell back. There was nothing they could do. They had one chance, and now, if they didn't win, they would die. *I can't let that happen,* Nora thought. This was for the people of Magisis, the people of their entire solar system who had died for this cause. This was for Uncle James.

Uncle James.

The others looked nervously at each other, only Pat understood.

"Guys, I think Nora knows what to do," she whispered, shushing them.

Nora took a deep breath, her friends believed in her. She could do this. Power surged through her veins, *this is what you meant*, she thought. They could do this. She harnessed her new-found power, drawing it from the ground below. An invisible shield seemed to stretch around them, neutralising Jabez's attack.

She screamed with all her might, pointing at Jabez, "*TUER!*"

Jabez roared in anger, his energy fading away. Suddenly, all the voices around him were too loud. They didn't make sense. His eyes blurred and legs gave away. This was how he was going to die. At the hands of the powerless—he didn't live long enough to finish that thought. His eyes closed and his breathing faded away.

"We did it!" Nora cried. "We did it!" She started sobbing. But her tears weren't sad, they were tears of joy and happiness.

Hannah stood alone. "But, even for somebody as bad as Jabez, was it right to take his life?" she whispered.

The happiness deflated. "We know it was wrong, Hannah. But sometimes, even the good people have to use bad spells. After all, not one person is truly good and pure," Hilary said. "But for now, we have brought peace and happiness to not only our planet, but the entire galaxy."

EPILOGUE

Jabez's army suddenly turned powerless. The zombies disappeared. One moment, they were there and the next, they were gone. The guards remained, but there were too few of them to do anything once the magic was gone, so they surrendered. Slowly, everyone started cheering. The cheering turned louder as everyone realised what they'd accomplished.

Even though there was a lot to celebrate about, everyone had to contribute to cleaning up the battlefield and all the damage Jabez did. They had to clean up the entire city. And there were, of course, the burials.

And that totally took away everybody's happiness. It was decided that everybody's burial would take place together, with everyone present.

***

The afternoon heat dawned on the Saveup. They were at a burial ground, especially arranged for them and their families. Hilary clapped to get everyone's attention. The chatters faded away. Everyone's eyes were on Hilary now.

"It's fine," Ruby whispered to Hilary. She squeezed Hilary's hand.

Hilary gulped. "Uhm. So, everyone. We're all gathered here today for the burial of our loved ones, our friends. They gave their lives to protect us from Jabez. But this day will not only be remembered as their passing away. This day will be remembered as their victory. Our victory.

"The day we defeated Jabez. Jabez killed our loved ones, to make us weak. But their deaths only made us stronger, gave us a bigger purpose to live for, to fight for. For our friends, our second family. And today, as we stand here, mourning their deaths, we shall always remember that they died heroes."

Everyone clapped and cheered. Soon, the burials were over. People cried, laughed, talked. But they were happy. They were surrounded by people they trusted, even if everyone was deep in sadness. Slowly but gradually, peoples' lives returned to normal. A week after the battle, the Saveup all gathered.

"Today, we're here for our last ever Saveup meeting," Hilary said.

"*Last*?" Jane echoed.

"Now that the war is over, we all need to return to our daily lives—" Ruby said.

"No way!"

"What?"

"I've not finished, guys," Ruby cried.

The cries died down.

"Don't worry, this isn't the end of the Saveup. Hilary and I are going to sell these headquarters and use the Magisos to make a school in Jafrer. We'll have many different courses. If your parents or guardians are fine, you all can join us at the school," Ruby continued.

"Today is the last day." Hilary's voice cracked. "We're going to have a farewell party and by tomorrow, your families will come to pick y'all up. To go away, forever." She broke into sobs.

"Shh, it's okay," Ruby shushed Hilary, patting her.

"It's okay, Hilary. We'll meet again, in your school. After all, our education doesn't end here," Jane cried.

"Yeah! We'll all do our BEST to join your school," Luna said.

"You'll be our best students. We won't show our favouritism though. But remember, that you all are our favourites, no matter what." Ruby glanced sideways at Hilary. "My favourites, at least."

Hilary laughed and punched her arm. "Of course, y'all will be my favourites too."

"So, let's do the boring packing and crying stuff later. For now, let's PARTY," Pat cried. She jumped into the air.

Everyone screamed 'yes' and so, the party began. First, nobody knew what to do but then Olivia played some music on her recorder. She started doing a funny dance and then Chloe joined in. A while later, Scarlett went into the kitchen and made some snacks for everyone. The party lasted till around midnight. Exhausted but happy, everyone went to bed.

***

The next day, there was noise in the HQ. Everyone was bustling about, packing things, laughing, talking and making memories.

"SIA, THOSE ARE MY PYJAMAS. COME BACK!" Mia cried, running after Sia who had taken her clothes.

"Scarlett, OWW! You just put your heavy suitcase on my leg. OW!" Luna screamed.

The screams, laughs and cries continued. Near five o'clock, all the boxes were outside HQ. All of the Saveup had gathered together for one huge hug.

"I hope we'll see you in our school," Ruby said to all of them.

"Yeah, y'all better come," Hilary agreed.

"We will try," they all promised.

"Pat, Nora. Your dad is here," Mia cried out.

Nora turned, hope filling her. Her father, he came back. But then she remembered that it was her new father. Her adoptive father.

"DAD! CRYSTAL!" Pat cried. She ran towards them, dragging Nora with her. She gave them a bear hug.

Nora nervously joined in. She knew she was part of the family since they'd adopted her, but she was still nervous.

"My sweethearts. My three little angels," Mr Kawse said.

Crystal pulled herself away from the hug. "Pat, I bet you that Nora is a better elder sister than you," she teased, sticking her tongue out at Pat.

Pat laughed. "Sure, Crystal. But just wait till we settle in as a normal family. Then you'll see that Nora isn't so 'Oh my God, I am so innocent!'."

"Hey," Nora cried. "That's mean, Pat."

"Ha-ha," Pat said.

"Okay, that's enough, girls. I better not have to deal with you three fighting every day. Now, let's go and take these huge boxes back home," Mr Kawse said.

***

Settling in wasn't as easy for the Wells sisters. They had to face their parents and tell them about Lucy. Their parents knew, yes, but the sisters needed to tell them the *entire* story. So, when they reached back home and told everything, there was a lot of crying, anger, guilt and regret. Mrs Wells was very shaken up and the rest of the family did their best to support her.

The neighbours were less helpful. They were demanding the Wells family to leave, thinking that Lucy's behaviour might reflect on them and be dangerous for their community. After a whole lot of drama, the Wells family moved to Jafrer. They settled in a new house and started a new life.

They went to Hilary and Ruby's new school, where they knew they would get support. Everyone from the Saveup was also attending the school.

Slowly, things started getting back to normal. Everyone cheered for their heroes from the Saveup. Even though there were a lot of deaths, Magisis started to feel like a safe haven again.